TO CLEAR AWAY THE SHADOWS

BAEN BOOKS by DAVID DRAKE

The RCN Series
With the Lightnings • *Lt. Leary, Commanding*
The Far Side of the Stars • *The Way to Glory*
Some Golden Harbor • *When the Tide Rises*
In the Stormy Red Sky • *What Distant Deeps*
The Road of Danger • *The Sea Without a Shore*
Death's Bright Day • *Though Hell Should Bar the Way*
To Clear Away the Shadows

Time of Heroes Series
The Spark • *The Storm*

Hammer's Slammers
The Tank Lords • *Caught in the Crossfire* • *The Sharp End*
The Complete Hammer's Slammers, Volumes 1–3

Independent Novels and Collections
All the Way to the Gallows • *Cross the Stars*
Foreign Legions, edited by David Drake • *Grimmer Than Hell*
Loose Cannon • *Night & Demons* • *Northworld Trilogy*
Patriots • *The Reaches Trilogy* • *Redliners*
Seas of Venus • *Starliner* • *Dinosaurs and a Dirigible*

The Citizen Series with John Lambshead
Into the Hinterlands • *Into the Maelstrom*

The General Series
Hope Reborn with S.M. Stirling (omnibus)
Hope Rearmed with S.M. Stirling (omnibus)
Hope Renewed with S.M. Stirling (omnibus)
Hope Reformed with S.M. Stirling and Eric Flint (omnibus)
The Heretic with Tony Daniel • *The Savior* with Tony Daniel

The Belisarius Series with Eric Flint
An Oblique Approach • *In the Heart of Darkness*
Belisarius I: Thunder Before Dawn (omnibus)
Destiny's Shield • *Fortune's Stroke*
Belisarius II: Storm at Noontide (omnibus)
The Tide of Victory • *The Dance of Time*
Belisarius III: The Flames of Sunset (omnibus)

Edited by David Drake
The World Turned Upside Down with Jim Baen & Eric Flint

To purchase any of these titles in e-book form,
please go to www.baen.com.

TO CLEAR AWAY THE SHADOWS

DAVID DRAKE

To Clear Away the Shadows

Copyright © 2019 by David Drake

A Baen Books Original

Baen Publishing Enterprises
P.O. Box 1403
Riverdale, NY 10471
www.baen.com

ISBN: 978-1-4814-8402-2

Cover art by Stephen Hickman

First printing, June 2019

Distributed by Simon & Schuster
1230 Avenue of the Americas
New York, NY 10020

Pages by Joy Freeman (www.pagesbyjoy.com)
Printed in the United States of America

10 9 8 7 6 5 4 3 2 1

To Mark Geston

AUTHOR'S NOTE

There were earlier examples, but the nineteenth century was the great age of scientific exploration. Wealthy amateurs sometimes funded their own expeditions, but most were carried out with government support.

This activity greatly increased knowledge of the natural world. For example, what is still believed to be the deepest point in the oceans, Challenger Deep, was plumbed by the 1872 Challenger Expedition—a joint effort by the Royal Society of London and the Royal Navy.

More important for my purposes, these expeditions were often described by highly literate individuals who left personal accounts of amazing adventures. (*The Voyage of the Beagle* is one example.) I've read a lot of these both before and after I decided to use them as a model for this book.

The complexity of the political situation was extreme, and the risks and discomfort these scientists were undergoing in their researches are truly remarkable. It's with reason that this period is sometimes called the Heroic Age of Science.

A note on the dedication. When I began writing in the 1960s, Mark Geston was one of the writers who were making waves in the SF field. By the time I left law in the eighties, Mark had become a full-time attorney. We've kept up a low-key correspondence over the years.

Recently Mark sent me an anthology of British Great War poetry.

Many of the selections were familiar, but some were not; among the latter, Robert Graves' "To Lucasta on Going to the War—For the Fourth Time." Graves was a scholar and a poet of note, but when Germany invaded Belgium in 1914 to start the war, he joined the British army as an officer of the 7th Welch Fusiliers.

The fusiliers were originally raised to guard the artillery. They were equipped with fusils—flintlocks—instead of matchlocks and pikes. They had their own traditions and even a marching pace different from that of other British infantry. They were a picked force.

Exactly what that means is here in Graves' poem:

> Lucasta, when to France your man
> Returns his fourth time, hating war,
> Yet laughs as calmly as he can
> And flings an oath, but says no more.
> That is not courage, that's not fear—
> Lucasta he's a Fusilier.
> And his pride sends him here.

I understand perfectly; because I rode with the Blackhorse in Viet Nam and Cambodia.

—Dave Drake

Diogenes

A hut, and a tree,

And a hill for me,

And a piece of a weedy meadow.

I'll ask no thing,

Of God or King,

But to clear away his shadow.

—Max Eastman

QUAN LOI

Lieutenant Richard Grenville looked over the side of the aircar. They were travelling between West Haven, Quan Loi's main starport where the RCS *Far Traveller* had landed, and Helle, the much smaller and less developed port to the east of the mountain chain.

The only thing Rick could find positive about the land to the car's left was that it wasn't as boring as the sea they'd flown over to avoid the spine of the mountains. The highest elevation was three thousand feet. The car—really a truck with room for three in the cab and a considerable cargo volume in back—could climb to ten thousand if everything worked properly. Tech 2 Kent, the Biology Section driver, didn't want to test that and Rick, whose normal duties didn't involve travel of any sort on a planet, was happy to let Kent decide.

An aircar glided like a brick. If the fans failed, the vehicle would hit the ground with whatever velocity gravity could give it. Their current fifty-foot altitude was probably enough to kill the occupants, but Rick figured there was a chance.

"Why did he land at Helle?" Kent said. "There's nothing there. There's bloody little at Haven."

"I doubt Harper had much choice about it," Rick said. "He was assigned to the *Goliath*, but she landed with damage on Morroworld. Her captain arranged the best way to get Harper to the *Far Traveller*, and the choices aren't great here in the back of beyond."

Rick was wearing a brand new second class uniform in honor of the man they were picking up. The collar rubbed, but he supposed he was lucky that he didn't own a first class uniform. Captain Bolton would have insisted he wear full dress to greet their new officer. A utility uniform with a saucer hat were as much formality as any officer should need for duty on a survey vessel on a distant station.

"Sir?" said Kent as he lifted the car slightly to clear a stand of trees with snaky, reddish branches. "If you don't mind me asking? This guy's Biology Section, right? So I see why I'm picking him up since I'm the Bio driver...but why're you along? Was he a buddy at the Academy?"

"I don't think that Lieutenant Harry Harper even attended the Academy," Rick said. He wasn't angry about it, just maybe a little envious. "He's a boffin like your Doctor Veil. The reason *I'm* here is that his dad's a senator and owns half of Ruislip County; at least that's what Bangs, the adjutant's clerk, tells me."

Kent whistled in surprise.

Rick nodded with a twisted smile. "Yeah," he said. "You know how Captain Bolton is about the nobility. I half thought he was going to come along and greet the new addition to the *Fart*'s complement himself, but he finally decided that I would do. I hope Harper won't want me to tug my forelock."

That was probably a little more informal than Rick should have been with a technician, but third lieutenant on a survey ship wasn't what he'd joined the Republic of Cinnabar Navy for. Being sent out to nursemaid some well-born amateur made the situation even worse.

"Look, if he's got that kinda clout...," said Kent. Below, a surface ship, really a timber raft, was hugging the shore as it headed in the same direction as they were. "Then what's he coming to us for?"

"Hell if I know!" Rick said, but the situation suddenly struck him funny. "If it was me, I'd get assigned to a pirate chaser since that's the only kind of action the RCN's got so long as the treaty with the Alliance holds. If Harper's not really a naval officer, I can see that might not be something he'd look forward to. But why the *Far Traveller*, that I sure can't say."

"I think we're getting there, sir," Kent said in a different tone, swinging the steering yoke to put the car into a climbing turn which heeled them over. Rick looked down over his side of the hull toward a shallow bay into which long piers thrust. In the center was an artificial island—possibly floating—with a causeway and tram to the shore which was encircled by sheds roofed with corrugated steel or structural plastic.

Three starships were anchored near the island. One was so small that it might be intended for transport within the Quan Loi system; another was a standard freighter of about two thousand tonnes displacement when it was floating as now on the water of the harbor. Rick figured that was the *Belleisle*, the tramp which had hauled their intended passenger here from Morroworld, where the damaged *Goliath* had landed.

"What's that tub on the outside?" Kent said. "It looks like a barrel and I'll bet it handles like one."

"Put us down on the shore as near as you can to the causeway," Rick said. If their passenger was still aboard the *Belleisle*, he supposed they'd have to walk up to the island unless he could get the port authorities to give them a ride on the tram.

"As for the ship," he continued, looking critically at the oddly shaped vessel, "I suspect that's from the Yamato Cluster, the Shining Empire they're calling themselves now. They're pretty active in this region, from what I can figure out from the briefing material. We don't even have proper charts of this region. Well, that's why Navy House sent a survey ship, I suppose."

Rick guessed he shouldn't complain about being on a survey ship. If this post hadn't appeared, he'd have been on the beach where hundreds of other young officers had ended up when Navy House decided that peace with the Alliance was going to hold. Half pay for a junior lieutenant was a license to starve, and Rick didn't have family money or rich friends he could touch.

The RCN hadn't operated in the galactic north during the forty years of warfare with Guarantor Porra's Alliance of Free Stars. The region wasn't entirely under Alliance control, but the practical routes into it were, so there was no Cinnabar-flagged trade into it. Peace opened new markets for Cinnabar merchants, and the RCN had decided to map routes to aid them. In addition to the civilian benefits, it kept skills current in the ships' complements involved and it could remind senators at appropriation time that the RCN was a valuable asset even during peace.

"Okay," said Kent. "I think there's room right at the south edge of the causeway. If it's wet, I may be throwing up some mud, though."

In fact Kent brought them in smoothly on what turned out to be dark-brown ground cover rather than bare dirt. The truck was used to place collectors to gather biological material for that portion of the *Far Traveller*'s survey, so Kent must have a lot of experience landing in places that got very little traffic.

"Good job, Kent," Rick said as he opened the cab door. "Now all we have to do is find Lieutenant Harry Harper."

"That would be me," called the man standing in front of the nearest shed. He must have been sitting on some of the considerable amount of luggage sheltered within.

And by the Almighty, he was wearing a first class RCN uniform, Dress Whites!

Joss, the *Goliath*'s Biology Section hunter was hoping to transfer to the *Far Traveller* with me. She got up from the box she'd been sitting on and said, "D'ye hear it? That's a forty-five twelve or I'm Guarantor Porra!"

"What's a forty-five twelve?" I asked, getting to my feet also. The short answer was, "One more thing Harry Harper was going to have to learn about." There'd been a lot of those already during my short passage on the *Goliath*.

Joss looked over her shoulder at me. "Sorry, sir," she said. She was always polite but she gave me the willies anyway. The right side of her face looked like somebody'd scraped it with barbed wire, and her body was tattooed; at least as much as I could see beneath shorts and a utility shirt. A jacket, the RCN called the garment.

Many of the spacers on the *Goliath* were tattooed, but the heavy knife Joss wore under her belt was as unusual as her scarring. I guess she had it for her duties collecting specimens on the ground. It made me uncomfortable around her also, but it was just something I had to accept now that I was in the military.

"A forty-five twelve is a utility aircar," she explained, "basically a light truck with two pairs of fans. They're standard in the RCN—Bio Section on the *Goliath* had one, so I'm guessing this is our ride."

She pursed her lips and added, "The Alliance has the same

sorta vehicle, but they're called Fourriers, no matter which company made them."

I looked up in the direction Joss' eyes were turned toward and saw an aircar coming toward us. Until I saw the vehicle, I hadn't separated out the note of the lift fans from the general racket of the harbor area.

"You've seen Alliance cars, then?" I said. I didn't focus my eyes on Joss as I spoke to her. She seemed to be a perfectly nice person, but I worried that I'd let something show on my face if I looked directly at her.

"Yeah, I was in the army for about ten years," Joss said, her eyes still on the aircar. "A mercenary, I guess, in a drop commando. Heyer's."

I didn't know what a drop commando was, but I decided not to ask for an explanation. I hadn't heard any emotion in her words, but there was something in her voice that bothered me. Maybe it was just the *complete* lack of emotion.

I'd taken the appointment with the Navy simply because it was a real biology job that sounded interesting. Straight out of the Xenos Science Faculty I wasn't likely to get much without using my family connections, and if I did that I'd become a decorative wall plaque in a lab's reception room. I wasn't going to be dazzling the audience at academic conferences, but I'd read biology because I was interested in it and I wanted real work.

Then my tutor, Professor Equerry, called me in for a conference. A former student of his, Doctor Margot Veil, was working in the Biology Department of the naval survey service. Doctor Veil had written to ask Equerry to keep an eye out for a wellborn graduate who might be interested in distant travel and *really* exotic life forms. It would be a chance to do unique work at the very beginning of a career.

I frowned at the birth requirement, but Equerry explained that the position was on shipboard and the Navy was more class conscious than Academe. Doctor Veil's captain completely ignored her. She hoped to have a junior in her department who could interact with the captain on equal terms.

That wasn't precisely what I wanted, but no one else was going to give me the position I wanted either. I didn't need the money—the real money in the family had gone to my uncle's branch, not my dad's, but we weren't short. Regardless, I wanted to *do* something and analyzing the biota of planets which had never before been visited by a Cinnabar scientist certainly sounded like something to do.

I'd initially joined the survey ship *Goliath* on Wittenberg, intending to transfer to the *Far Traveller* in six months' time. In fact I had only about a month on the *Goliath* before the ship was badly damaged while surveying routes, losing two antennas while in sponge space.

I learned later that it had been a very dangerous accident and that the hull itself might have broken up. All I knew at the time was that something had gone wrong and that the *Goliath* was making an unplanned landing on Morroworld.

Captain von Hase of the *Goliath* sent courier missiles to several locations and also canvassed starships in Morroworld and its system. I was completely out of my depth, so I could only listen and hope I understood—or at least that I looked like I did—when von Hase or one of his juniors rattled off information about my status.

In ten days after the *Goliath*'s emergency landing, I boarded the freighter *Belleisle*, bunking with the crew on the large bridge because she had no passenger compartment. To my surprise Joss came with me. I knew the hunter to look at on the *Goliath*—she was unmistakable—but I'd never spoken to her. The rest of the *Goliath*'s crew would stay aboard and limp back to Cinnabar when the rigging had been patched up sufficiently.

I had the impression that von Hase was at fault for the *Goliath*'s condition or at any rate feared he was. He seemed to think that my father was Senator Harper, a mover and shaker in the Senate though out of power at the moment. That was my uncle, Harper of Forwood. He and my dad were on good terms, but I very much doubted that anything I said would cause Uncle Ted to interfere in a Navy House decision to punish an officer for dereliction.

The only concession Captain Blasey of the *Belleisle* would make after we arrived on Quan Loi was to radio the *Far Traveller* which was several hundred miles away. He announced that someone would pick me up, and that the *Belleisle* was no longer responsible for my meals or anything else to do with me. I had plenty of money for my keep, and being cut off from the monotonous rice and fish on the *Belleisle* was no hardship;

but I wondered what I was supposed to do if transport didn't arrive before dark.

As it turned out the transport—the 4512—was arriving while the sun was barely beyond midsky. That at least had been a needless concern.

The aircar settled to the ground in front of us. I hadn't been sure there was enough room: The fan housings and plenum chamber made the vehicle considerably wider than the wheeled trolleys the port staff used to transfer cargo. The path was hard surfaced, but it lay beneath water-weed which the most recent exhaust surge had lifted from the harbor surface.

I stepped forward as the cab door opened and heard the officer in a gray uniform call back to his driver, "Now all we have to do is find Lieutenant Harry Harper."

"That would be me," I said. I wondered if I was supposed to salute now.

The officer straightened up like I'd jabbed him with a stick. His eyes focused on me and he said, "Harper? Well, if you are, this isn't as hard as I was afraid."

He walked toward me, a fellow in his early twenties. His hair was darker than mine and curlier than mine, but there wasn't much to choose from between us. Except that he probably knew what he was doing and I certainly did not.

I met him and thrust out my hand. That might not be protocol, but it was friendly and positive so it couldn't be very badly wrong.

"Good to meet you, Harper," he said, taking my hand and shaking it firmly. "We'll get you to the *Far Traveller* where Captain Bolton will sign you in. I'm Rick Grenville, third lieutenant on the *Far Traveller*. I suppose you've got luggage?"

"Well, yes, I'm afraid I do," I said. I pointed into the shed where my seven cases were stacked. "I didn't know what I was going to need, so I'm afraid I overpacked. Will this be a problem?"

"All of this?" Grenville said, staring deeper into the shed.

I turned my head and remembered Joss, standing quietly a little behind me. But I'd deal with that after this. I repeated, "Is it going to be a problem?"

I wondered if I could pay for extra luggage. Probably not on a warship. It hadn't been a problem on the *Belleisle*, since the freighter had only a half cargo at the time.

The driver had gotten out and walked over to us also. He said, "Sir?" He was looking toward Grenville, which made sense. "Bio Section has a lot of pressurized specimen storage, so unless Veil has a problem—which I don't see happening—it'll be fine. And there's stowage on the outer hull for anything up to a couple aircars. You didn't bring an aircar, did you, sir?"

"No," I said, "but I was beginning to wish I had before you arrived. At least if Captain Blasey would've told me which direction to drive to find the *Far Traveller*."

"Well, we'll get you there fine, Harper," he said. "Let's start shifting this luggage."

He paused and looked straight at me. "Say," he said. "What ought I be calling you? Your lordship?"

I cleared my throat, feeling embarrassed. "Well, technically," I said, "I'm Lord Harper or I guess Lieutenant Harper. What I'd much prefer, though, is Harry—if that's proper in the Navy. What I'm not is Harper. While my dad is alive, that's him, Harper of Greenslade—or my uncle, Harper of Forwood. When dad dies, my sister Emily will take over the Greenslade title."

Grenville smiled broadly at me. "Not something I'd ever had to learn about before," he said. "And I'm Rick. Harry is fine for me, though Tech 2 Kent here"—he nodded to the driver—"will call you El-Tee or sir."

"Right?" he added, looking at Kent, who nodded agreeably.

"And a bit of info for you, shipmate," Rick continued, "since you probably don't know much more about the RCN than I do dinner parties in Great Houses. We're RCN from the inside. 'The Navy' is what civilians call us—or Land Force pongoes, I suppose. Okay?"

"Thank heaven somebody's teaching me things for a change," I said. For the first time I could imagine doing something other than trying to keep out of everybody's way aboard ship. "Some of these cases may need two of us, so if somebody will grab the other end, we can get me to the *Far Traveller* while it's still daylight."

"I'll help," Joss said, reminding me again of her presence. "And Lieutenant Grenville? If you can fit me in, I'd really appreciate it. I'm hoping to sign on with the *Far Traveller* myself as a Bio Section hunter."

Rick looked at her. The scars and tattoos should have made

her conspicuous in any company, but she stood as quietly as the posts supporting the shed roof and aroused no more attention.

"If you don't mind riding in back with the gear," Rick said, "I don't figure you'll add more to the load than the fans can handle."

"Sixty-three kilos," Joss said with a grin which the scarring made grotesque. "And a time or two I rode *in* a plenum chamber, being *very* bloody careful not to let my legs slip."

"The mass and volume aren't a problem," Rick said. "But I can't promise you a lift back here if Doctor Veil turns you down."

"This isn't a place I want to come back to," Joss said, taking the other end of the packing case I had touched. I started to lift and found that the hunter was at least as strong as I was. "We'll hope that he doesn't turn me down."

"She," I said, duck-walking toward the open back of the car to keep from banging my knees. "Doctor Margot Veil is a woman."

Rick and the driver grabbed the next case in line. "I wonder, Harry . . . ," he said. "Have you got other uniforms than your Whites there?"

"Oh, goodness, yes!" I said. "Did I do wrong? I thought I should wear my best for reporting to a new ship."

Nobody aboard the *Goliath* had said anything, but they—the officers, I mean—were all so busy after the ship lost two antennas that I don't think they even noticed me. If it came to that, they pretty much didn't notice me before the trouble.

"No, you didn't do anything wrong," Rick said. "But on board we pretty much wear utilities, and they're good enough for the places the *Fart* mostly lands too. Sometimes the locals don't even wear pants, so there's not much point in dressing to impress."

Joss and I got another crate. "I'll be glad to get out of this cummerbund," I said. It was especially awkward for shifting luggage now, but I hadn't expected to be doing that when I dressed this morning. At home I'd always had servants and I'd expected that to continue on shipboard, but apparently Biology Section personnel were outside the ship's company. It hadn't been a serious problem on the *Goliath*, though I had to keep reminding myself that I was responsible for my own clothes, for example.

We got the seven large crates moved. Kent got into the back of the truck and adjusted them slightly for balance in the air.

While he did that, I picked up the document case that I would carry in the cab with me.

"Guess we're ready to go," Rick said. "You want the outside or middle seat?"

"Outside if you don't mind," I said. "This is the first time I've been off Cinnabar you see, and it's, well, exciting."

"We'll hope that Kent keeps it from being too exciting," Rick said. "You're welcome to see as much of Quan Loi as you care to, though."

He glanced at the document case and said, "What's that, if I can ask?"

"Captain von Hase gave me data chips to carry to Captain... Bolton, he thought? Of the *Far Traveller*. And Doctor Howe of Biology Section is sending information to Doctor Veil."

"Well, let's do it, then," Rick said. He hopped up the step in the plenum chamber and slid over to the middle of the seat while Kent boarded from the other side. Joss was in back, visible through the rear window.

The driver checked his instruments, then ran up his fans. We slid off the slight slope toward the harbor, then gained speed and zoomed up to fifty feet while curving eastward.

I was finally on the way to a career!

The aircar had dual hand controls rather than a central yoke, so Rick had to watch that his left knee didn't get in the way if Kent brought his right arm down fast to bank to the right. There was plenty of room, but he had to be careful.

Harry seemed a decent fellow, despite wearing his Whites. It was hard to believe that a lieutenant didn't know *that* much about protocol, though.

Aloud Rick said, "How long have you been in the RCN, Harry? If you don't mind my asking."

Harry gave an embarrassed laugh. "Well," he said, "I don't know that you'd say I ever was. What happened is that when Doctor Veil accepted me for the position, the personnel department from Navy House sent me a message saying that I'd be ranked as a lieutenant with seniority dated from my twenty-first birthday—that's three years ago. And I asked dad's secretary to pick up the sort of uniforms I was going to need."

Rick laughed whole-heartedly. "Look," he said, "if that's the kind of life you've had and you're still willing to muck in and haul baggage, I'm glad to have you on the *Fart*. Ah, that's the *Far Traveller* to us and probably to everybody else in the RCN."

"I'd figured that out," Harry said cheerfully. "Some civilian skills *do* transfer to life in the RCN."

He furrowed his brow as he thought, then said, "Come to think, I'm a lieutenant in the Sheet Island Space Fencibles. But that's just because my uncle owns Sheet Island. We have a very pretty parade uniform, and I did get some training in ship handling. I sincerely hope that we won't have to serve as Cinnabar's last line of defense, but I'm sure we'll die bravely if it comes to that."

It was a moment before Rick was sure that Harry was joking. When he decided it had to be very dry humor—humor you could build a desert with—he laughed. He hadn't been around enough nobles to be sure how common Harry's sort was—but not very common, he'd guess.

"How did you happen to join the *Fart*?" Rick asked. He knew he was going to be grilled about the new lieutenant by every other officer on the ship, starting with Captain Bolton. Since Harry seemed happy to chat about himself, this ride was a good way to answer their questions. Rick had stories which would keep him in drinks at every RCN bar he entered for the rest of his life.

They continued to chat for the next three hours. Harry was getting sleepy but willingly talked about his family—two elder sisters: one a politician under their uncle's protection; the other a colonel in the Land Forces whom Harry said would be Chief of the General Staff someday if she didn't get killed first. Rick hadn't been looking forward to the duty, but he was thoroughly satisfied by the time Kent curved them down onto the landing stage near the stern of the *Far Traveller*.

The car was overflying a reed delta. From higher up it would be a blotch of bluish gray, but at only fifty feet in the air the individual reed stems were visible. Rick hadn't seen any signs of a watercourse on the flight from Haven. Now that Harry was peering down intently, Rick began to wonder what he might have missed.

"What?" Harry said. "Doctor Veil asked for me, so I was sent out to the *Far Traveller*. Since she was still working up, I was assigned to the *Goliath* which was supposed to meet you on Quan Loi, but it got wrecked on the way on Morroworld."

"I'm surprised that Doctor Veil had that kind of influence at Navy House," Rick said. In fact he was utterly amazed. Biology Section was very much the poor relation, even aboard the *Far Traveller*. That Veil would have a say in the appointment of someone classed as a commissioned officer in the RCN—which Veil was not—beggared belief.

"That bird flying there!" Harry said, pointing. "Do all the birds on Quan Loi have four wings?"

Rick shrugged. "You'll have to ask Veil," he said. "I'm not much interested in birds." He grinned. "Except the two-legged kind."

"All the vertebrates here have six limbs," Kent said. "The flying ones modify the first and last sets into wings. The boss says they're pretty well catalogued on Bryce, and she's got the files since peace with the Alliance."

Rick had been thinking of Kent as simply a driver. He suddenly realized that Tech 2 Kent was also a member of Bio Section and had been for long enough to have learned things—even though he had no more specialized training than Rick himself did.

"Oh, that's wonderful!" Harry said. "Do you suppose she'll let me...? But of course! I'll have access to all the department's holdings!"

He realized Rick was looking at him expectantly and said, "Oh, I'm sorry. Well, it didn't occur to me that there was anything unusual in a professor choosing his assistant. Hers, in this case."

Rick shrugged. "The ways of Navy House are beyond the ken of mortal man," he said.

Kent swung the car out over the sea. After looking down at the sandbanks longer than Rick had found them interesting, Harry turned to him and said, "I was told on the *Goliath* that the *Far Traveller* would be different but it probably wouldn't matter to me. Can you tell me *how* they're different, Rick?"

Rick pursed his lips as he thought about what he knew of the *Goliath*. "They're both modified from light cruisers...," he said. "I haven't been aboard the *Goliath* but when we're back on the *Fart* I can check and correct anything I get wrong off the top of my head. The main thing is that our missile magazines on the *Fart* have been turned into pinnace hangars. We've got four pinnaces aboard so the ship herself doesn't have to make all the soundings. From what I heard, it was while sounding that the *Goliath* lost two antennas."

Harry nodded. "I don't know the details," he said, "but the trouble happened while Bio Section was at the base on Morroworld. All nonessential crew were landed while the ship was sounding because insertions and extractions are so awful."

He looked up and added, "Do you get used to them?"

"Nobody I know ever did," Rick said. "Sorry."

After a moment, he added, "It's pretty unusual for a gradient between two bubble universes to be so steep that a ship loses an antenna. A well-found ship, anyway, and I know the Survey Branch is inspected to regular RCN standards."

"There was something funny about what happened," Harry said, "but nobody talked to me about it. Maybe it's in the report"—he patted the document case—"Captain von Hase sent to the *Far Traveller*?"

"Maybe," Rick said. It was as good an answer as any; he sure didn't have a better one himself.

"Welcome to your new home, shipmate," Rick said with a broad smile.

The ship in West Haven looked enough like the *Goliath* that I would've believed they were the same if I hadn't known better. I'm sure an expert could've told the difference, but I was likely better at classifying sponges than the experts in spaceship design were.

Kent brought us in on the landing stage just above water. As he shut down, a crane extended from the hold. I saw a spacer in a cage with windows on the right bulkhead.

"Bio Section's down here on Level Three," Rick said as he followed me out of the car, "but first we'd better get you officially signed in on the bridge."

Kent pulled down the cable from the crane and was sliding its hooks over to a three-point attachment system in the car's roof.

Rick walked to a pedestrian hatch in the bulkhead to the left. The room onto which the landing stage opened seemed to be a hangar with a storage area at the back.

"Ah, Rick?" I said. "Will Doctor Veil be in Bio Section now? Because I think I'd like to meet her before we go up to the bridge."

"We can do that, but you ought to see Captain Bolton first thing," Rick said. He shrugged and added, "I don't think he'll care much, but Vermijo, the first lieutenant, can be a bear about things being done right. But sure, come on."

There was a corridor on the other side of the hatch. Numbers were stenciled on the opposite bulkhead. They didn't mean anything to me but Rick turned right and then rapped with his knuckles on the jamb of an open hatch just down the corridor.

"Bio Section?" he called. "I've brought your new officer. If you don't mind I'll stick around to take him up to Captain Bolton, but he wanted to see you first."

I followed Rick into a lab much like the *Goliath*'s. There were four work stations with genetic sequencers to the left on an aisle, and a counter with other equipment—including an optical microscope—across from them. A man in his thirties turned at one of the workstations and a woman of forty-odd came out of the enclosed office at the end of the aisle.

"Lord Harper?" the woman called as she came toward me. "I'm Margot Veil and I'm very pleased at your arrival. If you'll come into the office with me I'll bring you up to speed."

She looked at Rick and said, "Lieutenant Grenville, isn't it? You can come in too. I won't be but a few minutes; the last thing I want to do is irritate Captain Bolton."

We dutifully trooped into the small office. Veil closed the hatch behind us and slipped past to take the only chair, which was behind a workstation/desk. "Harper, what do you know about the Archaic Spacefarers?"

I frowned. "I've heard of the theory," I said. "That's about all I know, though. To be frank, I think it's about all anybody knows."

Veil looked at me. Her face had a wooden lack of emotion. She couldn't be more than fifty given that Professor Equerry had trained her, but she really seemed ageless. Not young, but never aging.

"I hope to change that ignorance," she said. "And I hope you'll be willing to help me?"

I swallowed. She obviously cared about my answer. I said, "Ma'am, I'm willing to believe in the Archaic Spacefarers if I see the evidence. I just haven't seen it as yet."

Veil nodded and the atmosphere relaxed. "Yes, of course," she said. "That's all I could hope for. The evidence will convince you, I'm sure, and between us we'll be able to convince all reasonable people. Starting with Captain Bolton, though I may be giving him excessive credit for the ability to reason. It may be that your family pedigree will be enough with him. That's why I hired you, you know."

I felt myself stiffen and my stomach turn icy. "No, ma'am," I said. "I certainly did not know that. I assumed that you looked at my high second-class degree and my tutor's recommendation. If you want me as a social coup, you'll have my resignation as quickly as I can write it!"

Rick was standing behind me, nearer the door. I heard him shift slightly, but I had to concentrate on Doctor Veil.

"Not at all, Harper," she said. "I misspoke as I often do. Your degree is fine; it fits you to take over from me—when you've gained experience. Which you don't have yet."

"I thought I was going to be your lab assistant," I said, calming down and grateful to be able to do it.

"I suppose you could," Veil said, "but Mahaffy out there with a certificate degree is better at the grunt work than you or I would ever be. What I need for you is entrée into the houses of local nobles who won't even answer a polite note from an oick like me. When I realized that, I contacted Professor Equerry. My experience already here on Quan Loi has proven it beyond doubt."

"You want dinner invitations?" I said, even more puzzled than I'd been angry a moment before. I supposed I could do that—Doctor Veil could go as my plus-one, and if I let it be known in local society that Lord Harper was hoping to meet locals of his own class, there'd be a line as long as Harbor Street.

"No, no, not that!" Veil said sharply. "Their collections are what I want to see. I'm sure that most of the old families throughout the region will have curiosity cabinets of plants and animals—and oddities that they've been gathering for hundreds of years. That's where we'll find evidence of the Archaics."

"Ah," I said. I cleared my throat. "I'm sorry I misunderstood. That's a very reasonable plan, and I'll help you carry it out to the best of my ability."

"Good, good," said Veil. "Now go off with Grenville here and take care of the naval niceties. When you come back, I'll fill you in on the details."

Rick and I returned to the corridor. I was inexpressibly glad that what Doctor Veil needed from me was something that I could provide.

✦   ✦   ✦

Rick led me toward the front of the ship, saying, "The aft companionways are closer, but Captain Bolton will be on the bridge so we'll save steps in the long run."

"Is 'companionway' naval jargon for elevators?" I asked.

"There aren't any personnel elevators on a starship," Rick said nonchalantly. "Elevator shafts twist with every insertion into sponge space and the cages would be trapped. A warship is even worse, because acceleration stresses can be so high—and battle damage can torque a hull into a pretzel."

"Just how much climbing does this involve?" I asked as we entered a rotunda with large lockers around the perimeter and four thick columns in the center. Rick opened the red-painted hatch in the base of one of the columns.

"Red means it's up," he said. "The blue ones are down companionways. And there's four more in the stern."

"If they're just stairs," I said, and I could see they were, circular staircases with perforated steel treads, "then don't they go in both directions?"

"They do," Rick said, "but the traffic doesn't. It'd be bloody chaos if people tried to go both ways, especially in action."

He turned his head and grinned at me as he started up. "And it's seven decks up from here to bridge level. But you will get used to this. After a while."

I concentrated on the climb. After a few steps I simply put my head down and kept going on. I could see the heels of Rick's soft boots. They were designed to be worn within suits on the outside of the hull. I found them adequately comfortable in general use, but I'd had almost no experience on the hull while under way.

Occasionally we paused when somebody entered through a hatch slightly ahead. I'm pretty sure that Rick was deliberately hanging back so that our—so that my—slow pace wouldn't delay others entering above us. It really wasn't practical to pass on the curling companionway.

I heard another hatch open immediately ahead of me. Rick said, "Watch the coaming when you step out, Harry," and only then did I realize we'd reached the bridge level.

I staggered as I stepped through the hatchway. I'd kept going by turning myself into a machine. When I tried to change the programming, the machine went to the verge of spinning out of control.

I opened my mouth to ask Rick to hold up for a moment, then closed it immediately. The fast climb—and it wasn't that fast—had made me queasy. My first priority as a member of the *Far Traveller*'s crew would be to practice climbing stairs. That hadn't been a problem on the *Goliath*, I guess because Biology Section was on Level 9 and my cabin was on Level 8 just below it.

I straightened up and got control of my breath. "Thanks for giving me a moment," I said. "I needed it, but I'm going to get into better shape."

"Then let's meet the captain," Rick said with a friendly smile.

The bridge was only twenty feet away, visible through the open hatch. There were half a dozen people among the consoles, in a quick glance. It looked exactly like the bridge of the *Goliath* except that the structural surfaces—deck, bulkheads, and overhead—were enameled a lighter shade of gray.

I thought we were going to enter, but Rick stopped instead at a cabin on the starboard side of the corridor. The light hatch was ajar. He rapped it with his knuckles, standing so that he could be seen from inside through the opening.

"Captain Bolton," he called. "I've brought Lieutenant Harper to join our company."

Rick stepped back and motioned me forward. Before I reached the hatch, it opened forcefully. A short man in a second class uniform burst into the corridor. I braced myself to salute, but before I could, he thrust out his hand to me and said, "Lord Harper? Welcome aboard, sir!"

I shook his hand, confused by the greeting but I was confused by quite a lot of the RCN's procedures. I said, "I'm glad to be here, sir," because it sounded harmless.

"Has Grenville treated you well, your lordship?" Bolton said, looking past me with an expression just short of becoming a glare. "If he hasn't, by the Almighty..."

I didn't know what the rest of that threat would have been, but I could guess. "Lieutenant Grenville has been a polite and knowledgeable guide," I said firmly. "He's going to get me enrolled and assigned a cabin, but he said it was important that I be introduced to you first, sir."

Bolton straightened abruptly. "Yes, of course, Lord Harper," he said. "I was going to suggest we adjourn to my stateroom, where I've got some rather decent bourbon from the Bryce

Highlands—there's nothing here in my day cabin, of course. But that can wait until you're straightened away."

He stepped back. I saluted and turned toward the stern with Rick. When we heard Bolton's hatch close, I muttered to Rick, "Is he always that enthusiastic?"

"Maybe he is when he meets nobles," Rick said in an odd tone. "Your lordship."

I grimaced. "Don't give me that crap!" I said. "I've got to take it from him, he's the captain; but I'm damned if I will from you!"

"Just making sure, Harry," he said. He smiled and I felt relieved.

"The Battle Direction Center's armored like the bridge," Rick said, "and it's in the far stern so the ship can be conned from it if the bridge is hit. That's the first lieutenant's action station, and his office and quarters are adjacent. That's where we're going."

"Ah . . . ?" I said. "I didn't realize that the *Far Traveller* was still a warship?"

Rick laughed. "Well, technically every RCN vessel is a warship, and the ship's crew—not the science crew like you—are RCN personnel just as sure as the admirals on the Navy Board are. But no, when the *Ajax* was converted to a research vessel and renamed the *Far Traveller*, her crew stopped expecting to see action. Bow dorsal turret is still active with a six-inch plasma cannon, but any ship going off into the back of beyond is armed. Ours is bigger and in a fancier installation than the four-inch gun on a freighter would be, but it was cheaper and simpler to leave the turret in place than rip it out during the rebuild and replace it with something less impressive."

We'd met half a dozen spacers going the other way on the corridor. In an undertone I said to Rick, "Don't people salute on this ship?"

"Not aboard in active service," Rick said. He glanced sideways at me. "Do you miss getting salutes?"

"Good heavens, no!" I said. "But I was expecting it. I thought the *Goliath* was just an exception because of the accident."

I saw the hatch of what must be the BDC ahead of us at the end of the corridor. Though it was open, its armored thickness demonstrated that it wasn't an ordinary hatch.

Rick led me into the end cabin to the left. Two steel desks with flat-plate workstations faced the hatchway. A woman in her forties sat at one, but a man of twenty at most at the other said brightly, "Lieutenant Grenville, how can we help you?"

"I'm just guiding Lieutenant Harper here around," Rick said, gesturing to me. "He needs a cabin and to be signed onto the ship's books."

"Roger that," the clerk said, bringing up data on his display. "He wants to be near the biology lab, I suppose?"

The older woman had looked up sharply when she heard my name. Still looking at me, she pressed something on her control field.

"Definitely," Rick said to the junior clerk. "Time he spends running up and down companionways is wasted from his real job: cataloging worms. Right, Harry?"

I returned Rick's grin and had opened my mouth to say something when the door to an inner office banged open. The tall, thin man who came out settled his officers' hat and said, "Lieutenant Harper, come into my office—*if* you'll be so good."

I stepped between the two desks, wondering what I'd done to so infuriate the first lieutenant. Rick had warned me that Lieutenant Vermijo could be a bear about protocol, but I hadn't expected that ten minutes with Doctor Veil would arouse *this* level of anger.

I followed Vermijo into the inner room and saluted. I probably did that badly, but I was trying.

"Close the bloody hatch, Harper!" Vermijo said from behind the desk.

I swung it closed; I hadn't been sure what he wanted or I'd have done that when I entered. "Sir," I said, standing as stiffly as I could, "Lieutenant Harper reporting!"

"I know who you are, Harper!" Vermijo said. "What I want to know is why you decided to go over the head of the RCN and use your political relatives to force yourself into a position which had already been awarded to a worthy candidate?"

"Sir," I said, trying to figure out what he was talking about. "I didn't know there was another candidate. My understanding was that Doctor Veil requested me on the basis of my tutor's suggestion."

"Veil isn't even RCN!" Vermijo said. "Why would you imagine that her opinion would matter to Navy House? If you were a real RCN officer, that would be obvious!"

"She's head of Biology Section on the *Far Traveller*!" I said. Remembering where I was I added, "Sir. All I knew of the position was what she and Professor Equerry told me."

"The slot had already been awarded to my wife's cousin Jorge," Vermijo said. "He has a zoology degree from Huntsman College on Maskelaine and was eminently qualified for the position."

"Sir, all I do is repeat that this is all news to me," I said. I could have said that a degree from a backwater college wasn't the equivalent of one from the Xenos Science Faculty, but that wouldn't have been useful. Besides, from what Doctor Veil had said about Mahaffy's certificate degree being sufficient for the job, the quality of my degree really hadn't mattered. "I didn't pull any strings."

"You *say*!" Vermijo said.

My skin prickled all over. For a moment all I saw was pulsing white light. When I was sure I had my voice under control, I said, "Sir, if you doubt my qualifications for the job, then you should take the matter up with Doctor Veil, my superior."

I swallowed. "But if you're calling me a liar—"

I'd been wrong about having my voice under control. To avoid choking up, I had to blurt out the rest of what I was saying: "—then I will meet you with pistols as a gentleman!"

"Where do you think you are, Lieutenant?" Vermijo said. He backed up slightly. Because of where he stood behind the desk, he bumped the bulkhead. "You know that officers of the RCN aren't permitted to fight duels!"

"I don't know anything of the sort!" I said. "I'm a biologist, not an RCN officer, just as you said. And if I were, it still wouldn't prevent me from responding as a gentleman should when a total stranger calls him a liar! I know *nothing* about any political shenanigans inside Navy House!"

That was absolutely true, but as I spoke the words I remembered I'd heard that Doctor Veil had a senatorial backer of her Archaic Spacefarer dream. If that senator had asked Uncle Ted for help, Ted would probably have put his considerable political weight behind the request. At the very least, Uncle Ted would have as little interest in bureaucratic game-playing as I did when a scientist of real stature was trying to put together a team.

But *I* didn't know about any of that.

Lieutenant Vermijo's face lost its angry expression as he took in what I'd said. He stiffened, then cleared his throat and said, "My pardon, Lieutenant Harper. I do not of course doubt your word, and I regret that I misspoke in a fashion to suggest that I did."

I cleared *my* throat again also. "I accept your apology, sir," I said. "I should have realized that I must be mishearing you."

I was trembling with relief. My sister Emily had fought a duel over some point of party discipline. They'd both missed their first shot and composed the matter. Emily told me after a night of heavy drinking that after the first exchange she'd found herself terrified that she was going to kill the other fellow, a junior whip—who'd blurted something out stupidly. In much the same way as Vermijo had, I now realized.

Vermijo let out his breath. "Yes, well...," he said. "Thank you for clearing up my mistake, Lieutenant. I'm sure that Brontop and her staff will take care of your billeting, but if there are problems just let us know."

I took that as my dismissal. I saluted again and quickly turned to exit the cabin. Everybody in the outer office was staring at me. I forced a smile and said, "Lieutenant Vermijo is confident that you'll take care of my housekeeping affairs. Rick, if things are under control, I'd like to be shown my cabin and get that squared away before learning more about my duties from Doctor Veil."

"We're set," said Rick. "You get more exercise in the companionway, but at least we're going down this time."

When we were a safe distance down the corridor, Rick said quietly, "Things go all right in there?"

I swallowed and said, "We reached an understanding. I think things will be all right if I concentrate on my job down on Level Three."

"You'll be eating in the wardroom with the rest of us officers," Rick said. "On Level Ten between the bridge and the BDC."

"Ah," I said. It would be an insult to Captain Bolton to take my meals in the lab as I'd hoped to do. "Well, I think it will be all right."

We reached a blue companionway. Rick paused for a moment at the hatchway and held his hand up to silence me. Gesturing me on when he was sure there was no one close below us in the steel column, he said, "Have you killed many people in duels, Harry?"

The door of Vermijo's inner office was thin. We might as well have left it open when the lieutenant brought me in to shout at me. The story would be all over the ship by this evening.

I took a deep breath. "I've never fought a duel," I said. "My family doesn't go in for them. But I would rather die than allow an insult to my honor like that."

Rick cleared his throat. "I'm sure Lieutenant Vermijo wasn't thinking about what his words meant when they came out of his mouth. And now he's truly sorry."

My knees were trembling in delayed reaction to the scene in Vermijo's office. I paused at the second hatchway down—the companionway expanded slightly where the hatches entered. I turned to Rick and said, "I've never killed anything but some birds. I'm a pretty good wing shot. I'm a biologist, that's all I am!"

"Well, personally I'm glad to hear that," Rick said. "Things can be dicey enough in the RCN without worrying about a messmate blowing my head off because I told him I didn't like his color sense."

I looked at him. "What's wrong with my color sense?" I said in puzzlement.

"Not a bloody thing, since you're in full uniform," Rick said. "Which made it a safe subject."

"Well," I said, "since we're mates, I'd even let you comment on my heliotrope pajamas."

Rick laughed, as I'd hoped he would.

The stern of Level 3 wasn't familiar territory for Rick any more than it was for Harry but at least a regular RCN officer understood the signage.

He wasn't sure how he felt about Harry's flare-up with the first lieutenant. There had been RCN officers who were famous duelists, but dueling had always been a violation of regulations and nowadays the general attitude of the service was to consider that sort of thing to be in bad taste. Rick certainly felt that way himself.

On the other hand, Harry wasn't a blustering bully using the implicit threat of death to dominate the folks around him. Vermijo had been out of line in using his rank to abuse a junior officer who had accidentally gotten in the way of one of his fiddles. Maybe there was more to be said for dueling than Rick would have guessed before now. Anyway, it'd all passed off harmlessly.

They reached Biology Section without a problem. Rick could see his companion brightening as he began to recognize landmarks.

Inside the section, Kent and the tattooed hunter, Joss, waited on the two jump seats folded out from the bulkhead in what amounted to the lobby. Both jumped to their feet when Rick and Harry came in.

"Kent," Rick said to the driver. They'd gotten to know one another slightly during the trip to pick Harry up. "Go get Lieutenant Harper's luggage hauled to Cabin 3P45. Draft a detail on my orders if you need to."

"Sir, it won't fit," Kent said. "You know that."

"No, but P47 is empty for the moment," Rick said. "Shift the overage there and Lieutenant Harper can sort it for permanent stowage as soon as he arranges for a servant."

The tech, Mahaffy, had gotten to his feet as soon as the officers entered. Now he nodded to call attention to himself and said, "Lieutenant Harper?"

When both officers looked at him, he continued, "If you just need ordinary redding up and the usual housekeeping stuff, laundry and all, I'm doing for Doctor Veil when I'm off duty. I guess I can handle you too at an extra florin a week."

Harry looked at his companion. "Rick?" he said.

Rick shrugged. "That's standard," he said. "If there's a problem I can line up somebody on the starboard watch to do for you."

"Very good then," Harry said. "Thank you, Mahaffy."

Doctor Veil stood at the entrance to her private office. She called, "You can go help Kent now, Mahaffy. You've got the latest marine intake processed, haven't you?"

"Roger, sir," the tech said, shutting down his console.

The hunter looked as though she wanted to talk to Harry also, but Doctor Veil said, "Harper, I've got a problem I'd like your help with. And you too, Grenville, if you don't mind. You've got proper RCN experience."

"Of course, sir," Harry said. Rick followed him, wondering what Joss had wanted to say. This wasn't the time to learn, though.

Rick closed the door behind him, though the panel wasn't any thicker than Lieutenant Vermijo's. "Harper," Veil said, "one of the message chips from the *Goliath* that you delivered to the bridge was actually meant for me. It's a message from Doctor Howe, the science officer."

"I'm sorry, sir," Harry said. "Captain von Hase gave me the case of data chips and asked me to deliver them to the *Far Traveller*. I didn't look at them, let alone sort them."

"Quite right," Veil said with a dismissive sweep of her hand. "But I want you to take a look at it now." She switched her console display to omnidirectional so that the document she'd been reading became legible to both the lieutenants on the other side of her desk.

"Doctor Howe is writing about the woman you came here with, Harper," Veil said. "It's a very odd recommendation, so I want your opinion about it before I make a decision. Both of you."

"*To head of Biology Section, RCS* Far Traveller," Rick read. "*Tech 1 Joss has been attached to my section as a hunter for four and one-half months. Her work has been unexceptionable during that time. Despite that, I fear that her reflexes from her military background may make her unsuitable for shipboard society. Dr. William Howe.*"

Harper frowned. "I don't understand what that means," he said. "Doctor Howe didn't say anything to me aboard the *Goliath*. Ah, I don't know if this matters, but Joss paid her own passage aboard the *Belleisle*. Captain von Hase didn't arrange it the way he did mine."

"I think I can figure out what it means," Rick said. "It means that Howe was covering his ass in case something happens but didn't have the balls to actually commit the other way either. Harry? Was there any problem with Joss on the *Goliath*?"

"What?" Harper said, frowning. "No, no problem at all, but she wasn't able to carry out her trapping program on Carside because the *Goliath* made an emergency landing on Morroworld instead."

"Right," Rick said. "So it's no problem, then. And on the *Belleisle*?"

"No," Harper said. "We weren't crew, of course, just passengers for the six days."

"Right, but six days on a tramp freighter is plenty time for trouble to start if there's going to be trouble," Rick said. "Professor Veil, you said you wanted my opinion. This Joss isn't a beauty and probably doesn't know which fork to use at dinner, but ships' crews don't run to little ladies and gents. If she'd done something Howe could've hung her on, you can bet he would've done that."

Harper had been leaning toward the holographic display. He

straightened and said, "I saw and heard of no problem involving Joss on shipboard or on the ground on Carside. When we were put off the ship here on Quan Loi, Joss understood what was happening much better than I did and was unfailingly pleasant and helpful."

He pursed his lips in thought and added, "It's not just her military background, understand. I'd never been off Xenos before I was sent to the *Goliath*. I'd have been completely at a loss when Captain Blasey told me he'd contacted the RCN ship and somebody'd be along to pick me up. And he'd offload my cargo, but that was the last business he had with me."

"All right," Veil said. "If there were no incidents, we'll take a chance. I don't suppose the local hunters I hire are anything but raw savages. Joss will be billeted on shipboard, though."

She nodded crisply, then said, "All right, I'll see her now."

"Shall we send her in as we leave?" Rick said, putting his hand on the door latch.

"No," Veil said. "I'll take care of it in the lab."

She followed the two lieutenants into the lab. Joss leaped to her feet when the office door opened. Rick would have gone out into the corridor, but before he reached the exit Doctor Veil said, "Mistress Joss, you wish to join the Biology Section of the *Far Traveller*?"

Joss kept her eyes front, probably focused at a point over the scientist's left shoulder. "Yes, ma'am!" she said. "I was classed as a Tech 1 Wiper on the *Goliath* and employed for the Bio Section under Professor Howe. He hired local hunters to collect specimens for their local knowledge. I was a scout with the Forces of the Alliance and therefore could size up and adapt to new environments quickly. Besides, I understood how to use the communication and collection devices, which the locals the *Goliath* hired never managed to do."

"That's certainly been the case with the ones I've hired also," Veil said. She grunted and stiffened her body. "Mistress Joss, you mentioned you'd served in the Alliance Army. As I assume you know, the *Far Traveller* is an RCN vessel. Will there be a problem with your former loyalties?"

Joss laughed, a broken sound; unexpected, and as ugly as her scarred face. "Ma'am, I'm sorry," she said. "It's an honest question. I'm from Api. I know now that we were in the Alliance Sphere of Influence, but nobody when I was growing up knew it. I left home when I was fifteen—pretty much had to. On Claiborne, that's kinda Alliance too, I guess, there was a recruiter for the Forces and I wound up sent to a drop commando, Heyer's Commando."

She shrugged. "Some of us was Alliance citizens, a lot of us wasn't. A lot of us enlisted to get out of jail. Nobody I met gave a crap about politics. That's still true."

Rick blanked his expression when Joss said she'd been in a "drop commando." These were the emergency reaction units of the Forces of the Alliance of Free Stars. They were more often used for internal policing than for ordinary military duties. They had a very bad reputation for brutality.

Granting that what one side in a conflict believes about the troops of the other side is likely to be highly colored if not completely imaginary, the scarred woman's passing admission was a shock. Rick found himself more sympathetic to Howe's mealymouthed warning than he had been when he first read it.

"I'll accept your assurance for now," Veil said. "At the least I hope you can take over the task of choosing and supervising local collectors on future landfalls. But I warn you, if there's any problem, you'll be put off the ship immediately!"

"Yes, ma'am," Joss said. "In all my time in service, I've never been a discipline problem. And sure, I figure I can handle your collector problems."

"Fine, then," Veil said. "I'll have you enrolled with the status and terms that you served on the *Goliath*. Ah, Grenville? Since you're more familiar with the naval business than I, could you take care of that as a favor to the Biology Section?"

"Happy to do so, sir," Rick said. Veil had no command authority over an RCN officer—except he supposed over Harry Harper, within her department—but courtesy is always proper, and he really didn't mind doing it.

The officers and Joss went out into the corridor. As soon as she'd closed the hatch, the hunter paused and said, "Sirs? Both of you?"

They looked at her. Rick noticed that she could have been an attractive woman—slim and blond—at least from the left profile. Though as the idea flitted through his mind, he realized that the tattoos were even more off-putting than the scars when you saw some of the things being depicted.

"Look," she said, "I owe you guys for not putting the boot in with Veil. I know you could've. And you, Lieutenant Grenville. You understood what Heyer's was, I saw it in your face."

"I know what Porra used drop commandos for," Rick said carefully. "I don't know anything about Heyer's specifically. And ground troops aren't my line of territory regardless."

"We were troops Guarantor Porra didn't care what happened to," Joss said. "Lots of wogs like me, like I said. Crooks and people on the outs with him politically, both of them folks he'd just as soon got killed. We got jobs that nobody else'd do because they didn't have the stomach for it, like enough. They sent us hard places because they figured we were harder and we were mostly—but if we got scragged instead that was no problem for the Alliance."

She wasn't looking at Rick now or at anything in the present. "But don't think we were out of control. Heyer's Commando was *never* out of control. The whole bloody universe was Us and Them, but your buddies were always *Us*. I'm a member of the ship's company of the *Far Traveller* now. You two, all of you, you're my buddies now. I may not like some of them, but they're still my buddies. There's nothing I won't do for them. *Nothing*."

Harry said, "Mistress Joss, I had occasion on the *Goliath* to sequence what were marked as specimens you had brought in. They were in flawless order and condition. It appears to me that Doctor Veil has made a very good decision."

"Right," said Rick. "Let's get you signed in, shipmate."

I tapped on the door of Doctor Veil's inner office, then opened it and said, "Sir? It took me longer than I expected because the captain asked me back to his stateroom to chat. Over a glass of bourbon. I hope that was the right thing to do."

Veil smiled up at me. Her display was still omnidirectional so I could see that she was viewing the genetic sequences of a batch of samples, though I couldn't tell whether the samples had been collected here on Quan Loi or during one of the *Far Traveller*'s earlier landings.

"Quite right," Veil said. "Convincing Captain Bolton that the Biology Section is a desirable part of the *Far Traveller*'s complement is one of the two important special duties which I want from you."

She gestured toward the chair, bolted to the deck like all furniture on a starship. "Sit down, Harper," she said. "You know that Bio Section's job is to gather data about life forms on the planets we visit, supplementing the route information which the sounding section is gathering."

"Yes, ma'am," I said. "The sort of information that would be in the *Sailing Directions* for better known parts of the galaxy."

"We are also searching for evidence of the Archaic Spacefarers," Veil continued. "This isn't in place of the duties which Navy House put on us, but rather in addition. Senator Blankenship has backed my interest in various ways, including having searches for other spacefaring cultures added to the expedition's mission statement."

"Yes, ma'am," I repeated. I didn't say that she'd already told me that. This was in greater detail than what she'd said before, though.

"Now," Veil said, "I want you to begin the other portion of your special duties, getting access to the collection of a local magnate, Porphyrio DaSerta. According to a colleague on Bryce, the DaSerta family owns a piece of Archaic sculpture which has not been examined by any scientist in the past hundred and fifty years.

"My own attempts even to speak with DaSerta have been completely ignored," she went on, giving a grimace of frustration. "The leader of the colony which settled Quan Loi was a Captain DaSerta. The current family claims direct descent from him. They're very proud of their family and their heritage. I'm not surprised that they ignored my request, but they have apparently refused to allow Alliance scientists to view the item also."

I nodded. "My father, Harper of Greenslade, is a member of the Society of Dilettantes," I said. "I can ask Master DaSerta if he would permit me to carry out a commission for my father and examine the DaSerta collection."

"That's exactly what I was hoping!" Veil said. "But—your father won't mind if he hears about it?"

"Dad wouldn't mind at all," I said, "even if he learned. And I'll give him a full report about the collection besides. He really *is* a member of the Society of Dilettantes."

I decided that for a communication like this, hardcopy was the only proper method of communication. The printer was on the bridge, so I went up there—I was already getting used to the companionways, though my calves ached in the morning when I awakened—to draft my note to DaSerta. I'd get Kent to carry it to DaSerta's dwelling.

The second lieutenant, Lieutenant Dogan, was on duty. We'd been introduced though no more than that, but he knew me as a friend of Captain Bolton.

"Sir," I called as I seated myself at a utility table which folded out from the rear bulkhead. "I just want to draft a document and I prefer doing it here rather than my cabin if that's all right?"

Dogan waved and went back to his course calculations.

I'd brought both stationery and calling cards with me, part of the reason my luggage had been so extensive. I hadn't expected that the fact I'm a gentleman was going to be important to my duties on the *Far Traveller*, but I *am* a gentleman. I was carrying the things that I'd believed a gentleman would need on a long voyage. I wrote:

> *Master Porphyrio DaSerta:*
> *I am the son and envoy of Harper of Greenslade, Member of the Society of Dilettantes.*
> *My father has requested that I view and make records of your Cabinet of Curiosities whose fame has reached him in Xenos on Cinnabar.*
> *May I call on you at your convenience to carry out my father's commission? I am travelling aboard the RCS* Far Traveller *and can be reached there by any means you choose.*
> *Harry Harper, Gentleman*

Someone came into the bridge while I was writing. I heard a low-voiced conversation but I didn't look around until I'd completed the note. I don't handwrite messages often enough to do it without concentration.

Rick had entered and apparently relieved Lieutenant Dogan on watch. Dogan was heading for the hatch. Rick came over when he noticed me looking toward him. He glanced down at the letter and said, "What in heaven's name are you doing, Harry?"

I folded the note's four corners together carefully. "Impressing a local nob with my high social status," I said. "On behalf of my boss, who wants me to search his collection for artifacts of Archaic Spacefarers."

I'd seal the envelope in my cabin, since I had to go back to Level 3 to give it to Kent anyway. "Say...?" I said to Rick. "Who do I need to tell that if there's a note or commo message for me from a local, especially if he's named DaSerta, that it's important? I need to see it ASAP."

"You tell the duty officer," Rick said, "which is me at the moment. I'll log it. This DaSerta?" he added. "Is he a relative of Romaine DaSerta, the Fleet officer?"

"I have no idea," I said. "The DaSertas are an old family on Quan Loi which wasn't a full member of the Alliance."

"We've got the RCN database even if we don't have full missile magazines," Rick said, walking over to the nearest console. I think it properly belonged to the navigator, but no one was at it. He brought it live, then turned with a broad smile and called, "Bingo! Full Commander Romaine DaSerta was indeed from Quan Loi. Say, you don't suppose I could go along with you, could I? He was really hot stuff. They may have a display or the like if it's the same family."

"I suspect I can arrange that," I said. I'd carried up several sheets of stationery because I didn't want any cross-outs on something like this. I took one of them—headed HARPER OF GREENSLADE—and carefully rewrote the request. This time I added an additional paragraph above my signature:

> As a personal favor, my friend and colleague Grenville of Hounslow is a student of naval matters. He hopes that if Romaine DaSerta was your relative, you will permit him to accompany me in hope of viewing memorabilia of Commander DaSerta.

I folded it as I had the other. "I need to take this down and seal it," I said, getting to my feet. "I'll give it to Kent to take." I frowned and added, "I hope that Doctor Veil will have DaSerta's physical address."

"Harry, do you think it'll work?" Rick said.

I shrugged. "I hope so," I said. "Doctor Veil will want to rethink her decision to hire me if it doesn't."

"And Harry?" Rick added as I reached the hatch, holding the note in my left hand. "Who's Grenville of Hounslow?"

I turned with a broader smile than before and said, "A young

Cinnabar gentleman, so far as somebody on this benighted world can tell. I hope that DaSerta can find data on the Harpers of Greenslade, but I doubt he has a complete listing of the families of the Republic available."

The response come within three hours of Kent's return to the bio lab, where Mahaffy was showing me the *Far Traveller*'s protocol for recording results of genetic sequencing. Doctor Veil had made it clear that she didn't care whether or not I could do the work of a lab assistant, but *I* cared quite a lot.

Somebody hammered on the corridor hatch. Before Mahaffy or I could get to the panel, it flew open to admit one of the watch from the entry hold. He held an envelope with a thick border of royal blue. "Lut'nant Harper?" the spacer said. "Got a message for you."

"Padko," Mahaffy said in an angry tone. "Why the bloody hell didn't you just call it up instead of banging like some bloody barbarian?"

"Because the fellow who brung it's waiting down in the hold for an answer," said Padko—not a crewman I'd met before. "Which isn't SOP, but Lut'nant Harper said that any message that comes for him"—he nodded toward me—"gets brought to him soonest or the captain hisself 'll burn somebody a new one."

I suspected there was some matter of protocol involved that I knew nothing about. Goodness knows I'd seen it often enough with servants at Greenslade, which is one of the reasons I hadn't made an effort to get a servant assigned to me when I joined the RCN. I'm sure that Uncle Tom could've said something to somebody. Regardless, my hopes for a life without precedence squabbles were falling short of perfect fulfillment.

I slit the heavy paper of the envelope with my pocket knife. Like my note it had been sealed, though the seal was of bright blue polymer instead of the red wax I'd used.

The card within was engraved with the legend:

HEREDITARY CAPTAIN PORPHYRIO DASERTA

My dear Lord Harper,
You and your esteemed companion will be welcome at DaSerta House at any time after midday tomorrow.

*I am pleased to learn that Lord Grenville is interested
in my uncle, Romaine DaSerta. The family collection does
indeed include Commander DaSerta's papers and various
items from his distinguished service with the Fleet.*

DaSerta

The document was so precisely hand printed that I suspected
the job had been done by an amanuensis. Otherwise DaSerta
himself had devoted himself to the activity with the wholehearted
enthusiasm of my great cousin Emanuel, who had modeled castles
with the corks of wine bottles.

I used the ship's intercom to route me to Lieutenant Grenville.
"Rick," I said, "we're invited for noon tomorrow. We can have
Kent drive us and my gear in the Bio Section truck."

I wondered if my search for Archaic artifacts would be as
successful as Rick's search for naval memorabilia.

The aircar was fifty feet up, approaching the location which
should be DaSerta House. Rick had plotted the location by comparing land records with imagery which the *Far Traveller* had
recorded—automatically—as she prepared to land in Helle Harbor.
Rick figured that the perfectly square three-hectare compound
surrounded by a stone wall was a solid identifier.

Harry was opposite the driver with Rick in the center as before.
Harry pointed and said, "Say, look at that double line of pink
trees lining the drive from the gate. Those're—"

The communicator on the car's fascia panel suddenly snarled,
"*Vehicle approaching DaSerta House, land at once or you will be
shot down! There will be no second warning!*"

"What do I do?" Kent said, turning his head with a desperate
expression.

"Land!" Rick shouted, grabbing the nearer control wand and
trying to swerve the aircar parallel to the front wall of the compound instead of overflying it. "Bloody hell, man. Don't you see
the turret on the roofline swiveling to track us!"

Kent immediately cut the throttles and banked the car properly
while reducing speed. He was a skilled driver, but he obviously
didn't have combat experience.

Neither did Rick, but he had the common sense which the
driver seemed to lack. There were ground vehicles on the street,

but the graveled expanse was wide enough for Kent to make a U-turn at idle and bring the car to a gentle halt in front of the barred metal gate.

"Would they really have done that?" Harry said. "Shot us down for encroaching on their air space?"

"Who the hell knows?" Rick said. "We're a long way from Xenos. I don't want to bet my life on what some wog in the sticks is going to do to a trespasser. The automatic impeller in that turret could shoot holes in anything that didn't have too much armor to fly."

Harry got out first and walked to the barred gate. He wore a dress suit of dark burgundy rather than an RCN uniform. Without having talked to him he could only guess at DaSerta's feelings toward the Republic of Cinnabar, and dressing as a civilian gentleman was probably the better choice anyway.

Rick followed a pace behind, wearing his second class uniform, his Grays, but without any insignia. He didn't have a selection of civilian clothing aboard—he couldn't have afforded them, and on most RCN postings (even to a battleship) a lieutenant would have nowhere to store them. This set of Grays were new and looked sharp, at least to Rick's own eyes.

He'd thought of wearing a suit of Harry's. They were pretty much of a size, but Harry was just enough taller and longer-limbed that he'd look like a clown until they were taken in. Many spacers were able tailors, but Rick balked at first begging a suit and then making alterations.

The two uniformed guards at the gate carried submachine guns. Rick thought they were Alliance standard, but the men kept their weapons politely slung behind their backs. Harry handed his calling card and DaSerta's invitation through the gate; Rick had his RCN identification card ready in his hand, but the guards had already begun to pull open the gates.

"DaSerta House welcomes you, gentlemen," the older, balding guard said. "Transportation will arrive momentarily."

Harry put the invitation away in his embroidered sabertache. "My research requires considerable equipment," he said. "May we carry it into the grounds in our vehicle?"

"I'm very sorry, sir," the guard spokesman said. Their uniforms were dull orange with brown piping. "Neither the vehicle or the commoner driving are to be admitted without special orders. The truck coming should hold as much as you need, and if it doesn't we'll call a larger truck."

An open flatbed, more of a motorized cart than a truck, was trundling up the paved driveway. It wasn't big, but it would certainly hold the imaging and testing apparatus which Harry had brought. The driver wore the same livery as the guards, but she wasn't armed.

Kent had opened the truck's cargo space and the armored specimen case welded to the deck within. The box of the vehicle would easily hold a dozen people—the same frame was used as a military transport—but a separate four-by-six-foot container with interior padding and tie-downs was built in to keep small items from bouncing around in transit. Harry's equipment was carried there.

Kent brought the imaging apparatus to Harry in the gate, then went back to the aircar with Rick to get the remainder of the equipment, a densitometer and an array of probes. It all fit easily in the back of the flatbed and the driver provided a blanket from under her seat to cushion them.

Kent returned to the aircar and the guards closed the gates; Rick and Harry took the leading pair of six seats in the center of the flatbed and the vehicle moved off, driving partly onto the lawn in its U-turn. Its best speed was a walking pace but there wasn't far to go. On the porch of the three-story mansion stood a slim man in black dress clothes awaiting them.

Harry looked at the trees—the trunks were dark green, but the foliage was a true pink, though the leaf veins were green. "Those are comfit trees from Wasatch," Harry said. "Their candied fruit is supposed to be medicinal."

"Wasatch is a day's sail from Quan Loi," Rick said. "We were figuring to meet the *Goliath* there initially, but they decided that they couldn't make it farther than Morroworld so we made the scheduled landing here instead. It's a better base for soundings, and that's what we've been doing."

He chuckled and looked at Harry instead of the trees on his side of the vehicle. "Which left you to whatever transport Captain von Hase could come up with. Sorry about that, but there's really worse than the *Belleisle* this far out from where anybody civilized wants to be."

There were birds in the high sky. Harry said, "Those all have four wings too and there's about a dozen of them. It seems that it doesn't matter much to Doctor Veil, but I *am* a biologist."

After a moment, he said, "Rick, Quan Loi *is* a long way from anything. Closer to Pleasaunce than it is to Cinnabar, but not at all close. How did somebody from here wind up at high rank in the Alliance navy?"

"Well, not *high* rank," Rick said. "Romaine DaSerta was a commander in his last battle. He wanted to be a naval officer and the Fleet was open to talented trainees from any bloody where. He had talent, all right, and if he hadn't been from this benighted place he'd have gotten a lot higher than commander when he died."

"Fighting us?" Harry said, and raised an eyebrow.

"No, fortunately," Rick said. "Because he was very bloody good. This was long before the war between us and the Alliance broke out."

Rick paused to marshal his thoughts. He'd reexamined the Battle of Seringapatam on the ship's database, but that wasn't as detailed as the accounts he'd first read in his Tactics course at the Academy.

"DaSerta had three escort vessels—they weren't destroyers, more like corvettes but without the sparring for fast passage. He fought a squadron from Montaillu long enough for the convoy they were guarding to escape. The freighters didn't have the crews to get under way quick enough to get away. The naval vessels could have, but they went for the raiders instead."

"And DaSerta was killed?" Harry said.

"He put his ship alongside the heavy cruiser with the Montaillu admiral," Rick said. "Pirate chief more like but the ship still mounted fifteen-centimeter guns. They shot DaSerta's ship to doll rags, but he took down four antennas on the cruiser and she headed back to base as bloody quick as she could. Which wouldn't have been very quick."

"I see that Commander DaSerta was very brave," Harry said. "But he wasn't alone on his ship, and the whole crew must've died with him."

Rick's expression went blank as he looked at his companion. "Well, I suppose that's true, but that's the way things happen in wars. It's just how it is."

Harry shrugged. "I suppose it is," he said. "And that was thirty or forty years ago?"

"More than fifty," said Rick. "So yeah, there's a good chance the personnel would've been dead by now regardless."

Harry nodded. "Common in many species," he said. "Individuals sacrificing themselves for the good of the race. All that really matters is what best helps the genes survive."

They had arrived at the full-height porch of the mansion. The driver made a wide turn that brought Harry's seat to within a pace of the entrance steps.

Rick followed Harry out, muttering, "Time to greet our host."

Master DaSerta had a goatee and a thin moustache. From a distance he passed for forty, but close up he was at least twenty years older than that. He bowed as the two younger men reached the bottom of the steps, then straightened and said, "Lord Harper? I am Porphyrio DaSerta."

He extended his hand. Harry took it and said, "I'm Harry Harper, sir, and honored to meet you." Turning to Rick he went on, "This is my friend and colleague Rick Grenville, sir."

"Honored, Grenville," DaSerta said. "You are interested in Uncle Romaine?"

Rick nodded. "Commander DaSerta is a hero whose exploits are taught even in the RCN Academy," he said. "I was thrilled when Harper here told me that he would be meeting a relative of the man."

DaSerta smiled thinly, the first expression he had shown since they arrived. "I was only five when I last saw Uncle Romaine," he said. "I thought of him only as father's younger brother, the wild one of the family. I didn't really appreciate the man he was until long after his death. There's a room devoted to him, a small shrine if you please. You're welcome to see it, Lord Grenville."

He turned. "But both of you, follow me now and I will show you treasures."

The doors whisked open behind him, pulled by a pair of servants in orange livery. Doors along the corridor beyond quivered closed. Rick had the impression of roaches scuttling away from a light, but it was probably children fleeing from strangers' eyes.

DaSerta opened the door to the first room to the right. A middle-aged man with a fringe of gray hair around a bald spot stood at the near end of a glass-topped display case. There were filing cabinets along the side walls and a full-sized console at the far end of the room.

"Swanny here will help you with any questions, Lord Grenville," DaSerta said. "I myself will guide Lord Harper through the main collection."

Harry and their host went off down the hall. Rick put himself in the attendant's hands, figuring he'd learn the most by doing that while keeping out of Harry's way. Harry, after all, was doing the real work of the mission at the moment.

Most of the material in the filing cabinets was of no interest except possibly to a biographer of Commander DaSerta. His family had obsessively preserved his childhood schoolwork, not in the expectation he would become famous but because he was their son. Rick suspected that his mother might have been the same way if she'd had the resources to manage it.

DaSerta's tactical simulations from Officer's Entry School on Euclid, copied to chip and probably found with his personal effects, were on the console. After six months at the Euclid feeder school, DaSerta was promoted to an Advanced Officer's Course on Pleasaunce. His graduation certificate as leader of his class there was in the files also.

From the beginning DaSerta's battle planning had been aggressive, but it took on increasing sophistication while he was still at Euclid. Even at graduation, DaSerta's simulations assumed that subordinate officers would obey his orders even when these put them into greater danger. It struck Rick that in reality this varied in direct relation to the quality of the navy involved. Even in the RCN at the height of the recent war, it hadn't been a hundred percent.

"Lord Grenville...?" Swanny said softly. Rick looked up from the simulation he'd been deep into, then followed the attendant's eyes to the door where Harry stood with their host. Harry was holding his 3-D imaging apparatus, which meant he'd returned to the vehicle without Rick noticing as Harry went by his door.

"I've made my record for Father," Harry said. "Master DaSerta is happy to give you access at a later time for further research into Commander DaSerta."

Porphyrio DaSerta nodded from beside him.

"Ah!" Rick said. "Let me shut down here and I'll be right with you."

"Your lordship?" Swanny said obsequiously. "I'll be happy to log you out..."

"If you'd be so good," Rick said. He gave DaSerta an enthusiastic smile. "In that case, if you wouldn't mind, Master DaSerta, I'd appreciate a glance at the main collection. I'm unlikely to be back on Quan Loi to see it again."

"Of course," their host said and led the way back into the room down and across the hall.

The objects included many biological oddities—there was the skeleton of a two-headed snake—and a considerable amount of memorabilia of Captain Romaine DaSerta. This included several uniforms; eyeing them Rick estimated that the captain had been slightly shorter than his descendent Porphyrio but with the same slender build.

There were also files of documents, mostly of a political nature dating from after establishment of the colony on Quan Loi. These were of no interest to Rick, but he browsed a few of them for politeness' sake. He'd gotten to the end of the long room before he'd repented of asking to see it. He certainly hoped that Harry had gotten more from the visit than he himself had, however.

The last item was on a freestanding table covered by a curtain supported by a frame. Rick's first thought was *Like a birdcage at night*, but he caught himself before he made what their host might have felt was a boorish joke. He was here as Harry's guest, after all.

"This is the great treasure that Lord Harper was particularly taken by," DaSerta said, nodding to Harry, who nodded back in solemn agreement. "This is an artwork left by the Archaic Spacefarers."

DaSerta whipped the curtain away. On the pedestal was a disk of quartz crystal a foot in diameter. Because it was displayed on edge, Rick could see the engraving on the back simply by stepping around the pedestal.

By looking at a shallow angle, Rick could read:

> THIS SCULPTURE WAS FOUND EIGHTY YEARS
> AFTER OUR LANDING ON QUAN LOI.
> IT DEPICTS MEMBERS OF A RACE WHICH
> INHABITED THE PLANET IN FORMER TIMES.

Rick moved around to the front again and looked at the two spidery figures there. The quartz had been polished after it was carved. The subject appeared to be a man and a woman on either side of a narrow-trunked tree with fronds rather than branches.

"I see," he said. He cleared his throat and went on, "Master DaSerta, may I ask who engraved the legend onto the back of the disk?"

"I don't have any idea," DaSerta said. "One of my ancestors, obviously, or rather one of his servants, but there's no record of which one. I don't suppose it really matters when it was found. Some of my ancestors have been very punctilious about inventorying the collections but others have not; and to be honest, I haven't been as careful myself as I might have been. Perhaps your visit, Lord Harper, will cause me to mend my ways."

He and Harry laughed mildly; Rick managed to force a smile.

The crystal disk was the condensing lens from the display of a Pre-Hiatus starship. Modern units used air-projected holograms for three-dimensional displays. Ancient consoles didn't have that capacity and used quartz crystal. This was an absolutely standard thirty-centimeter unit of Terran manufacture. Rick had seen many of them in the History of Space Travel course he'd taken as an elective at the Academy.

It was certainly ancient: two thousand years old at a minimum. But it wasn't the millions of years old that Archaic remains tended to run to, as best as you could date those elusive fragments; and it was of human manufacture.

Rick doubted whether he could convince Captain DaSerta that his cherished disk wasn't of prehuman construction, nor would there be any advantage in having done so. He'd tell Harry as soon as the two of them were alone so that Harry wouldn't be getting Doctor Veil's hopes up with nonsense.

DaSerta walked them out onto the porch. Harry said, "Excuse me, sir. Those comfit trees lining the drive?" He pointed. "They're not native to Quan Loi. Can you tell me anything about them?"

"Ah!" said their host. "In this case I *can* give you a solid answer. My founding ancestor, Captain Mortimer DaSerta himself, planted them. You knew that his ship, *Russell 974*, landed on Wasatch before proceeding here to Quan Loi, didn't you?"

"No, I did not," Harry said in a neutral tone.

Rick tried to hide his shock. That hadn't appeared in the *Far Traveller*'s course data either. Quan Loi was listed as settled directly from Earth with no mention of Wasatch.

"The initial plan was that the colonists on the *Russell 974* would supplement those sent to Wasatch twenty-three years before," DaSerta explained. "There was friction immediately, and before the year was out the later colonists reboarded the *Russell* and transferred to Quan Loi, which had been considered as an alternative destination. Captain DaSerta had become enthusiastic about comfit jelly by then and he brought the species with him to Quan Loi."

Rick thought about events hundreds of years ago—critically important to the participants at the time and now just a corner of local history. Remembered within the DaSerta family but probably unknown outside of it, even here on Quan Loi. Nonetheless probably true, since the comfit trees along the drive were certainly real.

"The species is very long lived," Harry said after consulting his handheld data unit. "Over a thousand standard years on Wasatch, so these may well have been planted by your ancestor just as your records indicate. But why is the third one down the left side stunted, sir?"

That was the tree Harry had remarked on as they were driven to the house. The others were all about sixty feet tall; this was only half that, and the trunk was spindly besides.

"It's always been that way," DaSerta said. "I'd have taken it out when I succeeded my father as Hereditary Captain, but that would leave a gap. Comfit trees take so long to grow that I decided to leave it the way it's been for twelve hundred years or so."

"Would it be all right if I made some densitometer readings, then?" Harry asked. He looked at Rick and said, "Lord Grenville? Would you mind fetching the extended probes that I left with Kent?"

Rick nodded and started down the drive at a fast walk. He'd been sitting as he went through the material on Romaine DaSerta. He was just as glad not to bother with the lowboy, and the vehicle wouldn't have gained him much time either.

By the time he got back with the bundle of meter-long rods, Harry was already taking readings from the stunted tree while their host watched in mild bemusement. For an instant Harry projected the meter's findings, then nodded. He said to Rick and DaSerta, "The number of rings is identical to that of the first tree in the row—indicating 1,182 years, Master DaSerta, confirming your records. Now—"

He turned to Rick. "If you'll help me, Lord Grenville, to set a constellation of these probes around the tree about six feet out from the center of the trunk, I'll activate them and they'll screw themselves in."

Rick was perfectly willing to be doing lift and carry for his friend. It was simple enough and would make Captain Bolton happy when he learned about it.

He pressed the sharp end of each half-inch beryllium rod into the soil, far enough to keep it from falling over when he took his hands away. He moved to the next one each time until he met Harry coming around the tree clockwise. Rick had never used the equipment before, but there wasn't much to learn.

"Now, step back," Harry said. "And you too, Master DaSerta, because occasionally these fly loose and it might take me a moment to shut them off."

Rick obediently stepped onto the paved drive. At least that way nothing would be coming through the ground at him.

Harry keyed his testing device with a small popping sound. The eight poles they'd set in a rough circle suddenly whirred and spun into the ground, throwing up piles of finely divided clay around each disappearing shaft. The heads were duplex, contra-rotating around their common axis.

One probe hit something about a foot into the soil. Rick felt the clack through his boots and the shaft stopped. The others sank in till only a few inches were visible.

Again Harry projected the display so that he and his audience could see what the probes had found. "That's very odd," he said.

"Lord Harper?" DaSerta said. "I don't understand what the image is."

"I've set it to show relative density as a color spectrum," Harry said. "Violet is highest. As you see, the soil is basically green with flecks of blue for pebbles—like the one that the fifth probe hit. The trunk is blue-green. And there's a ring of violet, there"—he pointed—"choking the tap root which has apparently grown through it."

DaSerta turned to the servant who'd accompanied him onto the porch and called, "Wesler, get the gardeners out here with shovels! I want this tree out of the ground in five minutes!"

To Harry he added, "I'll replace it with something local, maybe a spiked elm. They've got reddish foliage and I can put in a well-grown tree. I'd been thinking of doing that anyway."

Harry put his device away in its pouch and started removing the probes. Rick joined him.

"Tap the center of the top and it'll spin out on its own," Harry explained when he saw Rick gripping the exposed end with both hands with flexed knees and trying to draw the probe out by straightening his legs.

A touch on the button achieved what main strength had not. Rick caught the rod before it fell over when it had spun out. From stubbornness he pulled up by hand the one that had stopped a foot down.

A man in his sixties and a boy arrived, both carrying shovels and wearing coveralls. They dipped their heads low to DaSerta and immediately got to work on the ground around the stunted tree. Whatever the steward had told them had sparked their enthusiasm.

"Don't worry about the tree!" DaSerta said. "Just get the root of it up!"

"The ring appeared to be about eighteen inches down," Harry said from where he and Rick stood out of the way.

Rick had thought getting a backhoe in would have been faster in the long run, but in fact it was in less than the demanded five minutes that the gardener muttered to his assistant and they laid their shovels behind them. They gripped the tree trunk. Shifting together they worked the trunk in all four directions alternately, then lifted it out of the hole. They flopped it on ground behind the senior man.

They stepped back. Neither appeared to be breathing hard.

Rick got out his folding knife and knelt beside the lump where the tap root continued below a knotted halo of lesser roots. DaSerta stood beside him but didn't kneel on the dirt. Harry was adjusting his device.

Using the back of the long blade Rick scraped dirt from a smooth, clear object. Not a stone—

"That's silicon carbide!" Harry said, reading his display. "The clear variety—moissanite!"

"What's it doing here?" Rick asked.

DaSerta said, "The Archaics regularly used moissanite in their constructions! This may be one of their devices or what survives of it!"

"The ring is at least three thousand years old," Harry said, "but we can't prove it goes back any farther than that. Even so I'd like to clean it off and collect all possible data from it. And with your permission, I'll bring Doctor Veil to see it and I hope handle it."

"Yes, of course!" DaSerta said. "This is wonderful! Another Archaic artifact!"

Rick continued to scrape away dirt. *At least,* he thought, *he's breaking even for Archaic artifacts for the day.*

"Where's the boss?" Mahaffy asked as I entered the bio lab.

"She's still at the DaSerta estate," I said, taking one of the empty workstations.

"How long's it going to take you to finish up there?" Mahaffy said. "We're supposed to lift for Medlum as soon as the last pinnace gets back and it's due any time now."

"I think Doctor Veil's just going over the site again," I said as I looked at what I'd gathered. I had densitometer scans of the tree to either side of the stunted one and root sections above and below the ring of the tree that'd been pulled out of the ground. The actual wood was filed in specimen storage in the separate compartment where most of my additional luggage had been transferred by now.

So far as I could tell there was nothing to be seen at DaSerta House beyond what we'd already recorded in every fashion imaginable, but Doctor Veil was so excited to have an Archaic relic in her hand that she didn't want to leave it. I didn't say that to Mahaffy, just started sorting the electronic files.

"Did you really find an Archaic artifact?" Mahaffy asked. He'd turned away from what he'd been working on and was looking at me. I didn't meet his eyes.

"Doctor Veil believes we have," I said carefully. "I believe so also, though I might wish for additional supporting evidence."

I wasn't going to publicly disagree with my superior; and I couldn't imagine any other fashion in which a moissanite ring could have gotten into the soil of Quan Loi with a year of human settlement.

What I'd told Master DaSerta was true, though. The ring was

old, but as solid evidence it didn't any more prove the existence of the Archaics than the carved quartz lens did. Perhaps further study and analysis back on Xenos with a larger sample of experts could at least suggest what the object was intended for. Silicon carbide was extremely refractory, so it was anybody's guess how this ring fitted into a larger construct which had completely rotted away.

"You know, the Shinings...?" Mahaffy said. "The Shining Empire, I mean? They say they come from the Archaics. Their ancestors weren't from Terra at all. They say."

I smiled. The Shinings had built the barrel-shaped ship in Helle Harbor, I remembered. "I wonder what they cite as evidence for that, Mahaffy?"

"I dunno," the tech said. "I was just chatting with one of the Power Room crew who's served in this neck of the galaxy before. He's ex-Fleet, you see."

I closed the file I was working on. The visual and densitometer images were all tagged with full descriptions. I turned toward Mahaffy and said, "Well, without genetic samples I can't disprove that theory, but I will say that I find it most unlikely. Still, not for me to quarrel with another man's religious beliefs."

Doctor Veil entered the lab. "The third pinnace is back," she said. "We'll be transferring to Medlum within two hours, according to Captain Bolton."

She stepped over to me. I was afraid I'd done something wrong and started to get up. Instead she extended her hand and said, "Lord Harper, your skill and tact have gained me the greatest triumph of my career. Thank you from the bottom of my heart."

I shook her hand, feeling embarrassed. She thought I'd proven the existence of the Archaics. I certainly hadn't, and I would have to say so if I were questioned.

For now at least, Doctor Veil was pleased with her decision to hire me. I guess I could count that as a win.

MEDLUM

Rick tapped on the hatch to Bio Section but entered before there was a response. He'd become a frequent visitor to Bio Section since Harry joined the staff. Doctor Veil appreciated not only the help he'd provided on Quan Loi, but also his knowledge of *Far Traveller* and of the RCN generally.

The scientists were necessarily separate from the naval personnel, but there was no reason they should be hostile. Until Rick and Harry had become friends, that had been on the way to being the case.

Harry and the technician were at work stations; the hatch to Veil's office was closed. She was probably inside, but Rick didn't have any business with her.

"Hey, Rick," Harry called. "I hope you're here to offer me something more exciting to do than sequencing crustaceans from Beiderbeke, which I've never seen. Not that it matters whether or not I've visited Beiderbeke."

"Well, I don't know how exciting this is," Rick said. "I'm hoping that you can give me a little help. We—the *Far Traveller*—got underway pretty suddenly and Navy House didn't equip us with the background information that we'd normally have had. There isn't even a set of the *Sailing Directions* for this region. I'd like to know a little more about where we're operating than just route calculations."

Harry got to his feet and stretched. They were six hours

out of Quan Loi in sponge space. It didn't matter to a genetic sequencer, but to a human being it was a very lonely, boring existence. Nothing whatever would happen unless the hull were to fail catastrophically.

"Well, we've got quite a lot of background material down here," Harry said. "Our brief is to gather data on the life on planet, which meant we needed as much information about the planets as possible."

He sat down at the workstation to the left of the one he was using and brought it up. "I can't help you with the *Sailing Directions*," he said, "because they don't exist for this region. We do have the *Annotated Charts*, issued by the Fleet Bureau of Cartography on Pleasaunce. I don't guarantee that this is the most recent edition, but it's the most recent that the Science Directorate could find on Cinnabar before the *Far Traveller* set out."

He rose so that Rick could take the seat at that station. Rick called up the section on Medlum, the next base on the *Far Traveller*'s itinerary. He began scrolling into the data, then looked up and said, "This is wonderful! All we've got on the bridge are the coordinates and the course—and I can tell you, the course data is pretty rudimentary. Of course that's what we're here for—but we didn't even know that Medlum was self-governing with just an Alliance commissioner, a postholder this says."

He cleared his throat and said, "Ah, Harry—is there any way you can transfer this material to the bridge? It would be hugely helpful to us."

"Let me tell Doctor Veil," Harry said. He walked to the office door and rapped on it, then went in. Rick noticed that he'd said "tell" rather than "ask permission of."

A moment later, Harry and Doctor Veil came out of the office together. Veil said, "We don't have a physical connection—the science-side database is separate from the naval one. But if you think the information would be useful, you're welcome to any of it that you can transfer physically."

"That would be wonderful!" Rick said. "It doesn't matter while we're in sponge space, of course, but the *Far Traveller* has to set up a planetary base while the pinnaces do the sounding. Captain Bolton will be extremely grateful, mistress. And I shouldn't wonder if he'll be grateful to me for having thought to ask you."

Doctor Veil gave Rick a smile that struck him as wistful. "For my part, I would be grateful for a closer relationship with the naval side," she said.

Ten hours after Rick left the laboratory with data chips in a small satchel, he knocked on the door of Harry's cabin. It was a moment before Harry opened the latch. He was wearing utility trousers which he'd probably just pulled on.

"Is there a problem, Rick?" he asked.

"Not a bit," Rick said. "You got a moment to chat? And hey, I'm sorry if I waked you up."

"Come on in," Harry said. "Though I don't have much to offer here. Some white wine from Balgorod that isn't bad at all. I'm not sure where Mahaffy found it."

"Just as well not to ask where your servant finds things," Rick said. "We'll restock at Medlum and you'll be able to lay in your own cellar. But if you don't mind, I certainly would take a small glass as we talk."

"Pleased to do both," Harry said. He opened a small chest and took out two of the half-dozen ten-ounce glasses within. They were unadorned but sufficient for the purpose.

"So...," Harry said as he handed over one of the part-filled glasses, "what did you want to talk about?"

"Basically to thank you for the material you provided," Rick said. "We'll probably be getting invitations, us officers will, as soon as we land. Knowing that the Shining Empire and the Alliance both claim the right to rule Medlum is great, and learning that there's a Cinnabar mission there too is even better. We didn't realize there was any Cinnabar presence within ten days travel of Medlum."

"I didn't spend much time on the briefing materials myself," Harry said. "I guess the Foreign Ministry didn't brief Navy House as fully as they did the Science Directorate. At least they gave us the background materials. It sounded to me that they brought in Cinnabar to mediate because we *don't* have any stake in the region."

"I wonder if they knew there was an RCN expedition coming out here to sound new routes when they agreed?" Rick said, sipping his wine. He'd come down to see Harry as soon as his watch had ended. It was safer to keep his distance from Lieutenant Vermijo, and Lieutenant Dogan had no interest in anything but the RCN so there was no point in trying to discuss Medlum with him.

"I doubt that Navy House volunteers any more information to the Foreign Ministry than comes the other way," Harry said. Then he said, "Medlum seems to have at least a dozen major islands. I'll be flying around quite a lot choosing regions to sample. And Joss will have to set up collecting teams, if that's possible. Mostly the locals are cotton farmers, but if the plantations are anything like Greenslade, there'll be plenty of hunting for the pot to add protein."

"What I don't understand," Rick said, "is why the Alliance is negotiating with the Shinings to begin with?"

"What?" said Harry. "Well, the Shining Empire is a growing power in the region, rapidly industrializing. Why not become friends?"

"Because Guarantor Porra's normal reaction would be to slap down whatever fleet the Shinings have and take them over. If they're industrializing, fine. They can build ships for the Alliance, the way Pantellaria's been doing for the past thirty years."

"Ah," said Harry as he refilled their glasses. "Well, I guess we'll find out very shortly."

Some of the crew walked down to the corridors feeding the boarding holds while the *Far Traveller* was still making its descent. They squatted on the deck with their backs against the bulkhead. It seemed to me that if something went wrong on the landing, they'd bounce around like peas in a whistle.

Either the spacers didn't agree or they didn't care. I'd been around spacers enough even in my short RCN career to realize that fatalism was a major character trait. Probably a necessary one also.

The ship slowed almost to a halt while we were still in the air. We mushed for a moment, making me fear that something was badly wrong. Then we dropped another ten feet before fetching up with a greater braking effort that squeezed me hard against my acceleration couch in the lab. The actual landing involved severe sidewise rocking which didn't bother me the way the earlier greasy feeling had. That had seemed uncontrolled and I'd feared we were on the verge of plunging bow first into the ground.

Only then did I get up from my couch; Mahaffy and Doctor

Veil stood also. I called, "Doctor Veil, I'll head out and find the rep from the Mediation Mission!" She nodded toward me but didn't speak.

I didn't need to be in a hurry. We were down now, but it was a minimum of ten minutes after landing that the harbor would cool enough for the ship to be opened without poaching the spacers who waited in the hold.

The bolts locking the stern hatch into the hull withdrew with a series of clangs and the gears lowered the hatch to form a ramp. The line in the corridor started moving as soon as the hatch shuddered against the starboard outrigger, which meant that the team which would lay the floating extenders had begun walking across the ramp before it was fully down.

Many of the folks ahead of me started sneezing. I did the same a moment later as steamy air, sharp with ozone, flooded in through the open hatch. I slitted my eyes, keeping them only open enough to keep my place in the line of moving spacers. There was a stiff breeze when we reached the ramp and I was able to open my eyes wider.

The boarding ramp resting on the ship's outrigger had a width of twenty feet, but the floating extenders that connected the ship to the pier were only three feet wide with no handrail. This didn't appear to bother the spacers in the least, but I stepped to the side on the outrigger and let the crush at the extender empty out.

I looked around at St. Martins Harbor. Dominating everything to the north was the volcano. The lower slopes were green, but the top thousand feet of the cone were bare and a haze of smoke drifted from the top. Because of the ship's plasma exhaust I couldn't be sure, but I thought that the rasp at the back of my throat was from sulfur rather than just loose ions.

A trail zigzagged up to the top of the cone. Houses were fairly frequent at the base of the slope, but the numbers thinned out quickly.

Joss stepped to my side and nodded to me. "Sir."

She was wearing a light, long-sleeved shirt, but a tattooed serpent thrust its blunt head onto the back of her right hand and on the left hand was a stylized eye. I didn't see her bush knife, but I suspected the loose shirt covered the hilt of it and the blade was inside the leg of her shorts. I wasn't going to ask her.

The hunter's caution had kept her alive in difficult circumstances, but it was uncomfortable to think that she thought we might be in that sort of circumstance now. I wasn't trained for that sort of world.

"How do we get to the Mediation Mission?" Joss said. "Walk?"

"If we need to," I said. "I checked the location against the imagery we recorded from orbit. We've got quite a good optical suite even for a warship because we're expected to be choosing locations to sample even on uninhabited planets. But—"

I smiled at Joss. The last of the backed-up spacers were proceeding toward the pier. A few still trickled from the forward hatch.

"—the mission is supposed to send a car for us. I don't see a car, however."

"*Any* cars," Joss said.

When I looked at the traffic in St. Martins rather than just the buildings I saw that she was right. The street through the center of town to the base of the volcano was broad and likewise the boulevard running along the harbor, but the other streets viewed from orbit had been narrow alleys. I couldn't even see them from water level. What vehicles there were had spindly wheels and narrow, flimsy bodies.

We crossed the floating extension. Some harbors have solid bridges on the piers which they winch out to vessels' boarding ramps, but I hadn't seen any of these in the ports where the *Goliath* or *Far Traveller* had landed. A starship landing or lifting off does so on the power of plasma thrusters. Though less focused than bolts from the cannon which warships carried as defensive weapons, a multiple battery of thrusters—the *Far Traveller* had sixteen—was enormously destructive.

The concrete steps up to the top of the pier were slimy with harbor waste floated onto them by high tides and the surge every time a ship landed in the harbor. Each step was two meters long. The attachment bar slanting up the staircase allowed the extension bridges to move with changes in the tide.

I didn't see any cargo-handling equipment. I supposed that heavy cargo was lightered from the shore and hoisted aboard a receiving ship's own winch. I wasn't sure how heavy incoming loads were handled; maybe there were mobile cranes.

I kept a hand above the railing of steel pipe—not gripping it because it was slimed by the harbor water the same way the steps were, but hovering near and ready to grab if my feet went out from under me. Joss had skipped ahead—more fit than I was and probably less cautious as well.

Nobody hailed her at the top of the pier, but a woman called cheerfully when my head rose into sight, "You, sir? Are you looking for a ride to the Cinnabar Mission?"

The speaker was an attractive woman of about twenty, standing beside a large-wheeled tricycle parked on the concrete esplanade between where the *Far Traveller*'s two boarding holds connected with it. She had reddish hair and wore civilian clothes, though the fabric was a plaid of khaki and dull green.

I waved and called, "I'm Lieutenant Harper. Are you our ride?"

The tricycle had a saddle in front for the driver. Its rear compartment would hold four seated passengers or a modest load of cargo.

"Hop in," she said. She watched Joss approaching beside me. "Two of you, then?"

"Yes," I said. The woman's glance had been neutral—but determinedly so. Even though Joss' tattoos and knife were mostly out of sight, her scars couldn't be hidden. "This is Technician Joss. She and I are responsible for field collections. We're hoping that your mission will be able to help us find local help since you've been here longer."

"I'll do what I can," the woman said, taking my offered hand. "Oh—I'm Rachel Pond. I'm a research assistant for the mission. Which means general dogsbody, which is why I'm here picking you up."

The tricycle pulled out with a double whine from the hub-center electric motors in the rear wheels. Rachel pulled back onto harbor street—or whatever it was called—and then turned right up the central street. Our initial whining progress slowed to an amble as the slope steepened. None of the three of us was overweight and the vehicle was very lightly built, but even so we were underpowered.

I leaned forward and said, "Are there any roads on Medlum? I didn't see any on the orbital survey we made when we arrived here."

Rachel turned her head—not toward me, but at least so that she wasn't facing away when she spoke—and said, "No, not outside the town itself. The cash crop is Medlum cotton, a very long-staple variety. It's grown on the coast and on rivers, then transported to St. Martins by boat. As overgrown and mountainous as the islands are, cutting roads for a bulk cargo like cotton would be a pointless expense."

I strained to hear her. This was about the worst layout for conversation between driver and passenger that I could imagine.

I said, "Is the cotton so valuable then, that both the Alliance and the Shining Empire want it so badly? Badly enough to threaten war?"

Rachel laughed. I thought I heard bitterness. "The cotton is unique and valuable, yes, but of course not enough for a war. That's just boys being boys—male dominance behavior. The Shinings believe they were a great empire before the Hiatus and they're determined to regain their place. And the Alliance doesn't want to be insulted by some Johnny-come-lately yokels."

We were moving at a slow walk, but no amount of additional power would have allowed us to go faster unless we were willing to drive over pedestrians, many of them carrying packs or pushing carts. The feeders that entered the thoroughfare we were on were narrow and crooked, really what was left over after houses had been built rather than planned streets.

I wondered if Medlum had ever had animal transport? I didn't see any sign of it now except in the irregular road network.

Rachel's comment reminded me of Rick's question from the night before we reached Medlum. "Why is the Alliance negotiating?" I asked. "The Shinings may be a growing power in the region, but the Alliance of Free Stars is that fifty times over."

Rachel glanced back toward me again. "Let's wait until we're in the mission, shall we? It's not exactly a secret for us, but talking about it in the street might make a problem for Minister Blakeley. Or she might think it could have. She comes down on me either way."

"Understood," I said. I leaned back in the wicker seat and waited while we trundled through the traffic. I glanced at Joss, but she continued to eye the people and buildings—mostly courtyard houses with blank ten-foot walls facing the street. When she did meet my eye in a passing glance, she showed no emotion or even interest.

A man with two bundles balanced on a pole over his shoulder crossed in front of an alley to the right. Rachel paused till he was clear, then turned into it. We twisted halfway along before seeing a man in maroon shorts and a beige tunic standing in the passage. He stepped to the side, drawing a vehicular door open as he did.

Rachel turned around in the courtyard, then parked facing out. We were in the L of a two-story building, beside the blank wall of a similar building. The alley formed the fourth side.

"Come on in," Rachel said, leading us toward a door into the wall she'd parked against. "I'll introduce you to Milo. He's local and handles our supplies, so he should be able to introduce you to hunters and fishermen. We eat mostly on the economy here."

She entered the short corridor and stepped into the office just to the right; the panel door was open. The heavy man behind the desk inside nodded to greet her but didn't get up.

"Milo," she said, "this is Lieutenant Harper and his assistant Joss. They're on Medlum to take biological samples. I thought you could introduce them to people who can guide them to where they can find samples. Yes?"

"The guides, they will be paid?" Milo said. He got up and stood beside his desk to look us over.

"Yes," I said. "The rates will be determined ahead of time, after we consult with local experts." Which probably meant Milo himself if he did the bargaining for the mission, but anyway I was making it clear that we didn't expect to be held up for some wild amount.

"Very good," Milo said, nodding and walking toward us. "I will take you to meet some people now. You can walk, I trust?"

"Yes," said Joss before I could speak. She looked at me and said, "Sir, I can handle this. You had some business to take care of with Mistress Pond, right?"

"Ah...," I said, taken aback. "Well, if you're sure, that would be fine. Meet you at the ship when we're both finished, I guess?"

Joss and Milo went out through the corridor. Milo didn't bother to show any concern about leaving us in the room. I suppose I could've closed the door, but I said, "Do you have an office of your own, Rachel?"

"I have a cubby as part of Minister Blakeley's suite," she said, "but it's not in the least private. I think the Minister's in her office now."

"Good," I said. "Would you introduce me?"

"Well, if you'd like that, surely," Rachel said. "That's down the leg corridor. I think she'd have liked it to be on the upper floor, but she needs a full console and to get that up even the main stairs would probably require demolishing part of the building."

We went down the corridor and turned. We met two men in Cinnabar-cut civilian suits and a young woman whom I took for locally hired office help. All of them looked hard at my RCN uniform; the men muttered to Rachel and nodded to me, but none of them really spoke.

We entered the end office where a plumpish man in his forties sat behind a desk in the outer office. I'd decided how I wanted to handle this, so when the man looked up I said, "Good day, sir. Would you please inform Minister Blakeley that Lord Harper would like to speak with her. At her leisure, of course."

The secretary touched an intercom button and said, "Minister, Lord Harper is here to see you."

He had an earbud. I heard the response only as a hissing. He said, "I don't *know* what Lord Harper, mistress! Do you wish me to ask him his business?"

As he and I both probably expected, the door to the inner office flew open. A woman in a gray-blue business suit stepped out. She was younger than her secretary, probably in her midthirties.

"Ma'am," I said, extending my hand as I spoke. "I'm Harry Harper, my dad's Harper of Greenslade, you know. I'm here with the scientific team on the *Far Traveller* and I told the captain that I'd connect with your mission so that we don't put a foot wrong and cause you problems. You know what spacers can be like."

"Well, I—" Blakeley said, shaking my hand while trying to gather her mind.

"And Minister?" I said. "Let me add that Mistress Pond here has been extremely helpful to me and to the mission. She tells me that nobody can give me the answers I needed except you."

"Well, come into my office," she said. "Harper, is it? I'll see what I can do for you."

The Minister waved me to a chair and closed the door behind us. I sat, then said, "I don't—*we* don't aboard the *Far Traveller*— understand why the Alliance agreed to negotiation with the Shinings to begin with. We're very far from home if this is some sort of joke by the Guarantor Porra."

"So are we," Minister Blakeley said with a faint smile. "There are rumors that Porra is dying. At least the diocese governors believe he may be. None of them wants to be the first to test the rumor, but neither do they want to have their individual forces tied up in border wars when at any moment their neighbors might decide to strike at them to gain advantage in the scramble for the top when the Guarantor is confirmed to be dead."

"Do the Shinings know that?" I asked. I'd seen several of the angular Shining vessels in the harbor when I was viewing imagery of the St. Martins.

Blakeley shrugged. "At first I assumed they did," she said, "because otherwise their arrogance seemed insane. Having talked with them over the past four months, I've come to realize that they're not insane but their ignorance of the wider universe is colossal by civilized standards."

She turned and touched a control of the console with her behind the desk but at right angles. A constellation of about a dozen red dots sprang to holographic life in the middle of the room. "That's the Shining Empire," Blakeley said.

She touched another control and fifty or more amber dots appeared. At the lower edge they marched alongside the red clump. She said, "And that's the Fourth Diocese. They alone could easily crush the Shinings without needing to call for help from the rest of the Alliance, but the Shinings truly don't understand that. They believe that their race has been created to rule *all* races, and that their recent push toward industrialization is the beginning of an unstoppable rush to the top. The Gods will carry them to triumph."

"Then will you give Medlum to the Shinings?" I said. "If that's the case, then the *Far Traveller* isn't going to find itself in the middle of a war or be picked off by an Alliance squadron as the first prize of new hostilities between us and the Alliance."

Blakeley shut off the holographic display and faced me squarely. "You appear to have a low opinion of the diplomatic profession," she said in an ironic tone. "That's understandable, but in the present case my team will do exactly what the parties mutually have requested the Republic of Cinnabar to do: examine the evidence and determine to the best of our ability whether Medlum falls within the suzerainty of the Shining Empire or that of the Alliance of Free Stars. Does that surprise you?"

I cleared my throat. The minister didn't sound angry, though she had a right to be if I'd been so wrong about her ethics.

"Not exactly, Minister," I said. "But you're a Cinnabar official, and I would expect your first loyalty to be to the Republic rather than to abstract truth. Whatever the Alliance or the Shinings might want."

Blakeley sniffed. "I suppose I would," she said. "If I were sure what result would best benefit the Republic, which I am not. I therefore am doing my job honorably and keeping faith with both parties which asked Cinnabar to mediate...which"—she held my eyes—"is very possibly the action which is in the Republic's real long-term best interests."

I nodded to her. "Mistress, I understand and I even agree, though I don't suppose there's any way to know for sure."

"Not in our lifetimes, no," Blakeley agreed. She stared at her hands tented on the desk before her.

I stood. "I would appreciate, Minister, if you gave me access to your complete files. I give you my word as a Harper of Greenslade that I will not divulge the contents to anyone outside my fellows aboard the *Far Traveller* in the course of their duties."

"Granted," Blakeley said. "I'm sure the local staff which we *must* hire if we're to accomplish our task has leaked anything that either party may have been willing to pay for." She sighed and added, "I'll take you to the file room and tell the staff that you have full access."

There were three flat-plate displays in the adjoining room. Men in civilian clothes worked at two of them but the third was vacant; a woman was going through hardcopy files at a table.

"This is Lord Harper," the minister said. "Give him any help he needs."

When Blakeley left the room, I expected the three juniors to begin asking me questions. Instead they nodded to me with polite respect and went back to what they'd been doing—or at least the appearance of it; I had the feeling that they were all watching me from the corners of their eyes as if I were a spy left in their midst. That, or a potentially dangerous madman.

They should have thought of me simply as a young RCN officer. They couldn't know about my family connections—

But they might: The minister's secretary could—*would*—have slipped next door while I was in with Blakeley. I'd just used my name to get the minister to answer the question Rick had posed, while making sure that Rachel wouldn't be blamed for telling me. Heaven only knew what the mission staff had made of my sudden appearance, but it seemed to have frightened the hell out of them. There was nothing I could do about that now.

I skimmed through the evidence that the parties had brought to the Mediation Mission in support of their positions. These displays were linked to the console in Blakeley's office. I couldn't input data, but it was all visible.

The staff annotations illuminated the claims. There'd been a Pleasaunce post on Medlum since just after the resumption of star travel, nearly a thousand years ago. The Alliance claimed that the post involved political control, which was almost certainly an exaggeration. Until three hundred years ago, the most Pleasaunce traders could have claimed was immunity from local criminal jurisdiction.

The Shining Empire offered myths for which they could provide no corroboration on Medlum. On the other hand, the mission had uncovered a considerable amount of Pre-Hiatus trade between Medlum and some of the planets which now called themselves the Shining Empire. I wondered whether the researcher who'd documented that trade—the best evidence so far on the subject—was Rachel Pond.

I could ask her. Perhaps I could ask her at dinner.

A name that frequently occurred in the Alliance submissions was that of Postholder Bothwell. The name rang a vague bell: My mother was from Pleasaunce and I recalled her speaking of Bothwell relatives.

The mission files had Bothwell's background but none of course on Mom's family. He was from Pleasaunce and probably of a prominent family given the rank of some of his relatives; his cousin was an undersecretary in External Affairs.

I went back to the Medlum files for another hour. One of the local men went out with a short comment to the other staffers. Still nobody spoke to me.

I would meet Joss at the *Far Traveller*, though I didn't know how long it would be before she finished her business with Milo. I got up also, nodded to the staffers, and said, "Thank you," and went back to Minister Blakeley's office.

The door to the inner office was open, but I had no need to see her again. The secretary looked up and I said, "Do you know where Mistress Pond is?"

"Well, she's right here," he said, gesturing to the curtained corner of the room to my right. I turned my head and Rachel herself came out of the alcove.

I realized that she may have been as startled—in bad ways—as the other staffers were when I appeared as Lord Harper, but I decided to assume there was no problem and treat her as I'd done from the beginning. I said, "Hi, Rachel. I'd like you to guide me to the postholder's office and introduce me to him. Can you do that?"

"Well, the Alliance headquarters is only a few blocks away," she said. "But I won't be able to introduce you as I've never met Postholder Bothwell."

I checked my case and found I was carrying several visiting cards. "Well," I said, "if you can get me there, I can at least leave my card; he may be a relative, you see. And then perhaps you'd permit me to give you dinner as a thank you for your help today?"

"I'd be happy to guide you," she said, "or drive you in the cyclo if you'd prefer...?"

"I'd prefer to walk," I said. "Can we go now?"

She turned to the secretary and said, "I'll be out with Lord Harper, Griswold."

She took us out by the front door. That street wasn't much wider than the rear alley, but at least the building fronts were in the same line.

"And dinner?" I said. "If there are any places you recommend, that is?"

"This is quite a nice place," she said, pointing to the restaurant across the street on a corner. The sign read Steeling. "I can't afford to go there myself. But your lordship, I'm just doing my job and you don't need to feed me."

We turned uphill at the corner, proceeded two short, steep blocks and came to the next cross street. The two-story building on the corner had a broad veranda and was faced with pink stucco, bleached by long exposure to the sun. Where patches of stucco had flaked off, brighter plaster replaced it. Some missing swatches were still bare to the coarse dark-red limestone below.

There were two guards at the door, probably local men. Though they had Alliance uniform jackets, they wore sandals cut from worn rubber tires. Their carbines were in poor shape.

They stood up as we approached the open door, but when I

said, "Lord Harper to see Postholder Bothwell," they bowed us in without even asking questions. I was holding a visiting card in my hand as I stood in the circular entrance hall. For a moment I couldn't even see where to go next, but Rachel pointed to the doorway to our left. I entered what proved to be an outer office and handed my card to the receptionist.

"Lord Harry Harper," I said. "I'm hoping to see the postholder. I believe we're distantly related."

The woman goggled at me, but before she decided what to do the door to the inner office opened fully—it had been ajar—and a tall, heavyset man came out. He wore a vest but it wasn't closed at the front. He was probably in his sixties but looked worn enough to be older.

"You're Harper of Greenslade?" he said.

"He's my father, sir," I said.

"Come on in then!" Bothwell said. "You'll be Daphne's boy: She's my cousin's daughter. But what in heaven's name are you doing on this benighted place, boy?"

"Sir, I'm here as a biologist with the *Far Traveller* and recognized your name—well, the Bothwell name," I said. "And sir? May I introduce my friend and guide, Mistress Rachel Pond, from the Cinnabar Mediation Mission?"

Rachel had moved to the chairs on the wall beside the door. She came forward and joined us when I extended my hand to her.

"My goodness, good of you to bring her, Harry," Bothwell said. "My dear, is there some way I can bribe you on behalf of the Alliance of Free Stars?"

"What!" Rachel said. She didn't seem to know whether or not the postholder's courtly offer was serious. Neither did I, for that matter. "Sir, I assure you that I don't have any control over the mission's assessment. And I wouldn't be bribed if I did."

"Ah, well," Bothwell said. "You can't object to an old man trying, can you? I haven't really cared in a long time, and I'm pretty sure the External Desk in Pleasaunce doesn't care either. But do come in, both of you, and—Meisha, bring in glasses and a bottle of the Chatterton White."

"We really can't stay very long, Postholder," I said, but Rachel followed me doubtfully and we took chairs in the inner office. "I just wanted to say hello to a relative met in a far corner of the galaxy."

The secretary bustled in with the wine much more quickly than I expected from her blank-faced greeting when we arrived. I got up and poured for ourselves and the postholder, then handed Rachel's to her in her seat.

"Have my invitations arrived yet?" Bothwell asked. "Your ship's arrival is an opportunity to host a dance here at Alliance House. For the better sort of locals and for the diplomats—including the monkeys from the Shining Empire, I fear, but I think it's the diplomatic thing to do. And I *am* a diplomat, though I'm sure my superiors don't think I'm a very good one or they wouldn't have exiled me to this sump."

"Invitations weren't mentioned at the time I left the *Far Traveller*," I said. "If the ship is still on Medlum at the time, I will surely make an effort to attend, sir."

"Well, I set it for just two nights forward," the postholder said. "I realized that your ship may not be in harbor long, but this is a real opportunity for those of us on Medlum to interact with civilized people."

"We'll hope to attend," I said neutrally. I'd do whatever Doctor Veil asked me to do, but I suspected she would want to be at a social event which might gain us access to private collections.

The postholder and I made small talk for a polite length of time. The wine was palatable but not one I would tell my elder sister—the connoisseur—to lay in a stock of. Rachel stayed alert but said very little.

I rose and set my glass down on the tray. Bothwell and I shook hands and he followed the two of us to the door of his office. He and I made polite noises as Rachel and I went out.

Outside the building, I said to Rachel, "So—when and where shall I pick you up for dinner?"

She looked down and clasped her hands firmly together. "I hope you won't be offended, Lord Harper," she said. "I think I'd rather not go to dinner with you. I really was just doing my job."

"And doing it very well," I said truthfully. "But did I do something to offend you, Rachel? And I would prefer to be Harry, you know."

"You've been a perfect gentleman and quite exciting to be around, frankly," she said. Then she met my eyes again and said, "Harry, you're a perfectly nice young man, but I don't belong with you. We could spend a pleasant time, I'm sure, but even if you weren't a naval officer it could never be more than a dalliance. That's not what I want. I want a life partner, not a dalliance. Do you see?"

I sighed. "I see, Rachel," I said, "but you have to eat somewhere. That's all I'm offering."

That was technically true, but I certainly hoped that a good meal and a couple more glasses of wine might lead to more.

Rachel smiled at me—sadly, I thought. "Thank you, Harry," she said. "But no. I will take you to the mission, or you can go back to your ship directly from here. I think it's a little shorter to go directly to the harbor."

I sighed again and said, "I'll walk you back to the mission. Perhaps we'll see each other at the do Postholder Bothwell is putting together."

We walked off. I wondered how Joss had gotten on. Better than I had, I hoped.

"I don't see why we don't simply hire local transport like Captain Bolton and the other officers," Harry said as he followed Rick into the equipment bay. Rick was wearing his new second class uniform. Harry was in formal Cinnabar evening garb: black jacket with a high collar, black-and-white checked waistcoat, and white trousers.

The outfit was closely tailored and very uncomfortable, Rick would have thought. Harry seemed unaffected, though. He probably wore that sort of clothing often enough to be used to it.

"Well, the trucks won't be able to manage the streets of St. Martins," Harry said, "and the aircars don't have anywhere to land. I've seen the location."

"Wait and watch, my friend," said Rick.

The equipment supervisor was in his little office and the rear of the bay. He waved to Rick and said, "She's ready to go, sir! And thank you for the bottle! Where'd that stuff come from?"

"Nevermuch, I believe," Rick said. "Though I'm not entirely sure where that is."

He'd done a set of astrogational computations for Lieutenant Dogan, who'd offered a bottle of liqueur for the help. "Kiss of the Madonna" hadn't promised a must-have experience to Rick, but Tech 4 Pequod had been delighted to prep the utility runabout in exchange.

Rick gestured to the vehicle. "If you're all right with riding pillion," he said, "we're set. Otherwise I'll get some blankets and you can ride in the trunk."

"Pillion is fine," Harry said, walking over to the tricycle with large tires woven from beryllium mesh and a wire cage in back to carry the sort of odds and ends the ship might need to transport on a distant planet. The tires were suitable off-road, and the trike was as narrow as the local one Rachel had picked Harry up in two days ago.

It wasn't the sort of thing a senior officer travelled in, though, which is why it was available for a couple of lieutenants tonight.

"Want me to start it, sir?" Pequod asked.

"Naw, no problem," Rick said. "I'll need to start it coming back, won't I?"

Rick gripped the steering yoke and set his right foot on the starter crank, then kicked down with his whole weight. The little diesel fired on the first kick and settled into a ringing idle. Rick hopped aboard and gestured Harry onto the pillion seat behind him. The seating was tight but not impossible.

Harry leaned forward said directly into Rick's ear, "Rick, are you really taking this across the boarding bridge?"

"And up the steps onto the quay," Rick replied nonchalantly. "These mules really are all-terrain, you see. I got pretty good with them on the tender *Mandragora* when I was a midshipman."

There was a slight bump as they drove over the joint between the hold and the ramp, then down it to the end. The floating extension bridge quivered but didn't dip seriously. Rick kept to the center and drove off onto the long concrete steps up to the top of the quay.

He cramped the front wheel against the first step above the one they'd arrived on and said, "Hang on, buddy. This is going to bounce us."

The rear wheels sparked as they spun through the slime, then bit on the concrete. The front wheel lifted, then advanced until the rear wheels met the step and humped over more easily than the front had because they were larger in diameter. The trike repeated the process on the next step and then the three following until it leveled off on top of the quay. There Rick paused and looked over his shoulder at his passenger.

"How're you doing?" he said.

Harry smiled a little wanly. "I'm sure people pay good money at carnivals for thrill rides not nearly as interesting," he said. "All the same, I think I'll choose to walk down the steps when we come back."

"Deal," Rick said. He re-engaged the clutch and they rolled off onto Harbor Street.

They went up the median street, heading straight for the smoking cone of the volcano. The trike jolted. Rick blamed the jounce on the pavement but he saw three flowerpots fall from the upper-floor balcony of a house farther up the hill. Pedestrians scattered, one of them jumping almost in front of the vehicle.

Harry leaned close again and said, "Earthshocks. I'd thought of taking a volcano tour but they've been cancelled because of the activity. I wonder how safe it is to stay with the volcano like that?"

"I figure they know what they're doing," Rick said as he pulled into an empty lot to the rear of Medlum House. It was being used as a parking lot for ground vehicles of various sorts. There wasn't a proper usher to guide vehicles to places, but Rick went around to the back of the plot and drove over brush to find a spot.

When he and Harry had gotten off, Rick bent and removed a pin from the trike. He dropped it into his belt purse.

"What's that?" Harry said.

"It locks the collar joining the kick-starter to the drive shaft," Rick said. "They can still carry the thing away, but at least they're not going to drive off with it."

The sky was starting to get dim by the time they reached the back door of Medlum House.

The stairs at the back of the building were lit by an area light on the roof, which left the back tread largely in shadow from the tread above. At the bottom was a greeter with a hand light.

"Lords Harper and Grenville," Harry said before Rick could speak. The husky greeter nodded politely, but made no attempt to announce them. He was probably there to shoo away the riffraff; whatever that meant in St. Martins.

They hopped up the stone staircase arriving at the top a moment behind a heavy couple wearing the bright, loose clothing which seemed the local fashion on Medlum. Another greeter, this time a woman with a tablet on which she jotted names, stood at the doorway.

"Lieutenants Harper and Grenville," Rick said. It might have been necessary to be "Lord Grenville" to DaSerta on Quan Loi, but he preferred not to do so here. Lieutenant in the RCN was a very respectable status, all he wanted or should need.

The greeter made notations on her pad and they passed into a ballroom. There were sconces on both short walls, but most of the light came from glowstrips in the ceiling. They must have been very old because they were weak and had a faint greenish cast.

Rick stepped out of the doorway and said, "Let's split up. I'm going to see if any attractive ladies would like to know a dashing young RCN officer better."

His initial scan of the room wasn't encouraging, but as he walked to the refreshment table he saw a slender woman whose black dress would have stood out against the flashy locals if she hadn't been so petite that she was generally behind someone twice her breadth.

She'd picked up a glass of faintly pink punch and was looking around with a morose expression. Rick made a beeline for her and when she turned toward him, said, "May I ask if the punch is any good, madam?"

"It suits me well enough, I suppose," she said. Her eyes made a detailed survey of his uniform. Her expression didn't change.

"Well, I'll chance it then," he said with what he hoped was a winning smile. "And from the sound of the music, I gather there's dancing in the next room. Do you dance, ma'am?"

She finished her glass and set it on a tray with empties. In a very distinct voice she said, "Not with you." She turned her back and walked away.

Well, that didn't work well, Rick thought. He wondered how strong the punch was. Not as strong as he wanted it at the moment, he guessed, but he tossed off a glassful anyway. He wandered into the dancing room, which turned out to be the other half of the building's upper floor. A quartet had just finished the finale of a quadrille, and the dancers were drifting off the floor.

A girl in yellow caught Rick's eye. She was slender and quite obviously not a local. She'd separated from her dance partner with only a few words, so they didn't seem firmly attached.

"Ma'am?" he said, stepping briskly toward her. "I'm Rick Grenville, third lieutenant of the *Far Traveller*. Might I have the next dance?"

"It'll be a polka," she said, "which is a bit more energetic than I'm feeling up to at the moment. If you'd care to sit one out, I'd be happy of your company. I'm Rachel Pond, and you must be a colleague of Lord Harper, whom I met yesterday."

"I am," Rick said, "but I'm not nearly so elevated a personality. There are balconies off the other room"—he nodded—"and if you'll permit me, I'll get each of us a glass of punch to drink there. Does it sound like a plan?"

"A good one," Rachel said, putting her hand on Rick's elbow. "And frankly, I found it a little uncomfortable being with a nobleman. Though Harry was perfectly polite to me."

"He's a nice guy from anything I've seen," Rick agreed as they angled toward the refreshment table. "But we salt of the earth types have our uses too."

Not such a bad gathering after all, he thought as he, holding two cups of punch, shepherded Rachel out the side door. *Not at all!*

I had local women lining up to dance with the gentleman from Xenos wearing a dress suit. I wasn't much of a dancer, but you'd have thought I was a professional for the enthusiasm they grabbed me for each next set.

It didn't do any good to say that I wasn't from Xenos. Greenslade is in the far northeast; I was either a rural hick or an academic, and no partier either way. So far as women in St. Martins were concerned, I was the height of sophistication.

I saw Doctor Veil speaking with a group of local men. I hoped they were magnates and that she was making the kind of connections she wanted for her search for the Archaics. So far as I was concerned, I'd rather have been at Orontse on the other side of the island with Joss. I'd rescheduled for this party, so she'd gone on ahead yesterday. Well, tomorrow I'd join her.

I bowed my way past a gaggle of would-be dance partners and strode toward the refreshment table. I murmured nothings each time someone tried to accost me. My eyes weren't really focusing on people, though.

The woman ahead of me at the table turned. We didn't exactly walk into each other, but she spilled her cup of punch by jerking it sideways to avoid driving it into my chest.

"Oh!" she said. "I'm so very sorry!"

"No harm done," I said. "But can I get you another glass of punch? Which means I'll have to step past you, of course."

She returned my smile and moved aside, putting down the empty. I got one for myself when I replaced hers, then edged toward the side of the room to provide more space around the table. She moved with me.

"Your dress is from Pleasaunce, unless I miss my bet," I said. "May I ask what you're doing on Medlum?"

"What in heaven's name am I doing here?" she said, smiling wider. "And yes, the dress is from Pleasaunce, but after my brother Todd's death and my divorce, I moved here where my father is postholder. I don't expect to stay long, but I needed to have a calm place where I could think about the future."

"I've met your father, Mistress Bothwell!" I said. "We're even related through my mother!"

"Madame Hergestal," she said. "But Edwige. And you quite clearly aren't from St. Martins either."

"Well, I'm Harry Harper. Lord Harry Harper if you like, and I'm from Sheet Island on Cinnabar," I said. "I'm a biologist doing a survey of the biota of Medlum. I'd planned to go to Orontse across the island yesterday, but now I'm suddenly glad that I didn't."

I wondered if there was a place we could go to sit down. Since her father was the postholder, we could probably get somebody to open the lower floor offices.

"Orontse?" Edwige said. "Goodness. Are you going to the Meridan Spa also?"

"I'm not going to a spa," I said. "My understanding is that our hunter has established a base in a fishing village. She's going out with the boats and sampling the catches as they come in. I'm to deal with local hunters and I hope to go out in the field as well. Officially that'll be scientific research, but back on Sheet Island they'd probably call it a rough shoot."

"Are you here on your own yacht, Lord Harper?" Edwige asked, tilting her head quizzically.

"No, not on my branch of the Harpers," I said, laughing. "Possibly my Uncle Ted's side. I'm officially Lieutenant Harry Harper, RCN; aboard the RCS *Far Traveller*."

"So...," Edwige said. She didn't physically move away, but I felt the air between us freeze. "You are Republic of Cinnabar Navy.

The Republic of Cinnabar Navy killed my brother at Cacique. I loved Tomi and I wasn't sure I'd ever recover from his death. I'm still not sure."

"I'm very sorry to hear that," I said truthfully. I straightened away from her and crossed my hands behind my back. "It was a bad war."

I didn't mention that I'd had three cousins aboard the *Fiji*, lost with all hands in the First Battle of Cacique.

"Yes, it was." Edwige said as she walked away. Over her shoulder she added, "It still is for some of us. I wish you joy of your rough shooting."

I stood for a moment. I'd had a momentary urge to say that I wasn't really a naval officer, and that was true.

But it wasn't something I was proud of.

The RCN had been the Republic's bulwark against Guarantor Porra's mad arrogance. I couldn't claim the real status of Defender of the Republic, but my cousins had, and they had died for it. I wouldn't implicitly devalue their sacrifice in order to seduce a woman from the losing side.

Oh, well. I would find Doctor Veil and see if I could be of help to her. That was my duty as an RCN officer, after all.

It had been as long an aircar flight as that first one that brought me from Eastport to Helle, but there hadn't been any mountains in the way. Because we'd been over the ground at about a hundred feet the whole way, I'd seen a lot of jungle canopy and occasionally clearings, probably as a result of soil conditions.

I hadn't seen any animals, though. I didn't have much hope for what I'd see walking the region either. At least I knew that I was going to need my locator beacon to find my way back to camp if I entered the jungle—as I intended to do.

The beach was a broad yellowish arc of shells crushed into sand, showing up between the nearly violet sea and the deep green jungle we'd been overflying. The fishermen's shelters were pole-framed shanties covered by broad leaves. How recently each roof had been repaired showed in how green the leaves were.

"I'm going to put her down here," Kent said, bringing us to the ground thirty feet short of the nearest hut. "Closer and I'll knock over the shanties. This one's yours—Joss built it for the two of you."

The shelter was longer than most of the others but it was constructed the same way. Jungle seedlings grew up toward the light a hundred feet above. Chopped off at the base and bent over they became hoop staves when both ends were thrust into the ground. Joss had tied other poles onto them with withies to make a frame and had covered it with leaves gathered into clumps.

A boy of six or younger had hopped out of the shelter when our car landed. He stood staring at us. "Hi," I said. "I'm Harry. Who are you?"

"I guard the house for Mistress Joss," the boy said. "Valuable things here!"

"There certainly are," I agreed. Irreplaceable, at any rate. The refrigerator for specimens in particular. It was powered by a battery pack and probably would have been worth a great deal on the civilian market in any of Medlum's scattered settlements. "How do you guard them, sir?"

The shelter was open at both ends but it wouldn't be difficult to rip a man-sized hole in the sidewalls either. I looked around. I could see at least a dozen people, a few men but mostly women, in the settlement which straggled along the normal tide line.

There were a couple of boats drawn up on the beach. Each was fifteen or twenty feet long, undecked but occasionally with a roof of reeds over the central portion.

"I watch the house!" the boy said. "If anybody steal something, I see them and Miss Joss cuts their balls off! Or their tits if they're broads!"

"What if they sail away with what they've stolen?" I said, more curious than horrified. It doesn't suit a biologist to be horrified by the behavior of animals.

"Miss Joss track 'em down!" the boy said. "You think she wouldn't?"

"I certainly wouldn't bet on it," I said, "but I'm her friend."

"Is one of these the boat Joss went out in?" said Kent from behind me.

He was looking out to sea. Half a dozen fishing boats like those on the beach were coming toward the shore. The nearest pair were taking their sails in before they grounded while the others stretched back to the horizon.

I wasn't sure that the boy was going to answer, but it was unnecessary. When the nearer incoming boat scraped up on shore, Joss leaped from the stern where she'd been standing to raise the bow and splashed through the water to us.

"Sir!" she called. "We've got some unfamiliar fish from three hundred meters down. Usually that depth is barren Henk tells me, but there's a seamount five miles off shore and it's got a different biota."

"I'll help you process them," I said. "And you can fill me in about the region."

Joss had formal arrangements with three of the boatmen—brothers—working out of Orontse. Each of their boats had a locator beacon in it. She planned to go out with each of them in succession—today was the second.

When Joss was with a fisherman, she entered the time the net went in and the depth it was lowered to. The fisherman himself could have entered these details but realistically that wouldn't happen unless she did it. That had been the case on the *Goliath* also, she said. I could honestly tell Doctor Veil that Joss was earning her keep, though I didn't think Veil cared so long as the job was getting done.

The town of Orontse was three long houses on higher ground a half mile to the east. This was the nearest beach to them, but storms were frequent enough here that the fishermen preferred to walk rather than build substantial structures closer to their boats. These shacks along the shore were a matter of a few hours work—and probably less if an entire family worked on the project together.

While I took and recorded samples of the day's catch, two aircars and a surface yacht arrived at what was either a separate island or a very distant headland. "Joss?" I said, gesturing to the second aircar.

"That's the Meridan Spa," she said. "It even gets off-planet traffic that flies in from St. Martins. Dunno what they do in a storm, but maybe they have real bunkers there."

"Say . . . ?" she added after a moment. "Did you want to go over there? Kent and the car've gone back to St. Martins, but a boat goes over every day with fresh fish for the spa. You can ride along and come back the same way."

"I'm okay here," I said. "I like the hammock for sleeping and I'll like it more when I learn to get aboard without going over."

Food at the spa would be fancier and maybe better, but the woman from the village who cooked for us—the mother of the boy who'd been guarding the place when I'd arrived—turned out to be extremely good and the fish even fresher than they got across the bay.

I could see Edwige Hergestal at the spa, but if that never happened again, it was still too soon. I was sorry she'd lost her brother, but people die in wars. Her brother had enlisted, just as my cousins had. Or I had, if it came to that.

There are people who need someone to blame when things go wrong. I've found avoidance is the best way to deal with them.

Joss came back with another basket of fish from the boat she'd accompanied. "Do you want to come out with me tomorrow morning?" she said. "Or maybe on one of the other boats?"

"No," I said. "I'm going to go out into the forest tomorrow with my shotgun. I'm not sure I'll be able to spot anything even with the motion detectors in my RCN goggles, but it's worth a try."

Rick pulled the trike half onto the raised portion of the street in front of the Mediation Mission. One back wheel was still in the travel lane, though there wasn't enough vehicular traffic for it to become a problem.

The raised curb wasn't so much a sidewalk for pedestrians as a channel to direct rainwater into the axial street and down into the harbor. St. Martins was as concentrated as an anthill.

Rachel came out of the mission. Rick took off his commo helmet and waved to her. She looked startled but clicked down the steps to him. The idling diesel was quiet enough to talk over.

"I didn't realize you were going to be driving a cyclo," Rachel said.

Rick handed her the other commo helmet he'd borrowed and relatched the lid of the cargo box. "Put this on," he said, "and we'll be able to talk. Besides there may be stuff dropping outta the sky when we get near the top. Now, hop on behind me and I'll get outta the road."

Rachel pulled the helmet on and found that the internal band adjusted automatically to her head. She got onto the pillion seat by stretching her right leg over and then easing her body carefully to follow. The footboard for the driver extended far enough back for her to use it also.

"I thought you'd be coming in an aircar," Rachel said.

"And park where?" Rick replied. "Besides, the only aircar on the ship is the Bio Section one, and they're using that right now. They've got a sampling team across the island in Orontse. Now, hold on tight and we'll go see a volcano."

He let in the clutch and they started off toward St. Martins' central road with the diesel ringing. They had to pick their way down the street on which the mission fronted—Rick clutched frequently—but he didn't brush pedestrians or even the barrow being wheeled ahead of them by a tradesman who wasn't interested in giving way to the trike behind him.

Rick decided there was no point in getting angry about that sort of thing—any more than there was about rain or a new puppy behaving any of the ways a puppy behaves. That wasn't the sort of mood he wanted to put Rachel in as they picnicked on the volcano. He was very well aware of her warm body pressing against his back as they vibrated along the road.

They turned right on the axial street, toward the smoking cone. There was traffic there too, but more room to dodge.

"*Oh!*" Rachel said. "*I'd meant to bring an extra sweater.*"

"We can go back for it," Rick said. He clutched and checked the road, considering where the best place to turn would be. "Though I've got three or four blankets in the back of the trike for when we're stopped."

"*No,*" Rachel said, "*I left it in my apartment; and Rick, I'd really just as soon not show you my apartment. You're a nice fellow, surely, but you're going to be leaving Medlum in a week or so and not coming back. We're going to take a look at the volcano and have a picnic. That's all.*"

"Ah, well," Rick said. "If that's how you want it. But you can have an awful lot of fun in a week, you know?"

They were out of town. Instead of pavement they were driving on compacted volcanic ash. It seemed to have been sprayed with a plasticizer at some time in the past, but patches had slipped off to the low side as they climbed.

They came to a switchback. The cyclo's transmission shifted power to the outside wheel as Rick threw his weight into the turn—though the vehicle itself couldn't lean. They made the corner smoothly.

The trail must've been expensive to build and maintain. "How much traffic is there coming up here?" Rick asked.

"*There are daily tours, two or three six-seat cars,*" Rachel said. "*After every passenger ship lands, I mean. Folks who've come for Meridan Spa usually visit here first. But for the past month the ground shocks have been bad, and the tour companies have cancelled all trips. They're afraid that they'd lose a car sliding off the road. The tourist money's good, but the cost of replacing a car would break most of them. And a lot of tourists decided to wait till the cone had quieted down, too.*"

"But you were willing to come with me?" Rick said. They'd come to the reverse switchback. They shimmied around the corner, but Rick was afraid that the outside wheel was *very* close to the edge this time.

They made it safely. He opened the hand throttle a little wider on the straight.

Rachel gave an embarrassed laugh. "*Well,*" she said. "*I thought we were coming by aircar, remember.*"

"We'll be fine," Rick said. "I think we've got enough torque to go straight up the side if we had to. This is designed for a one-in-three slope. If the ash holds under the wheels, anyhow."

Behind them was a huge plume of dust, drifting back toward St. Martins. The dust would be following and probably catching up to them on their return. Rick wondered if the air filters had been changed recently.

"We'll be fine," he repeated, hoping that he sounded confident.

Even with the switchbacks, the slope was quite steep. As they climbed the next straight, Rick saw that the roadway was sprinkled with cinder that had shaken down from the higher levels. That wouldn't be a problem but beyond that he could see that a fuming vertical chasm had opened across the road, engulfing the corner and much of the next straight above it.

Bloody hell! Rick thought. Well, it was time to put up or shut up.

"Rachel," he said, his voice keying the intercom. "I want you to bend as far forward as you can get when I start up the hill."

If she replied, he was suddenly too busy to listen. He leaned left and cramped the front wheel up the hill, then opened the hand throttle full on. The back wheels dug in, their woven-wire structure stiffening as stress tried to deform them. Rick was bending over the front wheel, reaching back to keep the throttle open. If the thrust failed at this moment, they'd flip over on their back and skid down to the base of the cone.

"Whee-ha!" he shouted as they ground over the edge of the next straight above the one they'd left. He cramped the front wheel left again and they were back on the road and no longer threatening to tip over. He backed off the throttle slightly and said, "How did you like the shortcut, Rachel?"

"It scared me," she said.

Her quiet calm stabbed through his elation like a harpoon. "Love," he said, "it should have. That was bloody dangerous and I should never have tried it with you aboard. I apologize."

"Could you have gotten around the crack another way?" Rachel said, still calm.

"No way," he said, making the next switchback, this one a right-hander. "But we could've gone back and that's what we should've done."

"I wanted to see the top of the cone," Rachel said. "I never have. Let's go on."

He trusted the trike on this road more than he had before he'd had to take her off it, so they made most of the remaining two reaches with the throttle to the stop. He was smelling sulfur though it was an observation rather than a problem at the moment. He didn't look up while he was driving, but he knew that the peak and the plume were close above them.

Rick backed off the throttle when he saw a widening with pressed-steel picnic tables before them and they coasted to a halt among them. Now he looked up. The mild breeze was from the harbor, so the faintly iridescent smoke was slanting inland. It was noticeably warmer where they stood than it had been in St. Martins.

Rachel got off also and stretched. They took off their commo helmets. With her hands on her hips, she peered up at the peak. Rick noticed that there was a woven metal cable running up the slope from the ground to the lip.

"Well, let's go see!" Rachel said.

Rick would have been just as happy to have something to drink—his throat was dry from adrenaline and the touch of sulfur—but it was his plan to be agreeable. "Sure," he said, and started climbing steps cut into the cone.

Quite a lot of ash—grit to the size of pea gravel—had sprayed over the steps and the parking area below, but thanks to the cable the climb wasn't dangerous. A path four feet wide ran twenty yards in either direction along the top of the cone.

He looked into the crater without bending significantly over the edge. He'd thought he might be able to see the lava below but all Rick saw was stone, rough and stained in patches with a dozen different colors.

He checked the rock at his feet. It was solid, so he moved a trifle closer to the edge. No spacer who works on the rigging of a ship in sponge space could be afraid of heights, but neither did he want to have his footing give way and drop him hundreds of feet into a pit with molten rock at the bottom—even if he couldn't see it.

A ledge fifteen feet below seemed to run the circuit of the crater, as though a later, larger cone had been set on top of the original one. He could see a tree growing on the ledge far to the right. It was dead and bleaching now. The sulfur smell became sharper when he leaned over the edge.

"Oh, look at this?" Rachel said, crouching to his right. She was pointing at the splotches of flaky white on the edge of the rock.

"Mineral deposits, isn't it?" Rick said, walking closer.

"No, I think it's alive," Rachel said.

"Well, don't touch it with your finger," Rick said, taking out and opening his little pocket knife. He bent near the color. "If it's alive—and it sure looks like a lichen—it might be something people are allergic to."

With the tip of his knife blade he teased up the edge of a patch. "It's not just a stain, you're right," he said.

"Look, it gets blue deeper down," Rachel said, leaning over and pointing into the crater. The feathery patches of lichen seemed to cover quite a lot of the rock. Some of it shaded from gray to bright blue, mostly at lower levels. "Oh, what a lovely color!"

"Look, Rachel," Rick said. "Let's go back to the trike and have some lunch. I'll mention this to Harry, but he's the biologist, not me, you know."

He went down the steps, keeping his hand close to the cable but not touching it. If he started to fall he'd grab the line and risk getting stabbed by a broken strand, but only if it was that or a bad fall.

Rachel was coming down carefully behind him. He thought of offering her a hand, but that would probably make it more dangerous. He opened the trike's cargo compartment and got the tarps out.

"What are those for?" Rachel asked sharply.

"Rather than sweep off the table and benches, I thought we'd sit on the ground like we were on a beach," Rick said. "It'll be more comfortable. But if you like, I'll sweep the tables."

"Oh," said Rachel. She ground her toe into the ground. "Oh, you're right. Let me help spread them."

The sail-cloth tarps were ten by ten feet and he'd brought three of them. The fabric was extremely tough but not very soft. Rick hoped that stacked, the air trapped between layers would be cushion enough.

He hadn't packed a broom. Rachel's initial guess about his intentions had been quite correct.

The small duffle bag had a mixture of sandwiches: meat paste, egg paste, and sliced vegetables bought fresh on Quan Loi. Rick had no idea of her dietary preferences. There were also three bottles of wine charged to Rick's account at the officers' mess. They were from Keyser, two white and one red, and all proofed over fourteen percent.

"Also there's some fruit," Rick said, "but I figured if you wanted a more substantial sweet we could get something in town after we go back."

"This is very nice," Rachel said, taking a sip of wine as she considered the sandwiches. "You've thought of everything."

"Well, I've tried to," Rick said. Also, he had a good deal of experience in seducing women; which he did *not* say. Rachel was a nice girl, so the main thing was not to push too hard. The *Far Traveller* would be on Medlum another ten days, after all.

Rachel was crunching on a melon sandwich so Rick took one of the meat paste. He'd brought enough that they could both eat their fill from any of the varieties. He said, "Here, let me top off your glass. I won't be drinking much because I'll be driving us down. All you need to do is hold on, though, so drink up!"

She set the glass down and took another small sandwich. "I wanted to look down into the crater and I'm glad I did," she said. "But you know, the view down on St. Martins is even better and I hadn't been thinking about that. Look at the way the sea changes color as you go out."

"It *is* lovely," Rick agreed. "The part out there a quarter mile is such a dark blue it makes me think of cobalt glass."

He'd thought of cobalt glass when he realized he needed to

say something about the water color. Speaking of glass, he took a sip from his own—the tumblers and dishes were actually high-density thermoplastic which didn't mind being banged around a warship taking evasive action—before refilling Rachel's.

They talked about life on shipboard. "It's really pretty boring," he began, but when he got down to the tricks of astrogation and about working on the rigging in sponge space ("They tell you to always fasten a safety line, but sometimes you've got to work without one or a spar will carry you away. It's a long way down if you fall, because there's nothing else human in that universe with you.") he heard the enthusiasm in his own voice.

Rachel smiled and said, "You love your job, don't you."

"I wouldn't trade anything for it," Rick said, and as he heard his words, he realized that they were true. That embarrassed him a bit: He didn't want her to think he was a star-struck kid! Even if he was.

Rachel had refused a third sandwich and also another refill of wine. She got to her feet and walked at the edge of the parking area. She looked down at St. Martins. "It looks so pretty from up here," she said.

"There's a lot of prettiness in the universe," Rick said. He stood up also and stepped to her. "You just have to have the kind of eyes that see pretty things. Not everybody does."

He put his arm around Rachel's shoulder and tugged her gently to him. When she turned her face, he kissed her. She didn't fight him, but neither did she respond.

"No, Rick," she said. "I told you—"

She grabbed the hand he put on her breast and forced it down. "No! Stop that!"

He backed up a step. "Dear," he said. "This is a lovely place and a lovely time."

"No, I told you no!" She was flushed and breathing hard.

"No problem," he said easily. "We probably ought to be getting down before long anyway."

Rachel closed her eyes and squeezed her arms hard against her sides. Then she breathed out hard and looked at him again. "Rick," she said in a calm voice that barely trembled. "I'd like to borrow your little knife. I want to look at that lichen again."

He took the knife out of his pocket and opened the longer of the two blades. He turned it over and handed it to her handle first. It was a standard slip joint which she could have opened as easily as he had, but he was making a point.

Rick began to repack the unused food and the plates in the duffle bag, clearing the tarps. He didn't put the bag in the trike yet.

Rachel went up the steps holding the open knife in her left hand. She touched the cable repeatedly with her right hand. At the top she went to where she'd seen a blue lichen close to the rim. It was a lovely thing, and it was the right image to carry in her mind down to St. Martins.

The royal blue had shifted almost to mauve and the feathery lichen had swollen like the leaves of a desert plant. Rachel scraped the knife point against the rock with her right hand and held her left under the lichen so that it wouldn't drop into the crater when she separated it from the rock. Carefully she teased the knife under the base of the lichen the way she'd watched Rick do.

"Rachel, do you want a hand?" he called from below. They'd taken off the commo helmets when they dismounted from the vehicle.

The lichen lifted slightly. A mist of spores so fine that they looked like purple gas puffed from the purplish leaf she was raising.

Rachel gave a strangled cry and tried to stand. Her muscles felt liquid. She pitched forward, into the volcano's crater.

I went into the woods wearing a shooting vest. It was a perfect choice for my activity: loops for reloads, separate outside pockets for my beacon/compass and camera; inside pockets for little boxes to hold insects, minerals, or vegetable material; and large side pockets for any specimens I might bag. The last were waterproofed in case the specimens were leaking from the shot holes.

"Is your beacon synched, sir?" Joss called as I opened the chamber of my gun and loaded a light charge of number six shot.

She was being unnecessarily cautious, but rather than snap at her I set the gun down on my bunk with the breech still opened and got out the beacon. I thumbed it live. The tiny arrow in the tip began to pulse bright yellow in the direction of the base unit in the middle of the shelter.

"All as should be," I said. I put the beacon in its pocket again and started for the door with the shotgun. I wouldn't close it until I was actually among the trees.

"Good hunting, sir," Joss said. "I'll be going out on Hao's boat shortly."

Before I'd arrived at Orontse, Joss had chopped a hole in the undergrowth at the edge of the forest—basically at the point the sea reached at high tide and salt water prevented large trees from growing. Farther within the trees, the canopy stunted the brush and saplings in the understory.

There were no trails, but the only serious barriers to moving through the vegetation were occasional large fallen trees which hadn't yet rotted and been reabsorbed by the rest of forest. I had no place in particular to go, so if a tree blocked my initial path, I simply changed my path.

When I was far enough in that I no longer could see or hear sounds from the shanties on the beach—and twenty yards was more than enough for that—I stopped and put my goggles on. I scanned the forest at several wavelengths of light, then set the display to caret movement. Dull red light haloed more than fifty blips which proved when I magnified them to be Medlum's equivalent of insects.

Two slightly larger glows were insectivores prowling in the leaf litter. There were also creatures hopping about in the high branches, but they moved quickly and without any pattern. A shot would be at wild chance and would alarm the area. I might try one later if I didn't find a more likely specimen deeper in the forest.

For now I returned the goggles to optical clarity and proceeded, using my unaided senses. My hearing sharpened when I stopped using visual enhancement, though there wasn't any direct connection.

I heard a high-pitched ringing coming from ahead and to my right. After a moment it stopped. I moved in that direction, holding my gun muzzle up in front of me. I chose a path that would avoid big trees and tried to follow it while I concentrated on my surroundings rather than my feet. By shuffling I managed to avoid anything worse than stubbing the toe of my boot.

The tallest trees rose two hundred feet—two hundred and seven according to my goggles on a tree ahead of me where I caught a clear sight of the top. Buttress roots flared from the trunks like flowing garments, spreading twenty or thirty feet out from the edge of the trunk proper.

I came to a wide ravine. Its floor was relatively clear because the canopies overhead met from either side and the raw red clay hadn't been particularly hospitable to seeds. I heard the ringing call again, more clearly.

The gully walls were literally channeling the sound. I heard the same call louder but less clearly, from somewhere in the forest but the direction was lost in the tree trunks. It seemed to come vaguely from the left of where I stood now.

I started down into the ravine. A line of trees grew along its axis, a rounded trough into which seeds bounced and rolled down the raw steeper sides. There was probably a little more light there than within the forest to either side. *I* couldn't tell the difference, but the central trees showed by their growth that they could.

I saw a reddish blotch lying on the fan of roots at the base of one of the trees. I thought it was a fungus and squatted close to it. I got out a collecting box and a spatula, but when I pried at the lump I found that it wasn't attached to either the roots or the dirt.

Now that I was staring at it, I realized that I'd seen similar blotches on the roots of other trees. Those had been darker, deep purple shading to black. That was probably the way the substance aged rather than a different material.

I prodded my spatula deeper, planning to cut a section out to put in my collecting box. Something crunched faintly. I resisted my first impulse, to stick my finger into the mass and start pulling it apart; instead I got out a second spatula and picked the blob apart between them.

What I'd found was the chitinous internal support structure of one of the worm-shaped creatures which bored into tree roots. They didn't get much larger than a man's clenched fist, and this one must've been nearly fully grown.

Was the blotch I'd been looking at the excrement of a predator which had voided the skeleton? I took a small sample and recorded the data with my camera. The material didn't seem to be dried feces. It had a structure of parallel filaments which under magnification might tell me more.

The higher, thinner cry sounded again. This time it was very close, just a little farther down the central line of trees. I stood and pointed my gun in the direction of the sound. After an additional heartbeat of thought, I opened the breech and replaced the bird shot with one of the two solids which I carried in the loops on the upper left side of my vest.

I made the exchange quickly and smoothly, aware of how—briefly—embarrassing it would be if a predator attacked me while I was reloading. There wasn't anything about dangerous predators in the records of the fauna of Medlum, but the records were cursory and almost entirely limited to the south side of the island near St. Martins.

I whipped around the tree bole, presenting the shotgun. At the bottom of the third tree over was a creature that looked like an olive-drab mushroom, moving on a slender stalk. It was about the height of my leg at the knee. There were eyes and wormlike cilia around the circumference of the spreading top.

The thing gave another plaintive cry. There was a bright red blob of material on its top. I could see as a quivering in the air that a wire-thin cord ran from the blob to a branch over a hundred feet in the air.

A louder version of the same cry rang from the top of the ravine. I looked up sharply but saw only a quivering of brush as the creature that had called slipped back out of sight.

There was movement on the branch from which the trap had dropped. At first I thought the limb itself was sagging, but a black shadow had detached itself from the tree and begun sliding slowly down the line from which the sticky blob hung.

Magnification didn't help me see the black creature much better because the surface of the body drank light rather than reflecting it. There were many legs, both above and below the sack-like body, gripping the line. The trapped animal called out again.

I wondered what the physiology of the mushroom-looking thing was. The narrow base slid across the ground, but because of the sticky blob holding it, the trapped animal couldn't go far. A fang like a twenty-inch hypodermic thrust from the descending blackness, then withdrew again.

A larger version of the mushroom creature appeared at the edge of the brush and slid down the slope of the ravine. It left a track like that of a harrow through a plowed field. It called out again.

The cub answered its mother, straining against the sticky blob that held it. The mother's cilia extended and closed on her offspring.

I raised the shotgun to my shoulder and fired. There was a splash of yellow ichor. My slug swept the black predator away from the line that was both its net and its support.

Holding her offspring, the mother slid up the side of the ravine as swiftly as she had come down. The cub was held in a writhing mass of cilia. The cilia gave a concerted twitch and the sticky blob detached from the younger creature and flopped to the ground.

Before the creatures vanished into the brush again, the mother paused at the top of the ravine and called again; to me, I was sure.

I reloaded with my remaining solid shot and took a deep breath. After a moment, I walked over to the predator I had shot. I would prod it with my gun muzzle to make sure the specimen was dead before I touched it.

Rick turned when Rachel shouted. He was just in time to see her pitch forward into the crater.

He swore, which was useless. He ran up the steps without skidding as he'd done when he climbed more carefully when they arrived. That was probably useless also, but he had to do something.

His knife was still stuck in the lichen on the crater rim. *What the hell happened?*

He bent over the edge, wondering if he'd be able to see the girl's body. It would probably require an aircar to recover it and that would be tricky if even possible. He was pretty sure that Captain Bolton would refuse to risk any of the *Far Traveller*'s vehicles to bring back a dead civilian. Harry might agree to bend the rules if he were in St. Martins—but he wouldn't be back for a week.

Rachel was sprawled on the ledge fifteen feet down. She was limp. There was a bloody scrape where her forehead had hit the wall on the way down, but she might well be alive.

The RCN trained its officers to react well in crises. This wasn't the sort of situation that had been an example in the Academy, but quick logical thinking was the same in any crisis.

Rick couldn't climb down the rock wall unaided.

He couldn't get help or climbing equipment in the time available before Rachel rolled off the ledge half conscious, or simply suffocated in the sulfurous atmosphere.

So.

Rick pulled the knife out of the lichen and dropped it closed into his pocket. No point in jumping around with an open knife in his hand. He ran back down the steps to the trike and unfolded the first of the stacked tarps. He began cutting it into strips.

The fabric was tough and ripstopped every half inch in either direction. He nicked an edge and stressed the cloth with the weight of his foot, lengthening the cut by cutting each ripstop cord when he came to it.

He had two blades. They were short but of good steel, and he had working edges on both of them. It took time, but there were no short cuts that would increase his chance of success.

When Rick had finished tearing the first tarp, he took a break by knotting the twelve strips together. His right hand had been cramping from his grip on the knife.

He got to work on the second tarp, using the knife's shorter blade. He wished he'd brought a large knife; but if he were going to wish things, it was a pity he hadn't thrown a coil of half-inch line in the trike's trunk. Or brought Kent along; this job would be a *lot* simpler if there were two of them.

When he finished with the second tarp, he attached the crude rope to one end of the first—and then tied the other end of the first rope around the trike's triple clamps. Carrying the free end of the double length, he hauled it as high up the cone as it would stretch. By running the trike closer he could gain another ten feet, but this should work out. He needed not only enough rope to reach Rachel, he'd have to tie her to the line in order to lift her.

Switching back to the longer blade, Rick cut up the third tarp. He wasn't sure how strong the fabric was, but he figured strong enough. He could've cut these strips a little wider since he'd have sufficient length, but the combined line would be only as strong as the thinnest part of it.

Rick tied them together, then climbed up the steps again and tied the third length onto the end of the first two. He dribbled the makeshift rope over the edge and let it fall past Rachel's sprawled body. He gave a black chuckle. The way his luck was going, Rachel might wake up enough to grab the line herself—and inevitably lose her grip if she tried to climb on her own and go plunging into the crater before he could get to her.

He slid over the lip of the crater and let himself down hand over hand. When he got down as far as he wanted, he found that he was about to set his boots on Rachel's body. He kicked himself to the side enough to get to the ledge beyond her head. Supporting himself by the rope, Rick managed to stand firmly on the rock.

He was breathing hard from exertion but the sulfur fumes had gotten worse and deep breaths didn't clear his head. He lifted Rachel's body enough to feed the loose end of the rope under her, then tied it beneath her arms. There was enough length to knot the tail around her right thigh. Rick had first-aid training, but this exercise was a new one for him.

Rachel was definitely breathing, but she showed no signs of alertness. The fumes wouldn't be helpful, but one thing at a time.

Leaving Rachel on the ledge, Rick started up the rope with the strength of his arms alone. His attempts to grip the line with his boots were useless. Maybe he should've tied loops for his toes, but he wouldn't have been able to find them by feel alone. He crawled up, one agonizing lift after the previous one. He wasn't completely aware that he was back at the top until he realized he had to change the angle at which he reached for the next handhold.

He flopped over the lip. For a moment he lay on his back with his eyes closed, euphoric with the lack of strain on his arms. The job wasn't done yet.

The pause had allowed Rick's problem-solving mind to slip back into gear. If he'd been in normal condition, he'd have begun pulling Rachel up hand over hand as soon as he reached the top. His arms were trembling with fatigue and he was sure he couldn't get her up that way.

Instead he brought her enough up off the ledge to take a turn of the rope around his body. Continuing to use his body to belay the line, he repeated the process. He paused each turn to recruit his strength. After enough lifting—he'd stopped trying to count—Rick saw Rachel's head and torso appear at the crater edge. He gave a final heave and brought her over the rim. He lost his footing on the slope and rolled halfway down, tugging Rachel after him.

For what was probably a minute or two he lay chest down on the ash cone, breathing hard with his eyes closed. When he got up he managed to lift Rachel's torso and stagger with her to one of the tables where he laid her down again. He thought he saw her eyelids flutter, but that wasn't a concern at the moment.

The tabletop put Rachel at a height Rick could work on the ropes without having to bend over. His back had taken a lot of the strain of getting her out of the crater. Not as much as his arms had, but a lot.

If he hadn't dulled both blades of his knife already, he might have tried to cut the rope off Rachel. As it was, he used the larger blade like a marlinspike, forcing it between the strands of the knot on her thigh. When he'd opened that, he moved up to the loop around her torso. When he had that free, he left Rachel where she lay and freed his trike from the other end of the rope.

Rachel's eyes were open and she turned her head slightly to follow what he was doing. Her attempt to speak resulted only in a croak. He knew he couldn't have done any better himself. He turned and nodded to her with a broad smile.

The trunk of the vehicle was open. He gathered the makeshift rope into armfuls and dumped them into the trunk, gathering up the tag ends hand over hand. He'd have liked to arrange it neatly, but it would make as good a cushion this way.

Rachel sat up and started to get off the table. Rick shook his head and croaked, "No!"

He was feeling a lot better now than he had when he rolled down the side of the cone. He hoped that he was enough better. Standing beside the table, he put his right arm around Rachel's upper chest and slid the left one under her thighs. She was alert enough to grip his neck.

Rick straightened slightly to make sure he could handle the weight—*so far, so good*—he turned and shuffled back to the vehicle and set her as gently as he could in the trunk. He set one of the commo helmets on Rachel's head and put the other one on himself. They were too valuable to abandon, but if he'd thought that the woman might chatter while he was driving, he'd have switched them off.

He'd planned to leave the picnic gear where it lay, but the two bottles of wine caught his eye. He swilled a slug from the opened white around his mouth and spat it out, then handed the bottle to Rachel.

"Careful how you drink it," he said as he kicked the trike's diesel to clattering life. "Don't let it knock your teeth out on a bump."

He hauled the front wheel around, then drove off the edge of the parking area and headed straight for St. Martins instead of following the switchback road. He didn't need the throttle and kept off the brakes as well, letting the diesel's compression keep their speed manageable.

He took each road cut at a downward angle, then whipped the trike off the road again after he'd stabilized it. He didn't know what Rachel thought about what he was doing. Hunched in the trunk she might not even be aware. Regardless, Rick was doing the driving.

When they reached the extension of the road through St. Martins, Rick swung onto it and even opened the throttle a little because the reduced slope meant gravity no longer drove them as fast as he wanted to go. For the first time since they started down, he said, "Rachel, I can find the front of the mission building. Will there be somebody there to get you home? Because I don't think you can make it alone."

"Rick, take me to my apartment," she said. *"It's the next cross street from the mission going toward the harbor. To the left and in the middle of the block. I'll tell you where to stop."*

Then she said, *"I just want to get home."*

Rick wondered how much she'd drunk on the way down. Maybe none; he felt pretty much the same way and he was as dry as the air of the crater.

They got into traffic as they started seeing houses. Rick was too wrung out to get angry, even when a cyclo with a woman and three children aboard crawled down the left side of the street ahead of them and even turned into the cross street Rachel had indicated.

"Yeah, it's this one," she said. *"A hundred feet more and we're home."*

Rick parked with all but the right-side wheel out of the travel lane. There was still six feet of clear road for other traffic to use and he hadn't seen any local vehicles which were that wide.

Rachel stood up when Rick swung out of the saddle, but she would've fallen again without him grabbing her. "Here," he said. "I'll lift your legs out, and then I'll help you walk to the door. And I'll go away then, don't worry."

It took all his strength to set her down but he continued smiling. "Here we go," he said. "Just guide me."

"Straight ahead," she said. "I'm the back apartment on the ground floor."

Then she said, "Rick, how did you get me out of the volcano? I was really down inside, wasn't I?"

"You were inside," he said, "but not very far down. And as for how, it was a bloody near thing. Don't do that again, all right?"

He reached for the latch plate but saw that Rachel was holding out a metal key. He took it and guided it into the keyhole, then shuffled to the end of the narrow hallway with Rachel holding onto his shoulder. The street door must have swung shut by itself, or maybe Rachel had pulled it as she stepped in.

Rick stopped by the end door and inserted the same key. He pushed it open and paused.

"Go in," Rachel said. "Please get me to the couch."

He could see the couch across the room in the dim light from the hallway. He walked Rachel to it and set her down. Instead of a table lamp there was a wall sconce directly above the couch. Rachel turned it on and said, "Do you want something to drink? Coffee, maybe?"

"Dear," he said, truthful from fatigue, "all I really want now is a hot shower, and I'll have that as soon as I get back to the ship. I ache places that I didn't know I had any muscles."

"The door to the left," she said. "I've got a shower. Go on."

"You're serious?"

"Yes," she said, looking down at her hands. "Take a shower."

"Right," he said. She'd been banged around even worse than he had and was probably planning to shower as soon as he left.

The shower room sloped to the back, where there was a three-inch gap between the floor and the tile wall. The toilet was against the interior wall. There were soaps and lotions on a wall niche beside the toilet.

Rick stripped and adjusted the water from the dual taps so that it was hot but not too hot, then increased the flow and got under it. He didn't have a cloth and rubbed himself with the soap directly. It felt very good on aching muscles but the soap bit on places where he'd scraped the skin.

The door opened and Rachel came in naked. "I've decided to join you," she said.

"I, ah...," Rick said. "I'd be glad of that, but you don't have to."

"I see that you're glad," Rachel said with a giggle. She kissed him. Then in a serious tone she said, "Rick, you saved my life."

"And I'm even happier about that now than I was at the time," he said, embracing her.

I walked to the Mediation Mission from the *Far Traveller*. I could've gotten Kent to fly me to the uphill side in the truck, but I didn't mind the hike. Besides, I hadn't seen Rachel since I returned from Orontse last night and learned from Rick about their trip up the mountainside.

The guards knew my uniform—and possibly me—and waved me through. Mistress Blakeley was out as usual. I went straight to Rachel's little cubby and knocked on the doorjamb. She jumped at the sound but smiled as she turned and saw that it was me. "Hi, Harry," she said. "I'd heard you were coming back."

"For a bit, at least," I said. "I'd like to know what happened to you up on the mountain. Rick told me what he saw, but that wasn't much. I'm coming to the horse's mouth. It was a plant that knocked you out?"

"Well, I think so," she said, swiveling her chair to face me though she didn't get up. "A lichen, at least. Are lichens plants?"

"Partly," I said. "But partly fungus too."

We could have had a good time discussing the biota of Medlum...but that might have been jealousy talking. "But you touched it and it knocked you out?"

"I never really touched it," she said, frowning with concentration. "At least I don't think I did. I was prying it off the rock because it was such a pretty mauve. Then I felt cold and very dizzy. I don't remember standing up but I must have, because Rick says that when I shouted and he saw me, I was standing. And then I fell into the volcano."

"Could it have been a shock?" I said. "Static electricity? Or maybe just electricity from plant cells."

"I don't think so," she said. She looked at the tip of her index finger and held it out to me. "There's no burn and it didn't feel like a spark. My whole body felt cold."

I bent closer to the finger. I didn't see anything odd about it either.

"Rick had picked a sample of the white kind," Rachel said. "I wanted to get one of the purple ones too. Mostly they were deeper in the volcano, but I saw this one on the rim."

She smiled and said shyly, "I was getting it for you, Harry. I thought you might want to see it."

"Thank you," I said, thinking again that she and I might have had a lot of fun together. "The white lichen Rick gave me seemed pretty normal, but we think the colored version may be a reproductive change. A fruiting body."

"The leaves looked fatter," she said. "Besides the color. But they had the same shape."

"Well, thank you," I said. There didn't seem much more to learn from her. "Rick says he can take me to the spot where the lichen was, so I won't ask you to guide me. He's going to run me up on the Transportation Section vehicle, just like he did you. As soon as he gets off watch this afternoon."

I grinned. "He says we'll be taking a proper rope, but I don't guess we'll have that problem again."

"I can't believe that he climbed down into the volcano to bring me back," Rachel said. Her voice had gotten dreamy. "He's amazingly brave, isn't he?"

"I think the RCN selects for brave officers," I said. After thinking about it for a moment, I said, "I guess brave people select themselves for the RCN. It comes to the same thing. But Rick *is* brave, yes; and very clearheaded in a crisis."

I cleared my throat and added, "Look, Rachel. Rick's all those things and he's my friend. He's a good fellow, from everything I've seen or heard. But have you gotten serious about him for a romantic partner?"

She stiffened and glared at me. "And what if I have? We're both adults, aren't we?"

"You are indeed," I said. "Then I wish you both the best of good fortune."

I nodded to her and walked away, feeling sad. She was a nice girl.

I needed to get back to the *Far Traveller* so that Rick could run me up to the cone as soon as his shift finished. Any later and we wouldn't have time to get back with the sample before dark.

We wouldn't have time to do it tomorrow, because the ship would be leaving Medlum forever just after dawn.

ELKIN

I'd been ready to go up to the bridge five minutes before but Doctor Veil had said, "Not yet. Wait till we go into Elkin orbit."

I'd fed another sample from Medlum into the sequencer. While I waited, I took another magnified look at the mauve variant of the lichen I'd scraped free on the cone lip. It was genetically identical to the white variant; the color was from the spores with which the scale-like leaves were swollen to the point of bursting.

In fact several leaves had burst while we were on our way back to St. Martins, staining purple the inside of the clear container I was carrying them in. They contained bupivacaine and other compounds and were clearly psychotropic.

I noted the data on the entry, along with imagery and the genetic data. I was hoping to find the mechanism by which the spores were expelled by comparing lobes which had vented with others which had not, but I hadn't had a breakthrough before the High Drive went off and we went into freefall.

"Time for us to go up to the bridge," Doctor Veil said. She slid past me toward the door, and I scrambled to follow her.

Doctor Veil had been in space much longer than I had. She was more comfortable in weightlessness than I probably would ever become. She entered the Up companionway without a wasted motion and was almost out of sight by the time I got in behind her.

90 David Drake

This was why we'd waited until now: Veil was going up the companionway without having to fight the 1-g acceleration which mimicked gravity.

At bridge level, she headed toward the bow. When I tried to keep up by driving myself forward, I each time collided with the corridor walls and gave it up as a bad plan. I knew where she was going, after all.

The watch out on the hull was coming out of the airlocks in the rotunda as I passed. They'd gotten the antennas and rigging in so that we could land. The rigging is fully automated, but it always needs to be tweaked by human beings. The buffeting as a starship drops through an atmosphere is severe enough without mast and spars tearing themselves loose in the airstream.

To my surprise, Doctor Veil was waiting for me at the bridge hatch. I realized she must be afraid of being chased off with abuse by officers who felt she'd get in the way. My status with the captain was her protection against that happening.

Before I could lead Veil in, Rick joined us from the rotunda where he'd just stripped off his hard suit. "You guys need help with something?"

"We'd like to use the ship's optics to check a ground feature mentioned in the *Annotated Charts*," I said, raising my voice to be heard. Even coasting in freefall, the ship's interior was a noisy, echoing box.

"The gunner's console is vacant," Rick said, "and I'm off duty. Come on in and I'll set you up."

The third console from the bow on the right—starboard—side was vacant. Most of the others had a ship's officer at them. Instead of seating himself at the couch, Rick sailed past it and seated himself at the back side of the console, the striker's seat. He gestured Doctor Veil to the couch.

She maneuvered as smoothly in the air as he had. I wallowed along after her and managed to hook the couch with the toe of my boot. Otherwise I would have sailed through the holographic display.

Rick engaged active sound cancellation around the console. In a normal voice, he said, "What is it you're looking for?"

I stood behind Doctor Veil as she keyed in an eight-digit coordinate from the *Annotated Charts*. She said, "Lieutenant Grenville, there are one hundred fifty-six artificial pools at the edge of a bay here. We would like to view the pools as highly magnified as possible."

"Rick," I added, "that'll be Alliance notation on the coordinates if it makes a difference."

"It makes a difference," Rick muttered. The holographic display on our side of the console came live with a swatch of planetary surface which immediately dissolved and became a different portion of surface. "There. You can adjust it with the prompt on your side."

The image was a broad embayment at the edge of an arid landscape. There were round dots around most of the edge of the water. Veil used her joystick to center on one of the dots, then held down one end of the toggle in the top to magnify the image. According to the legend at the bottom of the display, the pond was circular to the limits of calculation and 23.6 feet in diameter.

Veil moved the prompt to the next pool sunwise. The diameter was the same, 23.6 feet, but on the land side of the pool was a square building with the ruins of several additional buildings to the side of it. When Veil raised the magnification again, we could see that the roof of the square building had fallen in. It was a ruin like the sheds beside it.

"These pools must be Archaic artifacts," Doctor Veil said, looking up at me. "Look"—she expanded the view again—"see the way the bay has encroached, submerging twenty or thirty of them. They're down there under the water. How long would that have taken to happen?"

One bad east coast storm, I thought, remembering winters on Sheet Island. Aloud I said, "Ma'am, may I take a look at that with the prompt?"

"Yes, of course," she said, sliding off the couch. I took her place and moved the joystick to the far left end of the line of pools. I thought I'd seen something there.

The sea's incursion had flooded many of the pools, as Veil had said, but it had also cut off a few pools from the remainder of the line. Behind the end pool there was a square building and three sheds in better condition than those of the first installation we'd checked.

Behind, inland, of the sheds were rocks arranged to block-print the word HELP.

"We may learn that the Archaics were here," I said. "Certainly there's been a more recent visitor, though goodness knows how long ago those stones were placed."

"Lieutenant Grenville?" Veil said. "Will it be possible to land beside that pool?"

"This bay looks like an ideal landing spot," Rick said, "and I'll point it out to Captain Bolton; but I suggest we set down on the other end? In this shallow water our exhaust will raise huge waves and if there *is* anybody living there we'd flood him out if we landed close."

"Yes, we have the aircar," Veil muttered, but Rick was already speaking on what I supposed was a private channel to the captain.

He paused and looked at me past the edge of the holographic display. "We'll be landing pretty quick," he said. "You may want to get onto couches."

Doctor Veil and I headed for the lab, though she could've stayed on the bridge if she'd wanted. Besides bracing for the landing, I wanted to tell Kent where we'd be going as soon as we were safely on the surface.

Lieutenant Vermijo was preparing to take the *Far Traveller* in to land in Pool Bay, as Captain Bolton had decided to name it. Rick, still off duty, was surprised when Bolton said over a two-way link, "*Grenville, you're slated to be in charge of the party setting up the temporary ground quarters, aren't you? Over.*"

"Yessir," Rick said. He'd remained on the vacant gunner's station on the bridge after Harry and Doctor Veil had gone down to their quarters below. "I've just come off the hull and figured to go straight to the transportation bay rather than to my quarters on Level 4. Over."

"*Do you think the watch can handle it without your presence?*" Bolton asked. "*Over.*"

"Yes," Rick said. "Bosun's Mate Veselka has done about a hundred setups between the *Boxer* and us. Over."

Besides which, he thought, *I've managed not to get in her way yet, but she always worries that I will.*

"*Doctor Veil asked if you could come along in the Bio Section truck while they check out some bloody thing they've discovered*," Bolton said. "*They thought you might be helpful. Since they're the ones you say found Pool Bay and I haven't seen such a good anchorage since we lifted from Harbor Three on Cinnabar, I'm inclined to do them a favor if you're interested in going. Over."*

"I'm very interested, sir," Rick said. "Shall I inform them I'll meet them in the transport bay as soon as we're down, over?"

"I've done that," said Bolton. *"And I'll also tell Veselka that she'll be doing the setup alone. Bolton out."*

The roar of the thrusters braking to allow gravity to shove the ship down into the atmosphere began to fill the world.

I was glad to be back in normal gravity. I knew that landing and lift-off were the most dangerous portions of star travel, but the sheer mental discomfort of insertion into and extraction from sponge space were the only aspects that I really disliked. I know that I'll die some day; and I know that crashing into a planet's surface would be quicker and less unpleasant than some of what has happened to relatives of mine over the years.

Doctor Veil and I were waiting with Kent in the glazed office of the transport bay. We could watch the techs getting the ship's four launches and our Bio Section aircar ready to haul crew and supplies for the ground site to shore. Rick entered the bay from a corridor and walked toward the car, then stopped when he realized we were all in the office.

I went out to join him just as he turned around. "They opened the outer hatch while there was still a lot of steam and ozone in the air," I explained. "We were just waiting under cover till it dispersed."

Rick laughed. "Well, you're RCN now and the standards are less ... delicate than you might've gotten used to in Academe," he said.

The tech working on the aircar got out of the cab and raised his thumb to us and walked over to the nearest launch. I glanced behind me and saw that Doctor Veil and Kent were coming out of the office also. The four of us walked together to the car.

There was only room for three in the cab, but Rick hopped over the tailgate of the rear compartment. That left room for me beside Doctor Veil, but instead I got into the back also. I heaved myself over the gate with more effort and less grace, but I made it in.

Kent opened the window in the back of the cab and shouted, "Ready?" I was about to shout back, but Rick gave the driver a thumbs-up. The car lifted as Kent checked the fan output and balance, then drove forward off the lowered ramp. We dropped abruptly to nearly the seething surface of the water, then swooped upward and swung left around the bay toward the far end of the line.

I looked down through the back gate. Rick joined me and brought his head close to my ear to say, "Are those pools lined with concrete?"

"Probably," I said, "but we'll need to check. Doctor Veil will want it to be moissanite because we know the Archaics worked with the stuff."

"And you?" Rick said.

I shrugged. "I'm just after the truth. I don't much care what it is."

Kent circled to kill his speed and dropped for a landing. During the turn Rick nudged me and gestured. I followed the line of his arm to see a man near the building. The fellow was wearing a loose garment that flared out as he changed direction: He was apparently trying to follow our maneuvers as we prepared to land.

We grounded with a small spurt of sand from beneath each of our four drive fans. Rick and I were trying to get out as quickly as we could, but the castaway was scrabbling at the cab door before we could. Kent wasn't opening for him.

"Here, sir!" I said. "I'm Harry Harper. Who are you?"

"You've got to take me off!" the castaway said. "You shouldn't've left me here so long! I ran out of food! I have to eat fish!"

"We'll get you off," I said. At least I thought we would. "We're surveyors from Cinnabar. But who are you?"

Kent still hadn't opened his door but Veil came around from her side of the cab. She didn't speak but the castaway turned to her and fell to his knees. "Ma'am!" he said. "You won't leave me, will you? You'll take me off surely, won't you? I've been gathering the weed just like I was supposed to but I don't care about the money! Just get me off!"

"Yes, of course," Doctor Veil said calmly. "We're not a passenger ship but I'm sure Captain Bolton can find you a place in the crew. What's your name, sir?"

"Ma'am, I'm Terney," the castaway said. "See all the weed I've gathered? When I filled the shed I covered it with brush."

Rick came with me when I walked to the shed Terney was gesturing toward. It was full of algae. It was so full now that the door must have been closed forcibly to compress it, though the algae had shrunk considerably in drying.

"What the hell is this stuff?" Rick said, prodding the stored algae. "It looks orange."

"That's algae from the pools," I said, repeating what I'd learned from the *Annotated Charts*. "When it's ripe it turns orange, yeah, but I think this has been stored for a long time and lost a lot of its color."

I walked over to the nearest of three mounds of brush behind the shed. The terrain inland of the beach was of crumbly soils. Cane-like plants grew in clumps linked by runners at about six inches off the ground. The soil under the clumps was held in place by a net of roots, but the winds gouged channels between the plants.

Terney had created round fences by driving a line of canes into the ground and had then piled cut canes on to cover—I checked—a mound of ripe algae. The other two piles appeared to be the same, though the one farthest to the east was small in comparison to the other two.

When we turned back Doctor Veil and Kent, with Terney hovering behind them, were bent over the pool. Kent was using a large screwdriver from the toolkit as a chisel and, striking it with an open-end wrench, knocked a chip from the liner.

"There are three more piles of the algae here," I called to Veil when she turned.

"Then I think we're ready to return," Doctor Veil said. "I have samples of the algae at various growth stages and we've just taken some of the pool material for analysis."

We walked to the car. Terney would have gotten into the cab but Kent sent him to the back with us. Rick offered Terney his hand but the castaway grabbed the tailgate with both hands and hurled himself aboard. He may have been afraid of being abandoned again.

When Kent ran up the engines, Terney relaxed noticeably: We were under way and he really was going to get off Elkin.

"Where are you from, Master Terney?" I asked as we lifted.

"From Hermogenes," Terney said. "I signed on with Kalish, a contractor who was going to supply weed to cosmetics companies. I was supposed to gather weed for a year and dry it, then the ship would take us and the weed off. There was twenty of us, I guess, and we'd get a third of the price of what we'd gathered when the weed sold back on Hermogenes. It's got to be ripe, you see, or it's worthless—and they assay each batch."

"You were an Away Man," Rick said. "You weren't wrecked here. You volunteered to stay?"

"Yeah, I did," Terney said. He hugged himself. "It was fine."

His voice sounded rusty, but he'd gotten enough control to speak normally. "I always liked to keep to myself, so I took the end place across the water from the rest. The others, I don't think they got together much neither. People who do don't take a job like that. And the ship came back, I guess in a year, I couldn't be sure. Only they forgot me, the other side of the water, you know. And when I saw they were closing up the hatches, I ran to the other side but nobody saw me. And they never came back, but I kept cropping the weed."

He started crying. He was wearing a piece of sacking; probably from the bales of food that had been left with the algae crew.

"You're all right," Rick said. "Don't worry. They'll find a place for you in the Power Room. Riggers need skills you probably don't have, but you'll do for lift and carry in the Power Room."

When we got back to the *Far Traveller*, Rick took Terney to the first lieutenant while I went to the *Annotated Charts*. I was looking not for information on Elkin (bare mention of the pools around Pool Bay is all there was) but to see what there was about Hermogenes, which turned out considerable trade in the region, both on its own bottoms and outside carriers. The Brotherhood— the regional combine which had provided the *Goliath* with the charts which almost wrecked her while I was aboard—was strong, but so were the Shinings and ships from a dozen other planets.

Hermogenes had light industry. It provided equipment which was cheaper and sometimes better suited to undeveloped planets than what was available from sophisticated worlds within the Alliance. There was no penetration of the region by Cinnabar manufactures, though that might change if the *Far Traveller*'s soundings were successful.

Hermogenes *did* export cosmetics. A rejuvenating creme was even sold on Pleasaunce as a cachet product. No information I could find went into the composition of the creme, but that note seemed to support Terney's story.

I went looking for Doctor Veil. Mahaffy told me that she was in her office with Lieutenant Grenville, which was a considerable surprise. I'd been at a work station, so lost in my researches that I hadn't heard Rick come in.

The office door was ajar. I tapped on the jamb and Veil called, "Bring him in, Grenville." They must've heard me talking to Mahaffy.

"Sir," I said to Doctor Veil, "I've found some support for Terney's story."

"Very good, Harper," Veil said. "And Grenville here has some other information from Terney."

Rick nodded. "He started talking about the dreams he'd been having ever since he found 'the room,'" Rick said. "I guess they were nightmares. He says animals were turning into fish, which doesn't sound so awful—but it was scaring the bejabbers out of him even to talk about it. But I figured Doctor Veil would want to know about this room, which he said is made of glass. It's about a day's walk inland."

"Glass?" I said. "Moissanite would look like glass if it was dirty."

"Yes," Veil agreed, nodding. "Do you suppose Terney can show us where it is?"

"Don't see why not," Rick said. "Besides, we can look for gullies from the air if we have to."

Captain Bolton had approved Rick accompanying Doctor Veil in the aircar. That meant he and Harry could be together in the back of the vehicle with Terney. Any husky enlisted spacer could have done the strong-arm part of the job, but there might have been more to it than that. Besides Rick got along well with the Bio Section and it would clearly please Lord Harper if the Captain allowed him to come.

Terney began to tremble when they brought him down to the transport bay. He didn't fight them when they helped him into the back of the truck, but he wrapped his arms around his torso and shook from the time they took off. He faced out the rear of the compartment, but it was pretty obvious that he wasn't really looking for the site he'd described to them.

Doctor Veil shouted through the cab window, "We're going to set down here. It's the ravine closest to Terney's hut, so it seems likely."

Kent eased us in perfectly, as usual. The cloud of dust settled quickly. Doctor Veil got out of the cab. Harry said, "Come on, Terney. You're going to guide us."

Terney huddled around himself, weeping again. He mumbled something which could've been, "Don't leave me."

Harry was murmuring in a reassuring voice, but Rick dropped the tailgate and gripped Terney by the shoulder, not harshly but firmly. He said to Harry, "Don't let him jump back," and pulled Terney from the truck. Terney yelped but again didn't fight.

Harry jumped down and took the other arm. They walked the Away Man—since he wasn't a castaway after all—toward the edge. The gully was about twelve feet deep and maybe forty feet wide. The clumps of cane growing on the gully floor were shorter than those on either side, so it must channel heavy downpours on occasion. Neither lieutenant knew where it drained, but it certainly wasn't to Pool Bay.

"Is this where you found the room?" Doctor Veil asked.

"It looks like it," Terney said. For some reason he responded to the woman's voice better than he did to the males. "It's on this side though so you gotta look over the edge to see it."

Harry walked over to the edge and looked in both directions. Something glinted on the inland side. "There it is," he called. "About a hundred yards is all."

Doctor Veil said something about getting the truck, but Rick let go of Terney's arm and the two lieutenants strode briskly toward the object. "It's not much to look at, is it?" Rick said as they peered down at the corner of something smooth sticking out of the side of the ravine.

"Well, it's not natural," Harry said. He had only minimal testing apparatus with him in the pockets of his equipment belt. Rather than jump directly to the ground, he hopped down to the visible corner and used it as a step midway, then hopped to the ground.

It might well be a room as Terney had called it. Much of the smooth crystal facade had been exposed.

"There's a shadow inside!" Rick said as he came down the steeply sloping wall to stand beside Harry. The shower of pebbles and grit he'd stirred up rolled along the gully floor beyond him.

Harry had an optical reading already but he tapped the crystal with a bit of stone to see what sound waves within the material told him. He said, "It's moissanite. That doesn't prove anything, I suppose. And it's a hollow cube just over seven feet on a side. I can't tell if there's anything inside, but maybe if we get powerful lights they'll be able to show us more than a shadow. If there *is* more than a shadow."

The aircar had lifted and landed beside them, blowing a blinding scud of grit down onto them. Doctor Veil walked over to the edge and looked over at them. "I'm not going to jump down," she said, "but can you send me imagery, Lord Harper?"

Harry linked his handheld to Veil's and scanned the front of the crystal for as far down as it was exposed. "Ma'am," he said. "I've already sent a full optical and sonic scan to the ship. As full as this little unit can do. I didn't see anything except there's a chip out of one of the corners at the bottom where it's still buried."

"This soil's so light we can lift it with a suction pump," Rick volunteered.

Doctor Veil considered for a moment, then said, "All right, we'll go back to the ship and get the equipment we'll need. Especially proper recording gear. I'll have Kent bring the car down to pick you up."

"No need," Rick said. He bent his knees slightly and made a stirrup of his hands. He nodded at Harry, who nodded back and stepped into the stirrup. "Ready," he said. He jumped and caught the upper edge of the crystal and hung there. With additional boost from Rick, he scrambled to the clear top, then bent and reached back down to catch Rick's hand as he jumped. They stood together panting at the top of the room.

"You know," Harry said, "I was willing to wait for a ride."

"And get sandblasted again?" Rick said. "Naw."

Together they scrambled up the steep slope to ground level. At the top, Rick said, "You're in pretty good shape, Lord Harper."

"I could've told you that," Harry said.

"Yeah," said Rick. "But now I know it, which might be important to me one of these days."

Laughing, they joined Doctor Veil at the aircar.

It was midafternoon before a crew set up a modified reaction-mass pump from one of the pinnaces. The crew running it was a mixture of Power Room techs and riggers who guided the suction mouth with long booms.

Doctor Veil and I watched, initially from nearer than we should have been. The output end of the rig put out an enormous plume of dust and grit. The crew serving it wore helmets, not for communication as I'd thought but because of the built-in filters. The grit fell out quickly, but the dust mounted high in the air and a shift in the breeze was likely to bring it onto anybody within a half a mile.

The howl of the fan, echoing to us from the opposite side of the gully, cut off. Veil was wearing a pocket communicator. It beeped. She checked it and said, "We can go down now. They say they've cleared the Room."

We joined Kent in the cab of the truck. Kent looked at Doctor Veil and said, "I'd rather wait a bit and let the dust settle. That stuff's like stone polish. It'll eat the fan blades in no time."

"Go on," said Veil. "We'll replace the fan blades, then. Don't you see how important this is?"

We lifted to a hundred feet instead of just swooping over the lip of the ravine and down to the work site. It struck me that Kent really was giving the dust as long as possible to settle, and was also trying not to fan what had fallen to the ground into the air again.

We dropped to the gully floor very close on the other side of where the suction pump had been working. It was probably as grit free as any site within a mile. Our lift fans shut off the instant we touched, though they continued to rotate slowly on inertia.

The crew had set up a coarse screen on the output end of the suction pump. It didn't catch items flung out of the pump, but it reduced their velocity so that larger items fell to the ground just beyond it. At first glance there was just a mound of dirt there, but we—probably I—would sift it soon.

The Room—Terney's word was as good as any—was a moissanite cube. Uncovering it hadn't really told us anything that my handheld apparatus hadn't. The cube was hollow with walls about five inches thick. Light into the cube wicked along the walls, but didn't illuminate the object inside. It was simply a blur standing three or four feet high.

The chip out of the bottom made no more sense when we could touch it than it had in imagery. It was about six inches long and wasn't a chip—it was more similar to a casting flaw or perhaps a mold. The complex shape was perfectly smooth and showed no sign of fracture.

I handled it after Doctor Veil had. I was quite careful because the edges could have been razor sharp, no matter what the imagery had indicated. I didn't want to lose a fingertip.

I helped Doctor Veil set up recording apparatus from three angles. Neither of us had any idea of what it might show, but the data was copied to the *Far Traveller* so we didn't have to be here in the dry wind to view it; if there should be something to view, which seemed unlikely.

Back at the ship I tried to talk to Terney about his dreams, but he didn't offer any details beyond what he'd said to Rick just after we found him. "They're just dreams!" he said when I pushed. "I dreamed that moles were changing into whales. I don't know why, I don't like to talk about it! I don't know!"

That was probably true. I didn't know why the business so interested me.

I did whatever work Doctor Veil set me, but Mahaffy was really much better using the sequencer than I was. Using a skiff, I serviced our traps set out in the bay. None of the catches were particularly interesting.

From orbit we'd seen that the interior beyond a range of hills to the east was much better watered than where we were on the coast, so Kent took Joss off in the aircar with her collecting equipment. The pinnaces were taking route soundings, the main purpose of the expedition; Rick had taken command of the third after the reaction-mass pump had been put back together and refitted after we'd used it to clear the Room.

I walked from the ship back to the Room, checking each of the pools along the way. Nineteen more of the sites had simple structures like the one where we'd found Terney. They were built of structural plastic, welded at the seams. All were in disrepair and a couple of them had blown away except for the base flange which anchored them into the ground. Terney had heaped additional sand around the one he inhabited, the only reinforcement he could make without tools or materials.

I looked frequently at the Room. Nothing had changed—of course.

Finally I hiked back to the ship. I probably could have made the request by communicator, but it seemed simpler to speak directly to Doctor Veil and the captain. Veil was delighted at the idea, as I'd expected, so I went up to Captain Bolton in his cruising cabin off the bridge.

"Sir," I said. "I'd like to spend the night at the structure we've uncovered. Doctor Veil has given me permission on her end, but to carry a tent and bedding and I guess a couple meals, I'd like to borrow a cyclo like the one Rick ran us around in on Medlum. I can bring it back in the morning. Or at once if you send a driver."

Captain Bolton laughed and said, "Well, I don't see what harm it can do. Sure, you've got my permission. It's certainly not a duty I envy you, though."

A tech from Transportation carried me to the site and helped me set up the little tent in the recently dug area between the Room and the remaining gully wall. I could check the cameras on my handheld, but there wasn't any more to be seen that way than there was with my naked eye, looking over at the back of the construction.

I hadn't come here to see anything, except possibly in dreams.

Pool Bay must be equatorial. Sunset was as sudden as a mouse-trap closing.

I normally don't remember my dreams, but tonight I was ready to record them on my handheld the instant I awakened. I'd learned that if I got the information out before I was fully alert, I could review it at leisure. Of course the dreams I'd recorded for about a week in a row—five years earlier—had been banal. For example, standing in a line which moved very slowly and appeared to have no destination—frustration dreams of that sort.

This time was different. I began to see colonies of small quad-rupeds living in woven structures in the treetops. They were communal and had a complex language which involved not only sound but color changes in the bare skin of their wattles.

They ranged a forest of trees with foliage dangling like ribbons from the branches. Their fruit grew at the base of the limbs, pulpy globs of varied color.

A population of the creatures suddenly froze in my aware-ness. The forest in which they had been scrambling grayed out, as though it existed on the other side of a thick crystal barrier.

The creatures changed gradually as though they were being squeezed into a subtly different mold. Then skin under their forearms bagged and grew into flaps attached along the sides of their bodies, becoming wings. At first they climbed and glided, but they began to fly with arm motions. Their skulls shrank and they no longer built structures together.

The flyers and the climbers coexisted for a time—there was no measure of duration in the dream—but the flyers reached the ripe trees more quickly than the climbers did. The treetop nests became less common, then uncommon, and finally vanished from the forest.

The flyers expanded their range. So far as the forest was concerned, there was no difference. The flyers spread seeds in the same fashion as the climbers had ... but they weren't intelligent and never would become intelligent.

I awoke as dawn was breaking as abruptly as last night's sunset. The recorder was ready, but I didn't need it. The dream was as crisply real as the moissanite cube.

The Room was suddenly horrible to me.

I struck my tent and left it with the bedroll and the two meal packs I hadn't eaten. I didn't wait for a tech to arrive with the cyclo, but he could pick up my gear. I hiked toward the ship myself.

Getting away from this place.

I asked the tech 4 in the transport bay to detail somebody to pick up the tent. I'm not sure I had the authority to do that, but I got along with the enlisted spacers. They took common courtesy to be something remarkable from a gentleman. Goodness knows I've met some of my peers who felt courtesy was a needless burden.

Then I looked up Terney who was off duty in the Power Room sleeping section. As a survey ship, the *Far Traveller* had a much smaller crew than the warship it had been, so there was plenty of room. Only one other spacer shared Terney's eight-person bay and she wasn't in it at the moment.

Terney tightened when he saw me. He said, "Yeah?" in a half-frightened, half-hostile voice.

"Relax, Terney," I said. "I just want to talk." Then I said, "We'll be lifting off in a couple days. Then we'll never have to see this *damned* planet again."

Terney had jumped up when I entered the bay. Now he sat down again on the edge of his bunk. "You saw something too?" he said.

"I slept beside the Room," I said. "Monkeys turned into bats, more or less. It isn't anything awful, is it? But it was."

"I know," Terney said. He clasped his hands tight together and was shivering. "It shouldn't happen. It isn't *right*."

"No," I said. "But it won't happen again. The people, the *things* that did it, they're all gone thousands of years ago."

Terney looked up at me. "Are they?" he whispered.

"I hope so," I said. But I couldn't know for certain. Ever.

I went back to the lab and worked on sequencing samples from the traps in the bay.

A pinnace had landed early and for most of the morning the *Far Traveller* echoed with the squeal of winches hauling the pinnace close to the ship and then hoisting it aboard. It was about midday when Rick entered the bio lab and called, "Hi, Harry, how has Elkin been treating you?"

"It's kept me supplied with marine microorganisms," I said. "As a biologist, I'd have to say that I have a fulfilling life. How was sounding new routes?"

I'd missed Rick while he was off being an RCN officer; he was the only person on the *Far Traveller* I could talk to. None of the other officers were unfriendly, but I was always aware that they were interacting with Lord Harper.

Rick was aware of my family and respected it, but he didn't really care. He was a space officer, focused on the details of his job—and outside of that on women, in a friendly, casual fashion. The way he'd treated Rachel bothered me—but by his own lights it had been a fair exchange. He'd never offered more than he was ready to deliver; and if she had put more weight than he did on his readiness to risk his life to save hers, well, she was an adult.

It also bothered me that he talked—casually—about their relationship. That was my own problem. Rick was nowhere nearly as clinical as what was normal in a sporting club. I'd been raised according to the standard that a gentleman doesn't use names, but my father was stiff-necked compared to members of the family who spent more of their time in Xenos.

"We found some," he said. "Why anyone will want to use them is beyond me, given how benighted the whole region is. Anyway, we're off tomorrow for Mindoro where there's supposed to be some nightlife worth the name."

"And different marine microorganisms, I'm sure," I said. "Well, I won't be sorry to see the last of Elkin."

Doctor Veil's office door had been open. She stepped out into the lab proper and said, "Excuse me, Lieutenant Grenville. Did you say we're leaving Elkin tomorrow?"

"Bright and early in the morning, from what the captain says," Rick agreed cheerfully. "Do you have any teams out in the field still?"

"Kent is on the way back with Joss and her specimens," Veil said. "But that means we'll have to wind up our examination of the Room immediately."

Given that we had three cameras recording a block of moissanite as inert as the sand around it, "examination" struck me as an optimistic description. "Pick up our cameras, you mean?" I said.

I wouldn't be needed for that, and my distaste for the Room and its creators brought me to the verge of asking to be excused from the business, but Doctor Veil said, "No, we're going to break it open and see what it's holding."

I frowned and said, "Break how?"

"Well," said Veil. "I hate to do it but Captain Bolton informs me that we won't be able to carry the Room on the ship, so I'm going to blow it open by placing an electrical shattering charge in the niche at the base of the door. Chief Engineer Hideko said that one of his techs is very experienced in this sort of thing—she transferred from the Land Forces. The charge will break apart the door. We'll be there to record the whole event and take away the contents."

Destroying an Archaic artifact would have disturbed me a great deal a month ago. After my dream it...well, it didn't bother me at all. I now believed in the Archaic Spacefarers, and I believed the cosmos was better off without them.

I said, "What do you want me to do, ma'am?"

Doctor Veil, Rick—who'd asked to be present—and I were down in the open transport bay when Kent drove in with Joss beside him in the cab. Tech 3 Snedscott stood with us, though we hadn't interacted beyond introductions. Her equipment was a powerpack eighteen by eighteen by twelve inches, and a soft-sided satchel. Veil and I had only our handhelds; the cameras were already on site and linked to the base unit in the lab.

Kent pulled in and shouted over the idling fans, "There's plenty of room in back without offloading, unless you want us to."

"No, that's fine," Veil said.

I grabbed one end of the battery pack while Rick took the other; the forty-year-old tech grinned at us—and goodness knows, it was a lot heavier than I'd expected—but we got it up and into the back.

"Mahaffy, you ride in the cab with Doctor Veil," I said as he came around to join us.

When the four of us had climbed into the back, Rick leaned over and said, "Is Terney coming along?"

"No," I said. "He doesn't like the Room at all. Neither do I, but I'm sort of looking forward to blowing it up."

The fans grew loud and the truck shifted. We were wearing commo helmets—Snedscott had warned us we'd need them for the blast—but it still surprised me when it was through the helmet that Rick said, *"What's wrong with the Room?"*

The truck swept out of the transport bay and curved over the pools. I'd checked all of them on my way to and from Terney's site on foot, but none of the others showed signs of habitation for at least a decade. That in itself could have made Terney—odd.

I cleared my throat and said, "The place gave Terney dreams. It did the same to me though they weren't the same dreams. If they mean anything, the Archaics changed the genetics of life forms on the planets they visited."

There hadn't been time to speak to Rick about this since he got back from soundings, but I wasn't sure I'd been ready to talk until now anyway. I didn't know what to say.

"So...?" Rick said. *"They made chickens with bigger drumsticks?"*

I shook my head. "What I was seeing was a lot more complicated," I said. "They were making animals different in ways that didn't seem to help any way. Help the Archaics, I mean."

The fan note was changing again; Kent was preparing to land.

"Rick," I said, "they weren't even malicious. It's like boys throwing rocks through the windows of an abandoned house—they could break something, so they did."

"There's people like that," Rick said. *"I don't like them much, but there are."*

We landed. Joss dropped the tailgate and we piled out. I reached for the powerpack but Rick put a hand on mine and said, "Where do you want this, Technician? I want you to stand in that place, because you're going to be moving it yourself if it's got to be moved."

Snedscott straightened. "Understood, Lieutenant," she said. She walked to the back of the Room and marked a rough square with the toe of her boot. "I think it's close enough for my leads to reach and we don't have to dig the pack in then. The box itself will shield it."

Rick and I hefted the powerpack and shuffled to the spot with it. Rick obviously thought that the tech had been taking too much pleasure in watching a couple officers do physical labor. From Snedscott's muted reaction, he'd been correct.

With the powerpack placed, we backed away while the tech ran a pair of thick leads to the corner where the chip was missing from the Room. She knelt in the soil and pressed a wire into the divot with the leg of a pair of pliers, then squirted foam from a spray can into the opening to hold the wire. A tag of wire stuck out of either end.

Snedscott attached a lead to each end, then walked back to the powerpack where the rest of us were standing. Doctor Veil had checked the camera set at the back of the Room.

The tech connected one of the leads to the powerpack but then looked at her audience and said, "When the wire goes off, the cables may whip around to the back here. I think it'll be safer in front but about twenty feet back. That's where I'll be standing."

We all scurried around while Snedscott made the final connection and walked around to join us. I stepped around the parked truck and squatted down beside Joss. My back was turned and I was watching the camera aimed at the front on my handheld. Doctor Veil and the others came and joined us, even Snedscott.

She held up the controller so that we could all see what she was doing, then pressed the EXECUTE button. I'd opened my mouth and the helmet had sound cancelling, but my whole body felt the slap of sound.

The image of the Room on my handheld suddenly *glowed*, then cleared. The crystalline roof and sides of the Room had powdered. The unsupported door—the floor had vanished also—fell back into what had been the interior. The moissanite powder fell out of the air, giving the ground around where the Room had been a sheen.

The camera had jumped at the blast but it quickly stabilized:

the mounting column was sunk several feet deep. I switched to the camera behind the Room. I scrolled forward at a crawl starting from the moment Snedscott raised her controller.

When the blast occurred—the camera jumped to mark the instant—I saw a figure sitting on the floor of the Room. It flashed into powder the instant the air hit, seconds before the toppling door slammed onto the ground where the creature had been. I wondered if we'd be able to take DNA samples from the dust which the moissanite slab was protecting.

Doctor Veil had run to where the Room had been. Kent followed her. When I moved forward Rick came with me; I noticed that Joss stayed behind. Her face was expressionless, but her tattooed fingers were toying with the hilt of her bush knife.

"Bloody hell!" Snedscott shouted. "I didn't do anything wrong!"

I didn't speak the words that were on the tip of my tongue—*Then the explosion you set didn't destroy the Room and the object inside it?*—but instead said, "Doctor Veil? We've got imagery that shows an animal inside the Room, but the touch of air destroyed it. It's an animal I remember from a dream I had."

"A dream?" Veil repeated in puzzlement. She was obviously ready to flash out in anger, but I felt that it was my duty to speak anyway.

"Yes, ma'am," I said. "It was a tree-climbing quadruped that seemed to be covered with fine down. Or hair, I guess."

Veil was checking the feeds from the cameras herself. She seemed to calm down a little; it was obvious that opening the Room had destroyed the specimen, not the way the Room was opened.

"Look, I tamped the wire right!" Snedscott said. "I shock-foamed it and made sure it had time to set. You saw me!"

"Mistress Snedscott," I said. "You could have danced widdershins around it and none of us would've had any better notion of what was going on. We're not demolitions experts. I suggest you keep silent while the rest of us figure out what to do with the situation we're faced with."

She straightened to an attention posture.

Rick said quietly to me, though I suppose the tech could have heard him, "The funny shape of the cavity may have made the blast reflect funny."

"It doesn't matter," I said. "Actually, we probably have better imagery this way than we would have if only the door had shattered. We had cameras on both sides as well as the back and if the sides hadn't been turned to dust, we'd have had only the front shot."

"Sir?" Joss said. "And ma'am? There's a specimen you ought to look at. Here in the back."

"Now?" said Doctor Veil.

I followed Joss without asking questions. I'd decided quite early after meeting her that she didn't speak unless she thought it was necessary.

Joss jumped into the back and said, "Just stay there and help me get it down for the boss, all right?"

She lifted and slid a refrigerated container to the back of the bed. Between us we set it on the ground, though it wasn't as heavy as the pack that had carried enough of a charge to vaporize a tungsten wire.

Joss opened the case to its bottom compartment while Doctor Veil and I watched. Stored in that tray was a winged animal covered in gray down. Joss reached in and extended one of the wings. It was about half again the length of the body. There was no tail and the skull was narrow and low.

"I had to use the carbine because it was too high up for a charge of shot," Joss explained. "It reminded me of what was in the box."

"This is a smaller animal," Veil said in puzzlement. "And the other didn't have wings."

"I know," Joss agreed. "But the jaws and teeth made me think of the image."

"I saw these," I said. "In my dream. Yeah, they're a lot like the climbers, only they've got wings. And they've got little brain, but because of the wings they out-competed the climbers. They'll stay where they are till climate wipes out the trees; and they won't be able to go down on the ground, so they'll die out."

"I don't understand?" Doctor Veil said.

"There's nothing to understand," I said, feeling sick. "Why does a boy smash a window? He just likes to break things."

Rick was with us. I don't know how much he'd understood of what was going on. He said, "Well, on to Mindoro in the morning. I wonder what you'll find there?"

MINDORO

The *Far Traveller* had extracted 1.1 million miles from Mindoro. Captain Bolton had put Rick in charge of the approach. They weren't short of reaction mass and they could have cruised to the planet on High Drive, but Rick figured he needed practice on short-range—in system—astrogation, so he calculated a path through sponge space and announced, "Bridge to ship. We will be inserting in one, repeat one, minute. Bridge out."

Rick knew that Captain Bolton was observing from the command console but he didn't interfere in his junior lieutenant's choices. Rick wasn't surprised: He wasn't making the most conservative decision, but neither was he taking any real risks.

"Inserting," Rick announced as he pressed EXECUTE. Hearing his voice over the PA system gave him a feeling of power which he wouldn't have admitted in a million years.

The *Far Traveller* shimmered out of sidereal space like cold water being poured into a bowl of oil. Insertion was generally painless, though extraction had various effects ranging from unpleasant to death-would-be-better. It depended on the individual, but it was never nice.

The timer pulsed. "Extracting!" Rick announced and the *Far Traveller* was back in sidereal space. They'd come out within seventy thousand miles of the surface of Mindoro, a good piece—a *bloody* good piece—of astrogation. "Cleaning hull for landing," Rick said and started the telescoping and folding of the rig.

The outside crew remained on the hull to supervise the procedure: cables kinked or broke, gear trains stuck, and occasionally an antenna or spar had warped too badly to withdraw into the tube which was supposed to hold it. The riggers were there to correct mechanical faults, because a ship dropping through the atmosphere would be jouncing badly enough even if all the rigging was withdrawn and tightly clamped to the hull.

There was already a ship in Mindoro orbit. Rick had ignored it except to plot its course and see that it was nowhere near anywhere the *Far Traveller* was going to be, but the stranger hailed on the twenty-meter frequency: "*Unknown ship entering Mindoro orbit. Identify yourself and state your business. Mindoro control over.*"

Heimskring, the warrant officer on signals duty, replied. Rick focused on the ship. "*Conn,*" the captain said over a two-way link, "*this is Bolton. That's not a Mindoran ship on our database. Over.*"

"Sir, from the lines that's a Shining Empire ship," Rick said. "Do you want me to check the Bio Section files? Over."

"*Look, you're friends with Lord Harper, right?*" Bolton said. "*Have him come up and brief me as soon as we're in harbor. Bolton out.*"

Heimskring reported on the command channel, "*Sir, we're clear to land in Keelung Harbor as requested, out.*"

Rick had already set up an automated landing approach in the assumption that the landing would be approved. The *Far Traveller*'s thrusters were very responsive and the automatic program would bring the ship in as smoothly as something the size of a cruiser ever landed. Rick didn't think he could improve that response with manual control, and nor did he think the experience would be enough of a gain over what he could get from a training program to justify the risk in the event that he really screwed up.

"Ship," he announced on the general channel, "braking for landing on Mindoro."

He hit EXECUTE. There was a brief delay as some of the High Drive motors gimbaled. They had been driving the *Far Traveller* at 1 g toward planetary orbit; now they were preparing to fire at up to 3 g's to slow the ship until it dropped into the atmosphere, at which point the less efficient plasma thruster would assume the burden.

Rick had added a direct link to the intraship protocol. "Bio," he said.

A moment later his console replied, *"Harper here,"* in Harry's voice.

"Harry, the captain wants you to brief him on Mindoro in his cabin as soon as we're on the surface," Rick said. "Can you do that? Over."

Bolton could have made that an order, but he'd chosen to pass it through as a wish to Lord Harper through Lord Harper's friend. Rick had therefore delivered it to Harry the same way.

"Say...?" Harry said. *"Can you ask him to come down here? I can find the material in our system but I sure don't swear that on yours, though I know you copied it all in. And I'll tell Doctor Veil so she can sit in."*

Rick smiled. Harry might not know all there was about RCN protocol, but his natural courtesy was standing him in good stead. The captain might be willing to ignore Lieutenant Harper's direct superior—but Lord Harper himself was not.

The *Far Traveller* was beginning to get buffeted by the upper levels of the atmosphere. The buzzing High Drive was replaced by the lower roar of the thrusters.

The High Drive motors combined matter and antimatter to give a very energetic impulse, but the process wasn't perfect and any of the antimatter which didn't recombine in the motor was spewed out in the exhaust where it met—and destroyed the first atom of normal matter that it contacted. If that happened while the motor was filled with air, the energy release would damage the motor itself.

"Conn to Captain," Rick reported. "Lord Harper suggests that he can better brief you in Bio Section, sir. Can I pass on your reply? Over."

"Of course, Grenville," Bolton said. *"Turn the watch over to Vermijo as soon as we've landed. Captain out."*

Rick wasn't sure how Lieutenant Vermijo was going to take that, but he simply copied the exchange as a text to the first lieutenant in the Battle Direction Center.

The thrusters increased their output as the *Far Traveller* slowed to a near hover over the sea just outside the port of Keelung.

With Doctor Veil's approval I'd turned the lab itself into a briefing room. With the help of a signals assistant on Medlum, I'd reconfigured a workstation. Now it could project holographs in the middle of the room instead of just as a display for the person seated at it.

Kent and Mahaffy had been released with the first liberty watch. Joss would have been but she'd asked to stay for the briefing instead. Captain Bolton sat on the reversed seat of one of the work stations. Rick could have had the other—I'd taken over the middle one for the presentation—but he preferred to stand, so the seat went to Doctor Veil as a mark of respect.

I cleared my throat and said, "Mindoro and Aseel, which now calls itself the Shining Empire, have been regional rivals for hundreds of years. For most of this time the competition has been economic, but the two powers have fought three active wars during the past eighty years."

I'd thought of beginning by saying that I was a biologist, not a foreign ministry briefing expert, but they already knew my (lack of) qualifications. I was what was available to them aboard the *Far Traveller*.

"Mindoro has had a great deal of internal problems during the past century," I said. "Internal dissentions between north and south of the main continent which finally led to the overthrow of the Republic five years ago when the war with the Shining Empire was going badly, and the reinstatement of the royal line. The new king made peace with the Shinings, which was on pretty hard terms."

"From our data," Bolton said, "I don't see how the Shinings won a war. The Mindoran navy was much stronger, though you're talking about a clapped-out collection of makeshifts and Alliance castoffs on both sides."

I'd readied imagery to address the question and projected it here. "This is the cruiser *Spirit*," I said, "Originally the RCS *Bellona*—and eighty-five years old today. Despite her age, she was the most powerful warship in the region. Her captain was a firm Republican, however, and when the Royalists ousted the Republican government, he turned the ship over to the local representative of the Shining Empire. When word of that got around, a Mindoran squadron of transports converted to missile ships defected also. Though not to the Shinings. Basically the former transports reverted to their peacetime role. Their captains and crews decided they weren't interested in being soldiers for the king, and the political officers left the ships—sometimes on land and sometimes not. After that happened, making peace was the only Mindoran option, but it wasn't a choice that anybody much liked even before the Shinings started throwing their weight around."

"There's a couple Shining destroyers in harbor," Captain Bolton said, "and the Shinings seem to have taken over landing control, though the orbital control ship claims to be a Mindoran vessel. That was why I came to you. We've got nothing about this in our database."

"It's all pretty sudden," I said. "Nothing in the files from the Foreign Ministry mentioned that."

"It sounds like it makes no difference to us," Rick said. "The government still lets us land and use Mindoro for a base to sound from, don't they? And I guess Biology Section will still be able to take samples, can't you?"

"The royal government, yes," I said. "And the Shinings aren't objecting, at least not where we can see it. But there are a lot of people, in Keelung especially since it used to be the Republican capital, who don't like the government and *really* don't like the Shinings."

"Well, that doesn't matter to us, does it?" Bolton said, frowning. "We're neutral and Cinnabar *certainly* doesn't have a dog in that fight."

"You know that and I know that, sir," I said. "I'm not sure that everyone in Keelung knows it."

Joss, standing in a corner of the room, said, "Nobody's your friend when you're on liberty, sir. You go in pairs, that's all. They'll rob you just the same, but this way it's not so likely somebody'll smash your skull with a brick."

Captain Bolton rose. "The liberty party's had the usual warning," he said, "but we haven't opened up yet. I guess I'll add a special warning about the political situation."

I rose and gestured him to the console where I'd been sitting. "You can use this, sir," I said.

I thought about what Joss had said. To me travel had been an opportunity to see and learn things. The view that common spacers got was closer to that of the animals I saw when I was hunting: they were prey.

And here on Mindoro, I was in the same case as a common spacer.

✧   ✧   ✧

"So...," Rick said as he joined Harry in the forward boarding hold, the only one that was in use on Medlum. "Decided where you want to go in Keelung?"

The *Far Traveller*'s present complement was much below what it had been as a warship, so the forward hold was sufficient for the orderly comings and goings of the crew. The floating extension bridge that ran to the concrete quay had emptied by now, because Rick had some duties to finish up and Harry hadn't been in a hurry.

"There are some temples with colonies of flying animals that've been resident for hundreds of years," Harry said. "If you're willing, I'd like to combine business with pleasure and take some samples."

Rick laughed. "Boy, you're sure one for the fast life, aren't you?" he said, "but sure, if you're up for a good dinner and maybe a little barhopping afterwards. But say? Are they going to let you kill a sacred bird for a specimen?"

"Well, I wasn't planning to kill anything," Harry said. "I think the nests will be lined with feathers, though, which will give us the genes. And I'll certainly have dinner with you, but I'm not going to be closing down any bars."

Rick thought for a moment. "You know...," he said. "There'll be a verger, or something. And I'll bet that his bosses don't keep a close account of how many birds there are daily, so for a couple florins..."

Harry smiled. "The feathers'll be fine," he said. "I've got a map"—he raised his handheld—"to the main temple."

"And I've got the name of Rice Street," Rick said cheerfully. "Where we can find a variety of bars. I would say we're ready to go."

They strode off the *Far Traveller*, with a plan in mind.

Keelung's main streets were thirty or forty feet wide with a raised pedestrian median which they had to dart across a vehicular lane to reach. There wasn't a lot of traffic, so that wasn't a problem.

The route Harry had plotted from aerial imagery involved going down several of the connecting streets, however. The connectors were narrow and twisting, but the two officers were on foot and didn't think there'd be a problem until they reached the first intersection where they planned to turn.

The building on one corner appeared to be fortified and over-hung the street on two sides. There was room for two to walk abreast on the connector, but stone stoops at intervals on both sides jutted out from doorways. Mostly men, but women as well, sat on them drinking. When they realized Rick and Harry weren't moving on, they stared at the strangers. Even at midafternoon the passage was dark.

"You know...," Harry said, "I'd just as soon go roundabout. And get there."

"Right," said Rick. "That or draw submachine guns, which Captain Bolton probably wouldn't authorize."

They went up to the next major street and started down it. "You know," Harry said, "those people sitting and drinking may have been perfectly friendly."

"Yes," said Rick. "But they sure didn't seem that way to me."

The Temple of the Land sat in its own plaza. There was a heavy presence of peddlers, buskers and whores, but the officers weren't mobbed as Rick had expected from past landfalls.

With Harry slightly in the lead, they moved through the crowd and up to the high wooden doors. He rapped sharply with his knuckles while Rick faced around just to make sure nobody with a half brick in his hand was sauntering closer. The crowd in general seemed to be less interested—and possibly less hostile—than the folks sitting in the alley.

Harry knocked a second time. Almost instantly the small door in one panel of the great leaves opened. The man who opened it was in his fifties, bald and stooped. He was wearing cloth-soled slippers so they hadn't heard him.

He didn't seem to be about to speak, so Harry said, "We're scientists from the Cinnabar survey ship in the harbor. We're here to view the kalu birds in their nests. We have government approval."

The little man opened his postern door fully, but that was just so that he could step out to spit. "*That* for the government!"

He took a deep breath and continued, "But come in and bathe in the light of God. The king cannot change the true God, though he may try to starve her acolytes."

"Thank you, sir," Harry said, dipping his head in what was just short of a bow. "May we see the kalu birds?"

They followed the little man inside. Rick brought out his RCN goggles—they hadn't brought commo helmets which were too bulky for a day in which they intended to walk around the town on their own. The goggles provided a variety of viewing options; Rick chose light amplification and was at once amazed by the gilt and scarlet carvings which covered the walls and ceiling of the sanctuary.

In the middle of the back wall was a twenty-foot-tall statue of a female figure with a beatific smile and arms spread wide toward the nave and the entrance doors. Rick wasn't a religious man, but he felt unexpectedly peaceful when he looked at the big figure.

"Sir, you're the priest?" Harry was saying as he slipped a coin— Rick thought it was five florins—to the little man.

"The Goddess has no priests by order of the king," the little man said bitterly. "I am the caretaker. For three hundred years the Protectors supported the Goddess and the Goddess blessed the planet, but now the King worships at the Temple of the Sky as his ancestors did—and the Shining filth are our overlords!"

Harry nodded to show that he was listening, but he turned and adjusted his goggles as he scanned the high rafters of the sanctuary. Rick followed the line of his friend's sight. He'd noticed motion in the air above him. When he focused, he realized from tiny movements that some of the bumps on the rafters were the heads of living creatures.

"Sir?" Harry said. "Might I see the birds from closer up? I promise not to hurt them. Do I see a ladder there at the back?"

Rick hadn't noticed the two legs of a ladder sticking out at the edge of a hallway across the back of the building behind the sanctuary. There must be some provision for cleaning the carvings, especially if there were birds living among them.

Harry was holding out another coin. He said, "I would be pleased to support your work in preserving such a masterpiece of faith and beauty. And the *Far Traveller*'s efforts in determining the true genetic affinities of the kalu birds can aid in the preservation of the birds and also of the resurgence of the temple in which they live."

"Really?" said the caretaker. "Well, I don't see that it can hurt. They're so tame they eat out of my hand, you know?"

"No, I *didn't* know," Harry said brightly. "I would *love* to get imagery of that after I take genetic samples from the nests."

Rick wondered how much of Harry's hopeful enthusiasm was

just an act, but perhaps not much. Harry really was an enthusiast for the things he cared about.

Rick braced the castered feet of the ladder while Harry climbed and returned with a small bundle. "I think that this is really remarkable," Harry whispered as he reached the ground. "The kalu birds are supposed to be related to the species on the north continent!"

"And...?" Rick said as the caretaker returned with a plate on which sat a dozen tiny bowls.

"They're not even the same phylum!" Harry said. "They have fur, not downy feathers like the northern population!"

The caretaker turned his back on the two visitors and held his platter out at arm's length. The fluttering above resolved into individual gray thumb-sized creatures which settled on the rim of the plate and extended a part of their mouths to suck up the material in the bowls. Harry continued recording imagery as long as the meal went on.

Rick just raised the magnification of his goggles. One of the "birds" was actually perching on the caretaker's hand where he held the platter. Their wings were still while they ate, but when finished, they each rose back into the rafters in a double blur.

When the last bowl had been emptied, the caretaker bowed to his visitors. Harry handed him another coin and said, "Thank you, sir."

Rick surprised himself and slid a florin piece out of his belt purse. This wasn't really his affair, and he was none too flush with drinking money; but the creatures had delighted him. "And may I thank you also," he said.

As they left the temple, Harry said, "I'm not sure there are any similar creatures in the current Mindoran database. This is *huge!*"

"What's huge for me right at the moment...," Rick said, "is my appetite for dinner. Shall we find some?"

The restaurant Rick had been told was the best in town could be reached by the broader streets and was within three blocks of the temple. The staff was of young women wearing outfits of bright primary colors and smiling unemotionally. The first course was a vegetable in a tasty green sauce.

The vegetable itself was another matter.

"Maybe if we had sharper knives?" Harry said.

"I think saws are more what's indicted," Rick said. He'd whittled off a piece he could get in his mouth and was chewing, but the resulting fibers didn't encourage him to swallow them.

He did anyway. The wad didn't choke him, but neither had be noticed any flavor during the process.

"We'll see about the meat course," he said hopefully. Harry smiled back.

Their hope was misplaced. The meat was a flat, oval animal which a pair of servers brought to the table. There one held it with a pair of forks and the other very dexterously reduced it to thin slices. A microtome couldn't have done a neater job.

The slices could with difficulty be worried into mouth-sized chunks with the edge of a fork. The sauce this time was red and extremely hot, which was the only flavor either man drew from the dish.

"What do you suppose they offer for dessert?" Harry said.

"I suggest we skip it and find something to drink," Rick said. "I figure I can find some sacking back at the ship which will fill me as easily. It won't be as exotic, but long odds it'll taste as good."

They got up and walked to the front. "Rightly," Rick said, "I ought to pay for this abortion. I picked the place."

"I'll let you buy the first round of drinks instead," Harry said. "I suspect you're more of an expert there."

The bar was the third one we'd come to on Rice Street. I didn't ask Rick why he'd passed the first two since they'd seemed pretty much the same to me, but he really did have specialist knowledge here. I was sure he'd defer to me if we needed to create a seating chart for a formal dinner among the leading families of Mindoro.

Even I could tell this one was a spacers' tavern. Rick found an empty four-seat table toward the back. The bar itself was crowded and kept two tapsters busy, but the body of the room was only filled in patches.

"How's the draft?" Rick said to the cute, dark-haired server.

"Right now it's pretty good," she said. "The barrel we opened yesterday had gone off, but they won't finish that one off till late evening when the folks drinking will be too well oiled to notice. And I finish my shift in an hour, so ask me if I care."

Rick laughed and said, "Bring us two drafts then. And say? What do you do when you go off duty?"

"It depends on who's asking," she said. "I'll be back with your beers—and my name's Maddy."

She swirled off. Rick grinned at me. "She's hoping a fine RCN spacer will tip well," he said. "And I wouldn't be a bit surprised if she turned out to be right."

A cadaverous looking stranger appeared behind one of the empty chairs. "Gentlemen?" he said. "Could I buy you this round?"

"You bloody well can," Rick said. "And you can tell us why you want to?"

The stranger wore a jacket over coveralls which didn't look like the garments I'd seen on anybody else in Mindoro. He laughed genially and said, "The characteristic directness of an RCN officer. You are RCN officers, are you not?"

Maddy arrived with the beers. The stranger gave her a thick wad of the local scrip. The official exchange rate was about seventy to a florin from what I'd checked back at the ship, but I was pretty sure the top bill of the pile was a 500. "I'll have one also, and I'm paying tonight."

Maddy set our beers down and tucked the scrip down the front of her top. The stranger said, "My name's Dolio, you see. And if you *are* RCN spacers—"

"I am," Rick said with a hint of belligerence.

"—then I'm here to apologize to you. Your fellows on the *Goliath* were given dangerously bad course information. I opposed that plan but I was outvoted. Now that my colleagues have decided that I was right to welcome Cinnabar as a counterweight to the Shining Empire, they have asked me to make amends if possible."

Rick leaned across the table. "Who are you, Master Dolio?" he asked.

Dolio smiled wryly. "I am a member of the governing council of the Brotherhood," he said. "My fellows felt that we independent traders would be harmed by an influx of Cinnabar vessels into the region. *I* felt that the Shinings were a worse danger to us and to all independent traders."

He shrugged. "The future will be challenging for the Brotherhood," he said. "Cinnabar competition will hurt us. But if the Shinings continue to expand, they will destroy not only our trade but our very selves. They regard themselves as the only true humans. They believe they're descended from the Archaic Spacefarers."

"The Archaic Spacefarers are real," I said. "I'm convinced of that. But I'm not sure they're human. In fact the evidence is that they weren't."

Dolio shrugged. "The Shinings would agree that we and they aren't the same species," he said. "They would quarrel with our belief that we are human, though. Regardless, Aseel has industrialized to a degree that nothing else in the region has ever come close to. I think they'll overstep themselves—they truly don't understand how much larger the Alliance and Cinnabar are. But until that happens, they make very uncomfortable neighbors."

"I can see that," I said. "I think your colleagues were very shortsighted—but then, I was raised to believe that treachery is always shortsighted."

I realized as I spoke that Dolio might think I was sneering at him. I suppose I was.

Rick said, "We're lieutenants. If you want to apologize, you need to find somebody with real rank. Mind, they'd likely tell you that Captain von Hase got what he deserved for taking the word of a lying little wog."

Dolio's smile was very tight, but he smiled. "I understand your attitude," he said. "I suppose I would share it in your situation. In any case, words of apology wouldn't be real amends for the damage which the *Goliath* received."

He put a small silk bag on the table and slid it over to me. Maddy arrived then with three more beers though Dolio had only drunk half of his. There was a chip in the silk bag.

I looked at Dolio, who met my eyes over his mug. "It's a route chip for this region," he said. "Since your vessel sounds by pinnaces rather than making the transitions herself, there's no serious risk to you in checking the computations. When you do, I think you'll find that our courses will save considerable transit time on many routes."

I put the chip back into its bag and slid it to Rick. Dolio had apparently thought I was the senior officer, but if this was astrogational data it wasn't my affair.

Rick had apparently been paying some attention while he chatted with Maddy, because instead of reopening the bag he merely set his finger on it and looked at Dolio. "Why should we believe you now?"

"You shouldn't," Dolio said. "I'm a lying wog, after all. But since you can check the routes with no risk except to a pinnace, you would be fools not to check."

He finished his first beer and stood, then slid the untasted refill over to Rick. "Good evening to you, gentlemen," he said. "I think the money I left with your server will keep you drinking for a good while longer."

He nodded as he made his way out of the bar. Rick turned to me and grimaced as he put the chip in a pocket. He said, "At least it'll keep us going until Maddy ends her shift."

I nodded. I figured I'd be going back to the ship alone tonight.

I'd just gotten a response from Master Blenkins, saying that he would be delighted to show me through his cabinet of curiosities, when the intercom at my workstation peeped.

"Harper," I said, knowing it had to be Rick if it were my outlet alone. A call to Bio Section would have come through the central unit to the side of the entrance hatch.

"Just checking on how you're doing," Rick said. *"There was honest to hell rioting last night in the avenue outside Maddy's room and I wasn't sure when you'd gotten home."*

"I got back before there was any trouble that I saw," I said. "I figured you'd still be with the new girlfriend or I'd have checked to see if you wanted to visit another collection with me. You saved us some time IDing that console lens on Quan Loi."

"I'm off duty till 1600 hours local," Rick said. *"I'm doing check rides on tech 3s striking for 4 for the next few days. And* sure *I'd like to see what the locals' ancestors thought was worth preserving."*

"Then come on down and keep me company," I said. "It ought to be an easy walk."

"It'll be easier still with the trike," Rick said. *"I'll meet you in the transportation bay."*

The Blenkins mansion was smaller than some I've seen, probably because it was one of the oldest buildings in Keelung. It was on the water, six blocks west of the *Far Traveller*'s berth, with its own stone pier. As we pulled up in front of the steel gate, a pair of attendants pulled open one of the leaves so that Rick could drive through. He pulled up just inside instead of driving up the ramp to the porch of house.

"Can we leave it here?" he asked the guards.

"Certainly, sir," one of the men responded. "They're expecting you inside."

The attendants weren't carrying weapons, but a pair of meter-long batons leaned against the inside of the wall flanking the gate. When we'd started up the steps I asked Rick quietly, "Who was rioting last night?"

"Backers of the New Party and the Old Party," Rick said. "One's the royalists and the other's the republicans, but Maddy wasn't a hundred percent sure which was which. Down at her level, politics mostly means getting your head down when you see party heavies out looking for trouble."

The broad house door opened as we approached it. A pudgy sixties-ish man wearing an outfit of light-weight cloth with puffy sleeves and trousers greeted us, but there were two attendants in the room as well as the man who'd pulled open the door.

"Welcome to Blenkins House!" the older man said. "I am Blenkins of Blenkins and you are welcome here."

I shook his hand and said, "I am Lord Harper and my companion from the *Far Traveller* is Lieutenant Grenville."

All three male servants were built on the lines of the two on the gate. They were wearing white tops and black trousers, ordinary service garb, but they sure didn't look as though they'd been hired to carry platters of food.

I guess I'd let my eyes hang on the servants longer than I'd meant them to, because Blenkins grimaced and said, "I'm sorry, gentlemen, we've had some trouble recently in Keelung."

He paused and took a deep breath, then continued, "I don't agree with those who foment violence—I think it's likely to result in an even more blatant presence of the filth from Aseel. Regardless of my own wishes, there are others who do regularly use violence. Even those who claim to be Old Party like myself are capable of trying to intimidate anyone who doesn't support them without reservations. I have to be prepared."

"Sir," I said, "I regret the difficult situation you and your compatriots are going through. The Republic has had similar problems in recent memory. Regardless, my companion and I are here to view the Blenkins collection with your very kind permission, not to interfere in local politics."

"I appreciate your tact, gentlemen," Blenkins said with a bow. "Come then, to the third floor."

We followed our host up two flights of stairs. The first was stone and the treads had been worn sway-backed by centuries of feet; the second flight was wood and recent enough that I could smell the oil used to finish the wood, though the surface was slickly dry.

In the hallway at the top of the staircase, Blenkins unlocked one of the rooms and gestured us in. The room was ten by twelve with glass topped tables on one side and open egg-crate cabinets on two others. In the two back corners stood space suits. They looked clumsy and odd to me, but I wasn't an expert.

Rick went up to a suit and looked at it closely. He turned to Blenkins, standing in the doorway, and said, "Is this part of the equipment of the colony ship? Because it appears to be over a thousand years old. Certainly Pre-Hiatus."

"It is the suit worn by my ancestor, Navigation Officer Edmondo Blenkins," Blenkins said proudly. "We are truly an ancient family and have been among the first families of Mindoro ever since the settlement—though we've never given ourselves such airs as the Pilkeys have."

"The Pilkeys are the royal family, then?" I asked out of curiosity rather than any real reason.

"The Pilkeys are descended from Captain Pilkey," Blenkins said. "The royal family—the self-*styled* royal family, I may add—are descended from Commissioner Seba, the head of the civil colony and based in Langsam, a port on the west of the mainland. They lost power on Mindoro when we regained space travel and began to reenter the galactic arena. They are back now, but I doubt whether they would be except for the aid of the Aseelians. The Shinings, as they prefer to call themselves now. I doubt the royals would even be in power in Langsam."

"I see," I said, giving my attention to the open shelves. What I saw was that internal divisions on Mindoro had crippled it in its war with the Shinings. That was a pity, but it was none of my business and didn't affect the *Far Traveller*'s mission.

"There's a Shining orbital control...," Rick said as I recorded images from the shelving. "And Shining ships in harbor, at least two of them, are there not?"

"Yes," Blenkins agreed curtly. "There are far more at Langsam, but Keelung is still the main harbor and Mindoro's trade moves through us. The royal vicar is a puppet of his Aseelian 'advisor,' Lord Kindoro."

He grimaced and spread his hands. "What can we do?" he said. "Certainly rioting in the street as Pilkey is stirring up won't help. There was a riot last week in which an Aseelian was stabbed. As a result, the vicar has arrested a dozen petty criminals and street thugs, and proposed to torture them to death until someone turns in the real murderers."

"Why didn't he arrest you and Master Pilkey?" I said. "He must know who's running the Old Party."

Blenkins looked at me, I thought in surprise. I said, "I'm not on his side, but it just seems the obvious thing to do. Cut the snake's head off, I mean."

After a moment, Blenkins smiled at me. He said, "You are a very direct man, Lord Harper. The vicar is not—none of the Sebas were, which is why they were forced out of power five hundred years ago. There would be a general uprising—New Party supporters as well as those giving allegiance to Pilkey and me. The king doesn't have enough force at his disposal without calling on the Shinings, and the Shinings don't have enough troops on Mindoro or any way to get more troops here soon enough to matter."

I went back to the egg-crate shelving. It was full of knickknacks—bits of equipment which I generally couldn't identify and which weren't of interest when I could. There were weapons, knives as well as guns. The guns might have been in working order from anything I could see. There were coins and medals, statuettes, and pieces of graphic art.

Then I came to a crystal rod. "Sir!" I said. "Might I handle this?"

"Yes, certainly," Blenkins said. "I suppose it's glass, though, so don't drop it."

"I won't drop it," I said. "But I'm pretty sure it'll turn out to be silicon carbide and a lot tougher than glass."

I set the spindle on a glass-topped table covering documents with attached seals and ribbons, then hooked my handheld meter to it and asked for density and structure. As I expected, I was looking at a moissanite rod of unusual shape.

"Sir?" I said to Master Blenkins. "Do you have a record of the provenance of this item?"

"The only records I know of are for items I added myself," Blenkins said. "I didn't know that even existed. Do you know what it is?"

"I suspect," I said, "that it's an artifact of the Archaic Space-farers. Though I have no idea of its purpose."

"No fooling?" Blenkins said. "Does that mean it's valuable?"

I sighed internally, but all I said aloud was, "In terms of florins, no. Clear silicon carbide can be easily mistaken for diamond but it isn't, and it's not valuable for itself. But as a matter of science, *any* artifact of the Archaics is uniquely important."

Blenkins considered momentarily with a fierce expression. Then his face cleared and he said, "Well, you can look it over to your heart's content. I guess I'll make a better display of it if it really is a rare thing."

"Thank you, sir," I said. I got to work copying the artifact from every angle. There wasn't really much to see beyond the obvious, but I wouldn't be coming back to Mindoro in this lifetime. I was making as much of the opportunity as I could.

Rick spoke with Blenkins in a low voice. They left the room together.

When I finished making images, I put the artifact back on the shelf where I'd found it. As I stepped to the door to look for my host, Rick and Master Blenkins reentered the collection room.

"There's another room next door," Rick said cheerfully. "It's got a lot of plants and bugs in it, which makes it more your speed, right?"

"Well, I'll be delighted to see the rest of your collection, Master Blenkins," I said, though in truth I didn't have much hope for the rest of the collection. The first room would have been a waste of time—without the Archaic artifact; but that was a huge find and would thrill Doctor Veil. Ideally, the second room would have the preserved body of an Archaic, but I wasn't going to bet much on the possibility.

The second room had waist-height glass-topped chests of drawers around the walls. The creatures in the top layer had external shells; some but not all had come from the sea. I suspected that in life many had been brightly colored, but in the years or even centuries since they were collected they had mostly faded to beige.

On one cabinet was a flat creature about forty inches long and slightly pointed at both ends. Although this specimen was dried, I was pretty sure that the meat course at dinner the previous night would have come from something similar. I preferred it as a museum exhibit, but perhaps it was an acquired taste.

"The drawers pull out," Blenkins said and helpfully extended the second drawer on the right-hand cabinet.

I dutifully recorded all the items in the cabinets. I didn't ask to take samples for genetic testing because I didn't have a portable way to do that, and I was pretty sure that I wasn't seeing anything that wasn't already familiar from the Blythe Academy database which Doctor Veil had gotten through friends at the Xenos Science Faculty before the *Far Traveller* lifted on Cinnabar.

When I finished recording the contents of the drawers, I straightened and stretched. "Do you have more collections, sir?" I asked Blenkins, who was watching with apparent interest from the doorway.

"Well, there's the ones on the walls here," he said, gesturing.

I realized that I'd forgotten the invertebrates arranged on the wall above the cabinets in whimsical displays. The designs were of birds, fish, and even what looked like a stylized spaceship.

I began recording the four displays. They were all the Mindoran equivalent of insects. Each display was pretty much a single species, so I thought of asking Blenkins if I could have a specimen of each for genetic sequencing.

That would disturb patterns which really showed some artistry, however. Joss was already out collecting specimens and I would be joining her shortly; we could find as many of the insectoids as we wanted. Besides, none of the creatures looked very interesting.

The fourth display was of a bird largely made from creatures with biting mouth parts and multiple body segments which had allowed the artist to draw the tail feathers in sweeping curves. The head was a different insect. I magnified my image of it, then stared at what I had.

Good heavens.

I cleared my throat, then said, "Master Blenkins, will you come closer please? I'd like you to look at this."

"Look at what?" our host said. "The bugs?"

"Not exactly," I said. I was using my handheld to search the *Far Traveller*'s Biology Database. I gestured. "Take a good look at the item that forms the head of the bird drawing."

"Oh, it's not a bug after all," Blenkins said, reaching over the cabinet.

"Don't!" I said, forgetting for a moment that I was a guest in this man's home. Blenkins jerked his hand back though.

"Sir," I continued, "have you heard of the lourdis tree on Commonwealth? They called it the God Tree before the species was wiped out by an off-planet blight a century ago. The planetary government set a reward of a million Alliance thalers for a surviving plant, now that they have a vaccine for the blight."

"A million thalers?" Blenkins said. "A *million*?"

"I don't know that your seed is still viable," I said. "And the reward may have been cancelled, though it was still open about a year ago, the date of my information. In any case, I think it should be handled carefully. On Commonwealth, the lourdis tree has religious significance as well as popularly being thought to encourage feelings of mental well-being."

"A million thalers...," Blenkins repeated. He looked over at me with a worried expression and said, "If that's true, what will your share be, Lord Harper?"

I chuckled. I hadn't been able to imagine what was bothering Blenkins, but now I saw. "I don't have a share, Master Blenkins," I said. "The seed is yours to do with as you please. Eat it, for all I care."

"Sir...," Blenkins repeated. His face scrunched up and he dropped to his knees. "Lord Harper!" he blurted. "Lord Harper, this is unbelievably generous of you! How can I thank you?"

"You invited me into your home and showed me your family collections," I said. "The thanks are mine to give. Lieutenant Grenville and I will take our leave now."

Rick would be going on duty before long and probably wanted to get lunch before that. I could use a meal myself.

"Well, wait a moment at least," Blenkins said. He stood up and strode out of the room. I looked at Rick and said in a low voice, "You're ready, I assume?"

"Sure," Rick murmured, but Blenkins came back in the room before we could leave. He held the moissanite artifact. "Will you at least accept this?" he said. "It's of no value to me, but at least it means something to you."

"It certainly does," I said, taking the Archaic Artifact. I put it in my side pocket so that I could shake Blenkins' hand.

"My superior will be overjoyed with this, Master Blenkins," I said. "And I only hope that the lourdis seed will bring you as much pleasure as your gift does her."

Rick and I left immediately. I needed to get my artifact into Doctor Veil's hands as soon as possible.

Rick hadn't really intended to spend the night with Maddy, but they'd had a good deal to drink with dinner. "Say, dear...," he said as they walked back along Covici Street. "I go on duty at 0800 tomorrow, but I can have the signals tech call a half hour before on my intercom. If that isn't going to offend you?"

Maddy hugged herself closer. "I'm not offended," she said. She giggled. "So...? What did you have in mind?"

They turned into Temple passage. The sky was visible between the building fronts, but the passage was a shadowed grayness which Rick had gotten used to in the past three nights. As usual there were people farther down the alley, but he and Maddy would be going up to her apartment at the second staircase down the passage.

"Well," Rick said, "I admit to having the same evil intentions that I've inflicted on you every other—"

Two figures got up from a porch down the way, but Rick was muzzily unconcerned until a bag was thrown over his head from behind. Maddy screamed.

Rick tried to grab the communicator in his tunic pocket, but the bag's drawstrings were pulled tight and pinioned his arms. He tried to kick but at least two men grabbed his wrists and jerked him backward. More men—he supposed they were men—caught his legs when his feet came off the ground. He sneezed violently. The bag had been used as a dog blanket or a dog had been held in it. He didn't have enough air, and blasting out what there was in a sneeze didn't help.

The men holding Rick threw him in the back of a vehicle where more hands gripped him. He continued to struggle, but he didn't expect it to do much good.

His tunic pocket ripped open and the intercom was pulled out. He heard it or something like it clack on the pavement. Then the car door crunched shut and the vehicle started off.

I'd left Joss and Kent to deal with the containers and other gear—even though we'd been called back early to the *Far Traveller*, we had a considerable haul of specimens. Normally I'd have helped carry the items for processing over to the lab, but this time orders as well as my own inclinations were to go up to Captain Bolton immediately.

Kent said as I started up the companionway, "I'll call the bridge and tell them that you're on your way."

I didn't try to run up the helical stairs. I'd gotten in much better shape in the course of the voyage, but I still wasn't going to push a seven-deck climb. Besides, I was upset enough by the slight news Kent had given me that I could very easily slip and knock out my teeth on a higher tread.

I had my breathing under control by the time I reached the bridge. Lieutenant Vermijo was on watch with the couch reversed to watch me from the moment I came out of the companionway. He rose as I entered and gestured me to the captain's day cabin, then followed me in.

"What's happened to Rick?" I said. I knew I should be more formal. When the *Far Traveller* was in service, the crew dispensed with saluting, but blurting my concern on entering was discourteous even so.

"I don't know," Captain Bolton said. "He's been snatched off the street by locals, so I've cancelled liberty for the whole crew and recalled you and your assistant from the west so that nothing would happen to you as well. It seems to be a matter of local politics, an attempt to put pressure on the Mindoran government."

I swallowed. *That doesn't sound good.*

Bolton cleared his throat and went on, "A group calling itself the Citizens' Justice Front says that it will hold Lieutenant Grenville until the government releases three Mindorans who killed a Shining official in a brawl. Well, they're accused."

"Sir, what is the government doing?" I asked, keeping my voice calm. Or anyway, trying to.

"Well, I've contacted the palace," Bolton said. "I'm planning to make a personal appeal to Prince Abel, but frankly I was waiting for your return before I did so."

"Then let's go right now," I said. "I'm sure Doctor Veil will let us use the aircar, but whatever you decide is best, sir."

I doubted that the name Harper of Greenslade was going to impress a backwoods monarch, but this would let me learn what was going on and very possibly keep Captain Bolton focused on the problem. He was obviously worried about the kidnapping, but the fact that he'd let much of a day go by without taking real action was worrisome.

"Well . . . ," Bolton said. "Yes! As soon as I've put my first class uniform on."

"I'll meet you in the transportation bay," I said. I'd put on my dress uniform also. I didn't think it would make any difference to Prince Abel, but it obviously did to Captain Bolton. And who knew? Maybe he was right.

Kent was just going back to the truck for a last load when I arrived. I shouted in his ear over the echoing racket of the bay, "We need you again right now. Well, you and the truck. Do you need to be serviced before you run us out to the north side of town?"

I transferred the site location from my handheld to the guidance unit in the aircar's console. Kent checked it and said, "Hell, we're fine. I could run you out to your campsite in a pinch."

Bolton arrived then. The three of us got onto the front bench of the vehicle and Kent whirled us back out of the bay. I gestured the captain onto the middle seat without thinking.

There was still a case of specimens in the back and I'd forgotten to tell Doctor Veil that we were off in the aircar. I was very nervous about Rick. None of the branches of my family was political, but even so I'd lost cousins during the Three Circles Conspiracy. These things take on a life of their own that goes way beyond what anybody at the start had in mind.

And the nastiness feeds on itself also. Things happen that none of the people involved could have imagined doing a month earlier.

The aircar buzzed over Keelung, drawing the attention of people in the streets. Unless a ship in the harbor had an aircar, this might be the only one in a hundred miles. Keelung was a fairly compact city with little need of private vehicles, let alone aircars.

"The palace was a vacation lodge of the Seba family before the Republic," Captain Bolton said. "It had fallen to ruin since then, but when the king decided—or the Shinings decided that there should be a royal presence in the main starport, they decided to rebuild the lodge as the Vicar's Palace."

"That's it right ahead," Kent said. "Say, do you want me to set down outside the fence? They may get stroppy about us barreling right in."

He was obviously thinking about the DaSerta estate in Quan Loi where automatic impellers had tracked us. I was thinking about that too.

"Well, if they get stroppy," Bolton said, "then I'll call Vermijo and have him bring the *Far Traveller* in and see if they like that better. An RCN officer has disappeared!"

For the first time I realized that Captain Bolton for all his foibles and inadequacies was a member of the Navy which had fought the far larger Alliance of Free Stars to a standstill and forced Guarantor Porra to give up his dreams of hegemony over all human settlements.

Crews were erecting a three-meter wall around the perimeter of the property. It couldn't have been very sturdy because it fluttered like a banner when our aircar overflew it at twenty-five feet and descending. It must have been on a frame of some sort, though, because it didn't simply sail away. The construction personnel were wearing yellow-gray uniforms that weren't familiar to me.

Kent landed us on the lawn, about twenty feet short of the front steps of the one-story building. I heard whistle signals while we were still airborne, and when the fans shut off there were excited voices from all directions.

The front door of lodge burst open and two groups of soldiers spilled out, carrying carbines. The blue tunics and white trousers were Mindoran dress uniforms, and I was willing to bet that the troops in mottled beige battledress were Shinings.

They weren't precisely threatening when they realized that we were visitors, not an assault force, but they didn't hide their weapons, just stopped pointing them at us. The labor crews disappeared, either into the lodge which they'd been working on, or streaming toward the three inflatable barracks which had been erected farther back on the property.

What I had thought of as a wall was actually three stacked coils of razor ribbon covered with gray fabric as a visual barrier. I suppose the idea was to keep the number of Shining troops in Keelung a secret. According to Rick, there was at least one warship in harbor as well, but not enough Shinings in total to control a hostile city by force.

Officers, with a Shining in the lead, started over to the aircar as I got out but I said nothing to their questions until the captain had followed me. The Shining shouted, "You should not be here!"

Captain Bolton strode past. He looked to me as though he'd have pushed through the much shorter Shining if the fellow hadn't gotten out of his way.

"My officers should not be kidnapped on the street!" he said. "Yet one was! I'm Captain Bolton of the RCS *Far Traveller* and I'm here to discuss with the vicar as civil governor the steps he's taking to correct the situation."

The lodge's original wooden steps had been replaced by concrete so recently that some of the forms still lay beside the building. I followed the captain into the lobby. A civilian sat behind a desk there. He put down a handset and gave us a broad, false smile.

"The vicar will shortly be with you, gentlemen!" he said.

"Good," said Bolton and walked through into the next room without slowing. I followed. The Shining officer who'd tried to intercept us outdoors darted into the lobby and through a side door.

Vicar Seba was in the next room putting on a brocade robe with the help of two servants when we entered. "Good day, Excellence," Bolton said, "Captain Bolton of the *Far Traveller* and the ranking official of the Republic of Cinnabar on Mindoro. One of my officers was kidnapped in Keelung yesterday. What steps have you taken to rectify the situation?"

Two men entered through a side door. They wore Pleasaunce formalwear of a generation past: stark black over white. The older of the two was barefoot. I guessed the elder was about forty and his companion some ten years younger.

Seba's mouth had opened to stammer something, but he gratefully turned to the newcomers and said, "Captain Bolton, this is my friend and advisor Lord Kindoro and his aide Master Pretsuma. They represent the Shining Empire which has been very helpful to Mindoro in our recent troubles."

The Shining representatives dipped their heads slightly. I noticed that though Pretsuma lowered his face, his eyes remained fixed on the captain. I remembered Doctor Veil saying that the Shinings claimed to not be descended from Earth stock. That was genetically absurd, but these two men did make me think of reptiles.

"And my lieutenant, Lord Seba?" Bolton pressed. He hadn't looked at the Shinings.

"If I may interject here," Lord Kindoro said. There was no question whatever in his tone. "I have been largely concerned with this matter as it appears to be directed at the Shining Empire, demanding freedom for miscreants who murdered one of our brothers. Of course there is no possibility of releasing the murderers."

Captain Bolton whirled on him. "The Republic of Cinnabar does not negotiate with terrorists!" he said. "But my question was directed toward Vicar Seba as Mindoro and Cinnabar are the only parties to this matter. So, Vicar—what are you doing about the matter? And who is this Citizens' Justice Front?"

"The Citizens' Justice Front is a fanciful name created by persons wishing to stir up trouble between the Shining Empire and our friends, the ordinary people of Mindoro," Kindoro said. "The group exists only in the minds of a few malcontents. You should ignore the matter and leave it in the hand of the proper authorities."

"I would be happy to do so," Captain Bolton said, "if I had any confidence that my lieutenant would be returned if I did so!"

"Honored Captain...," Pretsuma said in a tone without honor. "This region of the galaxy is very far removed from where your Republic of Cinnabar ordinarily operates. In the interests of your own safety, may I recommend that you return where you belong. I assure you that the Shining Empire will very shortly have solved the problem of the Citizens' Justice Front whoever they may be in a thorough and complete fashion."

"Vicar Seba," Bolton said, "I'm holding you personally responsible for this matter!"

He turned and stalked out. I followed him, having said nothing during the entire encounter. There was nothing useful to say.

I didn't recall ever before in my life being so angry.

Rick slid around in the back of a van. There were others with him but he knew that only because sometimes he slid into their legs: They weren't kicking him for fun. Occasionally one or another of them spoke but it was always in a voice too low for Rick to understand the words.

His greatest immediate discomfort was the difficulty of breathing. He twisted enough to get his right hand under the mouth of the bag that covered his head and torso. With the freed hand, he reached carefully his trouser pocket and found his little knife. He paused for a moment. His wriggling hadn't aroused concern in his captors. There must not be a light where he was being held, and the way the vehicle was bouncing meant that his intentional movements were lost in the rest of what was going on.

The van stopped and the back door opened. Men talked in low, ill-tempered voices. Rick held himself very still. Hands grabbed him by the ankles and both arms through the bag. They passed him to more hands. A moment later they dropped him—into what was probably a boat because of the hollow clang he made when he hit.

One good thing was that he hadn't been able to open the little knife when he hit. The other good thing was that when the shock jounced the knife out of his hand, the bag kept it from going anywhere.

Men grunted and the boat scraped off the mud beach. People climbed into the boat over Rick, some of them stepping on him. He probably could have rolled over the side but he couldn't have gotten away. Unless his captors let him drown, which he wasn't to the point of considering a win. The boat's motor buzzed and they began to move. Almost immediately choppy water began to slap at them, jolting Rick each time.

He figured it was safe now to resume trying to open the knife by pinching a blade between his thumb and forefinger and bracing the opposite bolster on his thigh. He levered the blade half-open—which was enough for the purpose—and brought it up to his face. Carefully he stabbed the point through the cloth at the end of his nose. The air didn't gush through, but it was a relatively free flow and a huge relief.

With that done, Rick relaxed. He thought about hiding the knife. He didn't really have a way to do that. The kidnappers hadn't shown any intention of killing him, but they might if he managed to hurt one of them seriously.

This wasn't a good situation, but doing something stupid wasn't going to make it better. He closed the knife and wriggled again to put it away. His movements didn't arouse his captors this time, either.

Rick guessed that they'd been sailing about an hour when the buzz of the motor changed. Men spoke to one another for a moment.

The boat slid up on another mud shore. Men splashed in the water and the boat rocked. Then hands seized Rick and hoisted him out. He managed to get his feet under him, but he couldn't see his surroundings so he overbalanced. He fell into mud and water.

"Take the bloody bag off him!" a voice snarled loudly enough that Rick could make out the words. Two men pulled the bag off Rick without bothering to loosen the tie at his waist. Because he'd already slipped on arm out, the process didn't tear his ear off.

It was still dark. The forest came down almost to the shoreline, and the trees that stood up against the starlit sky were snaky.

"Good evening, gentlemen," Rick said. There were three of them; the fellow with the bushy black beard appeared to be giving the orders. "What's next?"

"Next," Blackbeard said, "we wait till the royalist puppets let go of our buddies; then we let you go. It's simple."

"I'm from the Republic of Cinnabar," Rick said, smiling as cheerfully as he could manage. All three men wore pistols and carried long knives. "This isn't my fight."

"Well, it's your fight now," said Blackbeard, "because if your buddies don't convince the royals, you won't be seeing Cinnabar again. Let's get back to the house."

Rick followed his captors. He hoped that by being polite and obedient, he could convince them not to kill him. He didn't feel confident about his chances on that.

They were better than the chances of Captain Bolton convincing the civil authorities to trade three murderers for him, though.

I resumed sequencing samples from Elkin, items which Mahaffy hadn't gotten to on the voyage. He was working on the intake thus far since we landed on Mindoro. That wasn't a long list but we could target our further sampling if anything striking showed up before we lifted. It was possible that a sample would display genetic material that didn't match the profile of the rest of the planet or which *did* match the profile of life on another planet.

I now believed that the Archaic Spacefarers had existed. Doctor Veil had been right. I'd kept an open mind and the facts had convinced me. I wasn't at all sure that we were going to find proof that would convince people who hadn't been with us on the *Far Traveller*, though.

Kent entered the biology lab. That was perfectly proper—he was a member of the section, after all—but he was rarely here unless he'd been summoned to help with transport. He came and stood beside my work station, and when I looked up he cleared his throat and said, "Ah, Lord Harper? Could I see you out by the aircar for a bit?"

I looked at what I was doing. The sequence would finish without my input. "Sure," I said. I didn't know what was going on, but Kent was a solid man and a very skilled driver.

I thought the transportation bay was too noisy for conversation, but Kent led us into the office. The tech in charge nodded to us and went out, closing the door behind him.

"Look, sir," Kent said, looking fixedly at me. "There's some of us, enlisted ranks, you know—Maddy, that's Master Grenville's girl, you know—she come to talk to us. Could you see her, sir? Because it doesn't do no good us knowing what she says. And we figured she might talk to you, being his friend, right? Will you see her, sir? 'Cause it's not right letting a gang of wogs play games with an RCN officer, all right?"

I took a deep breath and sighed it out. I *really* didn't want to get involved with this, but I didn't have a choice.

"Rick is my friend," I said. "I remember Maddy and I'll happily chat with her if that will help bring Rick back where he belongs. Will she come here?"

"No, we gotta go to her in town," Kent said. "But it's a room right on the water, not far. And she'll be there, never fear. Joyeuse is with her to make sure she don't wander off."

I recalled Joyeuse vaguely, a female bosun's mate. She was probably about forty, as squat and solid as the hydraulic capstans on the hull of the *Far Traveller*. I wouldn't try to force my way out of a room she wanted me to stay in.

We crossed the boarding bridge, nodding to the spacers on guard. They held their submachine guns openly instead of having them discreetly at hand as had been the case on previous landfalls, but the atmosphere was relaxed.

The shops facing the harbor all provided services to sailors. I thought Kent was exaggerating when he said that Maddy would be waiting "right on the water," but in fact we entered a dram shop facing the harbor. The wooden floor was covered with canes which should have been replaced some while ago.

There were no booths but several of the places at the half dozen round tables seated women. None who looked like Maddy or Joyeuse (if she was who I remembered), though.

"Come on, sir," Kent said, leading me to a curtained doorway at the end of the bar. There was no separate bouncer, but Kent exchanged nods with the one-eared bartender as he started up. Of *course* a place like this would have private rooms upstairs or in the back.

They turned right at the top of the stairs. There were half a dozen doors, several of them closed. Kent rapped on the first one and called, "Joyeuse? He's come!"

The door snatched open instantly and I followed Kent inside. The bosun's mate slammed the door behind me with her free hand. Her right held a pry bar.

"Good afternoon, Joyeuse," I said to the spacer. I nodded toward the girl on the bed; that and a straight chair were the only furniture in the room besides the overhead light fixture. "And good afternoon to you too, Maddy. I'm glad you weren't injured during the kidnapping. Rick has spoken very favorably about you."

"Lord Harper, sir," the girl murmured, a bare acknowledgement. "Sir, I *can't* go to Prince Seba with this. They'll kill me! I shouldn't even've talked to Louise."

She looked at Joyeuse, who apparently had a first name.

"Well, repeat to me what you told the bosun's mate," I said calmly. "We'll see to it that nobody is injured, all right?"

I thought the girl would eventually start talking, but she didn't do so quickly enough for Joyeuse, who interjected, "The guys who grabbed Master Grenville was heavies for a local nob named Pilkey. She won't come out in public about that, and Captain Bolton won't act when I told him about it, but we figgered that your lordship can convince him."

"Well, I'm willing to try," I said. "Exactly what did the captain say?"

"Well, I told him that the witness was sure of her story—"

"I've known Arno Danforth for the ten years I've been in Keelung," Maddy said. "He and his brother Enos has been Pilkey's top enforcers for the past five. Arno was running things when they grabbed Rick."

"Captain Bolton says even if she was willing to come forward...," Joyeuse said. She glanced sidelong at Maddy but continued, "Even if she was, a whore's word isn't good enough to start a war on."

I felt my lips twist. Personally I believed Maddy; but personally I believed in the Archaics.

"But tell him what Lieutenant Vermijo said," Kent prompted.

Joyeuse nodded twice and said, "Yeah, well, Vermijo said we ought to arm twenty of the spacers and back 'em with the two turret guns they didn't take out in the refit. And they'd turn Pilkey's house upside down till we found Lieutenant Grenville."

"He won't be there," Maddy said unexpectedly. "Pilkey's got his Garden House just outta town. They'll have stashed Rick in someplace like that or another one."

She looked up and met my eyes. "Look Lord Harper," she said. "I want Rick back as much as you guys do. He was always nice to me. But if you push things and raid the wrong place, that's worse, right?"

I was starting to like this girl more than I had when all I knew about her was that she wouldn't come to the authorities openly. "Yes," I said. "Captain Bolton won't chance it, and going in with both boots would be the wrong idea anyhow. If we want to get Rick back alive, anyhow."

I looked at Maddy. "Do you know where this Garden House is?" I said.

The girl looked blank. Kent said, "I'll bet I can learn. I can talk to drivers on the shoreline."

"And me too," Joyeuse said. "Most of us know a few of the locals so they'd tell us that."

I nodded. "Then I'll go back aboard and talk to Doctor Veil," I said. "She won't go against Captain Bolton, but I figure she'll let me use the imagery we made before we landed."

Kent and I left the room.

I *did* want to talk to Doctor Veil. But I wanted to talk to Joss also.

I opened the door of Doctor Veil's office a crack and said, "Ma'am, might I speak with you for a moment?"

She gestured to the chair across the desk. I moved the files there to the floor and took it. "Ma'am," I said, "the girl who was with Lieutenant Grenville when he was kidnapped says that the men who took him work for Lord Pilkey, the head of the Old Party—one of the heads, Master Blenkins who gave us the Archaic artifact, is another one. Anyway, Pilkey's too powerful for the vicar and his Shining backers to move against without a civil war—which they're not ready for. And Captain Bolton says the *Far Traveller* can't dive in on our own because we represent Cinnabar and he doesn't have the authority."

"Go on, Harper," Veil said. "Though I should mention to you that I have even less taste for politics that Captain Bolton appears to."

"Yes, ma'am," I said. "And my branch of the family isn't political either. The thing is, though, Rick is a friend of mine. This has nothing to do with the Republic of Cinnabar. This is me, Harry Harper."

"I doubt whether the captain would see things that way, Harper," Doctor Veil said.

"No ma'am," I agreed, "and I wasn't planning to discuss this with him. But I'm asking you personally if you're planning to micromanage the way I spend my free time?"

Veil looked steadily at me. Then she said, "No, I am not, Harper. And because Captain Bolton required that I cut short your collecting expedition, I suspect you will have a great deal of free time."

I swallowed. "Thank you, ma'am," I said. "And with your permission, I will check with Technician Joss about her plans for the immediate future."

"Good luck, Harper," Veil said as I got up to go. "If I were religious, I'd offer my prayers."

Rick's captors taped his wrists together behind his back but otherwise ignored him as they played cards and drank beer. The hut was built on an outcrop of coarse limestone a hundred yards from the shore and hidden from the water by the cane-like brush which grew down to the edge of the mud.

There was no major vegetation, though canes topped out in tufts twenty feet in the air. Rick tried to force his way through them but he couldn't manage more than his own height into the brush. If his arms hadn't been pinioned he might have done a little better, but not much. The leaf tips were hooked.

Power tools had cut the path to the shore, but that was growing up again. Rick wondered how often it had to be renewed. He wandered down it for want of anything better to do. There was a trough in the mud where the boat had come aground but it was filling in, and the prints of booted feet were already gone.

"Look to your heart's content," a voice said. Rick turned:

Blackbeard had followed him down the path. "Maybe if you're brave enough you can even get the cargo tape off your wrists and try swimming to the mainland. Otherwise, you better hope your captain convinces the Shinings to let our buddies go."

"I don't think I'm that important to Captain Bolton," Rick said, smiling in what he hoped was a friendly fashion. "Certainly not to the Shinings. How do you folks get off the island?"

Until Blackbeard's comment Rick had assumed he was simply ten miles up or down the coast. It didn't really affect his chances of getting free, because the canes were as effective a barrier as barbed wire.

"We call Willie to come pick us up," Blackbeard said. "I don't think that'll help you much unless Willie's three cousins are back home, though. After all, it don't seem like killing one of them Shining filth ought to be a crime anyhow."

Rick managed a laugh. "I don't disagree," he said, "but I'm not a politician. If you grab one of them, maybe you'd get somewhere."

"Above my pay grade, kid," Blackbeard said. "I guess you better hope that you're more important than you think you are. Or practice your swimming."

He turned and walked back toward the hut.

Rick sighed and looked out over the little bay where they'd landed. He didn't even know the direction of the mainland.

He had plenty of time to think.

He chuckled. He might very well have the whole rest of his life.

Joss was looking at the display with me. I had up vertical imagery of what the Deeds Archive said was Lord Pilkey's property ten miles north of Keelung. The intercom pulsed red; I responded.

"*Lord Harper?*" Kent said. "*I've got somebody you'll want to meet in the transport office. Ah, your lordship? This is going to cost money. Is that all right, over?*"

"Yes," I said. Within reason, of course, but there'd be time to say that in the unlikely case that the request was unreasonable.

"You're coming?" I said to Joss. She nodded. I couldn't be sure of expressions on her ruined face, but I thought she seemed cheerful.

Kent, Joyeuse and Tech 4 Witmer were in the office with a civilian. I'd gotten to know Witmer as one of the coleaders of the group working to return Lieutenant Grenville. Kent was a member of the group by virtue of his access to me, but I was pretty sure that he had very little authority on his own.

"This is Pohaska," Joyeuse said, nodding to the civilian. "He's got information about Pilkey's Garden House."

"But I gotta have five hunnert thalers before I say nothing!" Pohaska said. "Right now!"

"I'll pay you in florins," I said. "That's a sixty percent markup, so even if you have some trouble changing them you should come out well ahead. Thing is"—I took a hundred-thaler coin from my purse and held it out in the palm of my hand—"I'll give you this right now, but the other four hundred wait till we've seen the information's worth it."

"That's not the deal!" Pohaska said.

I put the coin in the hand that had stopped after it started to reach for it.

"We're on a ship now," Joyeuse said. "We drop garbage in the harbor."

Joss leaned forward and gave Pohaska her terrible smile. "Lord Harper's a real gentleman," she said. "You can trust him. And if you're stringing us with a story, you can trust me too."

Pohaska swallowed. "It's no story," he said. "I was one of the regular guards at the Garden House. There was four of us but I'd been there as long as any, three years. Then a week ago Enos comes and tells us our pay's being boosted to two hunnert lira a month and we got eight more guys coming. They closed off the room on the east side of the ground floor and mounted automatic impellers in both the end towers, east and west."

"Did they say why?" Joyeuse asked.

"'We got company coming' was all," Pohaska said. "Anyway, that jump in pay, that's pretty good, right? And I tied one on that night. No big deal. Only it seems like the man hisself, Pilkey, he comes by first thing in the morning and he freaked when he sees me. Bloody near parks on toppa me."

Pohaska shrugged. "If it'd been Enos or Arno, it'd've been okay. But with the Man screaming his bloody head off, well, I'm out on my ear. That's not right!"

"Didn't any of your mates stick up for you?" I said. "Didn't Arno? It's not like none of his people got drunk before, is it? And to lower the boom on you just after they bumped the pay up, that's pretty hard lines."

"Bloody well told it is!" Pohaska said. "Nobody said a peep for me. They're so scared of bloody Pilkey."

"So...," said Joss. "There's twelve guards now? Or is it eleven when they fired you?"

The discussion went on for another hour. We put Pohaska on the only seat in the office. Kent went out for a pot of tea from the galley. I was taking notes on my handheld but really looking forward to being able to add the data to the full-sized projection at my workstation.

It would've been better to see Pohaska at a bar in town, but it wouldn't be safe for him (which I didn't care about) or for us if Pilkey and his crowd learned that Pohaska was talking to us. When all of us had asked all the questions we could think of, I said to Witmer, "You can find him a bunk for the night?"

"Roger that," the tech said, nodding.

"Wait a minute!" Pohaska said. "I didn't sign on as a bloody spacer! I wanna get ashore now! With my money."

"You'll be released as soon as it's safe to," Joyeuse said. "Safe for us."

"And you'll be paid when we've verified your information," I added.

"That's not right...," Pohaska muttered. He was one of life's losers, always treated unfairly by those around him. He was a drunk and a traitor on his own telling of it, but it was no fault of his own that he'd been fired or that his new employers didn't trust him.

That said, I would leave four hundred florins with Doctor Veil, to be paid to Pohaska in the event that I was unable to do so after matters had settled down. I was a Harper of Greenslade and my word was good.

The biology laboratory became the war room for the operation to free Rick. Doctor Veil didn't object and Mahaffy continued his work. I think Mahaffy was mainly concerned that we were going to ask him to take an active role in a dangerous endeavor. We weren't: We had more than enough people available for that.

We might have been able to use the Battle Direction Center, but we didn't need better displays than we had with my modified work station. I honestly wasn't sure as to how much Captain Bolton knew about what was going on, and I preferred not to rub his nose in it.

The Pilkey Garden House was projected in the middle of the lab. The normal approach was from the south side. There was a forest track that came within a mile on the north side but nothing closer. The plantings which gave the house its name wrapped around the back and both sides of the house and were surrounded by a ten-foot wall. There were gates on both ends which would allow small agricultural vehicles to enter.

"We've got fifty volunteers easy," Joyeuse said. "Personal arms for sure and I guess we could borrow a couple automatic impellers without a big problem. The trouble's transport."

"Maybe not," said Witmer. "I made some friends at the bus line that serves Langsam. It wouldn't be real expensive"—he nodded to me—"and they're rated twelve passenger but they usually run with thirty aboard so two'll do us. We'll still have to slog through the woods, though."

"No!" I said. I hadn't meant to be so forceful. Well, I hadn't meant to start that way. "Look, we're not going to start a war."

I'd silenced the others, but I sure hadn't convinced them. In the silence Joss said, "Yeah, we don't need that. Kent, you can land the forty-five twelve here, right?"

She jabbed her finger at a spot north of the wall, about a hundred yards short. I peered closely at the image when she moved her finger.

"Yeah, I guess," Kent said. "You'll want me to keep dead low, though, won't you—below the top of the wall."

"Yeah," said Joss. "And you'll want to stay low from half a mile out to keep behind the tall trees out here"—she waggled her hand at the edge of the image—"so they don't spot you from the east tower. You can handle that?"

"Sure," said Kent. "Though it'll help if the guards are drowsy."

"It always does," Joss agreed. "But you bring me there with maybe four spacers backup—and they're just going to sit in the truck. I'll go in alone and bring the El-Tee out. Then we didlibop back to the ship, all right?"

"What if he's injured?" Witmer said.

"Then I bloody carry him, don't I?" Joss snarled. "I've done it before."

"You're going to open the gate in the wall when you get inside?" I said. "So you don't have to do it when you're coming out."

"How's she bloody going to *get* inside?" Witmer asked.

"Yeah," Joss said, looking at me.

"Then I'm coming in with you when you do," I said. "You're not going in without an extra pair of hands. You're in charge and whatever you bloody say goes, but I'm coming in."

"And I'm going over the bloody wall, spacer," she added to Witmer in a snarl. "Hit at a run and flip over, just like in training. There's nothing on top, Pohaska says. It's just me and this—" She patted her bush knife.

"And sir, all right, you come. But you got to carry a real gun."

"I'll take one for you," I said. "For myself, I'll use the one my father gave me when I turned eleven and I could kill birds with in my sleep. But I'll carry solids and heavy shot."

Joss laughed. "You're okay," she said. "And maybe you can haul a couple grenades for me besides."

We'd followed the Langsam road for almost ten miles, flying twenty feet in the air. I could have gotten a precise figure from my handheld but it didn't matter and it was more important that I concentrate on what I was going to do when we landed. There was no road traffic in the middle of the night.

When Kent pulled off into the woods, he slacked speed and began weaving through the trees. He was using light enhancement with false color added to make up for the lack of depth perception. I'd still have felt safer if he'd slowed down a little more, but I kept my mouth shut.

I was in the middle of the cab between Kent with Joss on the door. The three of us were silent, though occasionally the spacers in the back spoke loudly enough for me to catch the sound—though not the meaning—through the communicating window. This irritated me though there was nothing wrong with it. Nobody could hear them over the fan intake, and the treetops and breeze scattered even that.

I was nervous and becoming irritated with others who dealt with their own nervousness in a different fashion.

I kept my mouth shut. I've found that's usually a good choice, even when I'm right.

"We're going in pretty quick," Kent said out of the side of his mouth. He was concentrating on his driving.

"Roger," Joss replied.

A moment later I said, "Thank you." I'd seem a fool trying to copy military jargon.

The aircar lurched and literally splashed down, raising a great bulb of spray. It wouldn't be visible in the darkness but it startled the bloody hell out of me.

Joss opened the door and leaped out, landing ankle deep in the boggy soil. At least the car wasn't sinking, which was my first thought. This was a clearing because it was a low spot. Standing water killed the roots of saplings before they got to any size.

I followed Joss out and splashed clumsily to solid ground before I paused to organize my gear which was suddenly a lot bulkier than it had seemed back on the *Far Traveller* while we were planning the operation.

I was wearing my shooting vest with reloads. Grenades and a small grapnel on a monocrystalline line were in the knapsack which I now managed to shrug onto my back; I'd thought the grapnel and line were for going over the wall, but Joss said that we'd use it and the aircar to tear the new cover off the window if we couldn't get inside the house door for some reason. I could think of many reasons, but Joss seemed confident that we wouldn't have to take the brute force approach.

Following the directional beacon on my handheld, I stumped clumsily toward the gate. Joss had glided away through the trees, but we were headed in slightly different directions anyway. I'd slung her submachine gun over my left arm and was carrying my shotgun at the balance.

I'd thought I could carry the heavy pry bar by hooking it over my belt. I could do that, but it banged my left ankle at every step.

I hadn't thought things through carefully enough. Fortunately determination will make up for many mistakes. I slogged on.

The thick vegetation and the beacon absorbed my attention so completely that I almost ran into the gate before I realized I was close. I stopped and the right side of the double leaves swung open.

"Good timing," Joss said. She carried her bush knife in the other hand. The blade was stained.

She noticed my eyes on the knife as I slipped through the gate. "There were a couple guards back here," she said. "Two fewer to worry about in the house."

She wiped the blade on the trousers of a body lying on the ground, the torso hidden by the berry bushes planted on this end of the garden. The bushes were why we'd come in this way rather than from the west side where a swale provided an even better approach to the grounds.

I dropped the bag of grenades, shrugged the submachine gun off my left shoulder, and rearranged the pry bar slightly now that I'd gotten free of the rest of my load. I couldn't carry it in my left hand because I'd need both for the shotgun. If I needed the shotgun.

Joss sheathed her knife and dropped a couple of spherical grenades into the side pockets of the mesh tunic she was wearing. Then she picked up the submachine gun—she didn't sling it—and muttered, "Ready?"

"Yes," I said with a nod. We slipped forward among the plantings. I kept ten feet behind Joss, but there was no danger of me overrunning her. She moved with as little commotion as windblown fog.

Some of the paths were bordered by shoulder-high bushes. With time and better light I could probably have identified most of them. I was pretty sure of the highbush cranberries along the main aisle we followed from the gate. We stayed close to the bushes so that they broke up our outlines, and the stiff breeze made the branches tremble and hid the fact that we were moving.

The house had a tower—really a short third floor—on the end. According to the imagery there was a similar turret on the west also, but that shouldn't have anything to do with us. If anybody in the tower had been alert, the automatic weapon could have raked us on the way from the gate, but everybody was asleep.

There was a pedestrian door in the wall. A four-inch sheet of structural plastic had been bolted to the outside of the house wall, covering the window that must be there, but the door hadn't been affected.

Joss waved me to the side and gestured me down. I obediently hunched on the front corner. She leaned her submachine gun against the wall and drew her bush knife. There was a small window. Leaning close to the door she tapped on it and whispered, "Juan! Juan!"

The window shutter clacked open. The door was too thick for anyone to see anything but her back and hair if they looked through. A moment later the door itself unlatched and a voice snarled, "What the hell are you playing at?"

Joss jerked the door the rest of the way open and went in with the speed of a closing trap. I expected to hear a scream but instead there was a gurgling sound and a thump.

Joss vanished inside. The east tower and the guards sleeping on the second floor were her job. I entered the building and stumbled over the guard on the floor of the corridor. He was making wheezing noises and had both hands pressed to his side. The big knife had gone through a kidney, and coils of intestine were leaking out past his fingers.

I expected the door to the ground floor room to be locked, but the knob turned when I tried it. "Rick!" I said. "Time to go *now!*"

A woman screamed inside the room. I threw down the pry bar I'd gotten ready for the door and found a light switch. A very pretty girl in a frilly nightdress was sitting up in bed. She screamed again when the light went on.

Bloody hell!

I heard a grenade go off upstairs. I grabbed the girl's wrist in my left hand and dragged her into the hallway. She continued to scream. Joss came back down the stairs.

"Wrong room!" I shouted. "We'll take her because she must be somebody!"

Joss lobbed a grenade down the ground-floor hallway left handed, then clocked the screaming girl on the head with the butt of her big knife. The girl went limp and stopped screaming.

"You carry her, then!" Joss said. "And come bloody on! That's Willy Pete!"

Joss whirled though the outside doorway, snatching up the submachine gun left handed. I followed her, carrying both the girl and the shotgun across my chest. I heard the white phosphorous grenade go off with a *whump!* and prayed that I was clear of where the bits of burning phosphorous flew.

I got to the garden wall just as Joss shoved a leaf open. The house was aroused now. I turned, wondering if the gun in the west turret could bear on us. Smoke and flames wrapped the house so completely they hid the entire structure.

I staggered through the gate after Joss, who shut it behind us as a visual barrier. I hadn't planned for getting back to the aircar. I suspected Joss could find it and I would stagger along behind her carrying the prisoner. She wasn't very heavy, but I sure wasn't looking forward to that.

"Watch it!" Joss shouted, putting out her arm to stop me from taking the next step forward into the forest. I was so wrung out by what had gone on that I almost fell down.

The aircar swooped over the trees and twitched sideways as Kent saw us. He dropped down beside the wall in a strip that the residents had cleared with defoliant to prevent tree roots from running into the garden. The car's left side brushed the garden wall while the right edges of the fans chopped brush into wood chips.

Spacers jumped out of the back gate. Two of them went to help Joss; the other two more usefully grabbed me and the girl and hustled us forward to the cab. I wanted to tell them to put the girl in the specimen box in back but I couldn't get the words out audibly and they probably wouldn't have understood what I was talking about anyway. They shoved the girl into the seat and boosted me in after her, then scampered around to the back. I supposed Joss would get in with them, but I didn't know anyone for whom there was less reason to worry about how she was getting along.

I held the girl and held her against me to keep her out of Kent's way. The car lifted as it ran parallel to the wall. I could hear the left side panel rubbing.

My left arm was around the girl while my right still held the loaded shotgun. I'd need more room before I could open the breech and remove the slug cartridge.

Also I would need to get better control of my nerves and my breathing. Being back in the aircar and by now out of sight of the house was helping with both those things, but I had a ways to go.

I gave Kent some orders to pass on by radio to his buddy in the transport section. Then I got to work on the injured girl.

There was a first-aid kit in the cab as well as a canteen of water. I used light amplification so I didn't need to call further attention to us by lighting the cab. This had the further advantage of eliminating color so I didn't have to see how much blood I was mopping off the face of quite a pretty girl. It was a nasty pressure cut on her forehead where the skin had been smashed against the bone.

The antiseptic creme may have stung or maybe it was just cool—the water in the canteen was at the temperature of the muggy air. Anyway, something brought the girl around when I applied it.

When I felt her squirm under my fingers I said, "Ma'am, who are you?"

"I'm Ophelia Pilkey," the girl said, "and my father will have you flayed for this!"

"Let me get a bandage on that," I said. "Just hold still for a moment."

I set the bandage over the wound—trying not to press onto the cut itself—and stripped the backing off the adhesive fringe at the four corners. I realized I was sticking at least part of the fringe to her fluffy hair.

"Who are you!" the girl said when I lifted my hand. "And why have you taken me?"

"I'm Lord Harry Harper," I said. "Taking you was an accident. Your father has kidnapped a friend of mine and I was trying to get him back. We got the wrong room, is all. I'm sorry about that, so we'll have to get Rick back another way."

I'd had time to think about it and I'd come up with a plan. It wasn't much of a plan, but it was a way to go forward. The best thing I could find to say about it was that if things went wrong I was likely to die, which would mean it stopped being my problem.

"My father isn't a kidnapper!" Ophelia said.

"Well, the actual job was done by a fellow named Arno," I said. "I don't guess he'd have done that without your father telling him to, do you?"

I tilted the shotgun barrel out of the cab, which gave me enough room to open the breech and extract the load. I dropped it into one of my breast pockets.

"What are you going to do with me?" the girl asked in a much quieter voice.

"I plan to give you back to your father as soon as possible," I said truthfully. "I really regret that my friend wasn't under guard in that room like we thought."

"You'll really let me go?" Ophelia said.

"On my honor as a Harper," I said. She probably didn't understand how serious an oath that was, but I hoped I sounded reassuring anyway. "Just as soon as your father returns Lieutenant Grenville."

"I see Bertie," Kent said. "I'm setting us down."

I said to the girl, "I'm going to cover your head and put you in a box to move you. You know who I am and you know what I look like. This is entirely my own business and I'll take all the responsibility for it. I've put pressure on some people who don't know what I'm doing and I won't drop them in the stew, so I'll be the only one you can identify. That's all."

Kent brought us in smoothly on a stretch of road half a mile from the harbor. The trike was parked at the edge of the trees with the cargo box in the back open. Tech 3 Bertie came toward us, holding a tarp sewn into a crude bag—really just a blindfold.

"Get out and let me put this over you," I said. "I'm going to take you someplace and stash you, someplace more comfortable than a ship's bilges, I mean."

She got out of the car after me with her head bowed and her hands pressed tightly together. I handed my shotgun to Kent and said, "Tell Mahaffy to wipe this down and put it away till I come back."

I turned to Ophelia, holding the bag open.

She said, so softly that I could scarcely make out the words, "Please don't kill me."

"I'm not going to kill you," I said as I swept the bag over her head; it covered her down to her ankles. "I'll swear that."

What I added only in my own mind was, *And I hope to heaven that your father's reasonable so I can give you back to him.*

The tricycle was remarkably simple to use but I kept twisting the throttle on the right handgrip too much or letting it drop to an idle. Fortunately the little diesel engine was geared so low that my problems weren't very evident from the outside. Uncomfortable though the pillion seat was, I really wished Rick were here to drive.

The thought made me laugh, which must've startled Ophelia in the cargo compartment if she could hear me. She'd been completely agreeable to anything I requested, allowing me and the two spacers to lift her into the cargo compartment without a struggle. Either she trusted me or she was completely terrified.

I was sorry Joss had hit her so hard, but something had to be done about her screaming. I wasn't going to second-guess Joss, and even after leisure to consider it, I couldn't think of a better way to have done it.

Because Blenkins House was on the harbor road there was more traffic than in most of Keelung but at least I couldn't miss it. Nobody was expecting me, but when the attendants heard the trike ringing up the road toward them they opened the gate to peer out. One of them must've recognized me, because they flung the leaves fully open.

I pulled in and called, "They're not expecting me. Is it all right?"

The other guard was already on the intercom. He waved me up to the house with a cheerful nod.

I stopped at the bottom of the ramp to the porch this time. I didn't want a servant in the house to hear the girl if she started to make a fuss. Although she'd shown no sign of that sort of behavior thus far.

I strode up to the door, ready to knock, but before I got there Master Blenkins snatched it open. "Lord Harper!" he called. "You are very welcome here!"

"Sir," I said, stepping past him to keep the business as private at I could. "I have a very serious problem, and if you get involved as I hope, it will put you in a great deal of danger."

The plump man may have stood a little straighter, but his voice was perfectly even as he said, "Go on, your lordship."

The three sturdy attendants in the room weren't the same individuals that I'd seen on my first visit, though I thought maybe they had been on the gate that time. Blenkins must have a considerable staff of heavies.

"A man named Pilkey, Lord Pilkey, has kidnapped my friend Lieutenant Grenville to put pressure on the government," I said. Getting it out straight was the quickest way to put the information before Blenkins. "I attempted to free Rick and accidentally kidnapped Pilkey's daughter instead. I hope to exchange the girl for Rick, but I need a place to hide her in the interim. Do you have an out-of-town property where I can do that safely?"

"You've taken little Ophelia?" Blenkins said. "Oh, I hope she's all right?"

"I have her, yes," I said, feeling my heart turn to ice. "She was knocked unconscious during capture but I think she's basically all right."

"Well, I certainly hope so," Blenkins said. "She's a delightful little thing. How a man like Pilkey could have such a daughter is beyond me."

He cleared his throat and continued, frowning. "I have properties variously on the planet, but why would you want to place Ophelia in one of them?"

I swallowed. "Well, sir," I said. "I thought it would be safer for you. In case Lord Pilkey should guess where his daughter is and attack to free her."

Blenkins sniffed dismissively. "I'm not afraid of Pilkey," he said, "and I have my support staff here in the house where I am. It seems to me that if Pilkey had concentrated his forces you might not have her now. In any case if you'll permit me, I'll entertain Ophelia here in the house and undertake to return her to you when you request I do so."

I started to say, "That makes you party to a kidnapping!" which was true but not something I should be emphasizing to my host. Besides, I didn't know what the laws on Mindoro were. For people at the social level of Blenkins and Pilkey, probably pretty much everything was all right if they could enforce their will.

Because I was standing there with my mouth open, "I suppose you're worried about her escaping," Blenkins guessed incorrectly. "My aunt Hermione got to be a problem in her later years and stayed in a room in the subcellar on her bad days. There are no windows, so no need for bars."

"Sir," I said, "if you're willing to do this in any fashion, I'll be eternally grateful. I just hope that this won't cause problems for you in the future."

"Pilkey is threatening all of Mindoro with his antics," Blenkins said. "The Shinings will send in troops as long as there are riots against them. We've got too big a population for them to actually conquer us, but they can make Mindoro ungovernable. Chaos will suit them. It doesn't suit them now.

"The only plan for Mindoro is to stay quiet and unite internally. We haven't been able to do that in five hundred years, but I think that with the Shinings as a common enemy, we'll be able to at last."

I nodded solemnly to Blenkins. I liked the little fellow and he was certainly doing me a favor at considerable risk to himself, but I didn't think his vision of Mindoro's future was a very likely one.

"In any case," Blenkins said, "making a public fool of Pilkey makes it more difficult for him to win over the weak-minded people who've been gulled by his message of violent opposition to the Shinings. If I become associated with that humiliation, so much the better."

I suspected Blenkins was wrong about having more guards in his townhouse being enough to stop a raid like the one we'd carried out on the Garden House. On the other hand, I was sure that Pilkey didn't have anyone on his payroll as skilled and ruthless as Joss.

"Sir, if you're really willing to do this," I said, "I'll bring the girl in now. She's just out in the vehicle."

Blenkins murmured a word to a pair of his guards and they went out with me. At the doorway I turned and said, "Thank you, again, sir."

Now I needed to carry out the actual negotiation. But before I did that, I would shower and change into dress clothes. My clothing hadn't suffered too badly during the raid, but the bitter hint of phosphorous might be enough to remind Lord Pilkey of what I'd been doing.

I decided that on balance, that wouldn't be politic.

I took a leisurely shower, then dressed in my blue frock coat and tight red slacks. It was probably out of date on Xenos but it had been high formal fashion when I lifted from Cinnabar.

I went over to the transportation bay. Kent and Bertie stood by the trike. That wasn't a huge surprise, but half a dozen other spacers were there also. I knew Joyeuse and Witmer but I couldn't have put names to the others. There was something in the cargo compartment.

Everybody stood stiffly as I approached. Kent was wearing a civilian business suit which I recognized as one of mine, though it must have been extensively tailored to fit him.

I looked at the cargo compartment. The lid had been removed so that someone could sit upright on the cushioned seat that had been built in.

"What the hell is this?" I said loudly enough to be heard by all of them because I didn't have any idea as to who was in charge.

"You're not dressed to drive," Kent said. "I'm going to take you to Lord Pilkey."

"So we added a seat," Witmer said. "Wasn't no trouble."

I opened my mouth to ask who had told them I was going to see Lord Pilkey, then shut it again. I hadn't said a word about my plans; it was my duty to keep everyone else out of it—especially at this stage.

But these were senior people. They were used to not being told anything by their superiors—but being held responsible for whatever went wrong. They watched the man in charge and knew to anticipate what was going to happen next.

I shut my mouth and nodded. "Then let's get on with it," I said.

"The boarding ladder's on the starboard side," Witmer said.

I walked around the vehicle. I'd thought I was going to have to hoist myself into the box which would be a bitch of a job in tight formal clothes, but again the crew had been there before me. I wondered if that was Mahaffy's suggestion; he'd laid out the suit for me.

A three-step boarding stool pivoted out from the top of the compartment. I wondered if they would return the vehicle to its original condition.

Kent kicked the engine to life and boarded. "You ready, sir?" he asked.

I looked at the spacers surrounding the vehicle. "Thank you all, shipmates," I said.

I heard cheers behind me as we motored across the boarding bridge. I found that I was a little choked up. I guess that was better than worrying about the coming interview, as I'd expected I'd be doing.

The Pilkey mansion must have been on the northern side of Keelung when the town was founded, but development had enveloped it in the years since. It was still an extensive walled compound, however, and I suspected that the double row of townhouses on the western edge—within the line of the original masonry boundary wall—were occupied by Lord Pilkey's retainers and their families.

Kent pulled up in the broad carriage circle curving into the front wall of the property. He hopped off the saddle and dropped the boarding steps before I could figure out where the release was.

A concierge in red with maroon piping called through the gate of vertical iron rods, "Lord Pilkey isn't receiving!"

I wandered up to the gate anyway. "I hope he'll see me," I said to the concierge. "I'm Lord Harry Harper, and I've come about the interests of Lady Ophelia Pilkey."

Instead of answering, the concierge backed away to an intercom on the masonry gatepost. Because he kept his eyes on me rather than speaking directly at the unit, I heard him say, "Sir? There's a toff here saying it's about Ophelia. Says his name's Lord Harper."

The speaker gave a crackle of sound though I couldn't make out the words. The concierge came toward me and said, "There's somebody coming from the house, sir. It'll just be a minute."

A man in slacks and a sweater stepped around the gatepost. Though he wasn't wearing a uniform, his automatic carbine was standard military issue. I nodded politely to him and he vanished back behind the solid wall.

A four-seat runabout came around the back of the distant house and ran up to the gate. The driver was a slim man of fifty. He pulled up behind the concierge and said, "Get the postern open, Brevoort. *Now!*"

The concierge finished unlatching the pedestrian gate set in the left gate leaf. He pulled it open for me and jumped back out of the way so that I could step through.

The slim man offered his hand. "Lord Harper, we're pleased to see you. I'm Hagen, a consultant to Lord Pilkey. Allow me to run you up to the house."

I got into the passenger side of the runabout. "How long have you worked for Lord Pilkey?"

Hagen turned the runabout in a tight circle and started back to the house. "Technically," he said, "for about three weeks, but I only arrived on Mindoro two days ago. Lord Pilkey realized that he needed someone on his staff with off-planet security experience, but he decided to go ahead with already-planned operations in the interim."

I laughed. "I regret you didn't arrive last month," I said. "Though I'm pleased that you hadn't shaped up operations at the Garden House before the other night."

We pulled up at the front door. "I'll take you through to where his lordship is waiting," Hagen said. I was surprised that he'd given his name, and that it wasn't Smith or the like.

"May I ask, Lord Harper?" Hagen said as he reached for the latchplate. "What are your regular duties on the *Far Traveller*?"

"I'm a biologist, sir," I said. My guide simply nodded. I didn't know whether he believed me or not.

We entered a larger room than the entrance hall of Blenkins House. This one had a double-height ceiling. The squad inside were in sweaters and slacks like the six or seven of them I'd seen at the gate over my shoulder. I'd looked as we came up the drive.

These also had submachine guns and carbines. Their caliber as individuals didn't impress me, but there were a lot of them.

"Come on through if you please, Lord Harper," Hagen said. We went through the door into a study where a heavy man of sixty waited standing behind a desk. The door closed.

"Who the hell are you, and what have you done with my daughter?" snarled the man behind the desk—Lord Pilkey.

"I'm Lord Harry Harper," I said. "A Harper of Greenslade, and a friend of Lieutenant Grenville. If you check on us, you'll learn that the Harpers keep their word."

Pilkey glared at Hagen and said, "Colonel? You looked 'em up, right?"

"Yes," said Hagen. "The statement is true. May I say that there's very little information about Lord Harry himself, and certainly nothing to suggest that he'd be in this room now."

"On the word of a Harper, Lord Pilkey," I said, "as soon as Lieutenant Grenville is released, Lady Ophelia will be released."

"This lieutenant is nothing to do with me!" Pilkey shouted. "You'll give my daughter back unharmed or you'll bloody well regret it!"

"If Rick is not released...," I said. My mouth was dry and I was speaking very slowly and distinctly. "You risk having a friend return from Xenos and telling you that he met your daughter in a brothel outside Harbor Three. That's on my oath also."

"Do you think you're going to get out of here until I say so?" Pilkey said. His face had been red when I entered the room and when he started shouting, it darkened to maroon. "Unless you return my daughter instantly, I'll have pieces cut off your body until there's nothing left to send back to your ship!"

"During the troubles on Cinnabar during the late war," I said, nodding to Hagen, "two of my father's innocent cousins were seized and tortured to death in an attempt to locate friends of theirs—who *were* involved in the conspiracy. I suspect Colonel Hagen can tell you how that worked out for the torturers and the men behind them. But if you think the best way to get your daughter back is by torturing me, then you'd best get started."

"Lord Pilkey," Hagen said, "I do know the story. And Lord Harper's father was involved in the retribution."

Pilkey swallowed. "How do I know you'll let Ophelia go?" he said in a choking voice.

"Sir," I said, "you have my word. I'll bring her here to this mansion."

Pilkey collapsed backward into his chair. "I'll give orders," he said. "It'll take time, though. Maybe a day."

"I understand, sir," I said. "I'll leave you to it."

I turned. Colonel Hagen opened the door and escorted me through the foyer. As we got out of the runabout at the gate, I offered my hand.

"I'm very glad to have met you, sir," I said.

"I'm glad that things worked out as they did," he said as we shook. "It's the next best thing to having arrived in time to stop it from happening."

Kent burbled all the way back to the ship, but I only replied with a few grunts. I was trying to come to terms with the fact that I was still alive.

Rick had been unable to sleep except fitfully since his captors shackled him the day before, but he'd managed to drop off finally within the hour so the ruckus didn't itself rouse him. Blackbeard jerked him upright and shouted, "Come on! Get up, and you better not slow us down!"

"Boss, maybe it's just Willie!" the red-haired guard said.

"No, it's too bloody big!" said Blackbeard. "Move, you! And you better hope it's not your buddies coming to rescue you or they'll find your brains smeared all over the canes!"

Now that he was coming awake, Rick heard the throb of a large engine. He stumbled in the direction Blackbeard had shoved him, though for the life of him he couldn't imagine how they were going to get out of the sight of anyone landing on the shore.

For the life of him was the right word. He could well believe that Blackbeard would shoot him rather than surrender him to a party of armed spacers. Though how would Captain Bolton have figured out where he was being held?

Rick squeezed as far into the cane as he could get; his body was off the cleared path at least. He could still see the edge of the beach. His two junior captors had run back into the hut, but Blackbeard was right beside Rick with a pistol in Rick's ear.

The nose of a flat-bottomed boat slid up on the mud. It was at least ten feet across, wider than the skiff that brought Rick was long. A man jumped down into the mud and called, "Arno! We gotta leave soonest! Arno, it's Willie! Come on out and bring the prisoner!"

Another man jumped to the ground. He was slender and fit looking. "Master Arno, my name is Hagen and Lord Pilkey has put me in charge of this business. Come out at once. We need to get back to Keelung without delay."

"I never heard of you," Arno said peevishly.

"We can take care of that later," Hagen said. He pointed at the younger of Blackbeard's two flunkies. "Get the shackles off him. Now."

Willie pulled Blackbeard—Arno—aside and was whispering to him. The flunky ran into the hut and came back with keys looped on a bright green cord. He was coming toward Rick with them when Arno suddenly shouted.

He turned toward Rick and said, "You bastard! Your buddies killed my brother!"

"Arno!" Hagen said. "Drop that now!"

"Like hell I will!" Arno said. He swung his pistol's butt at Rick's head. Rick's wrists were still taped but he got his arms up in time to protect his temple. The blow knocked him to the ground.

Hagen shot Arno twice, high in the chest. Arno sank to his knees and fell over backward. Hagen shot again, this time upward through the throat into the big man's brain.

The canes drank the triple crack of the electromotive pistol. The puffs of vaporized driving band drifted away when Hagen lowered the weapon, its muzzle glowing faintly red.

"Get the shackles off him," he repeated to the boy with the keys.

Hagen opened a folding knife with his left hand and knelt to cut the tape between Rick's wrists. Close up, he was older than Rick had thought. As he rose to his feet, he said, "I suggest you wait to remove the tape until you can soak it with alcohol for ten or fifteen minutes."

The shackles clicked and fell way from Rick's legs. He stood up. He'd have a bad bruise on his forearm where he'd blocked the pistol butt, but the bone wasn't broken.

"Thank you," he said to Hagen.

The pistol had cooled enough for Hagen to replace it in the holster at the small of his back. He nodded to Rick and said to the others, "Come on, let's get back to Keelung."

"Sir?" said Willie. He glanced down. "What about the boss?"

Hagen said, "Does Mindoro have crabs? I suppose there'll be something. Leave Arno for them."

Then he said, "Arno stopped being the boss when Lord Pilkey put me in charge."

Rick, limping slightly, followed Hagen to the boat. He was glad the crew still aboard the boat had slung a boarding ladder so that he didn't have to heave himself up unaided.

I'd showered and was dressing for dinner in utilities when someone rapped on the cabin door. "Come on in," I said, figuring it was Mahaffy come to pick up the dress clothes lying on the bed. That outfit had turned out to be much more useful than I'd decided on my first day aboard the *Far Traveller*.

Joss entered. I hadn't seen her since before I drove the trike myself to Blenkins House. I'd been a little surprised, now that I thought about it, that she hadn't been around to see me off to Pilkey's with Kent.

She may have slept for the past two days, for all I knew. I'd been really stressed by the raid on the Garden House and she'd done a lot more than I had.

"I thought I'd check how things went with Colonel Hagen, sir," she said.

"Come on in," I said. She closed the cabin door behind her.

"You know Colonel Hagen, then?" I said as I finished closing the seam of my shirt. I couldn't imagine what she was doing here.

"Not to speak to," she said. "Heyer's briefing officer was always somebody from the Fifth Bureau. Never Hagen that I know about, but I saw him around a time or two."

She cleared her throat and added, looking into the corner of the cabin, "I was glad when I saw him come to the gate for you. It meant the adults were in charge. I didn't know what a rich dickwad like Pilkey was going to do."

"I was glad that the colonel was present also," I said. "The conversation—the negotiation—was conducted in a very reasonable fashion. To my great relief. Rick will return as quickly as possible, and Lady Ophelia will go back to her father."

"Figured it must've gone okay," Joss said, "when I saw the colonel go off with half a dozen yobs in Pilkey's big boat. They must've stuck Lieutenant Grenville somewhere offshore, which is why we didn't find him in the Garden House."

"You were watching the whole time?" I said. "I didn't see you at the Pilkey mansion."

Joss shrugged. "Don't guess the colonel did neither," she said, "or I likely wouldn't be talking to you now. I sure as hell wasn't looking forward to going in after you if you hadn't come back under your own steam."

"There was no need to do that!" I said. "That was a private business of my own, nothing involving the *Far Traveller* or the Republic of Cinnabar."

"There was *every* bloody reason, sir!" Joss said. It was the first time I'd heard her sound angry. "You're one of the good ones, El-Tee. I wasn't going to let you throw yourself away because you were too proud to ask for backup."

My tongue seemed dry and swollen. I wanted to speak, though I didn't know what to say and couldn't have gotten it out anyway.

"I guess now that it's settling down," Joss said, "I better tell the colonel where the charges are under the wall. But I think I'll wait till Lieutenant Grenville is back. Just to be sure."

I cleared my throat and said, "Thank you, Joss. And I think you're right about waiting, though I don't think there'll be a problem with the hand over."

She went out of the cabin. I stood for a moment to settle myself before going up to the wardroom.

I stopped about two blocks from the Pilkey mansion. It was still five minutes till time for the exchange. I dismounted and shut off the engine because the high-pitched ringing fed my nervousness. That was bad enough already.

"In a couple minutes, you'll be in your own bedroom," I said, forcing a cheerful smile to reassure Ophelia. The cut on her forehead had been cleaned and dressed. There was still a bit of swelling and redness around the small bandage, but Blenkins' doctor had assured me there wouldn't be a scar.

I hoped this wouldn't mean problems for Blenkins. He'd been the best friend Ophelia could have had, but I've seen enough of life to know that people don't always see reality when their emotions are involved. Still, I'd been honest with Pilkey and he seemed to be grounded firmly in reality rather than the ditz I'd taken him for when we met. I couldn't blame myself for risks other people chose to take.

"Thank you, Lord Harper," Ophelia said in a small voice. I hadn't heard her speak loudly since the night we kidnapped her. "You've been very kind to me."

That was complete nonsense. I grimaced and said, "Well, it'll be over with soon."

My handheld squawked. Joyeuse said, "*They're coming out of the front door.*"

"We're on the way," I said. I switched on, took the handgrips of the trike and kicked firmly on the starter. My formal tights weren't ideal for starting the engine, but it fired up instantly.

The street was of two-story buildings, generally commercial at ground level and residential above. Of the twenty-odd pedestrians I could see in the immediate vicinity, at least six of them were spacers from the *Far Traveller*. If I hadn't been able to start the trike myself, I'd been confident I could find help.

We puttered along the boulevard to Pilkey's mansion. Because of the stone wall I couldn't see what was happening within the compound until we were almost to the gate. Guards were pulling it open, and I could see Colonel Hagen driving the runabout up from the house. Rick sat beside him.

I pulled the trike in front of the gate and did a tight turn so that it was ready to head back to the ship. Shutting down I dismounted and walked around to the right side to lower the boarding steps. "Ma'am," I said, offering my hand to support Ophelia as she dismounted.

She darted off to the runabout. I could see Lord Pilkey waiting on the porch, but whatever Hagen had told him seemed to have sunk in. Pilkey wasn't doing anything to jeopardize the hand over.

Rick and Hagen were walking toward the trike; Rick was favoring his left leg slightly but he looked in pretty decent shape.

"You going to be okay driving this thing back?" I called. "I've got a bit to discuss with Colonel Hagen here."

"I'm fine!" Rick said. "Just a bruise on my ankle from a shackle."

Hagen said, "I regret that, but the person responsible won't be making future mistakes of judgment. Worse things happen in wartime."

I nodded and said, "Lady Ophelia has a cut and maybe a headache, which I regret also."

I handed Hagen the plan Joss had made for me. "These are the locations of the five mines buried under the front wall," I explained. "I'm told there are no anti-tamper devices."

Hagen looked at it, then glanced along the stone wall. "This was your doing, Lord Harper?" he said.

"I didn't know anything about it," I said. "It was to be a diversion if Lord Pilkey decided not to let me go on my first visit. The rescue party would have come in through the back gate while the explosions drew the attention of those inside the house."

A smile of sorts made Hagen's lips quirk. He said, "It might have worked if the extraction team was good enough. Judging from the way you took Lady Ophelia to begin with, they might have been."

"I'm glad it didn't come to that," I said, and that was true as any words I've ever spoken.

Hagen shrugged. "I am too," he said. "I need to get Lady Ophelia back to her father. May I ask, Lord Harper, will you be staying on Mindoro for long?"

"No," I said. "We've recovered all the pinnaces and Captain Bolton plans to lift for Zemlyn's World as soon as Rick, Lieutenant Grenville, is back aboard."

Colonel Hagen said, "Then let me wish you well on your future enterprises. And I hope that I'll never again be part of them."

Then he saluted me.

ZEMLYN'S WORLD

A day out from Zemlyn's World Rick entered the bio lab. Harry looked up and called, "Hey, Gimpy! How're you getting on?"

Doctor Veil was in the main lab discussing what she took for an anomaly with Mahaffy (who kept saying, "Sir, the sequencer is working perfectly."). Veil said, "Lieutenant Grenville! Very good to see you after your difficulties."

"That's thanks to Harry here," Rick said, "at least from what the riggers on the starboard watch tell me. Doctor Veil, I realize I must owe a great deal to your forbearance that he was free to do that. Thank you."

"I was glad to provide any help I could to Lord Harper," Veil said. She cleared her throat and added, "And your support of the Biology Section is noted and appreciated also, Grenville. Is there anything we can help you with?"

"Actually, I'm here hoping to learn a bit about animals on Zemlyn's World," Rick said. "I gather there's no political situation, which is why Captain Bolton chose Zemlyn as our next base."

"There're no permanent settlers on Zemlyn's World," Harry said. "I suppose that's what the captain is thinking about. Guarantor Porra *personally* owns the planet. It's not part of the Alliance of Free Stars. He leases the Grinder concession to a consortium, and the staff on the planet is on contract."

"The Grinders are the most interesting things on the planet," said Doctor Veil, "and not just economically. They're warm-blooded marine creatures which crop algae from rocks in the far north. There is a very similar creature on Broadstairs, twenty light-years away, and the algae they feed on is very similar to a Broadstairs variety also. We intend to take genetic samples of both animal and plant to compare with file records of those from Broadstairs."

"So they're hunted for their pelts?" Rick said, staring at the holographic image Harry was projecting above his workstation. Without the human added for scale, the Grinder could have been a small caterpillar rather than an animal twenty feet long. It was shown swimming by undulating the fins fringing the sides of its flattened body.

"Oh goodness, no," Doctor Veil said. "Male hormones are gathered in the breeding season. They're used to make an anti-aging drug which is very widely sold within the Alliance and to some degree more widely yet."

"There's a problem in the Cinnabar sphere," Harry said, grinning. "Given that the profits go straight into Guarantor Porra's pocket."

"The literature is mixed about the effectiveness of Zemlite," Doctor Veil said. "Some people swear by it, especially those who admit using it themselves. I haven't made an exhaustive study. But"—she gestured to the image of the Grinder—"the fact that the creatures and their food source have been transplanted here from Broadstairs implies that the Archaics thought that the hormones were valuable."

Or thought that the creatures themselves were ornamental, Rick thought. *Or that they tasted good, or a hundred other hypotheses, most of them not involving the Archaics.* He noticed that Harry was carefully avoiding a response to his superior's enthusiasm.

"Were you interested in the Grinders, Rick?" Harry said.

"To be honest," Rick said, "I just wondered if you had some sort of an overview of life on Zemlyn. You see, on Mindoro I found myself on a mud island with nothing to do but look at the local wildlife. There was a little fuzzy fellow about the length of my hand running about in the tops of the canes. One missed a jump and fell right on top of me. I got a good look before he scrambled back up a stem."

He cleared his throat. "I guess you think that's pretty silly," he said. "Me just wanting to know more about the animals we might be seeing on Zemlyn?"

"Not at all," Doctor Veil said. "I'm afraid that there aren't many of such records as you're looking for. I hope we may have gathered some before we leave the planet, though."

"You're not expecting to be abducted again, are you, Rick?" Harry asked, raising an eyebrow.

"I wasn't expecting it the first time," Rick said. "I do expect to be on the ground a fair amount here, though; and I guess the days I spent on the island made me, well, more interested in little critters."

"Well, I'll show you what we've got," Harry said. "Sit here and I'll copy you."

He patted the seat of the vacant workstation to his left. "The truth is," he went on, "that except for the Grinders, nobody's been very interested in the biota of Zemlyn's World. We're going to change that."

Rick pursed his lips. He sat down in the offered seat and said, "Say, Harry?"

"Yeah?"

"These Grinders on Broadstairs? Do they make this Zemlite too?"

Doctor Veil said, "No, they do not, Lieutenant. The algae on Broadstairs grows much nearer the equator in warmer water. One of the things we'll be checking is to see whether the Zemlyn's World algae has been genetically modified from the original on Broadstairs; or whether the reverse may be true."

A variety of small creatures living on or in the ground of Zemlyn's World began to appear on Rick's display as Harry sent files from his workstation. There was a worm a foot long—it looked like a worm—that had a long pointed head with jaws which split lengthwise into four segments. The jaw edges were toothed.

Rick wondered how it proceeded through the soil. Mostly he hoped that he wouldn't encounter one in the flesh.

If the Archaics had genetically modified the Grinders to form Zemlite, then maybe they really did use the stuff.

For *something*.

Captain Bolton had brought them into orbit over Zemlyn's World and had done a brilliant job of it: The *Far Traveller* was ninety-five thousand miles above the surface of the planet.

Bolton's ship handling was on the clumsy side but his astrogation had been casually flawless during this voyage.

The ship already in powered orbit above the planet contacted them by modulated laser though there was also a transmission on the twenty-meter band that was the default of all human spaceships. Modulated light was crisp and static-free over long distances, but the ship you were calling had a working twenty-meter receiver if it had any commo equipment whatever.

"*Zemlyn Corporation Vessel* Argus *to* Far Traveller," it said. "*State your business. Over.*"

Rick was on communications duty, viewing the *Argus* through the *Far Traveller*'s excellent optics. The *Argus* appeared to have even better optics than those fitted to the survey vessel in order to identify exploration sites from space. Being able to accurately identify the *Far Traveller* at a glance was remarkable.

"Zemlyn Control," Rick said, "this is RCS *Far Traveller* surveying the region for the general advancement of knowledge. We request landing permission, over."

"Far Traveller, *you are cleared to land in the harbor at Island One in the Grinder Archipelago,*" the *Argus* said.

A caret pulsed on a location in the far northern hemisphere of the local display inset of Rick's console.

The voice continued, "*You are to immediately check in with administration on the island. If you land anywhere else on the planet, units of the Guard Force will be directed to your location and you will be arrested. The Guard Force is not noted for the delicacy with which it deals with interloping traders—which is what you will be if you stray from the approved location. Over.*"

"Roger, Zemlyn," Rick said. *And if your optics are as good as they seem to be, they tell you that we've got two working plasma cannon, so good luck to any pongo sent to arrest us.* "Far Traveller out."

The exchange had been copied to Captain Bolton on the command console. Rick sent a *Communication Closed* note to the captain, but he could already feel the High Drive motors shifting to bring the ship's thrust in line with the axis of travel, for braking.

Next stop, Island 1.

Captain Bolton and I walked together the length of the quay and then the additional hundred yards to the administration building. The slips at Island 1 were designed for vessels much smaller that the *Far Traveller*, but Captain Bolton had brought us down farther out in the harbor and ran the extension bridge to the end of a quay instead of to the long side as a small ship would have done. It would make no difference to the Biology Section, as we'd be flying the truck off the stern hatch regardless.

"So...Lord Harper," Bolton said. "How are you finding life in the RCN?"

"Well, I don't think I can rightly claim to be RCN, sir," I said. "Certainly my biology career has been more interesting than it would have been as a junior assistant in a lab back on Cinnabar."

"What you're doing now is RCN business," Bolton said. I looked at him in surprise but he nodded when he met my eyes. "We need a base and this is a very good one from the standpoint of the soundings we're making. Furthermore, the facilities here on Island One are ideal for our purposes."

I missed a half step. "Sir," I said. My first thought was that he'd been joking. "This is a barren wasteland with stunted brush and no permanent human occupation."

"There are no theaters or art museums, that's true," Bolton said. "But the corporation provides liquor that won't poison customers, most of them its employees, and prostitutes about whom the same is true. That really covers the requirements of most spacers on liberty. For the exceptions, there are chapels of a variety of faiths—often sharing the same building but trading times of services."

"Ah," I said. "I hadn't been using the correct frame of reference."

Island 1 was a regimented—it wasn't sprawling—community of barracks, refectories, and business establishments. The buildings were to a common plan and solid. While not luxurious, they provided more comfort and privacy than accommodations on a starship did, even a ship as relatively under-crewed as the *Far Traveller* was as converted to a survey ship.

The front of the admin building was windowless except for the small panel at eye height in either panel of the double doors. There was an atrium beyond as a wind trap, and in the lobby within Commander Marinetti met us. He was a short man wearing an ornate uniform of green and gold.

"Pantellarian dress uniform," Bolton murmured. He was in uniform himself so he stopped and saluted. "Sir!" he said. "I am Frederic Bolton, captain of the survey vessel *Far Traveller*. As we reported to your guard ship, we have no commercial or political agenda whatever. We're here to advance human knowledge of the region, plot courses through it and assess the biota of the planets herein. This"—he turned to me—"is Lord Harry Harper, a Harper of Greenslade, you know; one of our biologists."

I wasn't in uniform, so I reached out and shook Marinetti's hand. His grip was firm but he didn't try the childish trick of trying to crush my hand.

"You're welcome, of course, Captain and Lord Harper," Marinetti said, "but I don't know what we can do for you. We don't get many visitors on Island One, and apart from Zemlite processing, there's nothing here. And the Zemlite is rigidly controlled of course."

"All we want is water to float the ship on," Captain Bolton said, "and the right of the crew to purchase beer and other entertainment at ordinary prices. And Lord Harper hopes to carry out biology research."

"Yes, sir," I said brightly to the administrator. "On the mainland, however. As you yourself pointed out, almost nothing is known about the biota of Zemlyn's World *except* for the Grinders. My assistants and I hope to get data which will fit Zemlyn's World into the community of galactic life forms."

"Well, that's all right," Marinetti said, "so long as you understand that starships are only permitted to land here. The Company— Guarantor Porra, that is—is a stickler about the Zemlite monopoly."

"Understood, sir," I said. "We'll be flying off to the mainland in a standard aircar with just the three of us"—me, Joss, and Kent—"and ordinary collecting equipment."

"That will be fine," the administrator said. "I'll make a note for Colonel Zemke who runs the Guard Force, but we don't have a detachment on the mainland. Just the islands where the Grinders breed, with the main body here on Island One."

"If I may ask sir," Bolton said, "how large is your Guard Force? As we were coming in, I saw a very extensive equipment park on the north end of the island."

"Yes, we've got several hundred vehicles," Marinetti agreed, "but I can't guarantee how many of them are going to be operational at any one time. They all have to be capable of flight in order to respond to interlopers anywhere in the archipelago. We've got about five hundred troops here on Island One and another two hundred or so spread out on the other twenty-two islands."

He grimaced and went on, "You see, the Zemlite is extremely valuable, but processing it from the bull Grinders is a complex job. The factory here on Island One has three hundred workmen. Thus most of the troops are here to guard the factory and warehouse. Raids on other islands can carry off a few carcasses, but we can have a large force anywhere in the archipelago within an hour. That's much too quickly for a small plant to dress out and process even one Grinder. Adults weigh several tonnes each."

"There won't be any problem with us taking genetic samples from Grinders after they've been processed, will there?" I asked. That was for Doctor Veil since the differences between Grinders here and the population on Broadstairs was critical to the theory that the Archaics had modified the original population.

"No problem," said Marinetti. "For that matter, the females will be giving birth in a week or two and some of the whelps always die."

"Well, that's very satisfactory," Bolton said. "We'll get on with it, I guess. Is there anything we can do for you, Commander?"

"If you and your officers would eat dinner with me while you're on Island One," Marinetti said, "I would appreciate the company."

He made a rueful face and added, "I am paid very well and the duties are not arduous. But the personnel are not in sympathy with how I was raised. The factory workers are factory workers and the Guard Force are mercenaries—mostly from rural Buckroth."

"We can certainly do a visit," Bolton said.

I added, "I'll be going off tomorrow, but I'd be delighted to come by tonight, if that's all right?"

Marinetti gripped my right hand in both of his. "Lord Harper," he said, "your kindness melts my heart. At 1800 hours here, then?"

Captain Bolton and I walked back to the *Far Traveller*. I for one was very satisfied with the way things were working out.

Pinnace *Gamma* floated in Zemlite Harbor at one of the slips. Rick had been in charge of warping her in, using the *Far Traveller*'s cables but the quay's winches and bollards. The exercise gave the spacers, including Lieutenant Richard Grenville, good practice.

"Testing thruster one," Rick announced on the general push, which for this instance was copied to the ten spacers of the pinnace crew and also to the communications console of the *Far Traveller* and wherever beyond Captain Bolton decided to send it.

Rick gave the forward thruster a two-second pulse at sixty percent output with the leaves flared. The pinnace bucked. Waves sloshed both sides of the slip, but not seriously. Even the small freighters which generally called at Zemlite Harbor were significantly larger than the pinnace. The *Far Traveller*, moored across the top of the slip, barely noticed the event.

Bio Section's aircar lifted from the stern boarding stage. Rick paused a little longer than he might otherwise have done before testing the other thruster. The plasma exhaust raised a cloud of steam sparkling with loose ions when it quenched in the cold water. That wasn't a risk to the aircar, but it wouldn't have been fun to fly through.

The car curved over Island 1, rising as it did. When Kent slanted off over the sea to the southwest, Rick announced, "Testing Thruster Two," and pushed EXECUTE. Again the pinnace rocked.

Rick thought about Harry going to the mainland. He'd miss his friend's companionship, but he sure didn't envy him this expedition. The mainland was almost as cold as the Grinder Archipelago. At this latitude it was covered with stunted trees, much like those of the larger islands; and unlike Island 1, the only habitation would be inflatable tents. Even granting that Harry was more of an outdoor type than Rick had any desire to be, this didn't sound a fun trip.

I'd plotted our course using imagery the *Far Traveller* had made herself from orbit. There were absolutely no charts of Zemlyn's World anywhere I could find in the data we'd gotten from the Foreign Ministry. I wondered if there were something recorded in Guarantor Porra's personal files. Probably not: Porra's interest had been purely financial, though he had supported academic institutions throughout his reign.

If there were charts we didn't have them, but for Bio Section's purposes the orbital images were fine. The Grinder Archipelago was a sharp hook. Island 1 was a good hundred and fifty miles from the mainland, but a number of the islands were considerably closer. We were flying to an estuary in the east coast of the mainland, but I hoped to visit one or more of the lesser islands on our return flight and take samples there to compare with those on Island 1.

Kent and I were alone in the cab; Joss had chosen to travel

in the unheated cargo compartment. She'd brought a one-piece weather suit along but she wasn't wearing it when we boarded.

I must've dozed off from the vibration of the drive fans, because Kent jolted me alert when he said, "I think that's the notch you headed us for, sir. Right ahead. The guidance system thinks so anyhow."

My mind was buzzing from just having awakened. I said, "I guess it has to be," as I squinted down at the body of land ahead.

The windshield suddenly darkened. There was a terrible roar. "Kent, what in the hell is happening?"

"Don't look at the exhaust!" Kent said. "It'll blind you if you get the light unprotected and the side windows don't darken!"

The windshield slowly cleared. I could see the notch of an estuary which looked like the one we'd been headed for. "What was it?" I repeated in a normal voice, having gotten my startlement—well, panic—under control.

"It's just a ship landing," Kent said. "Probably the guardship coming down to take on more reaction mass. They keep one gee on in orbit for the crew's sake so they have to refuel."

"Who's on guard right now?" I asked.

"Well, I guess Guarantor Porra's taking his chances," Kent said. "It's that or he has to stump up for another ship and crew. I guess he figures that nobody can steal very much if they sneak in during the pit stop."

He slowed the car and brought us to a hover. "I'm going to set us down here unless you want me to fly on," he said.

"Here is fine," I said. "I'm looking forward to stretching my legs."

It looked like a nicer spot than Island 1, at any rate.

Kent landed on the border of stunted vegetation between the fast-flowing water and the thirty-foot trees nearest the estuary, rising to fifty or sixty feet tall farther back from the margin. The watercourse was only a few feet deep at the moment, but it must swell considerably with the spring melt from the hills visible to the north.

Joss put up the tent while Kent unloaded the truck into it. I tried to help, but I was obviously in the way.

Instead I decided to be a biologist and gathered local plants, taking images of each in place before setting a sprig of each in a collecting case under the same number as the image. The foliage of all species of vegetation was of soft spikes. The ground was covered by fallen leaves, and a few leaves of most plants were turning gray and preparing to join them. I suspected that the process was yearlong and that the site would look the same in six months.

There were spore packets on many branch tips, but only on a percentage of any species. Reproduction was year round also.

Having made an initial survey of the vegetation, I decided to look at the large birds flying about the estuary. They were eating fish that had washed up on the shore and on rocks out in the water. I used my goggles to view them closer. They had six limbs attached to the body segment. The final pair was modified into skin-covered wings and the top two were long with grasping claws. The middle pair seemed stunted, as best as I could tell from a distance.

Joss joined me as I examined a cast-up fish. "I brought nets along that'll take the little birds eating fruit in the forest," she said. I'd almost gotten used to her mutilated face and tattoos, but seeing her unexpectedly when her left side was toward me was still a shock. "Those"—she nodded toward a bird on the shore ahead of us—"are going to need the gun."

I went back to the tent, where I put down the collecting case and donned the shooting vest over my weather suit. I loaded the shotgun with a charge of number two shot. I judged the largest of the birds to run less than twenty pounds apiece.

I walked back to Joss and together we approached the bird. It watched us with increasing focus, then agitation. It hissed angrily.

I said to Joss, "I don't figure to shoot one unless I have to—" As I got the last word out, the bird launched itself at my face.

I fired before the gun was firmly against my shoulder, so it gave me a hell of a whack. The bird's middle limbs weren't stunted after all and they gave the creature a powerful lift-off.

"Bloody hell," I said, reloading the gun reflexively. The shot had flung the creature backward, dead instantly. "I wasn't expecting that."

"Your reactions are pretty good, though," Joss said, picking the bird up by the neck. "Well, we were going to want a specimen before we left."

The initial extraction had put *Gamma* five hundred thousand miles out from Zemlyn's World. Rick had reentered sponge space briefly and extracted into orbit ninety-five thousand miles up from the planet's surface.

"*They don't get better than that,*" Tech 4 Guadalupe said over the command channel. She was fully qualified and would be taking the pinnace for the next sounding voyage, but Rick had decided to run this one entirely himself.

"Thank you, Guadalupe," he said. "Now just to bring her in."

Rick was pleased with the work also. His astrogation had been spot on during this run.

"Argus *to RCS* Gamma," the communicator announced, "*you are clear to land at Zemlite Harbor. Over.*"

"Acknowledged, *Argus,*" Rick said. *They sure seem in a hurry to get rid of us.* "We will land immediately. *Gamma* out."

Rick set up his approach into Zemlite Harbor but took his time about it. The *Argus* sent a tight-beam microwave transmission to the ground thirty seconds later. The pinnace's commo suite registered the fact of the message but couldn't read it, though it was possible that the *Far Traveller*'s own much more capable rig would be able to do so if Rick recorded it.

He had no intention of doing so, but the direction of the guardship's antenna allowed *Gamma*'s sensor suite to vector back to the intended recipient. As Rick expected, there was a small freighter on one of the islands of the Grinder Archipelago.

"Braking in five seconds," he announced to the crew. "Braking!" and pressed EXECUTE.

Their two thrusters snarled and rattled in the small hull of the pinnace. They were headed back for Zemlite Harbor.

And if somebody'd corrupted members of the guardship's crew and was robbing Guarantor Porra—more power to them!

"Well, Kent," I said as we cruised back from the mainland. "I'm pretty satisfied with the haul we made. It's just a page out of a thick book, but it's the only page anybody has opened on Zemlyn's World. We can be proud of ourselves."

"I'm glad to hear that, sir," Kent said. He was an extremely good driver, but it was a job to him. I was thrilled with the range of our specimens, and Kent was responsible for much of our success by hauling nets and buoys out to the mouth of the estuary. Joss had placed them, but the flying had been tricky.

The result of the exercise meant nothing to Kent. He was pleased that he'd done a good job, but he always did a good job—often in more difficult circumstances than these had been.

The advancement of human knowledge meant something to me—and I think to Joss as well. So far as Kent cared—he drove an aircar. Human knowledge wasn't part of his job description.

"I'll be glad to be back," Kent said. "The cafeteria at Zemlite Harbor probably wouldn't make guidebooks rave, but the food's better than the self-heating meals we packed along."

"As soon as I've got samples from Island Twenty-Three," I said, "we head straight back. It's not really out of our way."

"You're the boss, Lord Harper."

Kent made it sound as though I were a brutal slave driver, but he was obeying. The stop would cost us at most an hour, and there was a chance that it would turn all our findings on their heads. It had always been assumed that the Grinders and the algae they cropped were identical on all twenty-seven islands of the archipelago, but there might be differences among the islands just as there might be between the Broadstairs population and that of Zemlyn's World. It was worth an hour to me—and as Kent had said, I was the boss.

I'd tried to tell Island 23 we were coming, but I hadn't been able to raise them from the mainland. I tried again now, still without response. We were at fifty feet in the air as Kent normally flew. Maybe if we were higher we could raise somebody, but I didn't know what frequency the base on 23 was monitoring or if they were monitoring any.

"I think that's it right ahead," Kent said.

Grinders were visible through the clear water, massive spindles with their edges quivering to keep them in place against the rocks of the shore. Occasionally the back of one broke the surface and caused surface ripples in the still water.

The island ahead was wooded, and there wasn't a beach on which the Grinder females could crawl out and give birth. Perhaps that was on the other side. There wasn't even a place to land the aircar.

"Hang on," said Kent. "I'm going to take her up."

He adjusted the fans and swooped upward to a hundred feet. I saw our mistake: The island we'd approached was separated from the real Island 23 by a gap of several hundred feet on the left end and farther than that on the right, sheltering a shallow bay. The island behind—the real Island 23—had a broad beach of russet sand. A score of laborers in yellow fatigues were using winches to haul a dead Grinder onto a large skid plate. Several other figures in gray-green uniforms watched them, carrying carbines.

I saw buildings on the opposite side of the narrow island, and also a small freighter at the end of a track worn in the coarse soil. The ship was dragging by a cable the laden skid plate into its hold where the Grinder would be processed.

Kent started to land on the sandy shore. He must have seen what was happening, but the significance had escaped him.

"Lift!" I shouted. "Out to sea! Fast!"

One of the guards in gray-green presented her carbine. The aircar's windscreen starred and the slug sprayed me with powdered thermoplastic.

Kent hadn't reacted to my shouted orders, but now he whipped the car in a circle to port, heeling us over. At least three or four of the guards had started shooting when the first one did. I heard a dozen distinct *whacks!* as slugs hit the underside of the car, though only one of them came through the cab—between me and Kent, then punched its way out through the roof.

We straightened out, heading away from Island 23. There was a loud *bang!* and the car's rear fan blazed with blue fire. We vibrated fiercely for an instant before Kent slapped something on his control panel and with the other hand tilted the left handgrip while twisting it to maximum output.

The motor behind us stopped burning though I saw ghostly sparks dance along the frame of the windscreen. We were dropping at a steep angle, but Kent managed to keep the aircar balanced and upright on lift from the forward fan alone.

We came down into the six-foot trees of the islet that we'd overflown a moment before, crunching through the foliage and the stems themselves. The front fan tore itself to pieces but without the violent asymmetry of the rear fan when slugs unbalanced only one of the four blades. Trees had stripped the front rotor completely. The stems sagging under our weight set us down to the ground, though the impact slammed me against my safety harness.

I fumbled to open the harness release. When I finally looked down, I realized that it was twisted so that I was pushing on the back of the catch. When it finally popped open, I stumbled out of the cab and shouted, "Joss! Are you all right?"

"I'm fine," she said. She was standing at the back of the cargo compartment, holding my shotgun which she'd removed from its case. "Do you want me to take care of this, because they're probably going to come over to finish the job."

"I'll take it," I said. A lot of me wanted to give the gun to Joss, who hadn't brought one for herself. That was passing off responsibility, though. I couldn't depend on others to save me. *I* was in charge.

She handed over the gun and my shooting jacket. I put on the jacket and loaded a solid. I'd brought two solids in case I had occasion to shoot a Grinder. I didn't plan to do that, but I hadn't planned to shoot that bird back on the mainland. I was damned glad that I'd had a charge of heavy shot ready.

Holding my gun by the balance, I returned to the cab to see that Kent was all right. He was still in the driver's seat, staring at the hole in the windscreen. He turned to me and said, "What the hell happened? They were *shooting* at us!"

"Yes," I said. "They're selling Zemlite to outsiders, probably the Shinings, and they were afraid we'd come to arrest them. Maybe if they'd had time to think about it, they wouldn't have shot. They're too deep now to back off, so I guess Joss is right."

Joss came over and joined us. The scrub forest we'd landed in hid us from the shore of Island 23 and them from us. By worming our way to the shoreline but staying within the brush I figured we could see the bare shore opposite, at least with our RCN goggles.

"Sir, what do we do?" Kent said. He was still in the cab, but as he spoke he opened his door.

"We wait for the next pickup from Island One," I said, walking back to the cargo compartment to take out a case of the rations we had left. "They must make a circuit of the collecting islands regularly and haul the catch back for processing. We contact the boat when that happens and go home with them."

"But the radio doesn't work!" Kent said.

"I think it'll work fine at line of sight," I said, separating out an armload of meal packs. "If it doesn't, I'll fire a shot across the boat's bow—or some bloody thing. For now, let's get what we need out of the truck since it's a target for them if they turn out to have an aircar, which I doubt. I'm not sure they've even got boats, but they can certainly make rafts out of something so we'll have to watch out for them crossing. And they may have some good swimmers, the water's not rough."

Joss laughed. "They're welcome to swim," she said. "They won't be able to trust guns that they've submerged, and I promise you I'll be ready to greet them as they should be."

She tapped the hilt of her bush knife.

"I'm going to carry these rations straight across to the shoreline," I said. "I don't want all of anything we need to be in one place."

"Right," said Joss. "And I'll see what our friends across the water are doing. If they start to cross, though, sir—it's the gun we're going to need. And they're going to be shooting back. Sure that you don't want to let me borrow it?"

"I'm sure," I said. I hated the thought of shooting another person, but I'd been ready to do it to free Rick and I was ready to do it now. Maybe the boat from Island 1 would appear momentarily.

We had fishing supplies as part of the collecting kit. When sunlight warmed the water in the bay, it created a slight outward current. I hung three buoyed hooks at intervals on a twenty-foot line and set them to drift out. I didn't expect we'd need to supplement the remaining ration packs but it gave me something to do while waiting for the collecting boat to come by.

Kent had set up one of the tent sections in a swale and carried most of the truck's contents to it. He'd cut the brush with a saw of notched monofilament. A single unit was too cramped to hold the open cots, and the ground would be extremely rough to sleep on. I figured I'd find a place of my own and fit myself between the trees instead of cutting them off into sharp stumps.

I figured Joss was watching the far shore. I left her alone, hoping that she'd say something if she thought we ought to be doing things other than I'd thought of. I was completely at sea in this mess.

It had only happened because a guard had been trigger happy—and because I hadn't successfully warned the garrison of Island 23 that we were coming, Maybe if I'd insisted that Kent take us up to a thousand feet before we set out, the better radio propagation would have made the difference. It just hadn't seemed to matter.

I thought I heard something but decided it was just the weather. Joss called through my handheld, *"They're running up the thrusters of the ship! Over."*

"Great!" I replied, making sure that Kent was copied. "That means the Shinings are running before the security forces get here. They can pass off shooting at the aircar as surprise, so they're fine so long as we keep out mouths shut. Ah, over."

"They won't take that chance," Joss said. *"Out."*

The freighter's thrusters roared, overwhelming the voice on my handheld—if Joss was still speaking, which she probably wasn't since if I'd heard correctly she'd signed off. My goggles were self-dimming so I could watch the vessel rise out of the huge plume of steam without the plasma exhaust burning holes in my retinas.

The ship had risen about a hundred feet in the air. It looked odd. *They're in so much of a hurry that they haven't closed the hatch!*

The freighter wobbled and started back down—very rapidly at first but pausing in midair and resuming in a series of slow jerks. The roar doubled as the ship landed in the bay, so close to the shore of our islet that you could jump from the outrigger to the land.

The steam that boiled out of the bay dissipated more quickly than I was used to when ships landed. It was three hundred feet away from where I huddled. The thrusters had been run only a brief time and the hull hadn't been heated by reentry.

In the boarding hold appeared figures in yellow fatigue uniforms, the laborers who'd been manhandling the dead Grinders when we arrived. They were now carrying carbines and submachine guns. I didn't see any of the company's security force, but the guards had clearly provided weapons for the Shining work crew.

The Shinings threw a boarding bridge from the end of the hatch. They were crying and coughing from steam and the ions. The bridge pivoted on the end attached to the ship and banged in an arc to solid ground. They rushed across it in a mass.

A man wearing the more tailored outfit of the military officers I'd seen on Mindoro stayed on the boarding ramp where it rested on the freighter's outrigger. He was wearing some sort of vision-enhancing headgear and held a loudhailer through which he shouted orders to the laborers spreading out below.

He's got a better view than the others because he's several feet higher.

The Shining officer drew a pistol from his belt and pointed it in the direction I'd last seen Kent. He fired three shots. The laborers turned and began spraying the brush in that direction with automatic fire.

I rose from my crouch and fired when I had a clear view of the officer. A hundred yards was a decent range even for a slug, but I took him squarely at the base of his throat. The Shining officer pitched backward, flinging the pistol to one side and the loudhailer to the other.

I ducked back down and reloaded. The automatic gunfire continued, but none of it seemed to be aimed in my direction. I'm not sure most of the laborers even realized they'd been shot at.

There was a scream from some distance away. I wondered if the Shinings had managed to shoot one of their own.

There was another horrible scream. I risked a look. I couldn't see anything through the brush in the direction the scream had seemed to come from, but I noticed movement in the boarding hold of the freighter. A spacer was preparing to put his weight on the lever that closed the hatch.

I shot him without thinking about it. He flew sideways; a mist of blood hung in the air for a moment. I crouched and reloaded with heavy shot. I had more slug cartridges in storage aboard the *Far Traveller*, but it was only whim that I'd brought even two with me on this trip to the mainland.

The laborers had mostly stopped shooting. They'd probably emptied their weapons spraying brush. I didn't duck after shooting this time though I was ready to if somebody noticed me. They were running back to the ship, as best as I could see through momentary openings and by the way the brush wobbled.

The yellow uniforms crowded onto the ramp extension, then started up the ramp. My shotgun wouldn't carry that far, not usefully, so I started through the brush myself. I wasn't exactly running because the trees didn't allow that, but I was moving as fast as I reasonably could.

The ship was our best route out of here. If the crew still aboard lifted off, it was back to waiting for the boat from the base at Island 1. That had been a straw of hope when there was no other hope, but the ship was a much better one.

I was close to the east shore and had a good view of the ramp but from my low angle I couldn't see deeply into the boarding hold. I could see the raised hatch lever, but I didn't have a good angle on anybody trying to use it.

An arm reached up for the lever. The laborer was hidden behind several of his fellows. I presented anyway, planning to put a charge of shot into the yellow-clad arm. A carbine cracked from the brush. The arm dropped out of sight. Five more shots snapped out of the brush. Laborers milling in the hold dropped.

Joss appeared on the ramp extension. She'd drawn her knife but she didn't carry a carbine. A Shining within the hold leaped to his feet and grabbed the hatch lever, hauling it down with his whole body weight. The hatch started to grind closed. As the ramp proper rose, the extension fell into the sea. Joss caught the lip of the ramp left handed and hauled herself up, then dropped out of my sight within the boarding hold.

I fell to one knee and panted. I needed to get back out of the way in case the ship lifted now that the hatch was closed.

The ship had shut down the instant it landed on our islet. There'd be some warning before it could move: at least the sound of pumps starting up to cycle reaction mass to the thrusters.

I got heavily to my feet. When I figured I was able to move, I set off to the center of the island, calling, "Kent! Are you all right! This is Harper!"

Just in case one of the Shinings still had some fight in him, I kept the shotgun ready.

Kent was near the tent he'd set up. His right arm was bleeding—but, when I examined it, entirely from splinters. A slug must have come very close but hit brush and threw bits into Kent.

Nothing looked very serious but I got the first-aid kit out of the truck. As I opened it, Kent said, "Sir, what do we *do* now?"

"We wait for the ship to open up and see who comes out," I said. "If it isn't Joss, then I see if whoever it is wants to negotiate. I take about any offer they're willing to make."

I pointed to a carbine I'd found in the brush. "You take that when I've got a bandage on your arm," I said. "It's got pretty close to a full load. Mostly just shoot to make some noise if it looks like they're coming for you. It'll make them cautious."

The bolts dogging the hatch shut withdrew with clangs, then a gear train drove it down to become the boarding ramp. Before it reached the bottom—the port outrigger—I saw Joss standing in the hold. She was bloody red all over, skin and utility jacket both. There were bodies in the hold behind her.

"Joss, are you all right?" I called in case there was more going on than I could see.

"Not a scratch," she said. She'd wiped the blade of her bush knife; it flashed bright highlights when it caught the sun.

I ran to her holding the first-aid kit in one hand—because I didn't wholly believe her—and the shotgun in the other. There were steps in the side of the outrigger. Even before I started up the ramp, I could smell the slaughter within. Blood, too fresh to begin rotting yet, and feces that the dying had voided when their sphincters released. I swallowed and tried at first to keep my features composed; by the time I reached the hold, I was just trying not to vomit.

"No, really," Joss said. "Not a scratch. Well, maybe a *scratch*."

She tugged the flapping tail of her utility jacket. There was a broad tear in it and the edges were black under the soaking of blood. An impeller had gone off in contact with the cloth. The driving band vaporized by the powerful flux had charred a hole in the fabric, but the slug itself appeared to have missed Joss.

"The bloody carbine jammed," she said. "There wasn't any choice but to board and do the job that way. I didn't think there was any danger but one of 'em still had a gun and the balls to use it."

Then she said, "I think they're all dead but be careful. I mighta missed one. That bloody slug *spooked* me. I swear it did!"

It was the first time I'd heard her express emotion. There were six bodies in the boarding hold with her. The knife had killed two of them.

"I'm going to find their commo and try to raise the *Far Traveller*," I said. Kent arrived at the top of the ramp, looking like he was watching a tree start to fall on him.

I looked at him and said, "Kent, get these bodies out. Just toss them in the bay for now."

"There's more," Joss said, sheathing her knife. "Come on, Kent. I'll give you hand."

She's in shock herself, but she's trying to keep a shipmate on track, I thought. *And what am I doing?*

I took the central passageway forward to the bridge. There were four more bodies there. The trousers of one showed double streaks where Joss had wiped her blade clean of blood.

I ignored the bodies and concentrated on the command console. It was of unfamiliar layout but I thought I'd brought up the commo display. On RECEIVE I got only static. I switched to TRANSMIT and said, "Lieutenant Harper to *Far Traveller*. We are at Island Twenty-Three and have been attacked by interloping traders. Send help immediately. Harper over."

I didn't know which frequencies I should be using, but I found a red caret which I hoped was fifteen meters, the RCN hailing frequency. I tried that, then several more frequencies. When I checked incoming between transmissions, I continued to get static.

I heard Joss and Kent behind me as I worked, but it was only when I gave up for a moment that I realized that the bodies had been removed from the bridge. Joss was standing in the hatchway. Our eyes met. She said, "No luck?"

I said, "Not yet. We're close to the magnetic pole here. Maybe if I take her up to a thousand feet or so, I'll be able to raise somebody."

"Could you maybe just fly us back to Island One?" Joss said, her eyes narrowing.

"No," I said. "The training I got in the Sheet Island Space Fencibles will let me take this thing up. I hope to bring her down."

Joss smiled.

I paused for a moment, then laughed. "Yeah, I suspect gravity still works here. Put us down in one piece then. Thing is, if I'm going to be flying her, I won't be able to fool with the commo."

Joss shrugged. "I've run commo," she said. "Which station to you want me to use?"

"Either of them," I said. There were three on the bridge. "As soon as Kent sets clear, we'll try it."

"I'm not going back on the island alone," Kent said from the hatchway. "If you guys are going, I'm sticking with you."

"Then somebody close the main hatch," I said. "I'll get the show on the road."

I had the pumps cycling; I could hear their deep note. I remembered Warrant Officer Greim sitting at the striker's seat of the Sheet Island flotilla's only ship: a pinnace with a dual control console out of a scrapped destroyer. Greim was fat and had lost both feet to diabetes but he could still get about the rigging with a speed and assurance that none of us "young gentlemen" could match.

The thruster controls were in the same places they had been on the Fencibles' pinnace. I flared all six nozzles, then lit them in pairs at minimum output. The Shining crew had tested the freighter very recently, so I didn't think I needed to attempt to remember all the details of a by-the-book lift-off.

"Here we go!" I shouted. I wasn't sure how to switch on the ship's PA system or if there even was one. I opened the throttles to eighty percent output, then closed the sphincter petals, using my right hand for both operations.

I knew that a skilled officer would use both hands to accomplish the operations simultaneously. My way worked, which trying to display more skill than I had might not have. The ship bobbled on the surface of the bay for a moment, then began rising on an even keel. I didn't know what I would've done if the thrusters hadn't remained in balance. Chief Greim wasn't here to take over.

Purple block letters reading CONTACT flashed on the upper right corner of my flat-plate display. I looked over my shoulder and saw Joss gesturing with both thumbs up.

I reduced the thrust of the thrusters together. I almost lost control then: one of the units lagged behind the other five and the stern started to rise. I knew I'd overreact if I reacted.

It cleared in five seconds. I'd done the right thing—nothing—but I was gripping the throttle knobs so fiercely that my knuckles were blotched in the seconds before the problem self-corrected.

We continued dropping, a little faster than I've have liked us to, but the descent was smooth and I knew now not to trust throttle response. I kept the bay centered in my display. I really would have liked to engage an automatic landing protocol, but I wasn't going to fiddle with the console in the middle of this operation.

"Hang on!" I shouted.

The ship guided itself onto my point of focus. In the Fencibles I'd been taught to slant down to a landing. That was certainly the best method given normal skill and a ship landing from orbit.

I had nothing like normal skill for a ship's officer, so this was perfect for me. This freighter may have been built for short hops after an initial landing—which would be normal for an interloper trying to keep out if sight as much as possible. In any case, it was making my job much easier.

We hit the water hard. I shut the thrusters down at the first impact but we still rose to the surface like a leaping fish. The throttles closed completely, so at least we didn't flip over.

"Bloody hell," Kent said from his couch.

I didn't blame him. I wished I'd practiced more on Sheet Island, but at the time I hadn't thought that piloting a starship would be a necessary skill for a biologist.

Joss stood up. "I've come down harder," she said, which wasn't as positive a comment as it would have been from somebody who hadn't been in a drop commando. "I got Lieutenant Vermijo. They're coming for us. I didn't have time to go into detail."

She stretched. I glanced at her, then looked away by reflex. She saw my wince and said, "If you open the ship up again, I'll take a bath in the bay before we have company. It won't help my scars any, but I'll get rid of the blood."

"Won't the water be boiling?" I said. I was embarrassed, but saying so wouldn't help.

"Not from a landing as quick as that," Joss said. "Anyway, I'm going to swim to shore and find a change of clothes besides."

"Right," I said and found the override switch on my station. We were floating a hundred feet from the island where the truck had crashed. If she wasn't concerned about the water, there wasn't any reason I should be.

Myself, I was just going to wait for help to arrive.

I wondered what it would take to clean the interior of the ship. More than I could manage, certainly. I got up from the command station and walked out onto the boarding ramp. Kent was already there, standing at the bottom where it rested on the outrigger.

I joined him but neither of us spoke. The bodies he and Joss had flung overboard floated near the ship, some of them rotating in slow pinwheels. Their legs and heads hung lower than their bodies.

"How long d'ye figure it'll be before the ship gets to us?" Kent suddenly said.

"They'll probably send a pinnace if there's one on the surface," I said. "Otherwise they'll probably come in APCs from the security force. That'll take an hour and they'll have to negotiate with Marinetti."

I wondered if I could hear the console from where I stood,

if the *Far Traveller* tried to call us? Probably not. But then, we probably wouldn't be able to receive their signals anyway, at least until the pinnace got closer. I also didn't care if I never spoke to another human being in my life.

When I closed my eyes, I kept seeing the Shining officer flinging his arms wide; and the spray of blood behind him.

"What if the guards come over?" Kent said. He was scanning the shore of Island 23. I saw a man in gray-green come out of the brush, then duck back in when he realized I was looking at him.

"They won't," I said. "If they try to, we'll close up in the ship and I'll light a thruster."

The water of the bay began to dance. I still had the goggles on so I looked up. The glare of a starship burned like a nova; the goggles grayed it down to a level that wasn't dangerous. The sound came to us through the air a moment later.

"We better get inside!" Kent said. "That's the ship, not a pinnace and it'll kick up a *bloody* big wave."

We sprinted up the boarding ramp. Kent started the hatch closing while I ran to the bridge. The great wave that the cruiser-sized *Far Traveller* threw up when it landed threw us sideways so hard that our port outrigger grounded on the islet where the truck had crashed. I fell sideways to the deck from the unexpected impact.

"*Shining vessel!*" the commo speaker boomed. "*Open at once and prepare for boarding by the RCN! If you attempt to escape, you will be destroyed without hesitation! RCN over!*"

Bloody hell! I keyed the commo—probably still on fifteen meters—and blurted, "*Far Traveller*, this is Harry Harper! We've captured the Shining vessel and we'll open up as soon as we can."

I turned and bellowed toward the corridor, "Kent, open the hatch!"

Returning to the commo unit, I resumed, "*Far Traveller*, the guard unit on Island Twenty-Three is in league with the traders and shot down our truck. The Shining traders as well as the guards are hostile, but Technician Joss is on the island this ship grounded on and is one of our crew. Harper over."

I could see that the two guns in the *Far Traveller*'s bow turret were pointed directly at us. I heard the ship tremble as Kent started to open the hatch.

"*Roger, Harper,*" the commo said. "*Are any friendlies on Island Twenty-Three, over?*"

On the display I saw the turret rotate away from us. I took a deep breath. Seeing those twin muzzles had really shocked me. I remembered Joss mentioning that the shot through her tunic had shaken her. I wondered how she was doing but I didn't have any way of checking.

"No friendlies," I said. "I don't think they really meant to shoot at first, we just startled them. But they gave guns to the Shinings to finish the job. Over."

The ship's plasma cannon fired twice with a tiny interval—maybe a second—between the shots. The largest building on the back of the island flew apart in a pair of fireballs, scattering support beams and chunks of the roof in all directions. The *crack!* of the discharges was sharper and louder than I would've guessed.

A boat came around the stern of the *Far Traveller*. Rick and Captain Bolton were in it with three spacers. One spacer ran the motor in the stern while the others held stocked impellers.

"I'm going down to the ramp to meet Rick and the captain," I said to Kent. I heard him following me out.

I knelt at the bottom of the ramp and as the captain pulled up to the outrigger said, "Sir, I'm *very* glad to see you. I wasn't expecting the ship herself to arrive."

"The fact that I'm commanding a glorified short-haul freighter, Harper...," Bolton said, climbing the integral ladder nimbly. "Doesn't mean that I'm not still RCN. Foreigners attacked my people. The Republic expects me to respond appropriately, and I bloody well will."

He looked at me and Kent. His eye lingered for a moment on the shotgun I still held in my left hand. "There should be three of you, shouldn't there?"

I saw Joss gesturing from the islet. She wore a set of my shorts and a utility tunic which was probably Kent's. They didn't look anything like the Shining garments, though she carried one of the carbines.

"She's right there," I said, nodding toward her. "Ah—could your boat fetch her?"

Rick spoke to the helmsman and the boat purred toward the islet with the three spacers aboard. It had just reached the shore when a pair of aircars arrived from the northeast. I expected them to go to Island 23, but to my surprise one landed on the rear stage of the *Far Traveller* and the other curved straight for us. There were more aircars on the way, including several which were noticeably larger because they had eight fans instead of the two on normal cars: armored personnel carriers.

The car coming our way landed on the freighter's ramp which can't have been designed for that use but didn't collapse or even sag. Administrator Marinetti hopped out and joined the four of us already on the outrigger. He was dressed in full uniform except that he appeared to be wearing slippers.

"Captain Bolton," he said, "thank you for your prompt aid in this matter. Do you have any personnel on Island Twenty-Three at the moment?"

"No, but I have my crew mustered with small arms and can provide you with another hundred people at will."

"Thank you, sir," Marinetti said, "but I believe Colonel Monson has the business under control. It's after all in his bailiwick."

He looked at me. "You're Lord Harper, if I recall. This is the interloping trader, I gather. Where is its crew?"

"In the bay," I said. The *Far Traveller*'s landing had scattered most of the floating bodies, though one was still caught between the hull and the outrigger we stood on. "I guess some are on shore, and I'm not sure that the whole crew boarded on Island Twenty-Three, which is where the ship was when we landed."

"There's nobody alive over there," Joss said, hopping up from the boat. "None that I could find, anyway."

"This is Technician Joss," I said. Marinetti wouldn't have seen her before now—she didn't flaunt herself in front of strangers. "She was instrumental in our survival. And may I say that your guards on Island Twenty-Three probably didn't plan to attack us."

"You may say that, Lord Harper," the administrator said, "but they certainly planned to sell Zemlite to the Shinings."

The newly arrived guards, backed by the automatic impellers of the APCs, were lining those they'd captured on Island 23 up on shore. There were twenty or so prisoners mixed between guards and Shinings wearing yellow garments.

I started to ask what Marinetti intended to do with them but the shooting broke out before I got the words out. All of the prisoners crumpled. The bay beyond—they were shooting at an angle to us, thank goodness—danced with bullets and body fragments. Some of the executioners had aimed high and the heads exploded on impact.

Marinetti saw my expression. "Lord Harper," he said, "this is much easier than explaining to Guarantor Porra why I didn't do it."

"I see," I said. Then I said, "Administrator Marinetti? I'd appreciate the loan of one of your vehicles to transfer my specimens from the islet where we crashed to the *Far Traveller*. Our truck was destroyed when the guards attacked."

"As a matter of fact, sir...?" Rick said. "I suspect that you and the establishment of Zemlyn's World can find a use for the ship we're standing in, which Lieutenant Harper here captured from the pirates who'd been stealing Zemlite from the Guarantor. Isn't that so?"

"As a matter of fact," the administrator said, "a direct means of communicating would be much better than depending on messages sent with the ships which pick up the Zemlite, but I don't have a budget for large expenditures."

"This major operation against interlopers could easily have cost two aircars," Rick said. "In fact, it did cost the one which your guards shot down and you'll need to replace. And a second one could be very useful to the *Far Traveller*, couldn't it, Captain Bolton?"

Marinetti turned to Bolton and shook his hand. "Done, sir!" he said.

"Kent," Captain Bolton said, "you'll come to Island Twenty-Three with me and we'll pick out a pair of aircars, if this meets the administrator's approval."

Marinetti nodded, smiling broadly.

Rick had bought the first round in the commissary on Island 1 so he was musing as he waited for Harry to bring the next pair of mugs. Rachel kept coming to his mind, which surprised him.

She hadn't been startlingly beautiful, nor what you'd call a bedroom athlete; but he'd *liked* her. When he'd told her that the ship was lifting at 1500 hours the next afternoon, she'd looked as though he'd just driven a truck into her. In a calm, reasonable voice she'd said, "Of course. I knew you'd be leaving."

He'd thought, *Well, that went better than I'd expected...*

Whereupon Rachel broke down in tears, rushing out of the restaurant and blundering into a couple just coming in.

He'd paid the bill and left. Similar things had happened in the past, but for some reason this one seemed to bother him. She'd said it herself: She'd known he would be leaving.

Harry set down the mugs. The commissary's lager was pretty good. It had a faintly bitter aftertaste, but another swig of beer quickly drowned that.

"You're looking thoughtful," Harry said.

"I'm just wondering if you've got anything on for the next couple days," Rick said. "We ought to check out the new trucks with a hunting expedition, it seems to me. I can get the time off."

"I suspect Kent and I can too," Harry said with a wan expression. "Doctor Veil was really impressed by our collections on the mainland—and the fact that we got a newer truck and the captain's blessing out of it too. Which was really your work, Rick. I owe you one."

"You captured the bloody ship," Rick said and took a deep draft. "Which I suspect is over and above for field biologists."

"Bloody is right," Harry said. "If I never see another sight like the boarding hold, it'll be too soon. But they *were* trying to kill us."

Both men carried handhelds. They pinged together. The text crawl said: ALL RCN PERSONNEL RECALLED TO SHIP. ST MARTINS ON MEDLUM HAS BEEN HIT BY A DISASTER. THE *FAR TRAVELLER* WILL RETURN THERE SOONEST TO PROVIDE HUMANITARIAN ASSISTANCE AND TO SUCCOR CINNABAR CITIZENS. BOLTON, COMMANDING.

"Bloody hell," said Rick as they and at least a dozen more crewmen in the commissary got up and headed for the door.

He thought, *I wonder if Rachel will be willing to see me again?*

MEDLUM

The crew of pinnace *Beta*, from Rick on down, had nothing to do during the launching from orbit, except to hope that the *Far Traveller*'s launch crew didn't screw up in the process. Mostly the pinnaces were launched from the surface where air and water buffered the process. If a clamp or cable stuck, the pinnace could be flung out of the bay spinning wildly. Then the enlisted crew could only hope that the lieutenant piloting her reacted quickly to a situation which was as new to him as it was to them.

Rick grinned crookedly. If you wanted a safe life, you didn't become a spacer. And you *sure* didn't join the RCN.

The cables at bow and stern tightened on their spools, sliding *Beta* neatly out of the bay, which had been converted from the light cruiser's forward missile magazine. "Slicker'n snot, crew!" Rick said over the intercom. It was just him and four techs; they wouldn't be inserting. "Stand by for braking."

He paused to check that St. Martins Harbor was locked in the center of his display, then pressed EXECUTE. The single thruster began snarling and the pinnace dropped deeper in the gravity well.

Rick lost direct view of the harbor almost at once but the *Far Traveller* transmitted imagery from its higher orbit to the pinnace for as long as possible. *Beta* wasn't using automatic landing, but the console would guide her down to a hundred miles west of the harbor, whereupon Rick would take over for the final stage.

The unscheduled freighter *Astoria 37* had been orbiting Medlum

193

with the intention of landing at St. Martins Harbor. An instant after the captain had begun braking out of orbit, the volcano above St. Martins blew its top. It sprayed a fan of glowing gas and rock down over the city and its harbor.

Astoria 37 had aborted its landing and proceeded to the next planet on its itinerary. The freighter made no attempt to land on Medlum and offer help, but she did announce the event when she reached Island 1 on Zemlyn's World. In fairness, there wouldn't have been much a tramp freighter could have done.

The *Far Traveller* had returned to Medlum to bring help but the first requirement was to figure out just what had happened. *Beta* and her crew of a lieutenant and four techs were doing that.

The buffeting was worse in a pinnace than aboard a larger ship. Rick gripped the locked controls mainly to have something to anchor his hands while *Beta* shuddered her way deeper into the atmosphere. Vibration degraded the display into a colored blur without sharp edges, tan or blue depending on whether they were over land or water at the moment.

Beta slowed further. The sea became a surface rather than a blur. Land approached ahead but the sea was a greasy gray plain prickled with waves and table-sized chunks of floating lava.

They were over St. Martins Harbor and *Beta* moved forward at a walking pace. The console was preparing to set them down in a slip. The entire harbor was covered with floating ash, in which ships floated like marshmallows in a cup of cocoa.

The pinnace hovered on its single thruster, about to touch down, when the display cleared enough for Rick to see that the slip contained not a mass of floating ash but rather a ship which had sunk and filled. Cakes of pumice would have shattered and dissipated under the plasma blast, but a ship's steel hull would have met the pinnace's with a crashing impact.

Rick eased open the throttle and hopped over the slip, finally settling to the surface in the open harbor. He shut the thruster down.

"Bloody hell," said Baxter, who'd been echoing the display on her handheld.

Merganthaler opened the boarding hatch. He and Hironi prepared to haul out the extension ramp.

The console suddenly spoke: *"Pinnace with RCN markings, this is Cinnabar Ship* Althea. *Our reaction mass pump has choked and we can't retract it. Can you help us repair this so that we can lift off soonest? Althea over.*"

The *Althea* was the Cinnabar-chartered vessel which had brought the Mediation Mission to Medlum. Rick, and so far as he knew, the rest of the *Far Traveller's* officers hadn't had any contact with it on their first visit to St. Martins Harbor, but some of the regular spacers may have.

"El-Tee!" Hironi called from the hatch. "There's somebody on one of the ships waving I think a tablecloth at us!"

I waved a hand in Hironi's direction and said to the console, "*Althea*, this is *Beta*. We'll take a look at the situation as soon as I've reported to the *Far Traveller*. How can we contact the authorities? *Beta* over."

"*There's no bloody authorities!*" the console said. "*Thank heavens the RCN's here! Althea over.*"

"Wave back to them, Hironi," Rick called. "We'll be over to give them a hand as soon as I've reported to the captain."

I was coordinating communications for the *Far Traveller* because I could do the job and the regular officers—the real RCN officers—were fully occupied by the recovery work that the crew was doing. I had the rank and I was a gentleman by birth as well as by declaration of Navy House.

Besides, I was pretty good at it. Organizing Captain Bolton's needs and priorities wasn't as hard as genetic analysis of species in a new biota.

"Master Womble?" I said when the secretary completed the connection. "This is Lieutenant Harry Harper, of the *Far Traveller* at St. Martins Harbor. We're coordinating relief for the government. We see you've got a fabric mill at Kelway, and we need cloth for tenting. We're hoping that you can help us here before the weather turns."

I'd been making calls like that all morning. A surprising number of residents had survived the explosion by fleeing when the volcano had let off a gush of steam while the earth shook violently. Many had swarmed aboard ships in harbor; many others had simply fled in one direction or the other along the coast road.

Six hours later, while *Althea* watched, the volcano had blown a hundred feet of its cone into a blast of rock and gases down the remainder of the slope and over St. Martins. RCN personnel were now running temporary power lines from our fusion bottle into the town, providing not only household power to returning survivors but also powering equipment being used to excavate streets.

A haze like smoke hung over St. Martins. Some of the ash was dust-fine and formed a layer along the whole track of the volcano's flow. The crewmen working in the ravaged area wore respirators, but there were none available for civilians. Those who straggled in from camps along the highway hoping to dig valuables from their homes wore crude cloth masks wet with sea water. Spacers were setting up water points outside the town, but fresh water was still in too short supply for anything but drinking.

The console intercom blinked. "Go ahead," I said.

"*Sir, it's Mahaffy,*" the tech said. Bio Section personnel had been left out of the work crews—partly because the petty officers didn't know them and partly because they were regarded as without the skill for the jobs in hand.

That was more true than not, but Kent and Mahaffy controlled access from the transportation bay which was being used as an infirmary for injured civilians. Nobody wanted civilians wandering around the *Far Traveller*, especially when most of her personnel were absent.

Joss stood at the base of the stern boarding ramp. Those tramping across the extension bridge had to pass her before getting to the ship. I suppose some refugees simply wanted to board because conditions were more comfortable than in one of the camps, but I doubt whether any of them tried to argue if Joss told them they didn't qualify.

I was quite certain it didn't do them any good if they *did* try.

"Go ahead, Mahaffy," I said, wondering what on earth this was about. I wasn't concerned. The next thing on my to-do list was to call a factory in Mishtect where they extruded plastic tubing. Bolton wanted to use their tubes as tent frameworks, if we could arrange delivery in a reasonable length of time.

"*Sir, there's a woman here,*" Mahaffy said. "*Lady Hergestal. Her aircar landed right on the ramp—that's how she got by Joss. She says she needs to see you.*"

I didn't have to worry about her rifling cabins, I thought. "Send her up."

It would take Lady Hergestal a while to reach the bridge. I

grimaced and called Mishtect. If somebody replied and I was still on the call when Edwige arrived, she could wait for me to finish. This was, after all, my job.

I got a flunky—he may have been a watchman—at the tubing factory. He said it was the owner's birthday and supposed the owner would call me back when he visited the plant again, but nobody else could help me.

He obviously couldn't. I broke the call and figured I'd wait to try the factory again for at least a day.

Before I could decide who to call next, Edwige Hergestal entered the bridge. I was alone, but fortunately I was facing the hatch so I could scramble to my feet.

Try to, rather. My legs were asleep and I thumped back down on the seat instead of staying upright.

Edwige didn't appear to notice. Her features had a glassy calm. She said, "Lieutenant Harper, my father is missing. He remained at his post in the Residency after the first signs of the coming cataclysm. That's what members of his staff told me, those who ran. My father felt it was his duty to stay at his post instead of adding to the panic which was sweeping the town."

I nodded to show that I was listening. *How many lives would Postholder Bothwell have saved if instead he'd organized the town's evacuation while it was still possible to do so in an orderly fashion?* But that was looking at it with hindsight. *I* hadn't thought the volcano was dangerous when we'd been here before. I'd ridden up the mountain to collect specimens—which might now be the last of their kind.

"My father is missing," Lady Hergestal said again. "I think he must still be in the Residency, perhaps trapped and unable to make his way to safety."

She swallowed. "He may be dead."

I kept my face still. *He almost certainly* is *dead.*

"Lieutenant, until help comes from Formby or Escalante, the Alliance of Free Stars for which my father worked—and I'm afraid died—has no presence in St. Martins," Edwige said, her voice trembling with anger. "My own driver refuses to take me to the Residency to look for my father. I'm therefore coming to Cinnabar to ask for humanitarian help for a *good* man, a *decent* man."

"Lady Hergestal," I said, "I wish you well in your search for your father, but I have no operational control over the ship's personnel. Captain Bolton is coordinating relief efforts from the command post on the quay to which the forward boarding ramp is attached."

Edwige turned without speaking. I said, "Milady? We're not using vehicles in the town either, even ground vehicles. The fine ash would destroy moving parts almost immediately. An aircar which landed at the site of the Residency probably wouldn't be able to lift off again. When there's a heavy rain to lay the fines, it'll be possible again. *If* you know where the Residency really is, which I'm not sure I do."

Edwige turned. "Thank you for your opinion, Lieutenant," she said. "In my family, the idea of leaving one's father trapped or unburied till the next storm is repugnant."

She left the bridge. I sighed and started thinking about alternate materials for tent poles.

The blast of hot gas and molten rock had spared a slice of St. Martins. A knob of the cone, an ancient relic of an earlier eruption, had survived a fraction of a second after the start of the explosion, long enough to cast a wedge of impunity over an edge of the town. Fine ash had covered the buildings and the water lines had ruptured when the earth shook instants before the fiery cloud struck, but most of the buildings themselves had survived—and the people in them had survived.

Rick had a section of riggers laying power lines on tripods made from tubing while a Power Room team created a substation by repurposing spares from the *Far Traveller*. Another section of spacers under a bosun's mate was putting down water lines on the surface, feeding collection points where survivors could fill containers for use in their shelters. The camps east and west of the city had spacers providing basic services also.

Rick walked over to the techs who were adjusting the components of their substation. "We've got the line complete from the ship," he said to Tech 5 Grabble, in charge of the squad.

"We're a half hour to the point we connect it," she replied. "But at least we've finally got all the components. Unless one of these bitches fries, when we hook 'em up."

Rick returned to his riggers. He looked up what had been a boulevard before the blast. He could just see the apartment building Rachel had lived in. It was partially collapsed but part of it still poked up above the level which the superheated rock had found.

"Joyeuse," he said to the bosun's mate. "Are you guys willing to take a little jaunt up the street"—he nodded toward the apartment house—"with me? This is a volunteer operation, not duty. A friend of mine lived around here and nobody aboard the *Althea* has seen her since the lid blew off."

Joyeuse didn't even bother checking with her riggers. "Sure, El-Tee," she said. "Where are we going?"

"Right up there," Rick said, "the building on the corner you can just see the roof of. Her room was on the top floor. We'll need masks."

They hadn't been wearing their respirators for stringing wire, but they'd been issued them before the shift. Rick put his on and started toward the ruined building. On his third step the crust on top of the ash gave way and he plunged ankle deep to the pavement.

"Ouch!" Rick shouted, jumping back and shaking his right leg furiously, shaking as much of the ash off as he could. "We can't do that without rigging boots! Forget it, it was a bad idea anyway."

"We bloody well *can* do it," Joyeuse said. "Adams, Kopinsky—get the doors off all the houses. If we don't have enough, we'll walk the back ones forward as we go. Move it, spacers!"

"But what if some of the houses are still occupied?" Rick said.

Joyeuse seemed to carry a pry bar as a matter of course. She stuck it into the back joint of a door to the stairs leading up to upper-floor rooms. With a fierce twist she ripped out the bolts of the top hinge, then bent and repeated the process with the lower hinge.

She looked at Rick. "This is a bloody disaster, right?" she said. "Lots of worse things happened."

"They sure did," Rick agreed. They placed the door, then went back to help the two spacers with providing more pavement.

"Lord Harper," Edwige said. I jumped because I didn't realize that she'd entered the bridge. "I am here to beg you."

"Lady Hergestal...," I said because I couldn't think of anything else at the moment. My brain was numb, trying to decide where I was on the recovery work.

Supposedly there were ships that would shortly be under way

from three ports carrying food and shelter—of various kinds in both cases. I didn't trust the locals who'd promised me that, but there wasn't much I could do about it if they were lying to me.

"Lord Harper," she said. "I've spoken to your captain. He refuses to release any of his personnel to search for my father. He says—"

She stopped for a moment and closed her eyes, then opened them and resumed, "Your captain says that his duty is to the living and that my father is certainly dead. When Alliance officials arrive they can set their own priorities, but while he's in charge his will stand. The lieutenant with him said that the death of one more of Guarantor Porra's thugs wasn't a matter for regret. Perhaps you feel the same, Lord Harper?"

"My family isn't political, Lady Hergestal," I said. "And while I don't have the right to speak on Lieutenant Vermijo's behalf, he lost close friends in the war and is very fatigued at the moment with his work on behalf of the citizens of St. Martins. Regardless, Captain Bolton's decision is one that most officers would make—if they bothered to volunteer to help in the beginning."

"I see that," Edwige said. Her words and her expression both seemed glazed. "Lord Harper, I appeal to you as the son of my father's cousin, can you help me find him or at least recover his body? I've found a guide, a clerk at the Residency."

I opened my mouth to say that there was nothing I could do even if I wanted to, but even as I formed the words my brain went into planning mode. I closed my mouth.

Edwige turned away and leaned against the wall. She burst into tears.

I got up from the console where I was sitting. "Lady Hergestal," I said, "I need to check in person with the other members of Biology Section, especially with Doctor Veil, my superior officer. If you sit here"—I gestured toward one of the unoccupied consoles—"I'll be back as soon as I have something to report. I hope it may be good news."

The crew had a path of doors to the wrecked house like a game of dominos. Half a dozen civilians protested but none very strenuously, which surprised Rick considerably. The residents were so stunned by the catastrophe that they didn't have much energy to protest forceful spacers entering to rip off interior doors because there hadn't been enough outside doors to complete the track.

"Here we go," said Joyeuse as she and Kopinsky brought the door which would finish the job. It was light and the central panel was slatted, but it would keep their legs from sinking through the crust. "*Here!*"

She dropped the door at the end of the row and adjusted it with hands protected with air-suit gloves. Their work on the trackway had stirred up enough dust that the respirators were necessary, which Rick had earlier hoped they could do without.

"You first, El-Tee," Joyeuse said, gesturing him to the front.

They'd reached what had been a second floor window facing the street. It was open. The original residents must have fled immediately after the explosion. Rick wondered if they'd survived the freshly deposited ash. The interior of the piles was still oven hot after a week. The day it fell it was almost hot enough to ignite wood.

Rick scrambled in without difficulty. There was a door to the hallway at the right side of the room. It had burst open when the building collapsed. He went through.

The light beyond was bad, coming from the offset window by which Rick had entered. At the back end of hall a woman's legs projected from beneath the fallen ceiling.

"Joyeuse!" Rick shouted. "Spacers! We gotta lift the roof off a, a person!" He'd started to say "body" which it probably was in all senses, but he wasn't going to give up hope. They might need a jack if there were any that weren't already in use by other teams.

The spacers crawled in behind him. He put his hand on the woman's bare ankle. It felt cold.

"Here, let me try it," Adams said. Rick squeezed to the edge of the hall, wondering how he could best help the tall rigger.

Adams turned and braced his back and both hands on the sloping ceiling. His knees were braced. They straightened and the ceiling lifted from the woman's torso. Rick grabbed both the woman's ankles. He'd get his arms under her torso if he could, but—

There was a crackling. "Bloody hell!" Adams said.

Adams' feet crashed through the floor. He sat down on a stringer and the ceiling sagged back. "*Bloody hell!*"

More of the floor had given way as well. The ceiling no longer lay heavily on the woman's body. Rick slid forward and hauled her out on his knees, cradling her head and torso against his chest.

She was Rachel. Her neck was broken, and she was long dead.

"You got her, El-Tee?" Joyeuse asked.

"Yeah," Rick said. "Take her legs and let's get out of here before the whole thing flattens."

Then he said, "She's dead. Been dead."

They reached the window. "Lemme take her," Adams said. "I'll hand her out to you."

Joyeuse backed out ahead of Rick and said, "Well, it was worth a shot, El-Tee. Sorry."

Rick took as deep a breath as he could through the respirator. There was nothing to be done now. There hadn't really been anything to do a month ago either.

Doctor Veil had told me to go ahead with anything I thought might be helpful; I think the extent of the volcano's devastation had stunned her. Mahaffy and Kent said they were under my orders and they'd do what I said. I'd never met the machinist, Tech 4 Malanovic, and I hadn't known how he would respond, but in fact he was delighted to have something he could do despite a badly broken hand. Kent and Mahaffy joined him in the fabrication bay to do lift and carry under Malanovic's direction.

Now I walked out on the boarding ramp to explain the situation to Joss. Any interaction with her was a negotiation. It wasn't that I thought she'd object, but she operated in a different world than anyone else I've ever met.

"Sir?" she said as I approached where she stood watching the floating extension bridge quivering on the surface of the harbor. I hadn't seen her look around so I hadn't been sure she'd seen me.

"Joss," I said, "I'm going to try to recover the body of Postholder Bothwell from the Alliance Residency, using Biology Section personnel. This is outside your regular duties. Are you willing to come?"

She gave me a smile that made her face even more hideous than usual. "Sure," she said. "If you've got a way to do it. You're pretty good at figuring out ways to do things."

"The shop is fabricating a skid from a sheet of structural plastic," I said. "It'll have a winch on the bow. We'll run a cable ahead wearing rigging boots and set a grapnel, then wind the skid forward with the winch."

I ventured a smile and said, "We won't even have to kill anybody."

"Even without that," Joss said, "I'm in. But say—the woman who flew an aircar onto the ramp this morning—she's the one were doing this for?"

"More or less," I said. "The aircar can't operate in the ash, though."

"Hell no," Joss agreed. "But it can get me to the lake up the coast where I was collecting the first time on Medlum. I want to cut reeds there, because hell if I've ever managed to use those heavy boots."

"Yes," I said. I had no idea what she had in mind but I didn't figure it mattered whether or not I understood. "Lady Hergestal is on the bridge. I'm locking the inner hatches and I'll get one of the regular crew to retract this bridge."

"I'll let it loose from the shore end and set it to retract," Joss said. "You go up and tell Lady Hergestal to get to her aircar soonest, it's parked by the captain's HQ. You get on with it, El-Tee. I'll catch you up as soon as we get back."

"See you soon," I said.

I was confident that Joss would join us soon. I wasn't nearly as certain about the rest of my plan.

The machine shop had its own external hatch though that didn't have a landing pad for aircars. Kent and Malanovic said there wouldn't be a problem. I didn't disbelieve them but it was a relief to me to see Mahaffy aboard the skid connect the cable hanging from the hovering aircar and Malanovic at the controls in the bay release the crane hook.

Next to the captain's headquarters on shore, I donned a pair of rigging boots. They were intended to keep spacers safe when working among the sharp edges and broken cable strands of a ship's rigging. The would certainly protect me from contact with the hot ash.

They were also miserably uncomfortable to wear, let alone to work in. Well, I'd been uncomfortable before.

The aircar curved to shore near me with Kent driving and Mahaffy still in the body of the skid, steadying himself on a support cable and the side of the skid. It was boat-shaped and had an upturned prow, but the back was completely open.

Kent let the skid touch down to take the weight off the cables so that Mahaffy could release them. While Kent parked the vehicle where Lady Hergestal's car had been, I ran forward to take the grapnel already strung onto the hand winch.

I'd known the boots would be uncomfortable but I hadn't appreciated just how bad they would be. The tops galled my shins, and my feet in ordinary ship's boots—really high-heeled moccasins—slid around bruisingly.

"Wish me luck," I said to Mahaffy as I took the grapnel over my shoulder.

"Luck, El-Tee," Mahaffy said. "Say, isn't Joss up for this lark?"

"She'll be joining us later," I said and began trudging forward.

"Good luck, Lieutenant," Captain Bolton called as I passed his HQ. I waved with my free hand.

I'd plotted the course in fifty-yard stages, though there was a hundred yards of cable on the winch and we could splice in as much as we wanted from rigging spares. As I walked on, the ash changed from grit under my boots to a layer that I shuffled through—like running through the surf on a beach. But worse, and hot, and I was wearing the respirator.

The first waypoint which I'd chosen had been a substantial building at a corner on the boulevard I'd taken uphill on my first trip into St. Martins. I wondered how Rachel Pond was doing. She hadn't been among the Mission staff who'd evacuated to the ship in the harbor before the eruption.

The building had been steel framed and one of the corner posts stuck out in the air. It had been bared when the weight of ash made the building collapse and spread the stone cladding over the streets. I looped the cable around it, then hooked the grapnel to another steel beam.

I waved to the skid, then sat back on an ornamental lion which stuck up above the level of ash. I stretched my legs out so that the heels rested on a high spot. I wasn't sure that the crew had seen me until the cable went taut. My face shield was fogged though the air was warm and my sweat had rolled onto it also.

I took the respirator off carefully. I didn't think I'd stirred the ash up too badly where I was sitting now, and I *had* to get more air into my lungs even if it came with tissue-scraping irritants that would cause serious problems in the future. The future could take care of itself.

With the respirator off I could see the skid crawling toward me. Kent and Mahaffy changed off on the winch crank. That would be tiring work also. Neither of them did a lot of physical labor in their normal duties.

Nor did I, and I'd be spelling one of them as soon as the skid reached me.

I put the respirator on as the skid reached the base of the fallen building. We'd be skewing to the right on the next stretch, basically caroming from the left side of the boulevard to the right side as we cranked onward. This was the course I'd worked out with Sauer, the Residency clerk Edwige had found. He'd been out fishing the day of the eruption.

Sauer had absolutely refused to accompany us into the ruin. We'd used the current panorama and the imagery the *Far Traveller*'s log had recorded on our first landing to plot a course to the Residency. If he'd been a Cinnabar citizen—or possibly even a Medlum native—I might have ordered him to come along, but he was a native of Pleasaunce, the Alliance capital.

I didn't blame Sauer: The fallen buildings stank of death. There wasn't enough heavy equipment on Medlum to dig all the ruins out. What we could locate was supposedly on its way to St. Martins by ship, but I didn't hold my breath.

The city would probably be rebuilt in a decade or so: The harbor was just too good to abandon. People would forget the disaster, or they would convince themselves that the first eruption had let off the crust's pressure and there wouldn't be another. They might be correct.

"Mahaffy, your turn," I said as I unhooked the grapnel and held it out for him to take. I pointed with my whole left arm. "The route's on your handheld but it's a straight shot. Remember, the quicker we get there, the quicker we can get back to our bunks."

There was a large cooler of chilled water with electrolytes on the skid. I immediately sucked a mouthful and savored it before taking another. I'd been carrying a backpack canteen but that hadn't lasted very long. I wondered if we were going to wish we had more fluid than the five gallons in the cooler before we were done.

Mahaffy was struggling forward very slowly. If I hadn't just done the same—and probably at as slow a pace—I would have been scowling with anger. I still wished he was going faster, but I wasn't feeling uncharitable.

An aircar landed beside the one Kent had flown out of the

ship. Joss jumped out of it carrying what looked from where I was like a bundle of reeds. Edwige followed a moment later while Joss knelt to bind reed bundles—there were two of them—over her ship's boots. Then she set off along the track of the skid.

She wore shorts and a utility top plus a sunhat. Her sheathed bush knife was visible beneath the edge of the top. She moved with long strides and didn't appear to disturb the ash.

"He's signaling us," Kent said. Mahaffy was waving to us from a heavy stone sticking out of a hill of ash. It wasn't as distant as the waypoint I'd plotted, but it was something.

I put my respirator back on. "Then let's get cranking," I said. "I'll take first shift." I'd shut my eyes to all but slits to let me concentrate on my job: pulling the skid toward the point where Mahaffy had set the grapnel.

I began cranking and felt the skid shuddering beneath us. The winch was geared low. I'd thought it was too low, but Malanovic saw it was as much as we'd be able to handle. I understood immediately that he was correct, which I regretted. I kept on cranking.

My eyes were open but I saw only colors through my fatigue and the fogged face shield. I breathed in grunting gasps, each one an attempt to fill my lungs through the respirator.

When I tried to raise my left arm for another half turn on the winch, the biceps cramped. I lowered that arm and the right biceps cramped also. "Kent, take over!" I croaked and stumbled backward.

Joss slid past the skid as Kent took over from me. She nodded when she saw I'd looked toward her, but she didn't speak or wave.

I wondered how long it would take for my arms to recover. The skid grated forward with each millimeter that the winch took up on the cable. It would scarcely be visible to those watching from the shore. Was anybody watching?

I took over on the winch again before we reached the waypoint. I closed my eyes and visualized the winch rotating in front of me. It was easier that way, living in a world of my own—

"We're there," Kent grunted. I let go of the winch handles. We were a yard short of the anchor, but close enough. I backed off slightly so that Joss, standing in front of us, could release the grapnel. The bundles of reeds on her feet looked like boats. They were extremely awkward and probably heavy as well, but she didn't have to drag quantities of ash along with every step.

I grinned mentally though the expression didn't reach my face muscles. It was also true that none of the three men involved had been very fit while Joss was in remarkably good shape. I hadn't known how she got over the wall around into the Garden House.

I didn't remember how often I took another shift on the winch. Having three of us on the rotation made the job easier than it would have been with two—but having to slog through the ash to reset the grapnel had been an even more brutal job than turning the winch. The job wouldn't have been possible without Joss, and even with her I was having doubts.

"We're here," Joss said.

The words came from outside my consciousness. I continued cranking another half stroke until Mahaffy put a hand on my wrist and said, "Sir, we're there."

We were on a wasteland of ash with hummocks from which occasionally a twisted girder or large block of masonry stood proud. Those outcrops had provided the anchors by which we'd winched up from the shore. There were very few anchor points closer to the crater rim.

I checked my handheld. Joss had brought us to the point that Sauer and I had identified as the Residency back aboard the *Far Traveller*. Here on the ground I couldn't tell why we'd chosen this hump in the waste—but neither could I come up with a better choice.

"All right," I said. "Here we start probing."

Malanovic had made us two probes from two-inch steel piping with one end cut at a forty-five-degree slant. I guess I'd been hoping that the postholder's body would be in plain sight. That was naive, but it's why I hadn't paid much attention to the probes. Now that I was here, I wished we had four of them.

I took one and began driving it into the ash. Immediately I wished that there were crossbars on the probes. By twisting the shaft I was able to work it into what was already stiffer than a pile of gravel. At about four feet there was a clink and a scraping sound when I rotated the probe; it didn't go any farther down. I had hit either stone or the original ground level.

I brought the probe back up with only slightly less effort than it had taken to insert it. I looked about at the others.

"I think we'd better do this in pairs," I said. Joss immediately came over to join me. It was at least as much a matter of weight as strength to get the probe through the ash. All four of us were about of a weight, though Kent and Mahaffy were clearly unenthusiastic about the task.

I wasn't enthusiastic either, but I'd said I would find the postholder and I didn't know a better way to do it. I reset the probe—a little farther back in the pile—but before I started to work it in I looked around the former site of St. Martins. I thought, *It is completely bloody crazy to be out here doing this.*

Then I put my weight on the shaft while Joss gave it a half turn between the palms of her hands. Mahaffy and Kent got to work about ten feet away which seemed as good a place as any.

I didn't think I'd ever seen Joss enthusiastic, and I suspected I wouldn't feel good about it if I ever did. I'd never seen her put in less than full effort on anything she was doing, though, so it didn't matter how she felt about the job.

We ground into the ash. Like getting the skid to the site in the first place, it was a terrible job in which progress was measurable in extremely small intervals. We kept on for three hours with basically nothing happening. Even Joss was wearing a respirator.

Mahaffy suddenly shouted, "We got something. Soft!"

An instant later Joss said, "This feels like a body!"

She twisted our probe and brought it to the surface by herself. There was a torn swatch of black fabric caught in the edges of the point. Grinding the steel into gravel as we'd been doing had roughened hooked edges into the point.

I touched the cloth. "Dress clothes!" I said. "Do we have any idea what the postholder was wearing when it happened?"

We didn't, of course. Sauer had been out at sea and Edwige was on the other side of the continent. It seemed like a good bet, though. "Let's get the shovels out and start digging!" I said, sounding as cheerful as I felt.

That was unreasonable, but the whole job had been unpleasant and terribly, terribly hard. If I was being unreasonably positive, that was all right.

The *Far Traveller*'s shovels were fabricated from steel tubing and plates—much like the chairs and tables aboard the ship, saving only those in the captain's cabin and the officers' wardroom. The shovels were sturdy and, though heavy, worked well in soil and probably better in the ash than lighter tools would have done.

Mahaffy and I took the first shift of digging down toward the body while Kent and Joss spread the spoil at a distance so that it didn't just slide back into the excavation. I uncovered the shoes while Mahaffy was working down toward the torso. When I saw the condition of the shoes and feet—shrunken to half the size they must have been in life—I knew there wouldn't be an open-casket funeral. Still, Lady Hergestal was getting her father back.

"Get the ash off the top of him and we'll drag him out," I said. That meant digging down through four feet of ash in an area of several feet around the body. I wondered if Edwige had imagined that we'd find her father alive in a cavity, trapped in an angle of fallen walls. The rolling waste of ash, marked by occasional distorted remnants of human construction was as alien and empty as the bottom of the deep sea.

We had the body's arms and torso visible and the shape of the head. I'd been keeping clear of the head so as not to mutilate it with the sharp edge of my shovel. Flesh and bone would cut much more easily than the compacted ash did.

The legs were clear. I lifted them one at a time, then took the left wrist and raised it. I was wearing the gloves. The arm came loose at the shoulder though the dress coat kept it together with the rest of the body.

"Lemme get a shovel under his shoulders," Joss said. "You slide yours under his butt."

She worked her shovel in from the side which meant forcing the edge against the hard pavement and then levering up the body. I moved the right leg aside and slid my shovel blade under the hips. The body was much lighter than it had been in life.

"Kent and Mahaffy," I called. "Get the bag open! I don't want Edwige getting a look at this!"

"Ready, sir?" Joss said. "Lift!"

I was a trifle slower than her because I was trying to hold the left arm on; the posture made me awkward. I backed away; Joss came toward me; the right arm fell loose from the body but it still hung in the coat. We kept on shuffling toward where I hoped the others were waiting with the open bag.

I thought of rotating so that Joss could put her end in first but Mahaffy bent forward to work the black plastic bag over the right leg that was sticking out behind me. I stuck the left leg in and turned the shovel out of the way, then dropped the shovel beside me and supported the body with both gloved hands beneath the bag, working the torso deeper as Joss continued to shove it forward.

I was pretty sure the left thigh had separated at the hip joint. I didn't really care. The face looked as though it had been carved out of leather and shrunk to half normal size. We got it entirely in and stepped back while Mahaffy closed and sealed the bag.

"Now we've just got to get the skid back," I said, almost to myself. The thought of the grinding labor of winching the load back to the *Far Traveller* made my gut roil. I was *so* tired.

"Hey, look at this!" Kent said. He bought out the probe he and Mahaffy had abandoned when Joss found the body with ours. White cloth was clinging to the point. He untangled it from the point and said, "Hey, look! They're dinner napkins."

Another still clung to the probe. "It says Steeling on the corner," Kent said. I recalled the restaurant I'd seen with Rachel on the way to the Alliance Residency to meet the postholder. I turned and looked in the direction the Residency had been when we were passing the restaurant.

I swallowed and met Joss' eyes. "Let's get on back," I said. "Joss, if you'll haul the grapnel to the corner where we made the turn, the rest of us will get to turning the skid around."

She nodded and moved toward the corner with her long stride, holding the grapnel. I made sure that the winch was unlocked so that the line would pay out as Joss moved away. Then I added my weight and strength—such as remained—to helping face the skid back in the direction we'd come.

At the corner, Joss hooked the line to the same exposed girder that we used when coming and waved to us. Then as we started cranking toward her—I took first shift—she moved back toward the ship without waiting for us to meet her. She vanished almost immediately. The eruption-swept landscape looked basically flat, but in fact the dips and hillocks were almost as irregular as the surface of the thickly built city it had been before the volcano exploded.

"There's two of 'em," Mahaffy said.

I quit cranking. "Kent, take over," I said and only then looked forward.

Joss was coming back. Behind her, slogging through the ash in rigging boots as we had done initially, was Rick. Joss in her reed shoes carried another grapnel, and a line was paying out behind it.

"It's a straight shot from the corner back to the ship," I croaked.

"If Rick's brought a line, they can haul us in by a power winch! Bloody hell, we're going to make it!"

Apparently Kent was as elated as I was. At any rate, he cranked the sled up to the anchor himself instead of passing the task off to Mahaffy as he might have done. We arrived just as Rick and Joss, who'd taken the line from Rick and hauled it the rest of the way, arrived. They both looked as wrung out as Kent and Mahaffy did; and me too, I'm sure.

"I'm glad to see you, Rick," I said, leaving it to the other three to hook up the second line. "And surprised. Captain Bolton changed his mind?"

"I was coming anyway," Rick said. "I heard you were trying to rescue the postholder. Lady Hergestal spoke to Captain Bolton, pleaded with him, so I guess I'll have a career when we get back after all."

He checked the connection and found the new line anchored to his satisfaction. He stepped out to the side and waved his arms over his head, looking back toward the *Far Traveller*. The line became tight and the skid started grinding forward, powered by a motor at the ship. Rick hopped on as we passed.

As the power winch hauled us, bumping and grinding toward the ship, I fell into a gray daze. I hurt all over, but it was fatigue that was really getting to me. I think Rick spoke a time or two, and I may even have answered him. Possibly Kent and Mahaffy spoke also, but we were all exhausted.

Joss didn't speak, but she normally didn't. It would have been as surprising to hear small talk from her as it would have if the corpse in the plastic bag had joined the conversation.

We stopped with a jerk at the edge of the ash, about twenty yards from where the winch was mounted on a utility flat from the ship's stores, driven by one of the temporary distribution boxes we were providing for the refugees and survivors. I stood and grabbed our own winch to steady myself and tried to bring myself to alertness.

Captain Bolton and Lieutenant Vermijo were both coming toward us from their command post, but Lady Hergestal had been waiting beside the winch and had started forward as soon as the cable stopped running and the spacers in charge of the installation allowed her to.

That brought me around.

"Lady Hergestal!" I said in a raspy voice. I stepped into her path with my arms spread at chest height. "Edwige! You mustn't come closer now!"

She stopped. "Have you found my father?" she demanded.

"Lady Hergestal," I said. "Your father is dead. I'm terribly sorry." I was standing just in front of her. "Please, Edwige, as a favor to me, don't ask to see the body. The hot ash must have killed all the victims instantly, but it did terrible damage to the bodies. Bury him at once so that you can remember your father as you knew him, a brave servant of the Alliance who stayed at his post regardless of danger."

She stood where she was, drawn up to her full height with the expression of a porcelain mask. Suddenly she threw herself into my arms and began bawling.

I patted her on the back. Everything was going prickly white. I was murmuring something to her when I felt my brain switch off and I fell.

I woke up on the bed of a medicomp aboard the *Far Traveller*. I felt crappy, but my limbs moved normally when I wiggled them. The lights in the bay were low. I turned my head and found I was connected to the machine.

"Hang on!" Rick called. He came over, his boots scuffling on the deck. "Let me take a look and I'll turn you off so the probes retract if the dials say it's okay."

He looked over the controls on the side of the couch; the covering shroud available hadn't been activated. "You're good to go, Harry," he said and pressed the release button.

I felt probes retract from my body and sealants splash cold on the swatches of skin where they'd been injecting into my body what the medicomp thought I needed. "Mostly you were just down on fluids," Rick said as I carefully swung my legs off the couch. "Also your legs were in pretty bad shape, from abrasion more than the heat. Your boots were too loose and you're not used to wearing them."

"I want to go to my cabin," I said. Rick tossed me a singlet. I'd been stripped on the couch of the medicomp. There were slippers beside the couch.

"It's right down the corridor," Rick said. "We figured that's what you'd want and put you in this medicomp. You're easier to deal with when you're unconscious."

We shuffled down the corridor with me occasionally leaning on his arm. When we reached the cross corridor I knew where I was.

Rick opened my door for me. I started in. Edwige got up from the chair beside the little desk.

"Lady Hergestal," Rick said. "I'll be leaving now. I figure you can help Lieutenant Harper with whatever else he needs."

He closed the door behind him.

I walked to the bunk and sat down. Halfway through the process, my thigh muscles lost all strength and I flopped down the rest of the way like a sandbag.

Edwige glanced toward the closed door, then turned back to me and said, "Lord Harper, when you fell into my arms, I thought you'd died."

"No, I was just dehydrated," I said. "I . . . well, I'm all right now. Except that I'm tired. Really tired."

"Lord Harper," Edwige said. "You—"

She stepped over to the bunk and sat down beside me. She took my left hand. Her hands felt cool on mine, and I wondered if I had an elevated temperature from whatever the medicomp had been shooting into me.

"Harry, you risked your life to find my father," she said. "No one else would help, but you did and you almost died."

I met her eyes and said, "We weren't able to save your father, milady. And there were four of us; not just me. Five if you include Rick, and he was the reason we made it back."

"None of the others would have gone except for you," Edwige said and raised my hand to her lips and kissed it. Her lips felt cool also. "We can bury Father back home because of you. I'll fly the body to Meridan Spa and put it in the freezer there until I can arrange passage back to Pleasaunce for both of us. My family owes you for that, Harry. I owe you, whatever you want."

"Edwige," I said. "You owe me nothing. I just tried to help you the way I'd have helped anybody. And all I want now is some sleep. A lot of sleep."

"Thank you, Lord Harper," Edwige said. "Thank you for bringing my father back to me."

She leaned over and kissed my cheek, then rose and went out the door. I stretched out on the bed and was asleep in less than a minute.

✧   ✧   ✧

I saw Rick the next afternoon, when he came off watch with a work crew. He'd recovered much more quickly than I had, even though he'd accomplished what I think was a much more difficult task than I'd had. We met on the quay, where I'd gone to wait for him.

"I don't see Lady Hergestal's car...?" he said, making it a question with his raised eyebrow.

"She's taking the body back to the resort where she'd been staying when the volcano blew up," I said. "She thinks they'll let her keep it in their cold storage until she can get it aboard a starship going back to Pleasaunce."

Rick laughed. "I wouldn't be surprised if she did," he said. "A very persuasive lady. Look at what she got you to do. And me too, if it comes to that."

"I appreciate you arranging for us to be pulled back, Rick," I said. "That was a lifesaver—maybe literally."

"Hey, it's the least I could do after the way you brought me back on Mindoro," he said. "Say, did Lady Hergestal give you good value last night for the way you risked your life for her?"

I smiled, though I don't think the expression looked very cheerful. "Not like you mean it," I said. "I guess she would've, but I didn't think it'd be right. Look, Rick—don't put this around, but I'm pretty sure the body we found was the *maître d'* at the Steeling, not Postholder Bothwell. You'd have to do a genetic test to be sure, and I hope to hell that she won't do that."

"Ah," said Rick. He grinned briefly, then straightened his face. "It's funny if you look at it the right way. The wrong way, I mean. But look—you made her happy, and you bloody well did risk your life, I saw where your fluids had been when they hooked you up. I wouldn't be surprised but it might've done her some good too. If you were up to it, I mean."

I shrugged. "I don't know if I was," I said. "Anyway, it seemed too much like getting a girl drunk to screw her."

Mostly to change the subject I said, "Say, Rick? Were you able to find Rachel Pond?"

"Yes," he said; sharply, which I hadn't expected. "She's dead. Do you think that's my fault?"

"Hell no," I said. "Just about everybody in St. Martins is, including the *maître d'* of the Steeling. It was the Foreign Ministry as sent her here, so I guess blame them—if you're not satisfied to blame the volcano like any reasonable person."

I cleared my throat and said, "I'm sorry, though. Rachel was a nice girl and I liked her."

"Me too," Rick said. We weren't looking at one another anymore. "More than I realized till Mindoro. I had a lot of time to think there, and I was sorta figuring I might not have any more time ever."

He looked at me and forced a grin when I met his eyes. "And then you fixed things. Which is why I was around to carry a line to you."

I nodded. Rick was a good friend.

"Are we still on for Otko next?" I said. That was where we'd been headed when the eruption called us back to Medlum.

"Captain Bolton says we'll wrap up anything we can do here by midday tomorrow," Rick said. "So yeah, on to Otko."

"Well," I said as we walked together to the ship, "the *Annotated Charts* don't say anything about volcanoes."

OTKO

The *Far Traveller* landed with the usual sudden still silence. What supernumeraries like me noticed was that the thrusters ceased roaring and the hull no longer vibrated numbingly.

I'd have to ask Rick what he noticed. It would doubtless be very different from his viewpoint.

I released the restraints and brought my couch back into chair position. I'd already prepared the messages for the men whom my contacts on Mindoro had assured me were the most important residents on Otko; I sent them off. I'd follow up in a more personal fashion as soon as I could, but I was giving the local aristocracy a heads-up and an outline of my qualifications immediately.

My qualifications included my birth and the fact that my father was a member of the Society of Dilettantes.

Doctor Veil came out of her office. Mahaffy was bringing up his work station while Kent sat at the extra position, waiting to be told what to do.

Joss was in the office also, probably to have Doctor Veil give her tasks. More probably to approve the tasks Joss had chosen for herself: She'd been doing the job for long enough that she had a good idea of what things were useful and within her skill set. She didn't need to be supervised to make her work.

"I have something to say to you all," Doctor Veil said. She looked angry or at least uncomfortable. I turned my seat to face her and wondered if I should stand.

"I've gone over the briefing material on Otko more carefully than I had when we were on Elkin," she said. "It's an extremely dangerous place and I'm not comfortable with you going outside the fenced compound around Ssu-lung, the port where we're landing. The Otkan natives are not only hostile to strangers, they're headhunters and cannibals! The fenced region is of almost forty square miles, so I think we'll be able to get adequate samples without risking ourselves in the forest beyond."

"Ma'am," I said, forcing the frown off my face, "I really think that's overreacting. Otko isn't heavily populated, especially where we are on the north end of the main continent, and the fenced area is largely planted with Terran rice and not at all a representative sample."

Before Doctor Veil could respond, Joss said, "Ma'am, I talked to spacers on Mindoro who'd been here. The locals may be one step above monkeys"—she spread her terrible smile—"which is what they said about us on Api, where I come from—but like Lieutenant Harper says, they're thin on the ground except around the cities. For a young buck to get admitted to the council of his tribe, he's gotta bring a stranger's head. They keep squirming through the wire and snatching farmers. I don't figure I'll have trouble collecting like usual. And"—she smiled again—"if they manage to chop me, I deserved it. Maybe you can hire one of the locals to replace me."

Doctor Veil looked from Joss to me. After a moment she said, "Well, I'll wait to make a final decision until we've had an opportunity sort through the situation ourselves. But I request that neither of you go outside the perimeter until I approve it."

"As you wish, ma'am," I said. "I'm hoping to view local collections in Ssu-lung for a few days, though I don't think Otko has been settled long enough to have anything as interesting as we found on older worlds."

Joss nodded. "Yes, ma'am," she said. "I'll set traps inside the fence till you say otherwise."

I'd sent messages to three of the Landowners—that was the title of aristocracy on Otko. They all replied to me within the hour, saying they were delighted to show Lord Harper their collections immediately. I took them in reverse order of distance from the ship: Easton, Riddle, and Platt. Rick was going out with a pinnace, so Kent drove me around the circuit in the trike.

On the way I noticed that one of the twenty-odd ships in the harbor had a familiar faceted shape. "That's from the Shining Empire," I said to Kent over the ring of the engine.

He took a quick look and said, "Right, El-Tee. You want to see if I can find what it uses for a dock? But they probably lighter cargo and passengers to it on the surface."

"No need," I said. "But I was just curious."

The attendant who let us into Easton's razor-wired compound carried a slung automatic carbine. He didn't seem tense, but the gun wasn't just for show.

Otko's native population almost certainly dated back to near the beginning of human star travel, over a thousand years before the Hiatus. The planet had been resettled from Mindoro within the past five hundred years, and the folks we were visiting today were families from that second settlement.

The original population had sunk back to Stone Age level. The tribes lived as hunter-gatherers and, as Doctor Veil had noted, had some nasty habits. Though the entire settlement of Ssu-lung was fenced and patrolled, the wealthy clearly didn't trust the general security.

Easton was overweight and in his forties. Servants and a woman surrounded by children watched as he greeted me on the full-length porch. "Lord Harper!" he said. He shook my hand with enthusiasm while two of the servants recorded the meeting. "This is an honor, sir!"

He took me through his collection. The servants preceded and followed us, capturing the event for posterity. I hoped they were getting images they thought were useful. I certainly wasn't, though I recorded a few items for the sake of politeness.

Easton had hunting and fishing trophies, though nothing Bio Section didn't have records of already. I would check to be sure when I returned to the *Far Traveller*, but I didn't expect a surprise.

Riddle's house was much the same, though he didn't put his wife and children on display. I noticed that Riddle's servants were all young men.

His collection was largely of material from the ships by which Otko was resettled from Mindoro. He looked puzzled when I asked if there were artifacts from the initial settlement—though that was personal curiosity rather than of interest to Bio Section's mission. "Oh!" he said. "You mean the natives! Yes, I suppose they must have come from somewhere else, but it's hard to think of them in connection with machines, let alone starships."

Then to Platt, who was the same age as the first two men but clean shaven and almost totally bald. His house and collection were by far the largest of the three, and the latter included many pieces of Otkan pottery, delicately shaped and fired to black and shades of gray.

"They don't have potter's wheels, you know," he said. "The pots are built up in strips and then fired in dried manure, if you can believe that. I find them oddly attractive, but I don't suppose they're of interest to your study?"

"Not for Bio Section, no," I agreed, "but I like the look of them too. Where do you buy them?"

"Well, you have to know where to look," Platt said. "Some of them have scratched designs. This one"—he rotated a bowl—"looks to me to be a mother and child, just as though they were humans."

"That's what they seem to be to me also," I agreed, passing on to a wall of stuffed animals. A carnivore with eight legs, which was the normal number of limbs on Otko, wasn't familiar to me. These were very short, and I wondered at the creature's lifestyle.

"Is this a burrower?" I asked, touching the animal's long canines. It was at least three feet in head-body length.

"We call 'em diggers and they mostly live in holes," Platt said, "but they can climb too. They've taken babies out of cribs and carried them off, though mostly they stay in forests where there's no people. Well, no real people, just natives."

"I wonder if I could take enough fur for a genetic sample?" I said. "Or—is there a place we could hunt them ourselves? If it's possible to do that without being eaten by the natives."

"Oh, the natives aren't a problem if you keep your eyes open," Platt said. "You don't want to go into the forest alone, though."

He frowned and went on, "You hunt yourself, Lord Harper?"

"Yes," I said. "And another member of the Bio Section, Technician Joss, is a very skilled hunter."

"Well, I don't have two seats open," Platt said, "but I got one in my aircar. I've got one of my own, you see. I'm taking two of my buddies for a hunt tomorrow and you can have the last seat if you like. I was going to take another guard besides my driver, but you'll do fine if you can shoot and you can be ready here at five tomorrow morning?"

"I can shoot," I said. "And I'll be here at five in the morning local time!"

I was pretty sure that Doctor Veil would be happy with me to go off with three armed locals. If for some reason she wasn't, Captain Bolton would overrule her. I was willing to invite him to dinner at Greenslade after our return if I needed a bribe to win his agreement.

The guard at Platt's compound opened the gate as soon as Kent pulled the trike up. We drove through to where an aircar was parked. Platt turned from having set a gun in the cargo compartment between the driver's cab and the four-person passenger compartment.

"Good morning, Lord Harper," Platt said. "You're just in time to take your pick of seat, though I see Riddle's car just at the gates. He's bringing Easton."

The passenger compartment was roomy and the bucket seats looked comfortable. Certainly they were more comfortable than the pillion of the trike. I took my specimen box and cased shotgun out of the cargo carrier and brought them over to the car.

"Any seat would be fine," I said. "For choice I'd take one of the back pair because they're forward facing, but I'm grateful for your generosity regardless."

Platt's carbine was already clamped muzzle-up into the gunrack. It was a wooden-stocked weapon with gold inlays on the receiver. It was of military size but was much higher quality. The driver placed a carbine in the clip beside him in the cab, but it was a simple utilitarian weapon.

Easton and Riddle got out of a ground car driven by one of Riddle's young men. Both were carrying decorated carbines similar to Platt's. They were all large bore though their relatively short barrels wouldn't accelerate slugs to the velocities of a full-sized impeller.

I knew of no land animals bigger than a lamb on Otko. I wondered if there were feral cattle or the like, because I'd been expecting to use fairly light shot in my own gun. I had a pair of slug loads available if a charging bull seemed a possibility.

Platt gestured me to the seat in the back and took the one beside me while Easton and Riddle slid in facing us.

Platt keyed an intercom and said, "We're in, Abner. You have the plot?"

"*Yessir*," the driver said. "*It will take us about forty minutes, sir.*"

"Proceed," Platt said and switched off the intercom. We took off smoothly and headed south. Ssu-lung was on the north end of the island so I'd taken the direction for a given.

"Does Otko have positioning satellites?" I said, though I was sure Rick would have told me if the planet did.

Riddle snorted. "Do you know what that would cost, as small as we are?" he said.

"What we do," Platt said, "is use imagery from ships landing. Of course that's no good for changing conditions. Do you think your captain would agree to us using imagery from your ship?"

"Almost certainly," I said, "though I can't speak for Captain Bolton, of course."

A thought struck me and I said, "Say, what are your relations with the Shinings here? I saw one of their ships in the harbor and I know they've got quite a presence on Mindoro."

Easton opened his mouth to speak, then stopped and stared at Platt; Riddle was already staring at him. I turned toward Platt myself and tried to put on a neutral smile. I was strongly wishing that I hadn't asked what appeared to be a charged question. My interest was idle curiosity. In a matter of days I would leave Otko and wouldn't spare a thought for the place ever again. Certainly the planet's political constitution was no concern of mine.

"I think you should say that the question of Shining influence on Otko is a disputed one," Platt said. "The official position of the Shining Empire is that Mindoro exercised suzerainty over Otko, and that having defeated Mindoro the Shining Empire succeeds to Mindoran rights over Otko.

"The position of the Coordinating Council of Otko is that we on Otko were never governed by Mindoro, that we just had a shared cultural background. Further, that because of the danger of native Otkans, the civilized population is quite well armed, and the planet's gross domestic product would not justify a military expedition."

Platt spread his hands in front of himself, palms down. "So...," he concluded. "Shinings sometimes visit Otko, as a party are doing now at Ssu-lung. They do not interact with civilized Otkans by mutual choice. And if they want to deal with the natives, they're welcome to. The natives might find them an interesting change of diet."

"I think we're getting there, sir," Abner said over the speaker. *"I see the stream."*

I looked down through the side window and over the flare for the car's plenum chamber, but that was at such an angle that I could see only the expanse of feathery, dark green foliage. The driver could see straight down through his clear nose panel.

The car slowed and descended. The canopy was over a hundred feet from the ground with occasional emergents half again that high.

Abner slid us down through the boundary between treetops on opposite sides of a watercourse. The branches didn't interlock though the canopies bulged into the spaces between trees across the water.

Branch tips brushed the plenum chamber but nothing actually got into the fans. Abner was skilled and the vehicle probably had guards on the output side. That would rob them of some efficiency but it was necessary if Platt made landings like this as a regular matter.

I thought we were going to land on the stream bank but instead Abner kept us twenty feet in the air and eased inland over the heavy growth fringing the steam. The slight thinning of vegetation that allowed the aircar to enter the forest also let in enough light. The undergrowth on the streambanks was a tangle which the shadows only a dozen feet away smothered.

The windows in the passenger compartment were down—mine as well, though I didn't know where the control was. The humid air smelled alive and thick. Abner set us down and killed the fans. They hissed faintly as they spun down.

Abner jumped out with his carbine and tried to look in all directions. I followed Riddle out our side of the car. He had the luggage compartment open and had taken out his carbine.

"I'll get mine," I said sharply as he reached for the shotgun. It had been made for me when I'd turned eleven, a gift from my father. Riddle strode into the forest. Platt and Abner were several paces ahead, and Easton followed Platt closely like a trained dog heeling.

I stayed well behind. I hadn't been out with any of these men before and I didn't trust their gun handling. Not only did I not want to be in front of one of them holding an automatic carbine, I was ready to throw myself flat if one of them spun around while trying to follow a flying bird.

I still didn't know what we were after. I was carrying number four shot in a high-energy cartridge. I moved up a trifle and called quietly to Platt, "Should I load solids?"

Easton turned and hissed, "Shush, you fool!"

Platt shouldered his carbine and fired a short burst. There was a scream. Platt and Abner ran forward and the other two locals joined them, spreading out slightly.

I followed. The scream had sounded human.

The forest opened suddenly into a bright patch. The tree bark had been ringed to kill the trees. The boles remained like the pillars of a roofless temple. With no foliage above, enough light reached the ground to support patches of what I thought was maize. The only grain I'd seen in the compound around Ssu-lung was rice.

There were huts in the cleared area, beehive shapes about ten feet in diameter made of broad leaves on a framework of bent saplings. In back of the nearest hut, two women had been kneading something in a log trough. They had both fallen when Platt fired, but one of them was trying to get up and the infant in a fabric carrier on the back of the other was shrieking.

Platt aimed at the wounded woman. "What the hell are you doing?" I shouted and jerked up the muzzle of Platt's carbine. "That's a woman!"

"If we didn't keep the numbers down, they'd overrun us!" Platt said. "They're animals!"

Riddle and Easton were firing deeper in the settlement. They were both carrying bandoliers with extra loading tubes, which had puzzled me at the time. Now I understood.

Abner bent over the dead woman and brought the butt of his carbine down on the infant's skull, silencing it. "Stop this!" I shouted. "They're people!"

Platt jerked free and shot the wounded woman twice more through the body. I lunged at him but Abner grabbed me by the shoulder and spun me around. Platt must have buttstroked me from behind because everything went white and my limbs went rubbery.

As I fell forward, a thrown club hit Abner in the temple. Platt whirled but my outstretched hand fouled his carbine. I hit the ground and lost consciousness completely.

The last thing I saw was a nude man grappling with Platt.

✧   ✧   ✧

Rick Grenville had expected to be back by early afternoon, but it was almost sundown before he strolled up the *Far Traveller*'s stern boarding ramp. Soames, whom he'd been training to sound with a pinnace, was a capable bosun's mate and even well educated for a spacer, but his astrogation had proven so consistently wrongheaded that Rick wondered if there was something organically wrong with the man. His tendency to add when he should subtract and adjust right when he meant left was more consistent than random.

Rick had finally taken the controls himself and brought *Gamma* back down to Otko, having proven to his own satisfaction that Soames had no talent whatever for astrogation. For some reason the fellow wanted to remain on the rotation for course soundings. It would be Captain Bolton's decision, but it seemed pretty clear to Rick.

An aircar came in from the south and landed while Rick was still on the boarding bridge. He thought about it for a half second, then went into the transport bay instead of up to the bridge to report back formally. The trike was there but the tech on duty hadn't seen Kent, so Rick went on the Bio Section where he found the driver chatting with Mahaffy.

"Hey, Kent," Rick said. "Going to pick up Lord Harper?"

Kent straightened. "As soon as he calls, sir," he said.

"I'm off right now," Rick said, which was almost true. "I saw the aircar land. If you like, I'll run over to Platt's myself. I just feel like chatting with a friend. It's kinda been one of those days."

"Be my guest, El-Tee," Kent said. "She's got a full tank."

Rick motored up the harbor road at a leisurely pace, sharing the pavement with trucks and with cyclos very similar to his trike but with wheels in back instead of treads. There were probably aircars on Otko besides Platt's but the only other one he'd seen belonged to the Shining compound on the east side of the harbor.

A ground car from the house side reached the gate of the Platt compound just as the trike arrived on the road. An aircar rested on the lawn in front of the house. Rick waited for the ground car to exit, then started to pull in. The guard tried to close the gate, but Rick already had the trike's front wheel into the opening.

"I'm here to pick up Lieutenant Harper," Rick said. He wondered if he should have informed Platt that he was coming. The household staff hadn't gotten the word, obviously.

"Look, I don't know if I can let you in right now...?" the guard said.

"Well, you can let me in," Rick said, raising his voice a bit. "Or else I can come back in a pinnace and land on the front lawn. There won't be much lawn left if I do that, but whichever way you want it. I'm an officer of the RCN and I *am* coming in, one way or the other."

He could have got Kent to bring him in one of the ship's aircars, but he was peeved by this officious servant. Did he look like a savage with a bone through his nose to be barred from the compound for safety's sake?

The guard pushed the gate leaf wide again. Rick puttered through. He pulled up at the foot of the steps. Instead of going to the door, he called to the driver who was getting into the cab, "Say? I'm here to pick up Lord Harper. Will you fetch him?"

The driver's head was bandaged. Blood was leaking through, so the injury must be recent.

"Look, I don't know anything about this Harper," he said angrily. "Go ask somebody inside if you want to."

He opened the door of the cab.

"Look, buddy!" Rick said. "He went hunting with your boss this morning. You carried him! I'm here to pick him up, and I don't want a runaround!"

"Master Platt intended to go hunting this morning," the driver said, "but instead he had a stroke and died. Go ask inside if you don't believe me. If your Lord Harper actually did come here, he must have walked back."

He threw himself into the cab and switched on the engines. If Rick had wanted to continue the conversation, the fan howl deafened anyone standing close.

The aircar wobbled into the sky. Had the driver been a member of the *Fart*'s crew, Rick would have ordered him to a medicomp as clearly unfit for duty.

Rick considered options. He doubted he'd learn more in the house than he had from the driver, though they might be more polite about it.

He realized that Kent had said he dropped Harry off but hadn't said that he had stayed to watch the car take off with Harry aboard. Could something have happened to Harry walking along the harbor road?

Rick hadn't shut off the trike's little diesel. He swung around in the driveway. He wanted to talk to people aboard the *Far Traveller*, to Kent and to Captain Bolton; and also to Technician Joss.

I came around slowly. My face was on the ground. My head hurt, and it hurt a great deal worse when I tried to turn it. I touched the back of my head without moving anything but my right arm and found that touching my scalp hurt almost as much as turning my head. When I brought my hand back there was blood on the fingertips.

I remembered the blow to the back of my head. A lot of memory returned in a rush. I got my hands and knees under me slowly and carefully. My head throbbed so badly that my vision blurred with each pulse.

The bodies of the two women and the infant lay by the trough where I'd seen them killed.

Abner was gone. So was Platt but there was a bloody patch several feet in diameter on the ground where I'd last seen him standing. Two men had walked in the blood, and their footprints led beyond in the direction where we'd left the aircar.

The guns were gone, including the shotgun; though I still had the reloads in my shooting vest. I walked toward where we'd landed. I found two splotches of blood on the leaf litter, probably where Easton and Riddle had rested the body.

No one could have lost that much blood and still be alive.

The aircar was gone. Either Abner had survived the clout on the head he'd taken, or one of the hunters could fly an aircar.

I took a deep breath and leaned my weight on a fallen tree trunk. When I stopped moving, my stomach settled.

I walked back to the village. The relatively open sky felt good.

There were seven huts. The bodies of nineteen adults were scattered around them and there were about a dozen children. Many of the dead had been wounded and then finished off, either by a long burst of shots in the chest or a single round through the head.

Those were the adults. The heads of the younger children had been crushed, the way Abner had finished off the infant before I tried to intervene. Two of the men carried knives in wooden sheaths. I looked at one. It was made from a section of leaf spring. There was a belt woven from vines and I tried to put it on. The belt was too small for my waist, so I hung it over my left shoulder.

I searched the houses. I found wooden water tubs in each. Each had a gourd ladle, but I didn't find any small container in which I could carry water away. I drank deeply from the first one, though. My throat felt dusty until the first sip, and the water settled my stomach as well.

My head still hurt.

Most houses had one or more pieces of black and gray pottery like those I'd admired at Platt's house. More important suddenly was the fabric bag of corn meal mush. Excess water had leaked out through the close weave. I tried a handful and liked it.

I had a long way to walk, after all.

Riddle and Easton had left me to die—or maybe thought I was dead. In any case, they weren't coming back for me. My handheld had to be within a mile or so of a receiver for anyone to hear me.

The handheld gave me direction, though. I could have set it to guide me straight to the *Far Traveller*, but I hadn't. All I knew was that I was south of Ssu-lung and that if hiked far enough I would reach the sea. Then I would have to guess whether to turn east or west, but I'd deal with that when I got there.

This was a bloody awful situation, but complaining wasn't going to help. I drank more water, then started hiking through the trees. The handheld kept me from curving into a circle, and I tried to go around each tree bole in the opposite direction: clockwise one time, and counter-clockwise the next.

I'd been hiking about three hours—the handheld would have told me precisely, but why bother?—when I followed a trail through unusually thick undergrowth and realized from the brighter sky ahead of me that I was coming to another watercourse. I wondered if it could be the one by which we'd entered the forest. I was walking in a different direction, but I could only guess at how streams meandered in this jungle.

I felt a tug on my leading arm and thought I'd brushed a thorn. Then I heard the faint swish behind me. The deadfall hit me in the middle of the back, knocking me forward.

The blow set off my headache again. I vomited before I could even start to deal with my other problems. I spared a moment to recall the club knocking Abner down and to hope that he was in shape as miserable as mine.

I lurched up into kneeling on all fours. I closed my eyes. I think I was unconsciously trying to keep my brains from leaking out. The pain was making me nauseous. I pulled against the gripping vine which held my right arm. I managed to draw the knife and rotated my right wrist to saw at the vine. The knife wasn't particularly sharp, and when I managed to cut into the vine, more gluey sap oozed out and quickly stuck my hand to the knife hilt and the knife to the vine.

The sap was hardening. I paused for a moment to think, but time was obviously limited and I couldn't turn my head enough to see *how* I was being held.

I tried pulling my body loose, forcing my way forward against the grip holding my vest and shirt. I wondered if I could escape by leaving my clothes behind, but I quickly realized that the sticky mass gripped parts of my torso also. I probably could pull free, but I'd leave large swatches of skin behind. Apart from the pain, I'd lose enough blood to be dangerous.

A native suddenly came through the brush ahead of me as easily as if he were smoke drifting through the stems and thorns. He held my shotgun.

The native squatted down to put his face on a level with mine. "Why are you here?" he said.

I swallowed. The native must have been very confident about the strength of the adhesive in his trap.

"I came to hunt," I said. "Birds and animals. Not people. The people I was with intended to hunt people, but I didn't know until we were here."

I took a deep breath and said, "Where I live, people don't hunt people. I'm sorry this happened."

The Almighty knew *that* was the truth. I was also sorry that I was trapped and at the mercy of someone who'd just watched the men I was with massacre his family, but that probably went without saying.

I smiled. That probably surprised the native. It certainly wasn't what I'd expected to do, but it'd struck me that he had every reason to feel confident with his adhesive.

"I will take the knife," the native said. He took a bitter-smelling cloth out of the container on his belt it had been sealed in.

"I can't let go of it," I said, but he took my hand firmly through the cloth he was holding. When I wiggled my fingers and found the adhesive was loosening. I was able to pull them away from the knife hilt. The native took it.

"The gun you have there was given me by my father when I came of age," I said. "It's a very good gun, but is there anything I could trade you for it?"

I was getting ahead of myself here—I still had a long hike ahead of me—but things were moving in a good direction.

The native moved behind me. He'd thrust his cloth into its container and I smelled the astringent fluid as he took it out again. I felt the liquid on my back as he worked on the trap where it caught my bare skin.

"You are here to hunt birds and animals?" the native said.

"Yes, just that," I said. "Well, crystal buildings, but I didn't expect to find those."

"What will you do now?" the native said.

The deadfall pulled away from the skin of my back though it still clung to my vest and the loose shirt I was wearing.

"I'll hike back to Ssu-lung," I said.

"What then?" said the native. He seemed to be working on my vest but I didn't try to pull on it.

"Then I'll talk to the people who brought me here to murder human beings," I said. "I'll have friends with me when I do that. What happens after that depends on circumstances. And whether I'm still alive."

I thought about Joyeuse and Witmer and the way Captain Bolton had ordered the *Far Traveller* in to Island 23. I'd have friends. I'm RCN.

"You will not come back here?" he said. My left arm was now free. The native had refreshed his rag from the container twice more. I wondered how much of the bitter liquid he carried. He must be used to releasing game from his traps, but he probably didn't normally care about how painful the process was for his victims.

"No, I won't come back," I said. "I'm sorry I came this time. Very sorry."

"There is a crystal hut," the native said.

"What?" I said as I stood up.

The native had vanished. I didn't even know which direction he had gone.

There was a roar of fans. An aircar plowed through the heavy brush at the edge of the watercourse. It had come in so close that the top of a small tree knocked me down. The branches were wrapped with vines but these were not beaded with sticky sap.

I struggled to my feet. I saw the muzzle of my shotgun sticking up from the brush. I drew it out carefully.

Kent and Rick forced their way through the brush to me. Both carried submachine guns. Menta was working his way gingerly through the brush. The signals assistant also carried a submachine gun, but he didn't look comfortable with it.

"Are you all right?" Rick demanded. He was missing the right sleeve of his utility shirt.

"O-*kay!*" said Kent. "Guess I could make a combat insertion, couldn't I?"

"I'm all right," I said. "But I'm really glad to see you guys. But how did you find me?"

"Your handheld," Rick said. "We couldn't reach you, but we could home on it when Easton's driver gave us the coordinates."

"He did that?" I said in surprise.

"I talked to him," said Joss from behind me. I turned more quickly than I should have done, though the brief dizziness passed away when I forced myself to hold completely still. "He wasn't in shape to come with us, but Menta took care of that."

I took a deep breath and backed up along the animal track I'd been following when I was caught.

To Rick—since he seemed to be in charge—I said, "Do we have an extra gun? I want to leave one here?"

"Leave one?" Kent said in wonder.

Rick's eyes narrowed. Then he said, "Yeah, I guess. We're getting out of here right away, right?"

He looked at Kent, who said, "Hell, yeah. I didn't ding the fans when I brought her in."

Rick handed me his weapon, slipping his hand out of the sling. I put it on safe and set the butt on the ground with the barrel leaning against the crotch where a sapling forked near the ground.

"Let's go," I said. Rick followed me as I made a long circuit to where the aircar waited.

We piled aboard the car. I was in the cab between Kent and Rick. "I'm in!" Menta shouted from the back.

Kent reached for his controls.

"How the hell did he do that?" Rick said and gestured past me and Kent, into the jungle.

The native stood beside one of the large trees within the band of tangled undergrowth near the watercourse. He held the submachine gun I'd left behind. He pointed with it deeper into the forest.

"He wasn't supposed to get that till we were gone," I said, but I put my hand over Kent's on the throttle and said, "Shut down for now. I want to talk to him."

Kent's hand remained on the controls but he stopped advancing them. He said, "You sure, El-Tee?"

"If he'd wanted to kill me, he had lots of chances," I said. "Shut down."

The aircar settled. Rick opened the cab door and got out instead of waiting on the plenum chamber. I raised an eyebrow and he said, "I'm coming with you."

I unloaded the shotgun and replaced the charge in my vest. I put the weapon in the cab and hopped out to join Rick. We started for where the native had been standing—he'd disappeared as soon as he was sure we'd seen him.

"Where now?" said Rick. There was nothing but brush before us.

I smelled the bitter odor of the fluid which released me from the trap. I looked around carefully before I spotted it to my right.

"Here," I said, kneeling down. A scrap of fabric hung from the rough surface of a vine. It was actually the pith of a seed pod rather than bark cloth as I'd believed when I watched the native freeing my hand.

"What is that?" Rick said.

Instead of answering him, I pushed through the band of reeds in front of me. I went sideways but it was remarkably difficult. Vines like the one I'd found the cloth on raked the skin of my leading forearm. I would have switched to my left, but the reeds held me so tightly that I decided it would be better to push on.

I hit a hill that I hadn't noticed till my outstretched hand plunged into loam. It was the first hill we'd seen in this forest.

There was something very hard under the loam. I raised my eyes to the slope directly above my hand. A hole had been scraped in the overburden. I saw the gleam of crystal at the bottom.

I straightened and called to Rick, whom I heard trying to follow, "Go on back! We've got to go to the ship to get equipment!"

Then I shouted to my left as loudly as I could, "We'll be coming back, but just to clear this."

Then to my right, "We're coming back!"

Rick had checked as they flew in that Captain Bolton was in his day office. When the aircar docked in the transport hold, the tech on duty saw Rick and said, "Sir? Captain Bolton's waiting for you now."

"Good luck, Harry," he said to his friend, who was on the way to Bio Section to explain the situation to Doctor Veil. In all likelihood, Veil would be thrilled beyond words at the news.

Rick wasn't as confident about his own mission as he climbed the companionway to the bridge level. Still, there were things in his favor. He hadn't gone into details over the radio, but he'd said enough to pique the captain's interest.

And everything he'd said was true.

Lieutenant Vermijo greeted him from the bridge hatch and walked through to the day office with him, closing the hatch behind them. Rick started to salute but Bolton grimaced and said, "Just spit it out, Grenville. What's this about a threat to Lord Harper's life?"

"Lieutenant Harper accompanied a hunting party of locals into the jungle," Rick said. "They were attacked by natives and the surviving hunters abandoned Harry, leaving him for dead. I accompanied members of Bio Section and signals assistant Menta and was able to rescue Harry with pretty much ordinary wear and tear."

"Lord Harper is all right then?" Bolton demanded.

"Lord Harper is fine, because during his wanderings before we picked him up," Rick said, "he found an Archaic site. He's delighted with this. It put all thought of the danger he'd undergone out of his mind."

"You mean like Elkin?" said Lieutenant Vermijo.

"Yes, only this one's covered in jungle instead of being in a desert," Rick said. "He'll want a couple techs with chainsaws and probably lifting tackle to get a better look at it. That is, Doctor Veil will."

"But what about the locals who abandoned Lieutenant Harper?" Vermijo said.

"It sounded to me that Harry is too happy about this find to worry about revenge," Rick said truthfully. "Besides, I gather that the servant who actually laid hands on him has been punished to a considerable degree."

"If all he wants is a couple techs to clear jungle," Bolton said, "I approve. You'll be in charge of our end, Grenville?"

"Sir!" Rick said, bracing to attention with a smile. "If you approve it, I certainly will!"

I was in the cab of the aircar between Kent and Doctor Veil. Harry, Joss, and two spacers were in back with Joss and the tools.

Also with the guns. I wasn't expecting the natives to be a problem but I didn't object to the spacers—Rick included—being issued submachine guns, and I'd filled my vest loops with charges of heavy shot.

For that matter, I thought Joss had brought a gun also though she seemed to prefer her heavy knife.

"We should be getting close," Kent said. He was using the log from yesterday when they'd come to rescue me, guided by the signal from my handheld.

"Lord Harper?" Doctor Veil said. "Would you say that this artifact is the same size as the one on Elkin?"

"We won't be able to tell until we've uncovered at least one side, sir," I said. "I'm not even sure that it's a block of moissanite—I didn't have any equipment along and just saw crystal at the bottom of a hole six inches deep. It could be glass, for all I could tell. But..."

I cleared my throat. I didn't want to pump up Veil's hopes; but in all honesty, I couldn't think of a more likely answer to what was under the mass of dirt and leaf mold than an Archaic artifact like the one we'd seen before.

"...it *is* about the right size. Regardless, we'll know soon."

"This time we won't blow it up," Veil said grimly. She reached into the pocket of the white lab coat that she'd chosen to wear. She had the odd-shaped rod of moissanite that Master Blenkins had given me on Mindoro for identifying his Lourdis seed.

"*This*," she said, "is the key. I've compared it with images of the cube's door on Elkin and it would have fit perfectly. Perfectly!"

"Ah," I said as a placeholder. Then I said, "That's a wonderful deduction, sir."

I hoped she was right, but *I* sure wasn't going to bet on it.

"We're going in!" Kent said. We dropped abruptly. Even with Kent's warning, I didn't see the waving line separating the treetops on opposite sides of the creek until we brushed through them. Branch ends flicked against the car's sides. Doctor Veil hunched closer to me.

Then we were through and Kent flared us down onto the same spot he had landed to rescue me. The brush was already squished down and didn't pose as much as risk to our fans as another spot would've.

I felt and heard the spacers decamping from the back, but Doctor Veil didn't move. I wasn't quite keyed up enough to reach past her and open the door—but I almost did. I wasn't exactly afraid, but I really didn't like sitting here doing *nothing*.

When at last Veil stepped onto the plenum chamber, I slipped past and jumped to the ground. The three spacers were facing angles of jungle, thrusting their submachine guns toward the vegetation, as I expected.

There was no sign of Joss. I expected that too.

I reached in for my shotgun and loaded a charge of heavy shot rather than a slug. I didn't expect to need anything, but if I did it was going to be at short range.

I took the imaging equipment from the back—one pole in either hand—and led Doctor Veil over to the mound in question. The spacers continued to watch the landscape but the edge was off their concern. I think they were feeling pretty silly waving their weapons at the leaves.

I'd seen the way the native appeared and disappeared through the brush. He was obviously a hunter. No single one of us—well, maybe Joss—would have survived if he'd wanted to attack.

Veil probed the mound while I calibrated the two projectors. When they were ready to test, she came back and took charge. The combined readout told us what we'd assumed from the beginning: the core of the mound was a seven-foot cube of moissanite. Detailed examination of the scan indicated a discontinuity of the face nearest where we stood. This was consistent with a separate door on that face, like the one on Elkin.

Also as with the artifact on Elkin, there was a chip out of the top of the door. It certainly might be the same size as the piece Veil was carrying.

The artifact was covered with wood litter, much of which had already decomposed to loam. The roots of later vegetation ran into and through it but because the moissanite had been cast or molded as one piece, the roots did not prize the blocks apart as they would have done stone. The door fitted so smoothly into its socket that rootlets hadn't been able to enter though I'd seen them show the penetration of thin oil.

"Ready now?" Rick said to us. I nodded. Rick turned to the spacers he'd brought and said, "Weems, Willis? Break out the saws and start earning your keep."

Rick and I put our weapons in the back of the car along with those of the two spacers. We took out the spades and, while Doctor Veil guided us, began chopping at the soil. Because the moissanite was so refractory, we didn't have to worry about chipping the surface with the shovel blade or even the vibrating edges of the saws if they sank deep while cutting surface roots. Doctor Veil stayed at the readout, watching the progress as we removed the overburden.

After three hours, Rick and I had the door clear down to the level of the forest floor. We leaned our shovels against a tangle of uncut brush behind us and, working together, dragged a clot of saplings out of the way. Weems and Willis had cut them off near the ground, but vines laced their tops together and they couldn't be moved individually.

We were resting for the moment. I took off my gauntlets and worked my fingers to cool my hands, wondering how long Veil intended to keep us at this. Clearing one side of the cube had been heavy work. Clearing all four and perhaps the top as well would be impossible without a larger crew and more time.

Doctor Veil walked forward with the rod—what she called "the key"—in her hands and held it up, close to the cut in the door edge. The cavity was still packed with loam.

Rick and I watched her poise there, wondering what next.

As we waited, Joss—whom I hadn't seen since we landed, shouted, "Incoming! These aren't ours!"

I hadn't heard the fans, but two heavy aircars came in from the direction of the watercourse. One crushed through on the near side of the vehicle we'd come in; the other was near where Rick and I stood. Brush settled and I heard the shriek of a lift fan which was damaged and coming apart.

The vehicles were clearly built as troop carriers: their sides flopped down and infantry in the yellow-brown Shining battle-dress poured out. There were a dozen or more in each truck. They carried automatic carbines.

Rick had tensed to bolt for his weapon, but it was in the back of our truck—on the other side of the nearer Shining truck. I put my hand on his arm. He relaxed. Shining troops continued to point their weapons at us, but they didn't seem to be on the tense edge of firing.

Weems was standing on top of the mound. He laid down his saw and raised his hands. I couldn't see Willis but I hoped he was also showing good judgment. Doctor Veil turned and looked back at me.

A Shining official in civilian clothes got out of the cab of the nearer vehicle and walked carefully through the brush to where Doctor Veil stood. I recognized him: Pretsuma, whom I'd met in Prince Seba's court on Mindoro.

Pretsuma nodded, perhaps a tiny bow, to Doctor Veil. "I will take the key now, Doctor Veil. If you use indigenous communications systems, you must expect to be overheard by everyone who wishes to do so."

Doctor Veil held out the key. "Sir," she said, "you're welcome to share the knowledge inside. Our purpose is to advance all humans. There was no need to descend like armed bandits to get what I would willingly share with all men."

Pretsuma took the key from her with a motion that reminded me of a lizard snapping. He said, "I make allowances for your ignorance, Doctor. You see, we of the Shining Empire are the direct descendants of the Archaic Spacefarers. We are the *only* persons who have a right to the information in this cell."

"No, sir," Veil said.

I winced, but Pretsuma didn't seem to have heard the objection. He continued, "We were the ruling civilization of our time, but we fell into darkness and have only recently started to regain our former situation. Our priests tell us that our ancestors left teachers in crystal cells to speed us back to dominance when we regained star travel. This is the first we've found."

"That's all myth," Veil said, frowning. "The real science is wonderful enough, but the Archaics weren't human and can't be your—"

"Silence!" Pretsuma shouted, his face mottled with fury. He knocked Doctor Veil down with the side of his fist. "How *dare* you question the ancestry of your superiors?"

Rick lunged when Pretsuma hit Veil, but a soldier grappled with him and another soldier standing behind struck him with the butt of his carbine. Rick hit the ground on his face.

I hadn't moved initially because it was pointless. When I would have gone to support Rick I was already being held from behind by two soldiers. Rick had the right reflexes for this sort of situation. I was an academic.

He would have a headache in the morning. I would have to remember that I hadn't run to help my superior, an older woman, when a religious bigot struck her for contradicting when he talked nonsense. I would have preferred the headache.

Pretsuma called an order to troops on the aircar that he'd arrived in. Two of them ran to the moissanite cube, one holding a bladder of about a gallon of water and the other with a rag. They began scrubbing at the niche, wetting it and the rag—the sleeve of a torn garment—frequently.

Doctor Veil stood and walked over to me. Her pace was slow and halting. She had no expression but she reached up with her left hand to rub her cheek.

Rick lay where he'd fallen. I hoped he was just trying not to attract attention, but if he was seriously injured there was nothing I could do. The first-aid kit was in our truck on the other side of the nearer Shining vehicle.

Maybe it was because I was thinking about Rick that when Pretsuma moved toward the cube with the key held out, I said, "Sir? I was on Elkin when a similar cube was opened. It was a trap. The creature inside was a local species, not intelligent. We'll show you the imagery."

Pretsuma looked at me, then returned his attention to the cube. He set the key in the niche and wriggled it slightly with his fingertips. I heard a click.

The moissanite suddenly became so transparently clear that it seemed to vanish. Instead of a block of diffraction and reflection, I could see through it to the leaf mold and the growing roots where they pressed against the crystal of the roof and far sides.

Pretsuma was suddenly within the space, looking startled. Then the moissanite was back, surfaces of distortions and diffractions with occasional flashes of fire where a ray of sunlight had penetrated. Pretsuma had disappeared—he wasn't standing in front of the cube and I couldn't see him anywhere else. Guards were shouting in surprise.

The truck behind us blew up, a *bang!* When I twisted my head to look, there was a ball of pale blue hydrogen flame from the fuel cells which powered generators for the fan motors. The soldier gripping my left arm suddenly flew backward with a startled expression. He'd been shot through the bridge of his nose.

I grabbed Doctor Veil and threw her on the ground, covering her with my body. I heard a second aimed shot but I couldn't tell what the target was.

Shining soldiers began firing wildly. I doubted they had any more targets than Weems and Willis had when we first landed in the jungle.

I prayed that Doctor Veil wouldn't start clawing me to get off her. If we moved, the soldiers would have real targets. And as close as we were, they couldn't all miss.

There was a scream. The shooting paused, then redoubled. A slug ricocheted from the cube.

There was another scream. This time a soldier staggered backward and fell over the sapling Rick and I had moved just before we stopped work. The man's belly had been cut open and a coil of pinkish intestine stretched back into the brush where he'd been standing.

Three soldiers ran past where I lay, focused on the remaining Shining aircar. One of them dropped his carbine.

The hydrogen in the first vehicle had burned out, but the plastic and fabric of the interior continued to smolder. The second truck wobbled as the driver ran up his fans. More soldiers were trying to pile aboard. I wondered whether this or the other vehicle was the one that had bent a fan blade while landing.

The truck pulled farther inland, gaining height. The driver was looking for a place to turn around and reach the watercourse before he tried to punch through the canopy.

I heard the bang, muted by intervening forest. I didn't see the vehicle until a moment later as it plunged to the ground. I heard but couldn't see the crash itself.

I rolled off Doctor Veil's slight body. "Sorry, ma'am," I said.

"Thank you, Harper," she said, rolling onto all fours. "Thank you very much."

Rick had also gotten up. He grabbed a carbine, then handed me another. "Never a dull moment," he muttered. "Say, was that Shining bigwig in the first truck that blew up?"

Kent, Weems, and Willis were coming toward us from the back of the mound. Willis was limping.

"I don't think so," I said, "but I'm not sure of what happened."

Rick said, "Kent, does our car work?"

"It ought to, El-Tee," Kent said.

Rick's scalp was bloody. He dabbed it with his fingertips. He said, "Then let's get ourselves back to some medicomps. Since at least I need one!"

When Pretsuma's vehicle landed, it had knocked over quite a mass of vine-bound saplings like those we'd been clearing from on top of and around the cube. Some of the undergrowth had been knocked over onto our truck.

Doctor Veil stopped in her tracks when she saw the pile, but Rick turned and called, "Willis, Weems? Good thing you haven't put away your saws yet. Let's get going so we can get home!"

The two spacers headed for the tangle of brush. Rick started to join them but staggered. I put my right hand on his shoulder and said, "Rick, I think we can leave this to people who haven't been hit on the head recently."

I'd had a stint in the medicomp when I got back from hunting with Platt. That had allowed me to work on clearing the cube, but either the drugs had worn off or I was simply exhausted. I'd have joined Rick in doing more heavy clearance work if he'd gone, but I sure hoped we could leave it to the common spacers now.

"Yeah, you're right," said Rick, relaxing. Weems and Willis were probably tired too, but they hadn't been injured recently. Weems, an ox of a man, with a flaring red moustache, turned. He called, "El-Tee? There's guns here. What you want us to do with them?"

Rick paused and glanced at me. From behind us, Joss said, "Leave 'em. Atti—he's the native you met, Lord Harper—is putting together a new tribe and they'll come in handy."

"Leave the guns for the natives," Rick called to Weems. Then he said quietly to Joss, "Are you sure that's a good idea?"

Joss shrugged. "Atti was helping us," she said. "I don't think he could hit anything with a gun that wasn't in knife range, but he can *get* that close."

Rick shrugged. "They're not our guns," he said.

"If it makes civilized Otkans think a little before they fly into the jungle to kill mothers and babies...," I said. "Then I'm in favor of it."

Rick smiled wryly. "I guess I can go along with that," he said. "Say Joss? How did you get the aircars to blow up like that?"

Joss smiled also. I guess I was getting used to it because the expression no longer struck me as horrible. "The Shinings had grenades," she said. "And if you know what you're doing, you can set a grenade inside an oleo strut so that when the weight comes off and the strut extends, the fuse ignites."

She looked at me. "How did you make the high muckimuck vanish, sir? I was moving around for a shot but then *Zip!* and he was gone."

Before I could speak—saying that I hadn't done it—Doctor Veil said, "Lord Harper explained to Master Pretsuma that the Archaics placed traps which long outlived them. What I thought was a key was actually the trigger—inserting it armed the trap. When an animal of the correct size entered the target zone, it would respond."

Joss frowned and said, "But it couldn't be armed, then. It'd catch whoever tried."

"I assume there was a safety to prevent it from working on the Archaics themselves," Doctor Veil said. "As I warned Master Pretsuma, the Archaics were not of our species."

She rubbed her cheek and smiled. "I'm glad that he chose to test the device instead of leaving it for me to do, as I'd intended."

The truck's fans revved and the vehicle lifted slightly before settling back. Weems stood in the open back of the vehicle and shouted, "We're ready to load any time you are!"

"We're ready now!" I called back.

I was sitting in the back with Rick, Joss, and the spacers, leaving Doctor Veil alone in the cab with Kent. I'd felt really trapped when Veil stayed seated after our arrival in the forest this morning.

I suppose I could've asked her to take the middle seat, but she was my superior and preferred the outer place. There was plenty of space in back for five people, but the saws were recharging in the middle of the floor so foot room was obstructed.

Rick had slid the sides up so we could look out as we cruised back to Ssu-Lung, but I basically looked at my hands on my knees. I was physically tired but my real exhaustion was mental. There were spatters of blood on my left sleeve, I suppose from the Shining who'd been holding my arm when Joss blew his brains out. I hadn't been at risk from that shot, but it drove home to me what had just gone on.

"Hey!" said Rick, looking out to the side. "That's an RCN courier ship! What the hell is it doing here?"

We were curving in over the harbor to reach the transport bay on the starboard side. There was a largish ship docked near the *Far Traveller*. It looked odd but I wasn't familiar enough with ships to know why.

"I don't know what you mean," I said. We were losing height; the new ship was hidden behind our own.

"It started out as a light cruiser, like the *Fart*," Rick said, "but they took out hull sections, razed it, and left the original sparring. I've never heard of one where all the pipes and ducting worked right, but they're hell for fast when you need to move orders or high officers."

"They're meeting us in the transport hold!" Kent shouted through the window from the cab. He'd been on the radio but all I'd made out was the crackle of conversation. I wasn't sure I'd heard him right this time either.

"Who's meeting us, d'ye suppose?" Rick said. Neither of us tried to distract Kent while he was pulling into the transport hold.

We turned in the entrance aisle and landed in our usual place. Six or eight people, most of them in uniform, had been packed into the office. They rushed toward us when Kent shut the fans down.

Willis banged the tailgate open. Rick gestured me out. "I don't think they're waiting for me," he said.

There was no reason for them to be waiting for me either, but I hopped down. I didn't recognize the three officers in RCN dress uniforms—they weren't members of our crew—but the civilian woman in her sixties was Mistress Klausen, Uncle Ted's personal aide for as long as I could remember.

Captain Bolton in a second class uniform greeted me first,

but he immediately turned to Doctor Veil. "Mistress?" he said, shouting over the echoes of the bay. "May we gather in your lab? It's the nearest large quiet space?"

I didn't hear her reply, though I'm not sure it would have made a difference. Guided by Mahaffy, we wound our way through the corridors to the biology lab. I really wanted to shower and sleep, but that would wait until this was taken care of. Whatever *this* was.

When Kent closed the hatch behind us, it became reasonably quiet. I suppose I should've waited for one of the officers to say something, but I turned to Mistress Klausen and said, "Debra? Is Uncle Ted all right?"

Klausen's smile was no warmer than usual—Uncle Ted didn't keep her around for her nurturing qualities—but it was real. "Harper of Forwood is very well indeed, Lord Harry. He has been chosen as minister of commerce in the new government, and he wants you as his chief of staff. He sent me to fetch you."

"I don't know a bloody thing about commerce!" I said. I didn't bother saying that I didn't want to learn about commerce either: this was family, and my personal preferences didn't count.

"You'll have a staff," Klausen said. "Your uncle needs someone smart and able to think on his feet to run them. He's read Captain Bolton's reports and was greatly impressed. And of course he's known you all your life and he trusts you."

"*What* reports?" I said, looking from Debra to the captain.

"You saved the Republic from embarrassment," Captain Bolton said, "and you may have saved my career as well when you rescued Lieutenant Grenville on Mindoro without public incident. It was a pleasure as well as my duty to cite you for an award."

"I believe your uncle mentioned 'ruthlessness' as another reason for picking you," Klausen said. "I believe the words he used were, 'a true Harper.'"

I was processing what I'd just heard. Captain Bolton said, "I should mention that Doctor Veil proved her value to the RCN when she brought Lord Harper aboard the *Far Traveller*. In recognition of that service, I am granting her an in-service commission as a lieutenant in the Republic of Cinnabar Navy."

He turned toward Doctor Veil, smiled, and added, "You'll be eating with the officers from now on, Professor."

Bloody hell.

"The *Signal* is waiting to lift off now, sir," said one of the officers I hadn't seen before.

I said, "I'll need time to move my luggage. And I'd *really* like to take a shower."

"I shifted your gear while you were gone, El-Tee," Mahaffy said. "And let me tell you, that wasn't *half* a job."

"Welcome aboard the *Signal*, Lord Harper," said the officer who'd spoken before. "I'm Becarra, her captain. I can assure you that the hot water is still connected in the passenger suite."

I took a deep breath. "I don't have time to say the things I'm thinking." I said, "but if I prove fit for this new position, it's because of what I've learned in the RCN."

I looked around the room and added, "Not least what I've learned from Technician Joss, who doesn't seem to be here. She avoids crowds and strangers. I hope she will continue to flourish on the *Far Traveller*."

I bent my head and wiped my eyes with the back of my right hand. "One more thing," I said, hoping I wouldn't choke before I got the words out. "I would appreciate it if Lieutenant Grenville would walk me aboard the *Signal*. He understands naval matters far better than I do."

"Get him aboard, Grenville," Captain Bolton said. "I'm sure Captain Becarra will wait until Lord Harper has dismissed you."

We went out into the transportation bay, a lifetime after I had first entered by it.

BAEN BOOKS • JUNE 2019

To Clear Away the Shadows
David Drake

Pub. Background:	**A Baen Original**
Category:	**Science Fiction**
Author's Home:	**Chapel Hill, NC**
ISBN:	**978-1-4814-8402-2**
Price:	**$25.00** ($34.00 Can.)
Format: **Hardcover**	Spine Size: **7/8"**
Pages: **256**	Per Carton: **20**

The nationally best-selling RCN series continues with a trip to the outer reaches of known space by Daniel Leary, Adele Mundy, and an intrepid young crew of scientists who are about to learn the hard way that advancing knowledge has a price.

SUPPORTED BY:
- Review Copies (50)
- *Publishers Weekly* – group ad
- *Publishers Weekly* – online
- *Library Journal* – group ad
- *Booklist* – full-page ad
- *BookPage* – online newsletter
- Ingram – Advance – annotations & Easy Reads

"Rousing old-fashioned space opera"
—*Publishers Weekly*